The WEIGHT of a PEARL

by
Walker Smith

SONATA BOOKS

2018

For further information, you may contact the author at:
www.walkersmithbooks.com

or by email:
walker@walkersmithbooks.com

Cover: Photography: David Williams
       Design: Eli *The Book Guy* Blyden
       Model: Brittany Clayton

Printed & Published in the United States of America
The Weight of a Pearl
Category: Fiction / Multicultural
ISBN: 978-0-9904996-7-1

ALSO BY WALKER SMITH:

The Color Line

Letters from Rome

Mello Yello:
The Incredible Life Story of Jack the Rapper

Bluestone Rondo

Sing, Antoninus, sing.
~ Dalton Trumbo

For Ina and Pearl

A pearl is a beautiful thing
that is produced by an injured life.
It is the oyster's tear....

The treasure of our being in this world
is also produced by an injured life.
If we had not been wounded,
if we had not been injured,
then we would not produce
the pearl.

~ Stephan A. Hoeller

HARLEM

CHRISTMAS EVE, 1963

*T*hank you, ladies and gentlemen... Right now we're gonna slow things down and do a special little number called "Something to Live For." And Ronnie, baby, this one's for you....

Pearl's mind was beginning to tilt now. For a moment she actually believed that she was back onstage at the Red Regency Club dedicating a song to Ronnie; the next moment she was staring into Magda's pale blue eyes. Both thoughts were tangled in her memory, sometimes as vivid as a Technicolor movie; other times as elusive and erratic as cigarette smoke.

A sudden bite of cold wind brought her back to the present. Pulling up her collar, she fumbled in her coat pocket for her matches and cigarettes, then lit up and stared closer at the shop window that had captured her attention. It was a typical commercialized Christmas display, with one of those artificial silver trees everybody seemed to be buying that season. Standing stiffly around the tree was a family of Caucasian mannequins dressed for winter. Pearl gazed at the smallest blue-eyed mannequin that had made her think of Magda. But why had Ronnie walked across her mind? He didn't belong with this Currier and Ives family. Then again, they didn't exactly belong on St. Nicholas Avenue in Harlem either.

A door opened across the street and a jangling mix of sound blasted out: laughter, holiday pleasantries, and Johnny Mathis singing "I'll Be Home for Christmas." Pearl closed her eyes tightly until the door slammed shut and she could breathe again.

She raised her cigarette to her lips, but her hands were shaking so badly now that she could hardly make that simple hand-to-mouth connection. Flinging the cigarette to the sidewalk, she crushed it with her shoe, wiped the tears from her eyes, and then headed for the subway. "God, help me—it's time to stop this. I'ma go visit my friend and then I am goin' *home*."

Most of the shops she passed had already closed, and the few remaining lights were just random blurs of color reflected on the dark, icy street. About halfway to the subway she stopped and looked back over her shoulder at the street with no sign. On that street, a woman named Margaret was waiting for her in a fourplex that addicts called "the quarter house." Jerking up her chin, Pearl hurried to the subway. As she ran down the steps, her thoughts returned to Ronnie—before this damn mean world had done things to him.

Just put one foot in front of the other one....

1935

In a reversal of the Scottsboro Boys' guilty verdict, the Supreme Court rules in favor of Clarence Norris in *Norris v. State of Alabama.*

Paul Robeson and Albert Einstein meet, beginning a lifelong friendship and collaborative crusade against global fascism and racism.

President Roosevelt implements the Social Security Act, the Works Progress Administration (WPA), and the Wagner Labor Relations Act.

In Spain, organizers prepare for the upcoming presidential election.

Negro activist Oliver Law organizes the "Hands off Ethiopia" campaign to protest fascist Italian leader Benito Mussolini's invasion of Ethiopia.

PART ONE

PEARL

CHAPTER 1

CHICAGO

Pearl's eyes flew open and she jerked her head out from under the warm covers.

"Pancakes!"

She inhaled the cold air again to be sure she wasn't dreaming. Scrambling out of bed, she found her shoes in the dark and slipped them on, then pulled on her sweater and reached down to shake her little brother, who was emitting a soft baby-snore that sounded like a funny little whistle-song. It always made her giggle.

"Wake up, Ronnie! It's Christmas! ... Hey, wake up! It's Christmas! We got pancakes!"

Ronnie stirred and mumbled, but his eyes didn't open.

She leaned close to his ear. "Christmas, Ronnie," she said loudly. "Can'tcha smell them pancakes?"

Ronnie's eyes fluttered open and his face contorted with a goofy grin more befitting a drunken sailor than a five-year-old boy.

Pearl laughed as she pulled him up to a sitting position. She managed to get him into his sweater and shoes and he stood up, but he was still wobbly.

"Ain'tcha heard me, Ronnie? I said it's *Christmas*, boy! So put one foot in front of the other one and come *on*!"

Ronnie finally cooperated by holding his sister's hand and doing a zigzag stumble down the hallway. When they reached the front room, she felt him stiffen as if he'd suddenly been hit by lightning. "Hey! Christmas, Pearl!"

Pearl sighed and rolled her eyes. "No kidding."

Ronnie ran to the little spruce tree on the table in front of the window and began hopping around in a circle. "Christmas tree! Christmas tree!" he yelped. "Oh, boy! Look, Pearl!"

"I know! Ain't it purty?"

Their mother Alva stuck her head in and laughed. "I knew them pancakes would wake you two up. Merry Christmas, kids!"

Pearl ran over and threw her arms around her mother's waist. "Merry Christmas, Mama! Where'dja get the tree and the purty lights?"

"Just some Mama magic, baby, that's all. It's just a little tree, but don't it smell good?"

"Yes, ma'am! It looks purty too!"

"Loooook!" Ronnie squealed. "Presents!"

"Boy, don'tchu touch them presents till after breakfast," Alva said. "Them pancakes is gettin' cold. Turn on the radio, Pearl. Maybe they's some Christmas carols on."

"Yes, ma'am."

Pearl turned the knob on the old radio their father had left behind, and waited for it to warm up. After twisting the tuning knob past a series of buzzes and squeaks, the sound of sleigh bells rang through the speaker to introduce Benny Goodman's recording of "Jingle Bells."

"Turn it up, and come on in here," Alva called from the kitchen.

"Yes, ma'am!"

By the time Pearl took a seat at the table, Alva was leaning over Ronnie tying a small towel around his neck. He tilted his head back, closed his eyes, and puckered his lips, which always made Alva laugh.

"Oh, you want your kiss, huh, baby?"

Ronnie nodded without opening his eyes. Alva gave him a quick kiss on the lips, then on his left dimple, then his right dimple, and then rubbed her nose against his.

"You sho' like them Eskimo kisses, huh, baby?"

Ronnie giggled and attacked his pancakes, smearing his face with syrup. "I *love* skosamo kisses, Mama!"

"Not skosamo," Pearl said, "Es-ki-mo!"

"I got another surprise for you kids too," Alva said. "We got chicken for supper tonight."

"Oh, boy! Chicken!" Ronnie yelled.

"This sure is a good Christmas," Pearl said. "We ain't had no pancakes or chicken since Daddy left."

Alva leaned over and kissed Pearl's forehead. "I told'ja, baby. Mama magic."

Ronnie waved his fork in the air and grinned. "I like Mama magic mo' better'n Daddy!"

Alva laughed, and Pearl sat there a moment gazing at her. Her mother was breathtaking when she was truly happy. She was tall and graceful with a deep tan complexion, and soft kinky hair she wore in a high twist. When she laughed, the dimples that Ronnie had inherited showed in her pretty face, and her teeth formed a dazzling smile. Her eyes were large and round and black, and Pearl hoped that she would look like her mother someday. She closed her eyes and said a quick prayer: *God, please let Daddy be dead so he don't ever come home....*

It was a prayer Pearl knew she should never say out loud. If she didn't say it out loud, maybe it wouldn't be a sin.

Once breakfast was over, Alva began clearing away the dishes. "Okay, you two go wash your hands real good. Use soap, hear me? Get all the sticky off of 'em. And don'tchu open yo' presents till I get in there."

After Pearl helped Ronnie wash his hands, they ran back to the front room and sat on the floor staring at the Christmas tree as they waited for their mother.

"Hurry, Mama," Pearl called.

Alva walked into the room and put her fists on her hips. "Show me them hands first."

Ronnie sighed impatiently and stuck his hands high in the air. "All clean, Mama!"

"Oh, put yo' hands down, boy," Alva said, laughing. "You ain't under arrest!" She picked up a red-wrapped oblong package the size of a cracker box and handed it to Ronnie. "Okay, you each get two presents. Open this one first."

Ronnie started squealing as he ripped the red wrapping paper from the box.

"Help him get the box open, Pearl."

"Winter Wonderland" was playing on the radio and Pearl hummed along as she tore open the box. A green metal truck with red wheels rolled out and Ronnie grabbed it.

"A car!" he screeched.

"Nuh-uh, it's a truck," Pearl said. "A dump truck. I bet it works, too, just like a real one." She tilted the back section of the truck and then snapped it back into place. "See? The dirt goes inside right here, and then you dump it out the back right here, like this."

"But not in the house," Alva said. "Awright, now, Pearl. This one's for you."

Pearl grinned and took the long box from her mother's hands, then carefully unwrapped it. "Checkers! Jus' like Maggie down the street got! Oh, boy! Will you play with me, Mama?"

Ronnie pushed the truck aside. "I wanna play checkers!"

"You too little! Play with your truck!"

"Nuh-uh, Pearl! I wanna play checkers!"

"We'll teach him," Alva said. "But first, you got one more present to open. Here. They both the same. One for you and one for Ronnie."

Ronnie opened his, and crooned, "Baby Rooooof! I'ma eat you right now!"

Pearl didn't unwrap her candy bar. "If ya eat it now, it be all gone," she advised. "If ya save it, then ya got sump'm to look forward to all day, right, Mama?"

"That's right, baby… Hey! Let's play them checkers. What color you wanna be?"

Pearl began setting up the board on the floor. "I'll be… uh, the red checkers, I guess."

"Okay, then I'll be the black checkers. And Ronnie, you can move my checkers to the squares I point at. That's how you learn, see? And then you can play the next game with Pearl."

* * *

Pearl hated Chicago's raw, harsh winters. By January she decided that this was the worst winter she could remember. When her father had abandoned the family in late August, all it had meant to Pearl was an end to the beatings. But her mother had cried and stared out the front window for weeks after her husband's sudden departure. Pearl had done her best to comfort her, but secretly continued to hope that Victor Sayles was dead.

It took some time before Pearl began to understand her mother's grief. It began on the night the lights went out right in the middle of supper. Alva borrowed candles from their neighbors, but then the city shut off their water. The pastor at the church took up a collection to have the water and lights turned back on, but Pearl was sure that God was punishing her for wishing her father dead.

Alva began taking in washing, which she did in the basement, and then walked several blocks to a part-time job she found as a cleaning lady. Pearl had to spend those days inside with the curtains shut. Her main job was to keep Ronnie quiet. Ever since Alva's friend Millie had moved out of the building, she had no one she could trust to watch her children, and she couldn't afford to pay anyone. Pearl knew her mother was relying on her to take care of Ronnie without letting anyone know they were alone in the apartment.

Sometimes when their mother came home there would be meat for supper, but most times it was rice and beans, and plain bread for breakfast and lunch, with watered-down soup.

As bad as things were, the arrival of winter made things unbearable for Pearl's struggling family. After Christmas, there were no more pancakes for breakfast or chicken for supper. It was back to rice, beans, bread, and watery soup.

Then in early February, Alva bundled up her children and took them to a walk-up a few blocks away for a "surprise." They climbed four flights of stairs and a smiling brown-skinned man answered the door. He was thin and bald, and he was wearing thick glasses and an apron. Pearl decided that he must be very old, at least forty, but he seemed nice enough. Alva introduced him as Mr. Washington, and told the children that he had invited them all to dinner. Ronnie leaped into Mr. Washington's arms and thanked him, and everyone laughed. Then Mr. Washington hurried them all into a room with an enormous table crowded with food: a large turkey just out of the oven, stuffing, gravy, pies, cranberries, vegetables, buttered rolls, and a dish filled with chocolates.

"Just like Thanksgiving!" Mr. Washington said. Then he told them to take a seat and eat as much as they could hold.

So they did.

They ate so much that Pearl didn't even remember falling asleep on the living room sofa.

It was dark when she woke up and she was terrified because she had no idea where she was. She felt Ronnie asleep next to her, but her mother was gone. She was just about to call out when her eyes began to adjust and she saw something—shadows moving in a dim sliver of light under a door. She heard her mother's voice speaking very softly to someone, and she remembered that it must be Mr. Washington. Then the door opened.

Her mother walked out slowly and awkwardly because Mr. Washington's arms were wrapped around her from behind. His hands were roaming all over the front of her body, and he was kissing the back of her neck and pleading with her to come back to his bed.

Pearl shut her eyes tightly and pretended to be asleep. In her seven-year-old mind, a deep, instinctive sorrow took hold. She and Ronnie had just eaten the best meal of their lives, and her mother had just taught her the meaning of "Mama magic."

* * *

Dinners at Mr. Washington's apartment became a regular occurrence for a few weeks until suddenly, Alva told Pearl that Mr. Washington wasn't their friend anymore. "Grown folks' business" was her cryptic explanation. "But don'tchu worry. Mama gon' make a way. I got two new house-cleanin' jobs."

"Yes, ma'am." Pearl put Mr. Washington out of her mind. She would miss his cooking, but she would not miss him.

CHAPTER 2

Winter was slow to melt away that year, and Pearl was growing impatient for the warmth of spring. Alva's new jobs brought in enough money for pancakes, but only on Sundays, and they hardly ever had chicken for supper anymore. Pearl decided that it was still better than having Victor Sayles living with them, even if they never had chicken or pancakes again.

Early one morning after her mother had gone to work, Pearl stared out the window at the skeletal branches of a tree growing in the small patch of dirt in front of their tenement building on State Street. She was waiting for the tiny green buds to appear, but instead, all she saw were snowflakes.

She felt Ronnie tugging at her sleeve.

"Is it snowin', Pearl?"

"Yeah."

"Le's go make a snowman!"

"No, Ronnie. We can't go out till Mama comes home."

"Mama don't get home till dark and I wanna make a snowman—big den me!"

"No, Ronnie!"

Ronnie fell to the floor on his knees and pouted. "I wanna snowman."

"I'm sick'a stayin' inside too, Ronnie." She sighed and stared out the window. "Well… maybe we could go down to the park for just a little while."

Ronnie scrambled to his feet and began jumping up and down. "Yeah!"

"But we *got* to come home 'fore Mama, Ronnie. She gon' whup us *hard* if she catch us, hear me?"

"Le's go, le's go, le's *go*, Pearl!"

* * *

There wasn't much snow on the ground when they reached the vacant lot that served as the neighborhood park, but Pearl managed

to scoop enough together to help Ronnie build an emaciated looking snowman.

"He ain't fat, Pearl," Ronnie whined.

"Ain't enough snow for a fat snowman. He good enough.
Now, come on and help me find some twigs for his arms."

Ronnie ran toward a small mound of snow. "No! I'ma fix him."

Pearl glanced up at the darkening sky. "Come back here, boy!
We gotta go home. It's gettin' late and we gonna get a whuppin'!"

"Mama don't hit hard," he said with a devilish grin. He dropped
to his knees and began scraping together a small pile of dirty snow.
"Help me, Pearl!"

"No!" Pearl ran over and grabbed her brother's arm. "It's time
to go *now*. We been out here too long! Look, it's gettin' dark. So
put one foot in front of the other one and hurry up!"

"I can't hurry up! I's little!"

"You're five now! And you sho' could hurry up on the way
over here!"

"I ain't done makin' my snowman, Pearl! He too skinny! I'ont
like him."

"We'll finish him tomorrow!"

"Snow gon' melt, Pearl. You said so. Then he gon' be *real* skinny."

"I said *no!*"

Ronnie wriggled out of her grasp and fell backwards into the
muddy snow, giggling and flailing his arms and legs. "Make a
snow angel, Pearl! Come on!"

Pearl glared down at him and tried to be mad, but he looked so
ridiculous grinning at her with his wool cap twisted over one side
of his face. His hair was all black silky curls, not nappy like Pearl's
hair, and she was glad that their mother hadn't cut it short yet. His
eyelashes were just as black and curly as his hair, and when he
smiled, his dimples were irresistible.

And then there was his laugh. Ronnie's laugh had the impos-
sibly rapid vibrato of a clicking typewriter, but with the shrill tone
of a baby goat's bleat.

"Huh-uh-uh-uh-uh-uh-uh... Come on, Pearl! Make a snow angel!"

"A snow angel? It ain't no snow, Ronnie!" she laughed.

"Okay, a mud angel, Pearl!"

Pearl finally gave up and fell on the ground with him, laughing and tickling him until they were both out of breath.

"Now we're all dirty! We better hurry so we can clean up before Mama gets home!"

Ronnie ignored her and scrambled up onto his hands and knees. "Sing me a song, Pearl," he said. "You sing, and me, I'ma fix my snowman!"

"No!" Pearl grabbed him by the back of his coat and pulled him to his feet. "I'll sing you a song on the way home. Now, come on!"

Ronnie poked out his lip and began stomping toward the street. Then he turned around and grinned. "Well, what'cha waitin' for?"

Pearl grabbed his hand and pulled him along as fast as she could. "Okay, here go the song: When the red, red robin goes bob-bob-bobbin' along...."

"No, Pearl! A new song!"

"No! We gotta get home, Ronnie. We gon' get a whuppin'!"

Ronnie frowned. "When I's seven I gonna make a *real* good song!"

"Oh, awright! I'll sing you a new song if you hurry! Okay, what'chu like a whole lot?"

Ronnie closed his eyes to think about it. "Ummmm... I know! Pancakes!"

Pearl laughed. "A song about pancakes?"

"No, wait. Candy bars! I *love* Baby Roofs the best!"

Pearl rolled her eyes. "You jus' like sugah! Okay, here go my new song... Ronnie is my sugah-boy... Ummm... He got some little sugah-toys... He got a funny sugah-laugh—"

Ronnie giggled. "Huh-uh-uh-uh-uh-uh-uh...."

"Stop makin' me laugh, boy! Okay... He got a funny sugah-laugh... It go like this: Rata-tata-tat-tat-tat!"

Ronnie giggled. "Why'd you stop? Sing some more!"

"Hush, Ronnie," Pearl said as they turned onto State Street. "Mama's on the stoop."

Ronnie froze. "Uh-oh...."

Alva was standing on the stoop peering in the opposite direction. As soon as she turned and saw them, she hurried down the steps and headed their way.

"Sorry, Mama," Pearl called preemptively.

"Don'tchu sorry Mama me, girl!"

When Alva reached them, Pearl braced for the belt's sting, but Alva grabbed her shoulder and whispered, "Yo' Daddy's back."

"Nuh-uh...."

"He sho' is. He back and he mad you kids was gone and I–I couldn't find you!"

In the light from a streetlamp, Pearl saw the large red palm mark on her mother's face. "I'm sorry he hit you, Mama! But don't let him hit Ronnie! He hit him so hard last time."

"I won't," Alva said as she picked up Ronnie in her arms. "Now don'tchu start cryin', boy, you hear me? You do what I tell you."

Ronnie's lip was quivering. "Please don't let him hit me again, Mama."

"I won't. But you do what I tell you, hear? You pretend to be 'sleep. I'ma carry you in and put you in yo' bed. He been drinkin', so maybe he'll forget you two was gone. But Pearl, you better keep ya coat on in case he wakes up and starts in on you." Alva jerked up her chin and smiled at Pearl. "Soon as I get Ronnie to bed, I'll be right in."

"Yes, ma'am." Her mother's reassuring smile gave her courage.

Their apartment was just to the left of the foyer on the first floor, so Pearl could hear her father yelling as she climbed the outside steps, even with the door shut.

"Alva! Don'tchu make me come out there and hunt down them gotdamn kids!"

Pearl stepped in front of her mother and waited for a moment before walking into the front room. Her father was sprawled across his old green chair with a nearly empty bottle of whiskey clutched in his hand. His eyes were closed and he had already begun to snore. Turning quickly, she signaled her mother and then stepped closer to her father's chair to block his view of the hallway in case he woke up again.

Once her mother had carried Ronnie safely to the back bedroom, Pearl stood there trying to decide if she might be able to sneak away without a beating. Then she remembered his rage the last time she had tried it, and decided it was safer to wait at least a few minutes more.

Please don't wake up... please don't wake up....

He was wearing a blue plaid flannel shirt that was stained with blood from his meatpacking job. It was missing two buttons, and the rise and fall of his bloated belly was threatening to pop a third. Though the room was chilly, his dark face was shining with sweat, and his mouth was open. The unkempt stubble on his face was gray, but his arms still looked strong and young. Pearl indulged in a momentary fantasy that he would suddenly grow old and weak, so he wouldn't hit so hard. She stared at his turned-in ankle that made him walk with a pronounced limp. How many times had he told the story about his father throwing him down the stairs when he was nine years old? And how many times had he threatened her with the same fate?

Please don't wake up....

Suddenly, his arm jerked and his eyes opened. He was looking directly at her.

"I'm sorry, Daddy," she said quickly.

Victor Sayles turned up the bottle for one last gulp, then set it down hard on the small table next to his chair. He leaned forward crookedly and narrowed his eyes.

"That all you got to say for ya'self, girl?" he growled. "You and that sissy boy think you can jus' do whatever the hell you wants to 'round here. How that boy ever gon' be a man with you and yo' gotdamn Mama playin' li'l girlie games wid'im? ...*Answer* me, gotdammit!"

"I'm sorry, Daddy. I–I–umm... I got lost and—"

"Shut up! And don't you move from that spot. I'ma get'chu, then I'ma get him too. Where is he?"

As her father slowly got to his feet, Pearl began backing away. Then Alva hurried into the room and stood in front of her. "Please, Victor—"

Without even looking at her, Victor shoved Alva so hard, she slammed into the far wall and fell in a heap on the floor. "You stay down there, Alva, or I swear I'll kill this girl."

As he moved in Pearl's direction, she wrapped her coat tighter around her body and backed away from him.

"Stop it!" he yelled. "Don'tchu make me chase you on my bad leg, or I bet'cha I peel the gotdamn skin off ya narrah li'l ass."

His voice was booming like thunder and Pearl began to shake. She bit her lip to keep from screaming as she watched him stagger toward her, taking off his belt.

"Please, Daddy, I'm sorry, okay?"

He raised his arm high, preparing for the first strike, but then he froze. "Aw, you think you smart, huh? Take that gotdamn coat off, girl. Right now!"

Alva began crawling over. "No, Victor!" she whimpered.

He lunged at Alva, and she cringed in the corner. "You stay there!" Then he glared at Pearl. "I *said* take that gotdamn coat off!"

Sobbing quietly, Pearl began unbuttoning her coat. Just as she slipped one arm out of the sleeve, she felt the first blow strike her midsection. "PLEEEEASE... NO!" Crumpling to the floor in a fetal position, she covered her head with her hands and cried out each time the belt struck—over and over and over again.

Suddenly, Alva tripped Victor and he crashed to the floor, shaking the walls of the small apartment. In the violent blur of screaming and movement, Pearl crawled toward the front door.

* * *

Pearl woke up in the bathroom at the far end of the hallway, unable to remember how she had gotten there. The tile floor was freezing cold, but she didn't move from the spot she was in until she felt her mother's hands lifting her.

"Oh, Jeezus Gawd," Alva moaned. "Look what he done to my baby...."

Trembling violently, Pearl leaned into the warmth of her mother's arms. "Did he hurt you, Mama?" she whispered.

"Mama's okay, baby."

"Is Ronnie okay?"

"He's fine. Ya daddy done passed out cold and I had to come tend to you. N-now step out'a them flannels, baby. I got a fresh nightgown for you."

Alva was gentle as she helped her undress, and Pearl watched her eyes as they inspected the severity of the bruises and strap marks.

"Hurts right here, Mama," she whispered, turning to show her mother the bloody gouge just under her ribcage. "Real bad...."

Alva gasped. "Oh, Lawd, he done hit'cha with that buckle, damn his soul!"

Pearl shivered and wrapped her arms around herself as she watched her mother soak two washrags in soap and warm water. "Ya eye's all swole up, Mama."

Alva shook her head. "It–it ain't nothin', baby. Gimme ya hands."

She held out her hands and Alva folded one of the washrags lengthwise and gently laid it across the red belt marks that criss-crossed Pearl's hands and fingers.

"That feels better, Mama."

Alva pulled the other washrag out of the warm water and wrung it out a bit, then looked into Pearl's eyes. "Don't move, baby. This is gonna hurt, but I gotta clean it 'fore I can put the bandage on it."

When Pearl felt her touch the wound under her ribs, she jumped and let out an inadvertent whimper. "M'sorry, Mama."

"It's okay, baby. I'm sorry too." A river of tears ran down Alva's face as she carefully washed and dried the wound. "I was... See, I–I was tryin' to keep him from gettin' at Ronnie. He would'a killed that baby! But he started in on you 'fore I could stop him... I should'a sent you and Ronnie out in the street and just let him beat me... Oh, Gawd, what I'm gon' do?"

Pearl stood there silently watching her mother cry as she bandaged, and then cry some more. When she was finished, she helped her into a clean nightgown and kissed her.

"Mama loves you and M–Mama gon' fix everything. You'll see... I got me a plan."

Pearl looked up at her. "What plan, Mama?"

"Well, I need you to help me with it, baby. I need to get you and Ronnie out the house real early in the mornin'. You think you can do that? Take Ronnie out'a here?"

Pearl stared at her and nodded. "Yes, ma'am... I will. But where do we go?"

Alva took a shaky breath. "When I wake you up, you keep Ronnie quiet and sneak across the alley to Miz Dundee's house. She'll keep you safe over there till ya daddy gone and I can come get'cha. Now, come on down the hall—I'll help you—and then I'ma get you to bed, baby."

"Mama?"

"Yes, baby?"

"What if, what if he kills you while we ain't here?"

Alva knelt down and hugged her gently. "I ain't gon' let nothin' kill me," she whispered. "I gotta stay alive to protect my babies."

"But Mama—"

"Shh. You and me, we gon' say our prayers, and everything gon' be awright."

"Yes, ma'am."

Alva and Pearl made their way down the hallway and slipped into the apartment, then headed to the back room. Alva helped her into bed and covered her with a blanket.

"G'night, baby," she whispered.

"G'night, Mama."

When her mother was gone, Pearl turned her face to the wall and wiped her eyes with the sleeve of her nightgown. After a few quiet minutes, she felt Ronnie snuggling against her back.

"Leave me alone, Ronnie," she whispered. "You made me get beat. I *told* you to hurry."

"I sorry, Pearl!"

Pearl heard the break in his voice. Then she felt his small hand gently patting her head, and she was glad she had saved him from being beaten.

"Pearl?"

"Mm-hmm?"

"Do it hurt... real bad?"

"No. Well, a little bad, I guess. But stop cryin' now and go to sleep."

"Okay. I sorry, Pearl."

"It's okay, Ronnie. Go to sleep."

"But I made a song for you, Pearl."

"You can sing it for me tomorrow, Ronnie."

"But it make you feel better."

Pearl squeezed her eyes shut. "Okay, but ya can't sing it right now. We ain't wanna wake him up. Just whisper it—*real* soft."

"Okay," he sniffled, "real soft... Here it go... Pearl is my sugah-girl... She a purty sugah-girl... She take care'a Ronnie... like a real good girl...."

Pearl let out a muffled sob.

"Don'tcha like my song, Pearl?"

"Mm-hmm. It's real purty, Ronnie. Now go on to sleep, okay?"

"Okay," he whispered. "I'ma make ya a new song tomorrow."

"Ronnie, listen to me. You gotta be good when we wake up in the mornin', okay? We gotta sneak out to Miz Dundee's house. And you gotta be real quiet, you promise?"

"Okay, Pearl. I promise."

* * *

The instant Pearl felt her mother's hand on her shoulder the next morning, she jerked up into a sitting position. "I'm up, Mama," she whispered. "I'm ready."

"Hush, baby," Alva whispered. "He–he done gone. Let Ronnie sleep."

"But Mama—"

Alva shook her head, reached for Pearl's hand, and led her to the kitchen.

In the light from the window over the sink, Pearl saw the puffy gash over her mother's left eye and her split lip, and she began to cry again. Alva tried to smile at her and Pearl saw that one of her front teeth was missing. "I'm sorry, Mama!" she cried. "He knocked your tooth out!"

21

"It ain't your fault, baby. See, I–I picked a fight w–with him on purpose."

Pearl felt a new rush of tears spilling from her eyes. Her mother always stammered for a few days after a bad beating. "Why, Mama? Why you *do* that?"

"So–so he'd get mad, baby, an', an'–an' leave! An', an' he got *so* doggone mad he said he ain't *never* comin' back. S–see, baby? I told you M–Mama was gon' make a way."

"Oh, Mama!" Pearl sobbed.

"Shh-shh-shh. Hush now, baby. Look at Mama… Look at me, Pearl." Alva attempted a smile. "You… you 'member why I named you Pearl? 'Member that story I told you?"

"Mm-hmmm. But you could tell me again…."

Pearl leaned her face against her mother's body and felt her arms around her. Closing her eyes tightly to keep from crying, she listened to the steady heartbeat and the soothing sound of her mother's voice telling the story she loved so much.

"When I was a little girl, jus' about your age, m–my grandmama told me—she told me a story 'bout a pearl. She—she said a pearl means a symbol. It means—not jus' love. It means *pure* love. An', an' you was my first baby! And I was *so* happy you was a girl so I could name you that. And look at'cha! You jus' the sweetest, purtiest pearl I done ever seen, baby."

* * *

Later that day, Alva dragged Victor's smelly chair out into the hallway. Then she marched over to see Mr. Dundee. Mr. Dundee was a gentle giant of a man, who worked as the superintendent for Alva's building as well as his own. Since he lived directly across the alley, she took the shortcut, and knocked purposefully on his door.

When he opened it, his customary smile faded quickly. "Lord, Miz Sayles," he said softly, "what did that man do to you this time?"

Alva smiled with closed lips to hide her missing tooth. "It don't matter, Mr. Dundee. He gone. That's all that matters to me and the kids."

Mr. Dundee sighed. "Well, I hope he stays gone for good this time so you and the kids can get on Relief. Do you need help with sump'm? Did he put another hole in the wall?"

Alva shook her head. "All I need is for you to get rid of his ol' chair with all that liquor stink on it. I dragged it out into the hallway, but if you could get it down them stairs and put it on the street so the trash man can haul it away—"

"Lead the way, Miz Sayles," he said, smiling broadly. "And I'ma do sump'm else while I'm over there. I'ma change your locks so he can't come bustin' in on you again."

"Thank you, Mr. Dundee. I—I sho' wish there was more fellas like you in the world."

"Happy to do it for you, Miz Sayles."

* * *

The next few months passed quickly for the children, but Alva was struggling to find ways to feed them. When enough time had passed, she claimed abandonment, which allowed her to apply for the Government Relief program.

Several days later, a gray haired white woman knocked on the door. Alva had been expecting her. " 'Mornin', ma'am," she said, gazing at the woman's clipboard.

The woman peered over her glasses at Alva. "Mrs. Sayles?"

"Yes, ma'am. I'm Alva Sayles."

"I'm Mrs. Ellis, your case worker," she said as she walked in.

"Yes, ma'am," Alva said nervously. "Uh, have a seat, ma'am. Would'ja like sump'm to drink? Oh, uh, I'm sorry. All we got is water, but I can get'cha—"

"No, thank you. I'm just going to take a look around and make some notes."

Mrs. Ellis said very little as she walked through the small apartment scribbling notes. When she got back to the front door, she finally spoke to Pearl. "How old are you, dear?"

"Seven, ma'am."

"Mrs. Sayles, why isn't this child in school today?"

23

"Oh, um, well, I been plannin' on gettin' her in school, ma'am. It just been—"

"She's already behind, Mrs. Sayles," she said. "She'll have to enroll in first grade, but she really *should* be in second grade. Well, unless she can read. Can you read, dear?"

Pearl looked at the floor. "No, ma'am."

"Speak up, please. I couldn't hear you."

"No, ma'am. I can't read yet."

"That's my fault," Alva said quickly. "She real smart though. Could she catch up?"

Mrs. Ellis was shaking her head. "No. It's first grade for this child. Here's a form with information on how to register her at Ward School."

Alva looked at the paper. "Is it very far, ma'am?"

"It's right here in your district. She can walk to it. But get her registered this week."

"Yes, ma'am. I sho' will."

* * *

Ronnie cried when Pearl left the house for her first day of school, and he waited on the stoop every afternoon to hear her stories about all the things she had learned.

At the end of her first semester, Pearl hurried home, smiling. "Hi, sugah-boy," she called.

"What'cha learn today, Pearl?" Ronnie shouted as he climbed down the steps to meet her.

"Sump'm good," she answered. "I got a surprise for you, too. Come on in the house."

Ronnie followed her inside and they went into the kitchen. Pearl opened the book bag her mother had made from a pair of khaki pants her father had left in the laundry basket. Smiling proudly, she pulled out a book and pointed at the picture on the cover. "See this bunny right here? This is a story about a bunny. Want me to read it to ya?"

Ronnie's eyes widened as he stared at the book. "Yeah, Pearl! Read it right now!"

"Okay ... Hey, where's Mama? I wanna read for Mama, too."

"Gettin' a chicken."

Pearl's eyes lit up. "Chicken for supper! Oh, boy! I'm so sick'a beans I could spit!"

She pulled out two chairs. "Okay, you sit right there and I'll read till Mama gets home."

Ronnie climbed up onto the chair and stared down at the book. "Did'ja steal it?"

"No! I get to borrow it for three whole weeks. This is what'cha call a liberry book. Wait, I mean ... a lib*rary* book. Miss Danbury— she's my teacher, 'member? Anyway, she said I gotta stop sayin' words wrong."

Ronnie sighed. "I can't wait till I get seven and go to school."

"You ain't gotta be seven ... I mean, you *don't* gotta be seven. You only gotta be six to go to school, Ronnie. I started late, 'member?"

Ronnie nodded, still staring at the book. "When I'm gon' be six, Pearl?"

"Umm, let's see." Then she counted her fingers. "Hey! Only four more months!"

"Oh, boy!"

"Okay, lemme read now." Pearl opened the book, turned two pages and began to sound out the words: "The ...Vel-vuh-teen ... Rabbit ... by Marger-ee W-will-eemz."

"What that mean, Pearl?" Ronnie whispered. "Bel-buh-teem?"

"I don't know. All I know is it's about a bunny rabbit. We'll ask Mama."

Turning two more pages, Pearl went back to reading: "Chapter One. There was ... once a velvuh-teen rabbit, and in the beee... the beee—"

She froze when she heard the sound of the front door opening, as she always did, until she was sure it wasn't her father. She still worried that he would find a way to knock down the door, new lock and all. But it was Alva who walked in carrying a grocery bag. "Hi, Mama!"

"Got that chicken?" Ronnie asked.

"Just like Mama promised," Alva said. "What'cha tryin' to read, Pearl?"

"The Vel-vuh-teen Rabbit."

"What that mean, Mama?" Ronnie asked. "Bel-belbuh-teem?"

"Oh, velveteen. It jus' material, like what I sews with, baby, but softer and fancier."

Pearl sighed. "I was tryin' to read it to Ronnie, but I ain't very—I mean, I'm *not* very good yet. I gotta stop sayin' ain't, Mama. That's what Miss Danbury said."

"Well, ya gotta do what your teacher tells you, Pearl. Okay, scoot over and I'll read a little to get'cha started. Then you can read to me and Ronnie while I cook. How that sound?"

Pearl and Ronnie grinned at each other. "Thanks, Mama!"

"Here we go ... There was uh, once a velveteen rabbit, and in the beginning ... he was really splen... Oh! Splendid." She winked at Pearl. "Mama needs to practice readin' too, huh?"

Pearl grinned. "You read real good, Mama!"

"Read some more!" Ronnie shouted.

"Okay, here we go... He was fat and bunchy, as a rabbit should be...."

* * *

The next few months were happy ones for Pearl. She had worked hard to improve her reading skills, and that improvement carried over to her other subjects, as well. The best evidence was in Miss Danbury's smile as she handed Pearl her second-semester report card: An "A" in every subject, with the exception of one "C" in Arithmetic.

Pearl loved Miss Danbury, not only for her patience and gentle voice, but also because of something that had happened on the first day of school. Miss Danbury had leaned over to point at a word in her book, and when their arms crossed, Pearl saw that her arm was the same shade of brown as Miss Danbury's. Pearl had never liked being brown, and wished that she had inherited her mother's tan coloring. Ronnie was only a shade darker, with soft, curly hair. Their father was dark-skinned, and Pearl recoiled whenever she saw anyone that dark, whether man, woman, or child. Pearl wasn't as dark as her father, but she resented that he had made her so brown.

Until she met Miss Danbury.

Miss Danbury's complexion was the color of a smooth pecan shell, and she smiled with her whole face. Her eyebrows bobbed up and down when she talked, and little crinkles appeared around her expressive black eyes when she laughed. Pearl was even charmed by the way Miss Danbury pushed her wire-rimmed glasses back up on her nose whenever they slipped down. Her mid-calf skirts and high-necked blouses always looked clean and freshly pressed, and her shoes were always polished. None of the women on State Street had nice clothes, especially not for going to work. When Pearl's mother left for work each morning she wore the usual uniform of most cleaning ladies—plain gray skirts and blouses, and those awful white rubber-soled shoes. The only time she saw her mother dress nicely was each Sunday. Alva had two church dresses, one blue and one brown paisley. But even in her church dresses, Pearl's mother never looked as elegant as Miss Danbury, and Pearl began to think that being brown wasn't so bad after all.

After Miss Danbury rang the 3:00 o'clock bell on the day the report cards had been distributed, Pearl waited until the other children had left and approached her teacher's desk.

"Miss Danbury?"

Miss Danbury stood up and came around to the front of her desk. "Yes, Pearl?"

"Thank you for my good grades, specially the 'A' for reading. I really like reading now."

Miss Danbury smiled. "You are most welcome, honey. But I didn't *give* you those good grades. You earned each one, and especially that 'A' for reading."

Pearl felt a big smile coming on, so she pressed her lips together tightly to hide her missing front tooth. Her mother had promised her it would grow back, but she was still self-conscious about it. "Can I ask you sump'm, Miss Danbury?"

"Not 'can I.' It's 'may I.' "

Pearl nodded. "May I... May I ask you sump'm?"

"Yes, you may."

"Could you... Uh-oh, that's prob'ly wrong too. M-may you?"

Miss Danbury laughed and patted Pearl's shoulder. "What is it you need, honey?"

"Well, I sure would like a list of books I could get at the liberry." She squeezed her eyes shut. "I mean the li*brary*, ma'am. You know, hard books—well, a *little* hard. So I could get—Wait… So I *may* get better with my reading."

"I understand. You mean that you're ready to try reading at a higher level, is that it?"

Pearl nodded so fast, she felt her braids bouncing against her ears. "Yes, ma'am! That's 'zackly what I mean!"

Miss Danbury went back to her chair and began writing as Pearl waited quietly.

"Here you are, Pearl. Take this list to Mrs. Monroe at the library, and she'll get you started. Now, they're numbered, so be sure she gives them to you in order. That's important."

"Thank you, ma'am!"

As Miss Danbury began stacking the books on her desk, Pearl cleared her throat.

"Was there something else, Pearl?"

"Well… Yes, ma'am. Uh, do you, maybe, need some help to clean erasers or sump'm? See I—" Pearl stopped and stared at her shoes.

"Speak up, Pearl. Don't be shy. Tell me what's on your mind."

"Well, see, I need to get my brother a birthday present, but me and Mama ain't got—I mean, we *don't* got no money."

Miss Danbury corrected her gently. "You *haven't any* money, Pearl."

"We sure haven't! But see, I was thinkin' that I could work after school for a nickel a day and save up. Ronnie's birthday ain't till—*isn't* till—one more month. I could get him a real good present with all them nickels."

Miss Danbury laughed. "You've really thought this out, haven't you?"

Pearl grinned and nodded happily, and didn't care that her missing tooth was showing.

"Well, I haven't much money myself in these hard times, but I think I can spare a nickel a day. So I'll make you a deal, Pearl. You go and pick out the present you want for your brother and write down the price. Then go home and figure out how many nickels it will take to buy it."

Pearl's smile faded. "Yes, ma'am... Um, that's Arithmetic, huh?"

"Yes, it is. But you can do it."

"Yes, ma'am. See you tomorrow." She turned and walked slowly toward the door.

"I guess it'll be all right if you ask your mother to help you with the Arithmetic. A little."

Pearl's smile was back. "Thanks, Miss Danbury!"

* * *

Each day after school, Pearl tidied up the classroom and cleaned erasers as Miss Danbury graded papers. She enjoyed having her teacher all to herself and loved chatting with her about the library books she was reading.

But one afternoon, Miss Danbury was strangely silent as she graded papers. When Pearl tried to start a conversation, she shushed her sternly.

Pearl worked quietly, sneaking glances at her teacher's angry expression and trying to think of what she could have done to make her so angry. When she finished, she picked up her school bag and walked slowly to the door. "Bye, Miss Danbury," she said softly.

Miss Danbury stood up. "Pearl. Come back and sit down, please."

Pearl walked back to her desk and sat down. Miss Danbury stood over her.

"Look at me, please."

Blinking back tears, Pearl looked up.

"I was very disappointed in you today, Pearl."

"Why, ma'am?"

"Don't you remember when Tommy was trying to read and you laughed at him?"

"But—"

"Don't interrupt. You rolled your eyes and snickered. And then *what* did you say, Pearl?"

Pearl wiped her nose with the back of her hand and mumbled, "I said... I guess I said... 'that's not even a word'... or sump'm like that."

"You said, 'that's not even a word, *stupid.*' You called Tommy stupid, Pearl! And then the other children laughed at him too. How do you think that made Tommy feel? Just because he's still learning to read does *not* make him stupid!"

Pearl was sobbing now. "I'm sorry, Miss Danbury!"

"Don't you remember how hard it was for you when you were learning to read?"

"Yes, ma'am."

Miss Danbury handed her a handkerchief. "Look at me, Pearl. Stop looking at the floor."

Pearl looked up. "I'm sorry. I'll tell Tommy I'm sorry, okay?"

"Yes, you will. And with more than words. Tomorrow, I want you to start helping Tommy with his reading, and encourage him the same way I encouraged you. That's the only reason to learn things, Pearl. Knowledge is not something to brag about. It's something to share."

Pearl nodded and wiped her eyes. "I'll never laugh at nobody again, I promise."

Miss Danbury extended her arms and Pearl ran over and hugged her.

"Now stop crying and go home. All is forgiven."

* * *

Ronnie's birthday fell on a Friday. Pearl brought her nickels to school in a sock so that she could stop on the way home to buy the book Mr. Tate was holding for her at his store.

After Miss Danbury rang the bell at 3:00 p.m., Pearl waited for the other children to leave and then ran up to her desk to show her the nickels.

"That's a lot of money, Pearl! I didn't pay you that much, did I?"

"I been helpin' Mama with her job on Saturdays. She gave me some nickels too!"

"Well, I'm very proud of you. So what present did you decide to get your brother?"

"A book! *The Ugly Duckling*. Ronnie *really* liked that velveteen bunny book so I know he'll like a duck!"

Miss Danbury laughed. "I'm sure he will! Do you have enough money there?"

"I even got enough left for two Baby Ruths. Ronnie *loves* Baby Ruths."

"All right, then. You'd better run along now and get that shopping done."

"But I have to help you with the erasers and clean up your desk first, Miss Danbury."

"Not today, Pearl. You go and enjoy your brother's birthday party."

"Thank you, Miss Danbury! You're so nice to me."

"You're welcome, Pearl. And I'm very proud of you for helping Tommy. He's really improved his reading, hasn't he?"

"Yes, ma'am! I'm teachin' Ronnie too!"

"That's good! You're a good little teacher. Now, go get your brother's gift."

* * *

Once Pearl had bought the book and the candy, she ran nearly all the way home. Hurrying up the steps, she threw open the front door, but then stopped to hide the book and the candy in her school bag. Then she skipped into the living room.

"I'm home, Mama."

No answer.

A chill crawled down Pearl's spine. The house was too quiet. "Ronnie?"

Again, no answer. The radio was off and the kitchen door was closed. "Mama?"

Only then did she hear her mother crying. She ran into the kitchen and saw Alva on the floor near the stove. Her hair was sticking out wildly, and her eye was swollen shut.

Pearl hurried over to her, already crying. "Mama!"

It took a long time for her mother to choke out the words: "Yo' daddy took Ronnie!"

"But, but how'd he get in, Mama? Mr. Dundee changed the lock!"

"Ronnie was out on the–on the stoop waitin' for you to come home. Then, then I heard him scream and I seen yo' damn daddy out the window! I ran out and tried to fight him, but he dragged me back in! I was hangin' on to Ronnie, but... Oh, my Gawd! He was screamin' for me to help him, but that damn devil... he... he beat me... and I couldn't get up! An' he hit Ronnie, Pearl! He hit him hard and made him bleed! An' he–he took him!"

Pearl collapsed in her mother's arms. All she could do was cry as she listened to Alva's screams growing louder and louder: "He took him! That damn devil!... He took my baby!"

1937–1938

Despite reversal by the Supreme Court, the State of Alabama retries Scottsboro Boy Clarence Norris and sentences him to death for the second time.

Paul Robeson, Ernest Hemingway, Martha Gellhorn, and Langston Hughes arrive in Spain to support the antifascist struggle in the Spanish Civil War.

Oliver Law, serving with the Abraham Lincoln Brigade in Spain, becomes the first Negro Commander of an international military unit.

Salaria Kea, a Harlem nurse and activist, becomes the first Negro woman to serve with the Abraham Lincoln Brigade in Spain.

The liberation of Spain from the oppression of fascist reactionaries is not a private matter of the Spaniards, but the common cause of all advanced and progressive humanity... Through the propagation of false ideas of racial and national superiority, the artist, the scientist, the writer is challenged. The battle-front is everywhere.

~ Paul Robeson

The loss of political freedom in Spain would seriously endanger political freedom in France, the birthplace of human rights. May you succeed in rousing the public.

~ Albert Einstein

Make the lie big, make it simple, keep saying it, and eventually they will believe it.

~ Adolph Hitler

DOC

All you colored peoples
Be a man at last
Say to Mussolini:
No! You shall not pass!
~ Langston Hughes

CHAPTER 3

SPAIN

From his prone position under a thick growth of roadside bushes, Doc stared past the border crossing at the overwhelming height of the Pyrenees mountains. Moon shadows cast by the jagged rocks twisted upwards to a seemingly endless elevation. As his eyes trailed up the face of the mountain, he felt his heart pounding. He looked over at Jimmy. "Damn, man," he whispered.

Jimmy nodded. "I know."

Clément, their French guide, motioned angrily at them for quiet.

Just then, two French border patrol officers walked past, not four feet away.

All three men flattened their bodies under the bushes and remained still for several minutes. Then Clément slid halfway out and peered after the officers.

"He isn't gonna try to get across *now*, is he?" Jimmy whispered.

The plan, as Doc had understood it, was to wait until an approaching bank of dense clouds covered the nearly full moon, and then make a break for the mountains. He looked at his wristwatch; it was 10:05. Their Spanish contact had been waiting for them since 9:30.

Jimmy nudged him as the clouds finally blocked the moonlight. The road was dark.

Doc nodded and kept his eyes on Clément.

With the slow fluidity of a snake, Clément had been quietly retracting his body until it was back to its original position under the bushes. As soon as he placed his right hand behind his back, the border patrol officers passed again. They were so close this time that one of the officer's shoes was no more than three inches from Clément's head.

Doc stared at Clément's fingers for nearly a minute before the signal came. Clément counted down five seconds, and then moved back out from under the bushes. Rising slowly to a crouch position, he looked back at Doc and Jimmy, mouthed the word *allons*, and then began running swiftly and silently across the road.

Doc followed immediately without turning his head to look at Jimmy or the officers. Only when he felt the rough embrace of the dense woods on the other side of the road did he look back for Jimmy. He felt Clément grabbing his arm and pulling him into a narrow pathway.

"Jimmy?"

"Right behind you, man!"

Doc stayed close to Clément as they moved quickly up a steep, winding labyrinth of dry brush and flying branches. After several minutes, he could feel sweat stinging the cuts and scratches on his face and arms, but he kept climbing. Just as he began to wonder if their guide was lost, they came to a narrow plateau. Clément stopped abruptly, then Doc stopped, and Jimmy bumped into him from behind.

Doc glanced back and exchanged a look with Jimmy. They were both gasping for breath, but Clément was breathing normally.

"This is hard work, man," Jimmy whispered.

"Yeah. And we haven't even seen any of Franco's boys yet. Still ready?"

Jimmy jerked up his chin. "Hell, yeah! Nobody said it was gonna be easy."

Clément was pointing at a hand-drawn map and staring at them with an angry look they had become accustomed to. It translated roughly into: *Crazy Americans talk too much.*

Doc and Jimmy took the cue and leaned in attentively to study the map. With his index finger, Clément traced the way to their contact's position, then pointed to a barely visible path leading upwards to their left. As he handed the map to Doc he said one word: *"Liberté!"*

Then he was gone.

Doc was still catching his breath. "Let's go, man."

"Damn, I'm dyin' for a smoke," Jimmy said.

"You're kidding, right? You see that steep, treacherous trail over there?"

"Yeah, I see it," Jimmy said. "But I still want a damn cigarette. Wish I would'a brought more from home. Hey, I wonder what Spanish cigarettes taste like."

Doc shook his head. "Two weeks ago, you were bitchin' about how hard it was to get a passport. And now you're bitchin' about cigarettes?"

Jimmy chuckled. "Message received, comrade."

Doc nodded and cinched up the straps on his leather backpack. "All right, then. Let's start puttin' one foot in front of the other one."

Jimmy shook his head and sighed. "Nuh-uh. Make that hands *and* feet."

"Aw, hell," Doc groaned suddenly. "There's our contact waving at us from the top of that ridge, and we're standin' around shootin' the shit like we're on the goddamn subway."

"Where?"

Doc pointed up to his left. "Right up there where Clément showed us on the map."

"Oh, I see him now." Jimmy turned for one last look over his shoulder. "Goodbye, France. Hope I get to see you again someday."

"Come on, man," Doc snapped.

"Right behind you."

Their contact was a lanky, gray-haired Spaniard who looked to be about fifty. Doc considered himself strong and tall—six feet, two inches—but the Spaniard was at least six feet, three inches—maybe four. Though he appeared slender, Doc noticed that his forearms were as thick and muscular as his own, and his calloused hands were evidence of much harder labor. His face was the color of burnished copper and still youthful in its structure, despite deep lines from weather, worry, and not-so-recent laughter. His eyes were light brown and startlingly clear, like the last light of sunset reflected in a clean pond. At the moment, he looked annoyed, but nodded a curt greeting at them. It was soon evident that he spoke excellent English.

"You are late, comrades. Five minutes more, and I would not be here. I am Enrique. Follow me and do not waste time to talk."

After climbing up the rough, rocky surface of the mountain for several minutes, Doc was winded again. He turned back to check on Jimmy, who was also struggling. Then he looked up at Enrique, who was still climbing with steady efficiency. "*Señor*," Doc called softly.

Enrique looked back at them and nodded. "We rest here."

He reached down and Doc gripped his hand. As he felt himself being pulled up to a level spot, he was impressed with the older man's strength. Then he watched him help Jimmy up, again with little apparent effort.

Enrique sat down, removed his backpack, and retrieved his canteen. "Sit and drink," he commanded, "but only a small drink."

They did as they were told, without question.

"Do not feel shame," Enrique said. "It is a lifetime of climbing that prepares a man for this. You will climb more distance in shorter time as we go."

Jimmy nodded quietly.

Enrique gazed at Doc and Jimmy in a contemplative once-over. "You are with the Abraham Lincoln Brigade, yes?"

"Yes, sir. We got separated from the others on the ship."

Enrique nodded. "They divided you for questioning. Your comrades told us of this."

"Yes, sir," Jimmy said. "We told them we were students headed for Paris."

"An honorable lie," Enrique said somberly.

"An honorable mission, *Señor*," Doc said. "I just wish there were more of us."

Enrique nodded sadly and fell silent for a few minutes. Then he stood up. "Come, comrades. We have much of this mountain yet to climb."

Doc got to his feet. "Will we be meeting up with the other Lincolns for training?"

"We were hoping to meet Oliver Law," Jimmy explained. "He's an activist from Chicago. He inspired a lot of us to come to Spain."

"He's with the Lincoln Brigade, like us," Doc added. "Have you met him or—?" He stopped talking when he saw the strange expression on Enrique's face.

"I never met him," Enrique said softly, "but I know his name. One of our Mexican comrades told me about Oliver Law. He was killed in Brunete only last month. I'm sorry."

"Oliver Law—is—is dead?" Jimmy stammered. "Are you sure?"

Enrique nodded. "Yes. I am sorry, comrade."

Doc heard the catch in Jimmy's voice and couldn't look at him. All he had talked about on the boat were the reports of Oliver Law's crusade to save Spain. And now he was dead.

Jimmy finally asked the difficult question: "How did he die?"

"He was killed by a sniper while leading the attacks in the Boadilla del Monte sector."

Jimmy looked up. "Leading? He was *leading* the attacks?"

"He was Battalion Commander, comrade."

"A colored man was a battalion commander?" Doc asked.

"Yes, comrade. With much respect from his men."

"Thank you for telling us," Jimmy said.

Enrique nodded. "The best way to honor your friend is to get to our mission. Your shipmates are in training with another unit that has moved on. You two will remain with us. We are a special unit. Our mission requires that we are small and unknown. We will train you at our outpost."

"Yes, sir," Doc said. "When will we be getting weapons?"

Enrique pointed into a high, dark distance. "Beyond that ridge we cross into Spain. Our outpost is a cave on the other side of the mountain, half distance from the bottom. A good place to defend air attacks, and a good place to watch the town below. Everything we need is there."

* * *

The area surrounding the cave was thick with fragrant pine trees, which had dropped a blanket of soft needles over the rocky ground. The entrance to the cave was framed by slopes of gray boulders and covered by a large burlap flap to keep out the wind and hide the interior light. All three men had to duck as they entered, but inside, the ceiling height was nearly eight feet.

The first thing Doc spotted was a huge banner draped on the wall of the cave with *¡No parasan!* painted in large red letters. He knew the meaning of those words: "No! You shall not pass!" It had been Madrid's battle cry, and it brought back an electrifying memory of sound and vision: A rally in Harlem. An impassioned Spaniard explaining the urgency of keeping Franco's fascist army from crossing into Madrid. To the people of Spain, Madrid was their final, inviolable line of defense. Crossing it would be an absolute act of war.

Doc closed his eyes. He could still see the Spaniard standing on the stage, his chest heaving with emotion. Out of words, he had appealed to the crowd with nothing but the desperation of his dark eyes. After a long, tense silence, he began screaming the words again and again, weeping and pumping his fist in the air until the crowd joined him in an eruption of shouts: *¡No parasan!... ¡No parasan!... ¡No parasan!... ¡No parasan!*

That chant had burned into Doc's memory. It had inspired him to join the Abraham Lincoln Brigade. As he continued staring at the words, he realized that Enrique was watching him.

"Since the fall of Madrid, it has become the battle cry for all of Spain. Rest now, comrades. There is food to eat."

Doc nodded, slipped off his backpack, and looked around. There was a rough wooden table just under the banner with two benches for sitting. The air was damp and musty, and heavy with conflicting smells: kerosene from the three lamps that lit the cave, and some sort of stew with garlic. A stocky man with a thick black beard and angry eyes was staring at him while stirring the concoction in an iron pot over a charcoal fire. His complexion was nearly as dark as Doc's, and his hair was blue-black, straight, and almost long enough to touch his shoulders. Enrique said something to the man in rapid Spanish and he filled three bowls without speaking or breaking his frightening stare.

Enrique seemed amused. "May I present Lobo—one of our Mexican comrades."

Doc nodded and took the bowl. "*Gracias. Me llamo* Doc Calhoun."

Jimmy smiled nervously. "And, uh, *me llamo* Jimmy Turner. *Hola.*"

Lobo didn't answer.

Enrique took a seat at the table. "Sit, comrades," he said, still smiling.

Doc and Jimmy sat down on the bench and began to eat.

"What is this?" Doc asked.

"Beans and rice, with peppers and garlic," Enrique answered without looking up. "It is simple food, comrades, but it fills the belly."

"Sure does," Doc agreed. "And it's good."

The bearded man came over and poured wine into two cups.

"You got wine?" Jimmy asked in disbelief.

Enrique laughed. "Wine is everywhere, comrade. Not *good* wine, but wine."

Doc nodded at Lobo. "*Gracias, Señor.*"

Again, Lobo didn't respond.

Jimmy cleared his throat. "Doesn't *Lobo* mean, uh, wolf? Is that right?"

Enrique nodded. "That is right. He is called that name because, like *el lobo*, he is a very talented killer, especially in hand-to-hand combat. His favorite weapon is the bolo knife."

Jimmy and Doc exchanged a quick glance, which made Enrique chuckle. "He is also a talented cook, comrades. Two days ago, a noble antifascist rabbit sacrificed his life for the cause, and Lobo honored him in a delicious rabbit stew. But no rabbits today."

The sudden, distant sound of a truck engine prompted Enrique and Lobo to grab their carbines and move to the cave's entrance. "The lamps!" Enrique hissed.

Doc and Jimmy moved quickly to kill all the lamplight in the cave, then waited in the darkness for something to happen. Enrique was peering out from a tiny opening at one side of the flap. "*¿Qué va?*" he whispered to Lobo as the truck noise grew louder.

Then, for the first time, Doc heard Lobo's booming voice: "*¡Armas!*"

He raised the flap, and beams from truck headlights flooded the cave. Three powerfully built men came inside, greeting Lobo and Enrique with back-slapping embraces, laughter, and rapid Spanish. Enrique spoke to them for a moment, then tossed a box of matches to Doc. "Light the lamps, comrade," he said, smiling broadly. "We have been waiting for this delivery for weeks! A truckload of weapons from our Mexican comrades."

Once Doc and Jimmy had relit the lamps, Lobo and the other three men hauled in three long, heavy looking boxes and placed them near the other supplies against the cave's right wall.

One of the men smiled broadly at Doc and Jimmy, then rubbed his hands together as he gazed at the food on the table. "*¡Hola, comrades! ¿Guisado?*"

"*Sí*, comrade," Enrique said. "Lobo!"

Lobo nodded and filled more bowls as Enrique introduced the new men. Pointing at the smiling man, he said, "That is Julio, a very happy man when there is food to eat."

"*Hola*, Julio," Doc called. "*Me llamo* Doc."

"*Hola*, Doc." Julio sat down to eat, then nodded at Jimmy. "*¿Usted?*"

"*Me llamo* Jimmy. *Hola.*"

"And there is Jesús and Miguel," Enrique said, pointing at the other two men.

Miguel reached into his pocket and offered Doc and Jimmy cigarettes.

Jimmy smiled. "*¡Amigo!*"

"Miguel was in Oliver Law's unit in Brunete," Enrique said quietly.

Jimmy's smile faded as he stared at Miguel. "Oliver Law was—your commander?"

Miguel nodded. "*Sí. Comandante Oliver Law… salvó mi vida.*"

Doc and Jimmy turned to Enrique for the translation.

"Oliver Law saved his life."

After a long silence, Doc said, "Thank you, *Señor*. I'm sorry. I mean *gracias*."

When everyone had finished eating, the men lifted the first box of weapons onto the table and pried open the lid. Inside were carbines, submachine guns and clips, and all types of single-shot rifles. Some of the guns showed more wear than others, but they all appeared to be in good working condition. Enrique pulled out two well-worn Remington rifles and handed one to Jimmy and the other one to Doc.

Doc inspected the rifle and smiled. "Is this—?"

Enrique nodded. "American Government issue. Your American military may not be with us, comrade, but a few of their weapons have made their way to Spain."

Doc grinned at Julio and held up the rifle. "*Gracias, Señor* Julio!"

Julio smiled at Doc. "*¡Salud!*"

* * *

Jimmy had first tried to convince Doc to join the American Communist Party on the basis of their defense of the Scottsboro Boys. Then he had stepped up the pressure after Benito Mussolini's attack of Ethiopia in 1935, and again when Franco took over in Spain. The link between the two fascist takeovers had become clear.

After reports that the United States would not send troops to assist in either struggle, Doc's frustration intensified. He and Jimmy could find no organized resistance to the Ethiopian attack. They had no money to travel and no connections in the region. Spain was another matter. When Jimmy told Doc about the International Brigades recruiting volunteers from around the world, he finally agreed to attend a meeting. When it was over, he had not joined the Party, but he and Jimmy had signed up to defend Spain with the Abraham Lincoln Brigade.

Their first revolutionary adventure was obtaining passports. Once the U.S. government became aware of the number of Americans volunteering to fight Franco, all passports to Spain were suddenly prohibited. Doc and Jimmy joined a group from Harlem and applied as students traveling to France. As they waited for word on their passports, they prepared by reading party literature on the anti-fascist struggle and every breaking story in the newspapers.

It wasn't until they were on Spanish soil that they learned just how much the newspapers had omitted, either out of ignorance or intent. For two days, Enrique not only trained them as fighters, he educated them about the war. From Franco's takeover after the election of 1936 to the long list of atrocities that followed, Enrique relayed eyewitness descriptions of some of the battles that had already been fought: Madrid, Teruel, Jarama, Badajoz....

American newspapers had reported the names of some of the guilty collaborators—Adolph Hitler and Benito Mussolini topping the list—but many Doc was learning about for the first time. Studebaker, General Motors, Texaco, and Nazi-sympathizer Henry Ford had provided oil, trucks, and equipment to Franco's army. Even the Catholic Church supported Franco's fascist regime. Enrique confirmed a *Chicago Tribune* story that had quickly been hushed up in America. A Falangist gang called the "Black Squad" had rounded up over 1,800 Spanish citizens in a bullfighting ring and turned their machine guns on them. Many were women and children. The Black Squad had also murdered an outspoken homosexual poet named Federico García Lorca, who had courageously condemned the fascist takeover in Spain. But they could not silence him. In death, Lorca's legend grew and inspired antifascists around the world.

After speaking to Doc and Jimmy at length, Enrique fell silent and searched their eyes with his eerie, vacant gaze. "What do you think constitutes an act of war, comrades?" he asked suddenly. "How does war begin?"

"Here's what I think," Jimmy said. "Here in Spain it started with the coup. That was the first act of war. Then Franco brings in Mussolini and the Nazis. That was the second act of war."

Enrique was already shaking his head. "This war began long before Franco. It began with the oldest story. Years of wealthy landowners stepping on the poor. It began with each man who carried the shame of failure when he could not feed his family. It was each hungry child who watched his father die in the streets. It was each grieving mother who fought like a man to save her children. Each day, each minute of suffering ... All these things together constituted an act of war against the people of Spain."

"I understand," Jimmy said softly.

"No, comrade, you do not. And you *must* understand before you are truly ready to fight as our brothers. Think of your own lives, your own wars. Each man fights many wars."

Doc was staring blankly at a flame in one of the kerosene lamps. "Our war … Our war began with the first chains on the first pair of black hands."

Jimmy nodded. "And the first rope around the first black neck."

"And slumlords."

"Cops beatin' us up for just … bein' alive… and bein' Negroes."

Doc looked at Enrique. "You're right. We *didn't* know why we signed up to come here—not consciously anyway. But we *felt* it, Enrique. We were *compelled* to come here."

"Because our wars are the same," Jimmy said softly.

Enrique nodded. "Now you are ready to fight as our brothers—*hermanos*."

He stood up and his voice shifted from a low, philosophical tone to a commanding sharpness. "Tomorrow morning you will begin your first mission. Your weapons will be picks and shovels for digging the nest for the machine gun crew."

Jimmy frowned. "But we'll carry these rifles though, right?"

"Of course. But for your first mission you are more useful with the shovels. You will watch and learn. There will be plenty of time to shoot and plenty of enemies who must die."

"Where will this machine gun nest be?" Doc asked.

Enrique shook his head. "You will know when we tell you to stop and dig. We do not tell you of all plans, comrades," he explained. "Only your mission, one day by one day. One order by one order. Do not feel dishonored by this. If you are captured—"

"I understand," Doc said. "I should have known better than to ask too many questions."

"You are young, comrade. A young man asks many questions, but few will be answered."

* * *

That night Lobo cooked a more substantial meal of rabbit with rice and beans in a spicy wine sauce. After they ate, Julio and Miguel strapped on their carbines and went out to their assigned posts. Jesús left in the truck to pick up men and equipment for the next day's mission.

Jimmy stretched out on a thin blanket on the floor and quickly fell into a deep sleep. But Doc was wide-awake, hungry for more of Enrique's stories. The more he learned about the war the angrier he became.

"We *must* win, Enrique," he said.

Enrique gave him a strangely dejected look. "Win?... There is no winning in war."

"But Enrique, that's all we've been talking about, isn't it? I don't understand."

"What do you think is the prize to win in a war?"

"I didn't mean it that way," Doc said softly. "I just meant we shouldn't *lose.*"

Enrique patted his shoulder. "You are right, of course, comrade. And yet, here in the middle of this war, at this time, I fight a war with myself."

"I'm sorry, Enrique. I still don't understand what you mean."

Enrique sighed. "War is a tragic thing," he began, "a two-headed monster of our beliefs and our needs. Each day we fight to survive. But there is a deeper war—the war for humanity." He glanced quickly at Doc. "But this is not the time to speak of this. War is not a time to feel."

"With respect, I'll try not to feel, but I *need* an answer to that question... *por favor.*"

"Very well, here is my answer. It is my *belief* that we share this world as brothers and sisters. But it is my *need* to have healthy children, food to eat, work, a warm place to sleep. And I even dare to hope for a small measure of justice and happiness... but I am a man. And men fight over ideas of need and belief. But we do not kill the ideas of men. We kill the men of ideas. And we become fools with a desire for power. And so we kill each other, forgetting that we are killing our brothers and our sisters... and our children... And so war is wrong."

Out of a long silence, Doc said, "So then... what's the answer?"

"Ah… now you learn the truth, my friend. It is not only young men who will fail to find answers. Searching for answers makes old men of us all. For now, I fight for one thing. Today. Today we fight to protect our children and to build a country of justice and shared power." He smiled. "You Americans call it democracy. As for me, a man who shares the world with you, I dream that this will be the last war. Because if it is not, then one day there will be one man with all the power. But he will be completely alone, because to have *all* power, a man would have to kill everyone." He turned his head slowly and gazed at Doc. "Pray that you are not that man."

Another long silence stretched between them. Then Enrique stood up and walked to the cave entrance. "Too much talk. Now we sleep. You have had enough of my *escuela* for tonight."

"You're wrong. Your *escuela* has given me a lot to think about. And *gracias*."

"I am not the wisest teacher you will know in your life, comrade, but it is my time to teach you. Your time will come to teach others."

He pulled aside the burlap flap and went out to sleep under the stars.

Doc blew out the last kerosene lamp and stretched out on a blanket next to Jimmy. He couldn't stop hearing Enrique's voice and seeing the emptiness in his eyes. Then, after several minutes of restlessness, he realized that no one's eyes are empty, not even the eyes of a blind man. What had appeared to be emptiness was actually Enrique's ability—or curse—to look perpetually inward at all the death and injustice and two-headed monsters he had known and would never forget.

Unable to find any peace in that conclusion, Doc nevertheless fell into a weary sleep.

I don't think things'll ever
be like that again—
I done met up with folks
who'll fight for me now—
like I'm fighting now for Spain.

~ Langston Hughes

CHAPTER 4

Doc felt increasingly uneasy as he and Jimmy followed Enrique down the steep, winding trail.

From the minute Julio had rushed into the cave earlier that evening, it was clear that they were all in imminent danger. Enrique issued urgent orders: "Carbines, ammunition, and grenades, comrades. There is word of a surprise attack. Be prepared to fight."

As they moved swiftly and quietly down the trail, Doc thought about all he had learned over the past ten months, and wondered whether this mission could possibly turn the tide. Despite Enrique's attempts to dispel any rumors of defeat, the news had been filtering through. In battle after battle, the Republicans were losing ground to the fascist forces.

After nearly an hour of descent, Enrique stopped and pointed to his right at a natural ridge. "Under there, comrades. That is good cover for you and easy to spot for me to find my way back to you. When I return from the gorge I will know our next move."

Doc and Jimmy scrambled under the ridge and settled in.

"Do not move from this spot, comrades," Enrique said. "If you hear shots, do not return fire unless you are directly attacked. When I return, I may come from another direction. If I do not return in thirty minutes, then return to the outpost. Take care that you are not followed."

Once Enrique disappeared up into the brush on the hillside, Jimmy nudged Doc. "I know you've been avoiding this, but we gotta talk about sump'm before we go back home."

Doc barely heard what Jimmy was saying. He was scanning the perimeter, still jumpy about what it was Enrique expected to find on the other side of that gorge. "Huh?"

Jimmy sighed. "Tell me you been givin' some thought to joining the Party."

"You want to talk about that right now?" Doc said crossly.

"You gotta join sometime, man."

"I don't *gotta* do anything but stay black and die. And I already told you, Jimmy, I'm not party material. I'm a musician."

Jimmy groaned. "You could've been a scholar, man! In college, I thought you'd turn out to be a lawyer who stood up for us! Always rattling off chapter and verse about justice, and all those constitutional arguments. Always with the books."

Doc shook his head. "I never planned to go to law school, Jimmy. I was just trying to broaden my mind with some college classes, that's all. But I was *always* a musician, even then."

"Yeah, I know it," Jimmy said bitterly. "You were *obsessed* with it."

"I'm *still* obsessed with it. I'll be a musician till the day I die."

"Yeah, but you didn't have to start runnin' around with fools like Rico and Hooper—"

"Rico looked out for us when we were kids. He saved my ass more than a few times."

"Yeah, and he ended up in prison! But even Rico wasn't as bad as that rotten pusher Hooper! That sonofabitch was almost your downfall. And you would've never met him if you'd kept away from those dope fiend musicians and stayed in college, man."

"Drop it!" Doc said sharply.

Jimmy's wounded silence reminded Doc of how they had fought when he dropped out of college to play jazz on the nightclub circuit. Then Hooper came along. Heroin had only started out as a curiosity, but soon Doc had become one of Hooper's regular customers. Although it had been years since he had quit, Jimmy never let him forget his mistake.

"You should be more careful who you pick for a hero," Doc said. "And *now* is not the time to bring that shit up."

Jimmy shrugged. "Okay, that was a low blow. Friends disappoint each other sometimes. I know I disappointed *you* when I joined the Party."

"Only at first. But when I learned more about it, I understood. I respect your dedication to the Party. It took guts to make that choice and I'll defend it to the death."

"I know you, Doc, and everything you believe in is right in line with—"

"*Don't* tell me what I believe in, man. I believe in music. That's the only thing I'm sure of in my whole life."

"Sounds like a cop-out to me."

"No, it's the truth, that's all."

"You can't just spend your life on the sidelines playin' your trumpet, man!"

"Who's standin' on the sidelines?" Doc snapped. "I'm fighting for Spain, ain't I?"

"I'm talkin' about when we get back to Harlem! Our people are still catchin' hell!" Jimmy let out a frustrated sigh. "Okay, look... You got two parties in America—"

"Goddamn," Doc groaned. "Here we go."

Jimmy persisted. "*One* party tells us right to our faces they don't want anything to do with Negroes. They shove us all into tenements to keep us from havin' any kind'a damn chance in life! And they sure as hell don't want us to vote."

"Yeah, I know all that, Jimmy, but this still ain't the time."

"And then you got the damn Democrats—"

"Roosevelt's not so bad."

"Roosevelt? What the hell's Roosevelt done for Negroes?"

Doc cut his eyes at Jimmy. "I know about fifty cats in Harlem who got jobs through the WPA! And what about the Relief program? That helps everybody, man. Not just white folks."

"Scraps, Doc! And you sure don't see Roosevelt's army over here helpin' Spain, do you? All those fat-cats just sit around in Washington while the fascists are takin' over the world!"

"It's not just them. Americans are scared, man! So they believe the liars till it's too late."

"So you're saying U.S. citizens would choose *fascism* over Communism?"

"I'm *saying* that most folks in America don't know the goddamn difference, Jimmy!"

"But *you* know the difference! And you're not scared!"

"I've never been scared of ideas."

"But you still swing with the Democrats!"

"Better than the alternative! So yeah, I swing with 'em on most issues."

"Shit. Nobody in Washington will *ever* let Negroes get a whiff of party leadership."

"What a surprise, Jimmy. Life's tough for colored folks. Let's all cry the blues."

Jimmy let out a hard, frustrated sigh. "The Party was good enough for Oliver Law!"

Doc glared at him. "I ought'a belt you for that."

"All I'm sayin' is that the Communist Party stood up for us when nobody else would."

"Drop it, Jimmy," Doc said. "I'm *not* a joiner."

Jimmy rolled his eyes. "Said the guy who joined up to risk his neck for Spain."

"Which is what I'm *trying* to keep my mind on at the moment. And it's time for you to shut up before your loud Communist mouth gets us both killed, man!"

Jimmy lowered his voice. "We're not finished with this conversation, Doc."

"Wait a minute. Be quiet," Doc said, peering out over the top of the ridge. "Hear that?"

"What?"

"That rumbling. You can feel it. Don't you feel that?"

"Oh, now I do," Jimmy whispered. "A truck."

"Shit, more like a convoy. These are the guys Enrique's lookin' for!"

Headlights suddenly emerged from a low rise about 100 yards away.

"Shit!" Jimmy hissed. "Let's go, man! Let's head up that hill where Enrique went."

"He said to wait, Jimmy. And I am *not* leaving here without Enrique."

"So let's go up there and get him before those trucks roll over our dumb asses!"

"They can't see us. We've got good cover and he *ordered* us to wait!"

The rumbling of the trucks was now an imminent roar. "Doc! The brush on that hill makes *better* cover! They can't follow us up there." Jimmy scrambled to his feet. "Come on!"

As Doc reached up to grab Jimmy's arm, he felt a bump against his left side. He jerked up his rifle, ready to fire, but saw that it was Enrique.

"It was a trap, comrade," Enrique said quickly. "They were reported to be on the other side of the— Where is Jimmy going? Stop him!"

Doc called out to Jimmy, but his warning was lost in a blast of machine-gun fire. He could only watch helplessly as Jimmy staggered to one knee under a shower of his own blood.

The next few seconds registered in Doc's mind as a series of cruel sounds and images he knew he would never forget: The urgency in Enrique's voice—*¡Dios Mio!* —followed by an immediate shift to action. Before Jimmy's body fully hit the ground, Enrique had yanked Doc back and was pulling him in the opposite direction. "Crawl, comrade! Stay low!"

Doc's reaction was unexpectedly foolish and emotional. He jerked away from Enrique and scrambled into the open toward Jimmy, who was trying to crawl back to him. Jimmy's eyes were wide with terror and he was choking out a gurgling noise as blood bubbled from his mouth.

"There is no help for him!" Enrique shouted. He grabbed Doc's foot and pulled him back.

Doc kicked at Enrique. "Goddammit! We can't just leave him—"

Then he felt a rock-hard pressure on his throat. Enrique had him by the neck and was dragging him away. They bumped along for several yards and then rolled down a rocky decline into a patch of tall weeds. Only then did Doc feel a release of the pressure, but only slightly.

Enrique leaned close to his ear and spoke three words that stabbed like cold knives: "He—is—*dead*!"

* * *

The trip back to the outpost was a blur. Doc suddenly found himself seated at the wooden table, staring at Enrique, who was calmly eating a bowl of beans.

"War is not a time to feel," Enrique said, without looking up from his bowl.

"Sorry. It's hard for me to turn off feelings like you do with such *ease*," Doc snapped.

After a tense silence, Enrique dropped his spoon and pounded the table with his fist. "Do *not* speak to me of feelings!" he shouted. "Spain has felt the pain of this war long before you came here, comrade! But today is war. And war is a time to fight! Tomorrow we will feel and we will cry and we will honor our dead. *Tomorrow*. That is the only thing to fight for in war."

Doc stared at him. It was the first time he had heard Enrique raise his voice in anger.

Enrique picked up his spoon and turned his attention back to his bowl. "Today is still war," he said. "And war is not a time to feel."

Doc said nothing.

"Eat, *Señor*," Enrique said. "Tomorrow we may have no food."

* * *

When Doc woke up the next morning, his first thought was not of Jimmy's death. The tomorrow Enrique spoke of was here. Julio was packing supplies and weapons, and Enrique was issuing directives about the day's mission as he adjusted the saddle on a large black gelding.

"You are carrying much needed supplies in that truck, and our men in Barcelona are waiting for you," Enrique said, without looking at him. "As for me, comrade, I am needed for a very special mission, or I would have taken them myself. So you see, I have much trust in you. You have been trained. You are ready."

"Yes. I'm ready," Doc said in a flat tone. "I've studied the map. I know the way."

"Barcelona is under constant attack from all sides. And as you learned last night, you must trust no one, unless they have shown loyalty. The betrayal of our informant was intended to kill all of us.

We are fortunate to have lost only one man. So now, I must trust you with this mission. There will be many decisions that you alone must make."

"I'm ready," Doc repeated. "And you can trust me."

Enrique put his foot into the stirrup and swung his body into the saddle. Taking the reins in his hands, he finally looked into Doc's eyes. "When you came to Spain, you came as a boy."

Doc gazed at him quietly, knowing there was more.

"You are no longer a boy, comrade."

Doc nodded and stepped back. "*¡Libertad!*"

As he watched Enrique nudge the horse into a gallop and ride away, Doc tried to ignore the sudden cold feeling running through him. He climbed into the truck and waved at Julio, who had just finished packing the last provisions for the movement of the outpost to its new position.

* * *

For the first few miles, the bumpy road was the only thing keeping Doc awake. He tried humming melodies and horn riffs from his favorite jazz records, but his mind went blank after "Caravan." He shook his head to clear it, then hit his brakes hard. He had nearly run over a large object in the road. Jumping out, he went to move it out of the way.

Then he stopped. There was an outstretched arm just in front of the truck's left tire. He walked slowly to the front of the truck until he saw the whole body. It was a woman, lying face-down in the road. She was riddled with bullet holes and covered in blood. He knew that she was dead, but he touched her neck to be sure. She was cold and there was no pulse.

As he stood there looking at her, he felt the same shaking he had experienced when Jimmy had been killed. Though he had never met this woman, he knew her. Her dress and headscarf were similar to those worn by the good women who had helped them with their missions. Bringing food in baskets and smuggling weapons under their skirts, the women of Spain were as heroic as any of the men.

Doc thought of Enrique's words just before he had ridden away on his horse: *There will be many decisions that you alone must make.*

With great effort, Doc reached down for self-control, and found it in a surge of anger. Climbing into the back of the truck, he pulled out a shovel. He had not been able to bury Jimmy, but by God, he would give this woman a proper burial.

"My decision, Enrique," he muttered. "My goddamn decision."

Checking the area, he found what looked like a good burial spot under a stand of pine trees a few yards from the road. He stuck in the shovel to test the soil. It was soft enough. Just as he was about to go back for the woman, something made him stop. Since his arrival in Spain, all he had noticed were the charred remains of churches and homes, terrain cratered by bombs, burnt trees and scattered bodies of dead humans and animals. He knew that hell on earth was still out there, lying in wait, but there was no sign of it here. Surrounded by sloping green hills, this spot seemed untouched by the violence of war. Lavender wildflowers grew in bunches under a warm yellow sun, and the breeze carried the fresh smell of the black, fertile earth and the pines born here. If there was a hallowed spot left in Spain, this was surely it.

Doc hurried over to rescue the woman from that dirty road and bring her to a better resting place. He gently turned her over, but then jumped back. "Oh, my God...."

Under the woman were two babies she had evidently been protecting with her body. One was an infant with the back of its head blown out, and the other was a little boy, one year old, maybe two. A loaf of moldy bread rolled out from under her skirt, telling her story. She had died trying to feed her children. Doc took a step back and squeezed his eyes shut as he swallowed back a sob. Then he forced himself to get to work.

Picking up the woman, he carried her to the pine trees and laid her down. Then he returned for the two babies. He knelt down and stared at them for a moment, then carefully picked them up, one in each arm. As he carried them against his chest, he felt his teeth clenching so hard he thought they would crack. Then he knelt beside the woman and placed each baby carefully in her arms, one on either side of her. He picked up the shovel and began digging.

With each stab of the earth, he struck harder and harder, working out his rage on a grave that never should have existed.

It wasn't until his arms began to shake from the exertion that he began to think about time. He had to get to Barcelona, and the sun would be going down soon. Hoping that the hole was deep enough, he moved the babies aside and carried the woman down the slope of the grave. After positioning her, he went back up and brought the babies down to her, gently tucking them between her body and her arms.

He tried not to look at her face as he covered her and her babies with the earth he had dug up. Instead, he heard himself talking to them in random, broken sentences, and wondered if his memories of Spain would cause him to lose his mind someday. He could feel a flood of tears and sweat dripping continuously off his chin, but he didn't stop to wipe it off. He kept working.

"You deserve a prayer," he muttered. "You deserve a prayer or sump'm... I should'a said that in Spanish, huh? Forgive me, Mama... I should'a learned Spanish quicker... You kids are–are sure gonna like heaven—if there is one... There *better* be a heaven for babies, goddammit!"

* * *

Doc stared at the road without really seeing it, only feeling its bumps. He remembered burying Mama and her babies, but somehow couldn't remember getting back into the truck and driving away. He forced himself to think about getting to Barcelona.

It had been hours since he had eaten, and his throat was so dry he could hardly swallow. His canteen had fallen off the seat and he reached down for it, but couldn't reach it. Rolling to a stop, he reached under the seat and retrieved it. As he took a swallow, he heard a distant droning sound and stuck his head out the window to take a look. Enrique had taught him the difference between the German Heinkel IIs and Junker 52s that had been bombing the last remaining Republican strongholds, but these planes were a little too far away to identify. All he could see was that they were approaching in V-formations from the east. And there were a lot of them.

He quickly pulled the truck off the road and bounced over the rough terrain until he felt the concussion of the first bomb. The truck jerked up on its two left wheels and Doc was sure it had been hit until it bounced back down in one piece. But before he could engage the gears, a second blast hit much closer, sending up a spray of large rocks and debris, and flipping the truck completely over.

Time is a strange creature when death is imminent. Doc felt the ticks of the next few minutes alternate between hard, violent jerks of resistance, and a calm feeling of compliant surrender. Like taking a ride to some unknown destination at the whim of some unknown force he was powerless to control. The darkness that swallowed him was gentle and black.

* * *

When Doc regained consciousness, he didn't have to open his eyes; they were already open. His hearing, what there was of it, was muffled. He wasn't even sure he could move. Slowly, he began to realize where he was—still inside the truck, pinned against the steering wheel. The smell of fuel and smoke filled his nostrils, and a sudden surge of pain and panic urged him to action. Turning his head, he was able to get his bearings. The only way out was the passenger window. He pulled and stretched his body until his fingertips caught the edge of the door, and he inched himself along until he could get a good grip. After a few hard pulls, he tumbled out. Only then did the pain really hit. His left arm was trembling with a radiating burning in his shoulder—as though a hot iron were being pressed into it.

After scanning the sky to be sure the bombers were gone, he touched his shoulder gently with his right hand and located the source of the burning. A jagged piece of shrapnel was embedded in his deltoid muscle. When he touched the pointed end, it was still hot, so he knew he hadn't been unconscious for long. He yanked it out quickly and tossed it to the ground. The burning eased up immediately, but he began bleeding heavily. Ripping off his shirt, he wrapped the wound as tightly as he could and secured an awkward knot using his right hand and his teeth.

The sky was getting dark.

Keeping close to the tree line, he made his way along the road. About an hour later he noticed the crunching sound of his boots in the gravelly dirt. His hearing was returning.

As hard as he tried not to think about death, he couldn't erase the grisly image or the choking sounds of Jimmy's young life bleeding away. Or Mama and her two babies left to die alone and helpless on a dirt road.

He caught himself shaking his head very hard, even though he knew that he would never shake out the images. *Keep your mind on the mission. Keep your mind on the mission.*

Periodically, he peered back down the dark road for any signs of approaching enemies, but there were none. According to his watch, he had been walking for two hours. His shoulder was beginning to throb. He turned his thoughts to Enrique and wondered if he'd ever see him again. Then he realized that he wouldn't. Enrique was already on his way to another tomorrow, whatever that tomorrow might bring.

Doc began to wonder how long he could keep walking and fighting the fatigue. Just as he was debating the wisdom of ducking into the woods on his right to rest for a few minutes, a sudden rustling sound from that direction sent him straight down into the dirt. He crawled as fast as he could with the use of only one arm, but he froze when the rustling sound took on the rhythm of footsteps. He looked around frantically for some kind of cover, but to his left there was nothing but the open road. And to his right....

A click. A metallic click just above his right ear.

He held his breath as a cold rifle muzzle pressed against the back of his neck. There was nothing to do but shut his eyes and hope that his death would be quicker than Jimmy's had been.

A deep, unfriendly voice from above said one word: "*¿Americano?*"

Doc opened his eyes, and decided that it would be safer to answer that particular question with his own question. "*¿Republicano?*"

When he felt the muzzle move away from his neck, Doc stood up slowly and looked into the bearded face of a young Spanish villager. His rifle was pointing directly at Doc's chest. Doc held his breath and once again cursed himself for not being fluent in Spanish. Very slowly, he raised his hands to show that he was unarmed, and nodded in the direction of his carbine, which was still lying at his feet. Only then did he speak. "*Me llamo* Doc. Uh, Lincoln Brigade."

"*¿Qué?*"

"Uh, International Brigades. Lincoln Brigade. *Me llamo* Doc. It's my name... *¿Usted? ¿Republicano?*"

At last, a look of perception and relief crossed the man's face. He uncocked the rifle and shifted it to his left hand, then grasped Doc's hand with his right. "*Republicano, sí! Me llamo Pablo.* Eez... eez my name."

Doc exhaled and smiled. "*Hermano....*"

"*Hermano, sí.*" Pablo smiled broadly, then gestured in the opposite direction of where Doc had been headed.

Doc hesitated. "But Barcelona is that way," he whispered, pointing back over his shoulder. "I mean uh, *pero... Barcelona está—*"

Pablo stared at Doc and shook his head sadly. "*Barcelona... Barcelona... no es.*" Again, he pointed up the road. "*Gerona ahora.*"

Doc nodded in understanding. Barcelona was lost, and the Republicans were making their last stand at Gerona. Though defeat seemed inevitable, he knew that there would be one more battle, one more chance to fight for Spain. As he walked quietly at Pablo's side, he came to the realization that this war had brought him full circle. Gerona offered only two possibilities. If he died, Spain would be his final resting place. If he survived, his only possible escape route would be the same as the one he and Jimmy had taken to get to Spain—across the Pyrenees Mountains.

A light wind began to blow, rustling branches on trees hidden in the dark. Doc closed his eyes and turned his face upward toward the breeze. He thought of that little grave under the pines and hoped that it was good enough.

When he opened his eyes, he looked over at the man walking next to him. Pablo was his only friend now. They would fight together and they would probably die together.

Then Doc aimed his eyes straight ahead at the road to Gerona. And in that moment he finally understood what Enrique had tried to teach him: War is not a time to feel.

Little eagles, I said,
where is my grave?
In my tail, said the sun
On my throat, said the moon....
                    ~ Federico García Lorca

RONNIE

CHAPTER 5

INDIANAPOLIS

Ronnie's body jerked in reaction to a sound, but he couldn't seem to force his eyes open. When he finally sat up, it took him a moment to remember where he was.

"Man, you were sleepin' so hard I was hopin' you died," a deep voice said.

Ronnie nodded and cleared his throat, still trying to shake off the cobwebs of sleep. He looked around the neat, new room. It still smelled like fresh paint. Then he glanced over at his older brother Trey, who was sitting on the edge of the other twin bed smirking at him.

"What was that sound?" Ronnie said softly.

"It's a heater, stupid. Ain't you noticed it ain't cold in here?"

Ronnie gave him a blank stare. "It's warm."

"Hell of a lot better than our old tenement, huh?"

Ronnie shrugged. "It's warm."

Trey rolled his eyes. "Ain't nut'n make you happy, boy. We' in the damn Lockefield Gardens! Them niggas from the old buildin' would be happy as shit to get in here."

Ronnie shut his eyes and wished Trey would disappear. "Yeah."

Trey threw a pillow at him. "Get up, dummy, 'fo I drag you out that bed."

Ronnie sat up and looked at the floor. "I'm up."

He waited until Trey left the room, then walked over to the window. His eyes scanned the playground and the fragile looking saplings that were sprinkled around the front of the new building. A large "Works Progress Administration" sign stood at the entryway on the corner of Indiana Avenue. Ronnie understood the importance of the WPA only in terms of how it affected him. His father was more agreeable when he had work, and he had worked for nearly a year on the construction of the Lockefield Gardens housing project. But it was Victor's wife Loretta who had put the family at the top of the waiting list. Loretta Sayles was the head administrator at Crispus Attucks High school, and she even owned her own car—a shiny, brown Buick sedan. It was four years old, but she kept it looking showroom new.

Ronnie shook his head and went over to the bureau drawer to find something to wear. It was Saturday, so he pulled out a pair of clean dungarees and a blue sweater that Loretta had folded so perfectly it looked as though it had just come off a display stack in a department store.

By the time Ronnie appeared in the kitchen for breakfast, he was steaming with hate for Loretta. She was serving her perfect breakfast and aiming her perfect smile directly at him.

Ronnie stared at her and tried to force a smile. She was what his father called "a healthy woman," a little on the heavy side, but her biggest parts were "in all the right places"—another thing his father often said. Her hair always looked perfect, dyed and styled at the beauty shop she went to every weekend, and she had a closetful of perfect dresses.

She was saying something to him, but he couldn't hear her. Ronnie's eyes were fixed on her starched white apron. His real mother had never even owned an apron, not that he could remember. When he finally tore his gaze from the apron and looked at Loretta's face, he felt a hard pang. After three years, it was growing more and more difficult to recall the details of his real mother's face.

"What's the matter with you, boy?" Victor Sayles barked as he came into the kitchen. "Don'tchu hear your Mama talkin' to you? Say good morning to her, goddammit!"

Ronnie felt his teeth clamp together as they always did in the daily battle he fought with his brain: *Just say it, stupid.* Then he saw his father's top lip quiver the way it always did when he was angry, and Ronnie finally mumbled, "G'morning."

"Good morning, *Mama*!" Victor shouted.

Ronnie sat down quickly and stared at his plate. "Good morning, Mama."

"Good morning, baby," Loretta said softly. "Don't be too hard on him, Victor. You know how quiet he is in the morning."

"Shit. He quiet all the damn time. Hey, where the hell's Trey anyhow?"

"Oh, he grabbed some toast and ran out to meet his friends. It's Saturday."

Victor was still staring at Ronnie. "Eat your damn food, boy!" he snapped.

Ronnie jumped nervously and began eating as quickly as he could. But every time he looked up, Victor's eyes looked angrier. And Ronnie knew exactly what that meant.

After Loretta cleared the breakfast dishes, she kissed Victor on the cheek. "Gotta go get groceries, baby. Be back in a while."

"Mm-hmm. Take ya time."

Then Loretta smiled at Ronnie and headed his way. Ronnie cringed, knowing what was coming. A kiss. Of all the things he hated about Loretta, he hated her kisses more than anything. One of his clearest recollections of his real mother was a sensory memory of her kisses. Her lips felt firm, warm, and velvety on his face, and then she would tickle him by rubbing her nose against his, which had always made him giggle.

Loretta's kisses were cold and greasy from the red lipstick she wore. He never said it out loud, but Ronnie had long ago decided on the perfect word to describe her lips: *slimy*.

He endured the kiss and finished the last bite of his toast. When he heard the front door close, he got up carefully. "May I be excused, Daddy? I was gonna go to—"

Victor's chair scraped the floor as he got up and unbuckled his thick belt. "You ain't goin' noplace, boy."

Ronnie nearly dodged the first lash of the belt, but the end with the buckle caught him across the mouth. "I'm sorry, Daddy!" he screamed.

He dropped to the floor and curled up, protecting his head with his hands. The belt was singing its whip-song in a rapid rhythm, punctuated by the pop each strike made on his body.

"I'm 'bout sick'a you cuttin' your eyes at my wife!" Victor yelled. "Can't even smile at her! After all we done for you! Got you out of that rat-trap your no-good Mama lived in! That bitch wasn't even my wife! You lucky me and Loretta took you in, you sorry little sonofabitch!"

He was just bringing the belt up over his head for another swing when Ronnie scrambled to his feet and screamed, "Don'tchu *ever* talk about my Mama again!"

Victor froze, clearly stunned. But after a moment he forced a laugh. "You nine years old and you think you gonna fight *me*? God*damn*, boy. I'ma make you wish you was never born."

Ronnie balled up his fists, and spit a mouthful of blood onto the floor, intentionally spattering his father's shoes. "I don't care if you *kill* me!"

Victor slowly aimed his eyes at the blood on his shoes; then he gave Ronnie a deadly stare. He still hadn't moved from the spot he was standing in, but Ronnie knew it wouldn't last. He was bracing himself for the worst when he heard the front door swing open and heard Loretta's quick steps as she hurried into the kitchen.

"Oh, my God, Victor!" she gasped. "I could hear you all the way downstairs! Look at this boy!" Running over to Ronnie, she snatched a handkerchief from her pocketbook and began dabbing at the blood on his mouth. "Victor, there are more and more people moving into this building, and they *aren't* the kind of people who are gonna put up with this kind of behavior."

Ronnie and his father were still locked in a hateful stare-down.

Loretta glanced up at Victor and smiled nervously. "I—I know you're just trying to discipline the boy, but please, Victor. This is a little extreme, don't you think? We don't want somebody callin' the law on you, now do we?"

Victor continued staring at Ronnie as he slipped his belt back through the loops and buckled it. Then, without a word, he walked out, slamming the front door behind him.

* * *

Ronnie was still awake when his brother got home that night, but pretended to be asleep.

"Wake up, Ronnie," Trey said. "Hey! Wake up!"

"What?"

"I heard Daddy worked you over again."

Trey turned on the lamp, and Ronnie saw his eyes widen. "Shit! He *really* worked you over, huh?"

"Leave me alone."

"Listen to me, boy. You're a pain in my ass and I don't like you much, but I'ma give you some advice anyway. You *gotta* learn how to deal with Daddy. If you don't, he gonna keep beatin' the shit out'cha till you crippled or dead. How the hell you think I got to be fifteen?"

Ronnie finally looked at Trey. "I hate him."

"Shit, so do I. But you gotta play him smart. Them WPA jobs are startin' to get thin, so he'll be gone drinkin' anyway. Just do like I do. Get out the house when he's here."

* * *

Ronnie decided to take Trey's advice. He managed to avoid his father for the next week by leaving early each morning. The public library was only two blocks from the school, so when he asked Loretta's permission to go there after classes, she seemed to understand, and even offered to pick him up on her way home every evening.

On Saturdays, he spent the whole day at the library. It had become his only true sanctuary, a magic place with books that transported him far away from Indianapolis, away from Lockefield Gardens, and away from his father, Loretta, and Trey.

He had checked out a new book called *The Hobbit* three days earlier, and he read each page feverishly. Bilbo Baggins was his new best friend, and Bilbo's Middle-Earth world was the most exciting place Ronnie had ever imagined. Alongside Bilbo, he had already encountered elves and trolls, and a wizard named Gandalf.

The hours ticked by like seconds that Saturday until Ronnie was suddenly and rudely yanked back from Middle-Earth by a hard tap to his shoulder. It was Belinda, the librarian's assistant, popping her chewing gum and telling him that the library was closing—right in the middle of his epic battle with a dragon that looked exactly like his father. Ronnie scowled at Belinda, dropped his sword, and then slammed his book shut. Without a word, he grabbed his coat and his book, and grumbled all the way to the front door.

When he stepped outside, Loretta's car wasn't there. After waiting for over twenty minutes he figured that she had forgotten about him, so he decided to walk home. It was dark, but Lockefield Gardens was only a few blocks away.

As he walked, Ronnie's mind went back to the fearsome dragon in Middle-Earth, and the night seemed to grow darker. He began walking faster. By the time he saw the entrance to his building, he was looking over his shoulder and running so fast he stumbled over the first step and dropped his book. Brushing off his pants, he picked up the book and hurried inside.

The foyer was usually well lit this time of evening, but tonight it was semi-dark. The only lights he saw were at the far ends of the hallways to his left and his right. As he started up the steps, he heard a frightful moaning sound from under the stairwell that stopped him in his tracks. His heart began to pound until he heard his brother's voice, but it sounded strange and breathless.

"Come on, Wanda, you know you want to, baby."

"Ooh, Trey, I do, baby, I *dooo*... but just not here."

"Nobody's around. Ooh, you see how you got me? I'm all hot and everything. I might... I might pass out or sump'm if you don't gimme some right now."

Wanda moaned again and Ronnie had to clap his hand over his mouth to keep from laughing. He had seen Wanda with Trey several times in the past few weeks. She was a "healthy woman," just like Loretta, only she was much healthier in the chest.

"You want me to do it with you—right here on the floor?" Wanda said.

"I can't wait, I told you! We can lay on my jacket. Come on, take off them panties."

Ronnie was now peering closely through the space between the steps, and his mouth dropped open. *Her panties?*

Nothing could tear him away now. He watched closely as Trey and Wanda tumbled awkwardly to the floor. Then Trey pulled Wanda's skirt all the way up to her waist. Her eyes were closed and she was still moaning that weird noise as Trey pulled down his pants and positioned his body over hers.

Ronnie's initial shock gave way to intense fascination. He began to feel a tickling in his belly as he watched the undulating movements of Trey's bare gluteus muscles. Something about those movements seemed to make Wanda either very happy or cause her great pain, judging from her chorus of erratic squeals and groans.

Ronnie was utterly spellbound until Wanda suddenly opened her eyes and gasped.

"Oh, shit, Trey! Somebody's watchin' us!"

Trey pulled up his pants and looked over his shoulder. "Ronnie! Git'cho ass down here!"

Ronnie shook his head and started up the stairs.

"Git'cho ass down here NOW!"

Ronnie slowly descended the steps until Trey yanked him under the stairwell. Squeezing his eyes shut, Ronnie braced for a smack, but to his surprise, Trey started laughing.

"You don't even know what we were doin', do you?"

Ronnie glanced over at Wanda, who had fixed her skirt, but was still sitting on the floor. She smirked at him. "What'chu lookin' at, punk?"

"Nothing," Ronnie said softly, but he couldn't keep his gaze from drifting over to Wanda's pink panties, which were still lying on the floor near her feet.

"Shit!" she said, grabbing her panties. "He was lookin' at my damn panties, Trey!"

Trey grinned. "I know it."

"So what'chu gon' do about it?"

Trey pulled Ronnie over to Wanda. "It's about time this boy got his first lesson."

"Oh, hell, no, Trey," she snapped, "I do *not* screw little boys. You must be crazy!"

"You ain't got to screw. Just let him touch you a little, that's all, baby."

Wanda folded her arms and shook her head, and Trey went down on one knee to whisper in her ear. Ronnie took the opportunity to start backing away, but Trey's head snapped back.

"You stay right where you are or I'll beat the shit out'cha, boy!"

Ronnie froze and stared at Wanda's smeared red lips. *Slimy*, he thought. Then he picked up a few words of what Trey was saying to her. Something about a silk scarf and some powder. Then he heard Trey moan again as he kissed Wanda's neck, and she giggled. "You promise?"

Trey nodded and reached back for Ronnie's arm. Yanking him down on the floor near Wanda, he said, "Gimme your hand, boy."

"No!" Ronnie cried.

"Shut up, stupid! It ain't gon' hurt! You ever touched a girl's nipple before?"

Wanda took the cue, slipping off the strap of her brassiere and uncovering one of her large breasts. She leaned forward with her eyes narrowed in a leer. "Come touch it, Ronnie."

"No!" Ronnie fought as hard as he could, but Trey had a strong hold of his hand and was forcing it closer to Wanda's breast. Ronnie shut his eyes and curled his fingers into tight fists.

Wanda laughed and grabbed him around the waist. "Don't you wanna touch it, baby?"

"No!" He was trapped between Trey and Wanda, and felt sick from the combination of her mushy body, Trey's sweaty hands, and the pungent heat filling the stairwell. He let out a loud sob. "Lemme go, Trey," he whimpered. "Please... I won't tell anybody."

Trey stood up angrily and shoved Ronnie. "What'chu mean you won't tell? You better not even *think* about tellin'."

Ronnie stumbled up a few steps, but made the mistake of looking back just as Wanda stood up and put on her coat. "I'm leavin', Trey," she said. "This shit's too crazy for me."

"Wait a minute, Wanda! We ain't finished yet, baby."

"Well, I am! I can't even believe I let you talk me into this crazy ol' mess! I'm leavin'!"

Trey glared at Ronnie and chased him up the stairs, catching him by an ankle. As Ronnie twisted loose, he slipped and fell to the bottom of the steps, then let out a scream.

Trey took off after Wanda, but Ronnie could hear him yelling over his shoulder, "Daddy's right about one thing. There ain't no hope for you, you little fairy!"

Ronnie made his way to the apartment, cradling his left arm with his right hand to keep it from moving. The pain was bad enough, but any movement was like a lightning strike to his arm. When he got to the door, he kicked it three times. He was sobbing when Loretta opened it.

"Oh, Lord! I forgot to pick you up! Wait— What happened to you, baby? Why are you holding your arm that way?"

Before he could answer, Ronnie saw his father walk in from the kitchen.

"Well, I ain't touched him, Loretta," he said with a smirk. "Can't blame me this time."

"I fell down the stairs," Ronnie said softly. "I hurt my arm real bad."

Loretta inspected his left arm. "It's broken, baby! We're takin' you to the hospital."

Victor grabbed his jacket. "Shit. *You* take him. I ain't sittin' around no goddamn emergency room all goddamn night. I got better things to do."

Loretta gave him a surprised look, but said nothing.

"You got a problem with that?… Yeah, I didn't think so. I'll be back when I'm back."

* * *

It was nearly midnight when Loretta and Ronnie returned from the hospital. The doctor had set the bone and sent Ronnie home with a sling and a plaster cast on his arm.

"I'm so sorry I forgot to pick you up, baby. I just got so busy. You want some supper?"

"No, ma'am," Ronnie answered. "I'm just goin' to bed."

"Well, let me help you get into your pajamas."

Before he could stop her, Loretta's fingers were touching his bare skin as she helped him with his pajama top. "I can do my pants by myself," he said quickly.

She smiled. "Okay, baby. You just call me if you run into trouble."

After she left, Ronnie worked up a sweat getting his pajama pants on and climbing into bed. All he wanted to do was read his book. But it wasn't on the nightstand. Slowly climbing out of bed, he went to Loretta's room and knocked. "Mama?"

She opened the door and smiled. "Yes, baby?"

"I forgot I dropped my library book when I fell down the stairs. I'm sorry."

"It's okay, baby. I'll just put on my coat and go get it for you right now. You wait here."

After she left, Ronnie stared at the door and made up his mind to stop hating Loretta. He even smiled when she returned and handed him his book. "Thanks, Mama. G'night."

"Good night, baby. Hope you feel better tomorrow."

But then she had to spoil it by kissing him with her slimy lips. He hated her again.

When he got back to his room, he wiped off her lipstick with his handkerchief, then got back into bed and propped up *The Hobbit* on a pillow. His father was still gone, probably getting drunk at a bar; Trey was probably off somewhere trying to get Wanda to take off her panties again; and Loretta was in bed. The house was perfectly quiet, and Ronnie quickly found his place in the chapter that Belinda had interrupted at the library.

After reading halfway down the page, he was back in Middle-Earth with his sword, preparing to slay the dragon that looked like his father. By chapter's end, he had beheaded the dragon, and Trey and Wanda and Loretta had vanished, along with the pain in his arm.

Now he was off on a new adventure with his friend Bilbo Baggins in the Misty Mountains in search of a magic ring.

1942

World War Two's Operation Torch is implemented in North Africa.

The Tuskegee Airmen are initiated into the U.S. Armed Forces.

The *Pittsburgh Courier* launches "The Double V Campaign" dedicated to Negro soldiers fighting for victory in the War while still fighting for human rights in America.

The Congress of Racial Equality (CORE) is founded by Civil Rights activist James Farmer.

Jimmie Lunceford hits the Billboard charts with "Blues in the Night."

CHAPTER 6

Pearl was sitting on the edge of her bed yawning when her mother walked into her room.

"Why you gettin' up so early, Pearl?"

Pearl gave her a puzzled look. "School, Mama."

Alva laughed and patted Pearl's shoulder. "It's Saturday, baby."

Pearl scrambled back under the covers. "I been workin' too hard if I forgot what day it is! I'm goin' back to sleep. I don't have to be at work till noon."

"Now, Pearl, if that job at Williford's is too much for you, then you just quit, baby. You can't let your grades slip. I want you to be somebody in this world. I don't want you cleanin' toilets for white folks, like me. We can get by on what I make, ya know."

Pearl opened one eye and grinned at her mother. "Thank you, Mama. G'night."

Alva kissed her. "Don't forget I'll be late tonight. Miz Lewis got that fundraiser at her house. I gotta cook and I'll be servin' too, so I don't know what time I'll be gettin' home."

"It's okay, Mama. I'll make supper."

Alva headed for the door. "Well, let me get goin' so I ain't late."

"Mama?"

"What is it, baby?"

Pearl peeked out from under the covers. "You look so beautiful with your tooth fixed."

Alva smiled. "Gettin' my ol' jack-o-lantern teeth fixed was better than gettin' a diamond ring! David sho' is my angel, huh?"

"Yes, ma'am, he is."

"You be sure to check the mail, Pearl. Don't forget!"

"If you get a letter from David I'll be sure and put it right on your pillow, Mama."

"Thanks, baby! Gotta go now."

Pearl went right back to sleep and didn't wake up until the alarm clock showed 9:35.

"Ooh, I'm lazy!" she mumbled. Glancing over at her library book, she wondered if she had time to read the last chapter before getting ready for work. But it was a sad book, all about the first World War, and she knew that the protagonist soldier would probably die at the end.

"Not today. I'll finish it tomorrow. I need a hot shower right now!"

She put on her shoes and bundled up in her bathrobe. It was only November, but the apartment was already freezing. Grabbing her towel and washcloth, she hurried out the front door, locked it behind her, and pocketed the key. As she walked down the chilly corridor, she heard the echo of someone singing in the bathroom. At this late hour of the morning, she had figured that it would be unoccupied. She turned to go back to the apartment, but something about the singing drew her back. It was spiritual and painful at the same time—a low, moaning hum, and she couldn't tell if it was a woman or a man. Then it changed back to singing. But this time it didn't sound spiritual *or* painful. She stood close to the door so she could hear the words.

...My new man just lef' me, just a room and a empty bed....

Pearl gasped and then pressed her ear to the door.

...Lawd, he could grind my coffee, cause he had a brand new grind....

Pearl clapped her hand over her mouth to keep from laughing. *Grind?* The older girls at school always said that if you were trying to protect your reputation, you should never let a boy slow-dance you into a corner, because that's when they'd get too close and try to "grind." Pearl had never heard any song like *this* on the radio. She leaned back against the door, but the voice had softened, so she could only make out snippets of the song:

...He a deep sea diver—with a stroke that can't go wrong....
...knows just how to thrill me, thrills me night and day
Lawd, he got that sweet sump'm—I told my girlfriend Lou
Now the way she ravin'—she must'a tried it too!
When my bed get empty—

The voice stopped suddenly and the door flew open. Pearl stumbled backwards. A large, dark-skinned woman was standing in the doorway laughing. Through the cloud of steam, she could see the woman's smile. She looked like a picture of Bessie Smith Pearl had once seen.

"I'm sorry, ma'am!" she said.

"Who you, baby?" the woman asked, wiping laugh tears from her eyes.

"I'm sorry, ma'am," Pearl said again. "I was just waitin' for the shower."

The woman was wearing a large pink bathrobe, tied at the waist. Her short hair was still wet, clinging in tight, black kinks all over her round head. She laughed again, and everything on her seemed to jiggle.

Pearl couldn't help smiling at her. "I bet you got a lotta boyfriends, huh?"

That made the woman laugh even harder. "Lawd, girl, you make me holla!"

"You sing real good, ma'am. I *was* listening. But I couldn't help it."

The woman bowed. "Thanks, baby. My name's Lucy Barnes, and I'm your new neighbor. I work around the corner at the River Boat Club."

"You're a nightclub singer! Ooh! I'm happy to meet you, Miz Barnes! But I never heard any song like that before."

"I bet you ain't. That's what'cha call the lowdown dirty blues. What's your name, gal?"

"Pearl."

"Aww, now, that's a right good name for a blues singer. How old are you, Pearl?"

"Fifteen, ma'am."

"Fifteen? Lawd! You *look* eighteen, at least. I bet'chu ain't understood nothin' about that song I was singin' in there, huh?"

Pearl grinned. "Oh, I got the general idea, ma'am!"

Lucy Barnes threw back her head and laughed, then gathered her belongings. "You sho' talk proper, don'tcha! I jus' love the way you talk... Okay, Miss proper-talkin' Pearl, the bathroom's all yours. Got a real nice echo in here too, in case you wanna try some singin'!"

"Thanks, ma'am!"

"Just call me Lucy, hear? And stop on by number 107 later. I'll play you my new record."

Pearl's eyes widened. "You made a record?"

"Sho' did. I just got in from Kansas City where I do my recordin', sugah. My agent got me lined up for some appearances here in Chicago so I can sell some records here."

"Oh, boy! Your life sounds so exciting!"

Lucy winked at her. "Tell ya what... Come on by after ya shower and I'll play you some mo' blues you ain't never heard befo'! Hah!"

* * *

Pearl began visiting Lucy's apartment every evening after work to listen to records and watch her pick out stage gowns for her performances at the River Boat Club. Lucy Barnes smoked French cigarettes in a long cigarette holder made of silver and rhinestones, and she waved it in the air with broad gestures as she talked about jazz and the blues. She opened her steamer trunks and showed Pearl her hand-beaded stage dresses, hats made of silk, and feather boas of every color. Pearl sat cross-legged on the floor, paying wide-eyed attention to Lucy's stories about all the stars she knew, the glamorous places she had been, her adventures with married men, jealous girlfriends, and singing to captive audiences under the bright lights.

"I sure would like to go to Paris someday," Pearl said. "Does the Eiffel Tower really look like it's made out'a diamonds?"

"At night it does, sugah. And Lawd, they sho' got a lotta nice nightclubs in Paris. But you know, every place has its own special magic. Even some'a these dives I'm playin' now."

"Is the River Boat Club a dive?"

"You ain't never been to the River Boat? It's right around the corner!"

"No, ma'am! I heard of it, but, umm... so has Mama."

"Oh," Lucy laughed. "Guess all nightclubs got a bad reputation with mamas, huh? But to tell ya the truth, I done sang in *much* worse places. River Boat's really pretty nice."

Suddenly, she stepped back and gave Pearl a long look. "Stand up, sugah."

Pearl stood up.

"You tall, and you *don't* look fifteen. Tell ya what... Next time ya Mama works late—"

"Tonight, Lucy! She's workin' late tonight!"

"Awright, then. Tonight you comin' to the River Boat with me."

Pearl's mouth froze in the shape of a large "O."

Lucy laughed. "But first, we gotta dress you right and fix ya hair and... Come over here."

Leading Pearl over to the vanity table, Lucy pushed her into a small chair in front of the mirror. Then she opened up a tiny pot of lip rouge. "Poke out'cha lips, sugah."

Pearl pursed her lips and Lucy dabbed on a few dots of red color.

"Now rub ya lips together like this: Mmmm-muh. That's right. Okay, now undo them plaits in that mess'a hair you got, and let me fire up my hot comb."

Pearl eagerly went to work on her plaits, untwisting them two at a time. "But Lucy, what should I wear? I don't have any sparkly dresses like the ones you have."

"Ooh, Lawd, you sho' talk proper, child! I just love the way you talk! And don't worry 'bout'cha dress. You got a black skirt, ain'tcha? Go get it and come on back here. I got a shawl in here someplace made out'a gold lamé. We'll drape it around your shoulders and pin it just right with my topaz brooch, and fix ya hair, and you gon' be a knockout!"

"Yes, ma'am!"

Lucy shook her head and bellowed, "Hold it!"

"What's wrong?"

"Ya *gotta* stop callin' me ma'am! Ya ain't supposed to be a kid! Now, let's see... You can be my cousin, and... you visitin' from—"

"Paris!" Pearl shouted.

Lucy put her hands on her hips and narrowed her eyes. "Can ya speak French?"

"No, ma'am."

"Then you from Kansas City, sugah. Now go get'cha skirt, and stop callin' me ma'am!"

* * *

82

By eight o'clock that night, Lucy had kept her promise and trans-formed fifteen-year-old Pearl into an eighteen-year-old knockout. As she stood in front of the vanity mirror, Pearl couldn't believe she was looking at herself. Her hair had turned out nicely, nearly touching her shoulders in shiny waves, her lips were rouged, and her eyebrows arched. They were dark enough that Lucy hadn't needed to pencil them. The gold lamé shawl left her right shoulder bare, with the topaz brooch pinned high on the left shoulder strap of her chemise.

Lucy was standing behind her, smiling over Pearl's shoulder as she assessed her project.

"Told'ja. You look eighteen, and ya sound older too, with that deep voice you got. You got some pretty shoulders on you, so that's why I got that shawl doin' that little peek-a-boo. Ya never show men too much right off. Remember that. Just enough to get 'em in-terested. Now. What else? ...Hmmm... ya ain't got very much in the chest department, do ya, sugah?"

"No, ma'am—I mean... no, Lucy. But I'm hopin' for some more chest by the time I really *am* eighteen."

Lucy laughed. "You *still* gonna knock 'em dead, sugah."

She handed Pearl a rhinestone evening bag and then wrapped a black feather boa around her own neck. Then she lifted her chin and posed like royalty. "Ready, Cousin Pearl?"

"Ready, Cousin Lucy!"

* * *

Pearl could hear the music inside the River Boat Club even be-fore the doorman let them in. As Lucy walked through the club, ripples of applause followed her. The men kissed her, the women hugged her, and Lucy introduced Pearl to all of them. Pearl said her hellos while sneaking glances at the stage until their voices faded from her consciousness. All she heard was the music. The drums, the horns, the bass... It was all so different from anything she had heard on a radio or a phonograph. She was still staring at the band when she felt Lucy nudging her.

"Pearl, this is Sam Paxton. He a college man! *And* his daddy use'ta play drums with Bix."

"Bix?" Pearl asked. "Who's Bix?"

Only then did she see the young, light-skinned man who was smiling at her with perfect white teeth. "Beiderbecke," he said.

Pearl couldn't stop staring at his smile. "You sure have pretty teeth."

Sam laughed and Pearl's face felt hot. "Uh, I'm sorry, your daddy used to play for who?"

"Bix Beiderbecke! The cornet player! My daddy used to play drums in his band."

"Oh!" Pearl extended her hand. "Well, it's very nice to meet you, Mr. Paxton."

"Call me Sam," he said as he pulled out a chair for her.

Pearl sneaked a "gaga" look at Lucy as she sat down, and Lucy grinned.

"I gotta go get ready for my set, sugah. This is my special table for my guests. And Sam here is gonna keep all them doggish drunks away from you. You two enjoy the show now!"

Sam began talking to Pearl, but she could only catch snippets over the loud music. She didn't mind. She loved watching him talk. He had light brown wavy hair—and that smile!

Then he reached for her hand. "Okay?"

"Uh, I'm sorry," Pearl shouted. "I couldn't hear what you said over the music."

"I said let's go outside and have a smoke," he shouted back.

"But isn't Lucy fixin' to sing now?"

"Not for a few minutes. Come on."

She stared hypnotically at his teeth. "Okay."

His hand was warm and strong as he led her through the crush of patrons and the thick cloud of smoke. When they stepped into the alley, the fresh air and the silence were startling.

"Woo," Pearl said, laughing. "It was noisy in there, wasn't it?"

"No more than most clubs," Sam said as he tapped out two cigarettes. "Have you ever been to Club Desire?"

"No," Pearl said, trying not to look awkward as she placed the cigarette between her lips. "Uh, I'm from Kansas City."

"Oh! There are some great clubs out there! Have you ever been to Rex Alley?"

"Mmm, no. Must'a missed that one." Pearl watched the lit match edging to the end of the cigarette. She inhaled, and then blew out the smoke with only a small hiccup of a cough.

Sam blew out a big cloud of smoke and grinned with his white teeth. "First cigarette?"

"No, but uh, I haven't been smoking long. Still getting used to it. I like it though."

"So, Pearl... You like the fellas?"

Pearl was trying to position the cigarette between her middle and index finger. Then she blinked up at him. "What fellas?"

Sam leaned close to her ear and whispered, "Men."

She reminded herself that she was supposed to be eighteen. "Oh! Of course I like men... *You're* a man aren't you?" She smiled, more at her answer than at him.

"I sure *am*." He tilted his head and kissed her, letting his lips linger for a few seconds.

"Mmm... That was nice," Pearl whispered.

"Sure was. I've been wanting to do that since the minute Lucy introduced us."

His face was still looming over her, and Pearl was trying to decipher his look when he suddenly threw his cigarette to the ground and wrapped his arms tightly around her. This kiss was much different than the first one. His mouth pressed hard against hers until his tongue pushed its way inside her mouth. Before she knew what was happening, she felt her back bump against the brick wall of the building, and then Sam's pelvis began pressing hard against her.

Pearl's eyes popped open. As she tried to push him away, she was trying to yell for help, but it just came out as muffled mumbling. He wouldn't let up the pressure on her mouth, and she felt as though she were smothering. Then she felt his hand sliding up inside the chemise she was wearing under Lucy's gold lamé shawl, and realized that he was pulling her to the ground.

She yanked her head around and let out a scream, but he clapped his hand over her mouth. "Shhh…" he said, and then grinned at her with his white teeth.

The next sound Pearl heard made her smile: "HEY!"

Somehow, Lucy Barnes was in the alley.

Sam had barely turned his head to look over his shoulder when a red umbrella came crashing down on his head. Pearl scrambled out from under him and got to her feet.

"Beat his brains out, Lucy!" she yelled.

After several swings that connected perfectly, Lucy raised the umbrella a little too closely, and Sam snatched it out of her hand. She stepped back.

"You black bitch!" he said. "I ought'a—"

Pearl had made her way behind Lucy, so she couldn't see what it was that had stopped Sam in the middle of his threat. His wide eyes were staring at something in Lucy's hand. Pearl leaned around to look. "A gun!" she yelped happily. "Shoot him, Lucy!"

Lucy raised the gun. Pointing it at Sam's crotch, she said, "You drop that umbrella, boy, 'fo I shoot you 'tween ya legs and leave ya so limp you can't rape nobody again! NEVAH!"

Without taking his eyes off the gun, Sam dropped the umbrella. "I didn't rape—"

"Shut up and RUN, boy!"

Sam took off down the alley and disappeared around the corner.

Only then did Lucy look at Pearl. "You okay, baby?"

"Yes, ma'am. How'd you know I needed help?"

"The bartender told me he saw that fool take you outside. I knew what he was up to." Lucy tucked the pistol back into her evening bag and wrapped her arm around Pearl. "Don't ever trust them pretty boys with the pretty smiles, sugah. 'Specially not them high yella ones. They love theyselves too damn much to ever love a woman right."

"Yes, ma'am."

Lucy fixed Pearl's hair and then tried to straighten up the shawl. "Damn that boy! I *knew* I should'a shot his ass! He done to'e up my gold lamé shawl!"

"I'm sorry, Lucy."

"Ain'tcho fault, baby," she said, walking Pearl out of the alley. "You sho' you awright?"

"Yes, ma'am. He really *didn't* rape me. He just grinded me."

Lucy's laugh slowly turned into a sigh. "Welcome to womanhood, sugah."

* * *

After that night, Pearl never went back to the River Boat Club, but she visited Lucy every day and began singing along with her records. Lucy told her that with her deep voice, she'd make a fine blues singer someday.

By mid-December the Christmas rush was on, and Pearl was working extra hours at Williford's. Lucy was usually already at work by the time she got home in the evening. There was nothing else to do, certainly no shopping. After Victor had taken Ronnie away, Christmas was not celebrated or mentioned. Gifts and a tree would only make the day more painful.

On the one evening she got off early, Pearl hurried home. When she got to Lucy's door, it was open, so she stuck her head in. "Lucy?"

"Come on in, sugah! Come help me pack!"

The bed was piled high with dresses and boas. The steamer trunks were open, and Lucy was hanging and folding at a furious pace. "I gotta catch my train, sugah. Come help me!"

Pearl began folding and handing clothing to her. "Where are you goin'?" she said softly.

"Back to Kansas City, sugah! Gotta record a few new songs and I got a real good-payin' gig at Rex Alley while I'm there! Just in time too, 'cause I'm runnin' out'a money!"

"How long does it take to make a record?"

"Well, we'll do more than one. I'll be there about three months or so."

"Three months?"

Lucy grinned and wrapped a red feather boa around Pearl's neck. "You keep this one. Looks good on ya! And don't look so sad, sugah! I'll be back. I promise. It's only three months."

Pearl tried to smile. "I'm really gonna miss you, Lucy."

"I'm gon' miss you too, sugah… Hey… You seen my pink sequin hat?"

"Here it is," Pearl said, handing it to her.

"Thanks, baby… And ya know what else? That River Boat Club *sho'* gon' lose business without ol' Lucy to pull in them crowds. Now you keep an eye out the window for that taxi driver and holla at him to come on up and get my trunks."

A little under an hour later the taxi arrived. Once the driver had loaded the last trunk, Lucy hugged Pearl tightly. "Well, this is it, sugah. Promise me you ain't gon' cry, now."

Pearl smiled. "I won't cry. But write me, okay?"

Lucy climbed into the taxi. "I sho' will, sugah! And I'll send ya my new records, too!"

"Oh, thank you, Lucy!"

"Now don'tchu let one'a them light skin'ded pretty boys get'cha in no alley again, ya hear me? And take care'a yourself and ya Mama too."

"Yes, ma'am!"

"Oh, Lawd! *Maybe* when I get back, you'll stop callin' me ma'am!"

Pearl grinned. "Okay… sugah!"

Lucy let out a loud laugh. "Hah! Now that's better! Bye!"

Pearl stood there waving until the taxicab carrying Lucy Barnes disappeared around the corner of State Street, taking all her color and music with her.

She moped around the house for days until she finally realized what was ailing her. As she was washing the dishes one night, she looked up and sighed. "Guess I got the blues.…"

She quickly finished the dishes, turned off the lights and went to bed, hoping that she'd feel better in the morning.

But when the early light woke her the next morning, she sat up suddenly. How had the days gotten away from her? Or had she intentionally forgotten that it was Christmas? After glancing out the window at the cold, gray sky, she dressed quickly. When she walked into the kitchen, her mother was standing at the stove, quietly making breakfast.

"Good morning, Mama," Pearl said softly.

Alva didn't respond. She didn't even turn around.

Pearl sat down. *Go on, Mama. Say it. Just say that one word and get it over with.*

The first year it had been eleven words: *The first. This is the first Christmas without Ronnie. My baby...* But each Christmas after that, it was only one word. A number. And then she'd cry and Pearl would spend the rest of the day trying to cheer her up.

Pearl sat there, trying not to stare into the past, but it was all she could do as she waited.

Finally, Alva turned around and gazed at her with red eyes. This year she had started crying earlier than usual. Then she finally said it: "Seven."

Pearl flinched, and wondered why. She knew it was coming. Was it the deadness in her mother's eyes? Or was it the number itself that turned every Christmas into a dreaded day of sorrow? The usual silence drifted down, so heavy, so palpable, that Pearl imagined she could feel it weighing their bodies down and smothering their souls.

She closed her eyes. She had finally finished reading *All Quiet on the Western Front*, and now a line from it echoed like a cruel voice in her mind:

Gas—gaas... The gas still creeps over the ground and sinks into all hollows....

She inadvertently held her breath, but then opened her eyes and fought her own brief, internal war to find something—anything—hopeful to say. But once again, she was defeated by that heavy silence. She ate her breakfast without tasting it, and each time she looked at her mother, her heart broke again.

Seven years.

CHAPTER 7

NORTH AFRICA

"It's that gas I'm scared of," Eddie whispered. "Them Germans use that gas. God*damn*, I hate them Nazis!"

"The Italians use gas too," Doc whispered. "And save your hate for Hitler and Mussolini. Some of those soldiers are just like us. Sucked into a war we didn't start."

Eddie scowled at him. "Nazis and Blackshirts, Doc! Baby killers! They ain't like us! We ain't killed no babies, have we?"

Doc sighed. "You are one morbid sonofabitch, Eddie."

Eddie ignored him. "It ain't like I'm scared to die," he said. "Hell, gettin' shot don't scare me near as bad. I just want it to be quick, that's all. And that gas is slow, man. Or some Nazi guttin' you with his bayonet. Now *that'd* be a *real* bad way to go."

The moon suddenly reemerged from a small patch of clouds, and its sudden brightness annoyed Doc almost as much as Eddie going on and on about all the possible ways to die in a war. The fact that he had not slept in sixteen hours also contributed to his evil mood.

He and Eddie were positioned in a natural shallow trench under a dilapidated bridge they had found after their truck conked out about a mile back. Sergeant Denton had ordered them to deliver the 2-½-ton truck to a unit in Algiers, but they had drawn fire just past the halfway point. The truck's engine had taken a bullet, resulting in a slow-death mechanical casualty. They had no choice but to leave the truck and take as many supplies as they could carry.

Eddie was still talking. "You seen any a'them pictures of fellas with their faces half-gone from that gas? It burns your skin clean off! I wish I'da never seen them pictures!"

"Shut up, man," Doc whispered. "There might be some Nazis standin' on this bridge."

Eddie's gaze drifted up to the underside of the bridge, and he stopped talking. Then a sudden barrage of machine-gun fire erupted nearby, and he raised up to return fire.

Doc grabbed his arm. "Hey! He's just probing, man."

He and Eddie flattened their bodies against the wall of the trench until the shooting subsided. After a few minutes, the drone of the truck engine faded away. "See? They're givin' up on this area now. If we would'a fired back at 'em, they would'a been all over us."

"Yeah, you're right," Eddie said. "And that sounded like at least three guns."

"No, it was one of those big truck-mounted guns. They echo like that. I heard 'em in Spain. Sounded like more, but it was just one."

"That's right, I forgot you were in that Spanish war too. Shit! This one's enough for me! Anyway, at least they didn't hit us with that gas."

"Would you stop bellyaching about that goddamn gas! Our immediate problem is dodging these bullets and bombs and makin' our way to that truck unit. Ain't that enough to worry about?"

"Yeah. I guess so. Sorry I been gettin' on your nerves."

Doc patted Eddie's shoulder. "Ignore me, Eddie. You're the best soldier I've met in this man's army. I'm just a goddamn bear when I don't get enough sleep, that's all. And the truth is, that gas scares the hell out'a me too! So we're both on edge. Shit! Wonder why?"

"Hey, Doc, look at that! A big, fat bunch'a clouds! Let's get out'a here while it's dark."

"Good idea."

The two men slowly made their way west, using the trees along the road as cover, until they spotted what appeared to be an abandoned farmhouse.

"Maybe we can hide in there and get a little shut-eye," Doc said.

"But what if they's some Nazis up in there, layin' for us? Sho' would be a good trap."

"Okay, you want to split up? You stay here and cover me. I'll go check inside."

"Shit, no! I don't want you walkin' into no ambush, man! Two guns is better'n one."

"Okay. But you know we'll be in the open when we cross that field. Those clouds we had earlier are long gone and that moon's pretty damn bright."

Eddie pointed to a ragged, overgrown section on the far right perimeter of the field. "We could duck down and make it through there, at least most of the way."

Doc sighed. "Back on our bellies again. Oh, well... all right."

They made the slow crawl to the farmhouse without incident. When they got to the door, they both saw the large bullet holes at the same time and exchanged a look. Doc opened the door carefully and they moved silently through the house checking each room. When they were satisfied that it was abandoned, they removed their backpacks and settled into the kitchen. It was the only room with furniture: a rough, wobbly table, one chair, and an empty wooden crate. They searched the shelves and cupboards for food, but found none.

Eddie spotted a small photograph on the floor and picked it up. "Hey, look at this."

Doc looked at the photo. It was a plain looking blond woman with a plump face. Eddie turned it over and read the writing on the back. "What the hell's '*mein liebling*' mean?"

"It means Nazis have been through here."

Eddie scowled and dropped into the chair. "Nazis got some ugly women, man! Hey, you got any K-rations left?"

Doc turned the crate on its side and tested it for sitting. "Just some'a those hard biscuits and a can of that questionable meat," he said. "And shit, you can *have* that."

"Hand it over," Eddie said. "Better than starvin'."

"Wait a minute," Doc said, jumping up suddenly. "You saw that old chicken house in the back, didn't you?"

Eddie rolled his eyes. "Yeah, but I ain't heard no chickens cluckin' in there."

Doc grinned. "Get your gun and cover me."

Crouching as low as he could, Doc ran to the chicken house. A couple of minutes later, he returned to the door, where Eddie was waiting.

"Told'ja there wasn't no chickens," Eddie said.

Doc held up five eggs. "Breakfast!"

Eddie grinned. "How'd them Nazis miss 'em? Hey! I got a packet of salt left, too!"

"Cool. Now let's see if that little stove works."

Opening the door of the small wood-burning stove in the middle of the room, Eddie said, "Looks like it. And there's a little wood left in here too—enough to fry up some eggs anyway."

"Yeah, and eggs cook fast, man. Not too much smoke."

By the time the sky began to lighten, Eddie had built a small fire, scrambled the eggs in a pan from his mess kit, and put out the fire.

"Man, these goddamn eggs taste like sirloin steak compared to K-rations," Doc laughed.

"Ain't that the truth!" Eddie said.

Doc closed his eyes and tried to eat slowly. When he finally looked up, he spotted an unexpected glimmer of color through a gap in the window shutter. He pulled it open just enough to peek out. Dawn was breaking in gorgeous streaks of gold and deep rose. Behind it, the top curve of a red sun glowed over a hill, shooting a spray of iridescent rays in a huge arc.

"Man, look at that, Eddie."

Eddie turned around to look, then shrugged and went back to eating his eggs.

"Just think," Doc said. "Somewhere there are some folks lookin' at that same sunrise."

"What's your point, man?"

"Well, maybe they're not thinkin' about war, that's all. It's nice to think that somewhere there are some folks who are *not* worryin' about gettin' shot after breakfast."

"Naw," Eddie disagreed. "Everybody's thinkin' about gettin' shot after breakfast, man. And if they ain't worried about gettin' shot theyselves, they're worried about their husband or their brother or their son or somebody. Whole damn world is thinkin' about this war. Ain't nobody studyin' no stinkin' sunrise, man."

"You're a cynic, Eddie."

"Whatever the hell that is."

"Let's get some sleep, man. Mind if I go first?"

"Go ahead and take your grumpy ass on to sleep!" Then he grinned and pointed over his shoulder with his thumb. "I'll be at the window, lookin' at all the pretty colors."

Doc laughed. "Shut up, Eddie."

They took turns sleeping in a small windowless room off the kitchen for the rest of the day. When the sun began to set, all was still quiet.

Doc had been on guard duty for nearly three hours. He was just about to wake Eddie when he saw him walking into the kitchen yawning.

"Damn, man," Eddie said. "I sho' wish we had some more eggs."

"Shit. We're lucky we got to eat at all. And we got some sleep too."

"Think we ought'a try the road yet?"

"Soon as it's dark. Maybe we'll get lucky and those clouds'll come back to give us some cover. Damn, we got a long way to go."

* * *

After walking for over ten hours, stopping several times to rest, Doc noticed that the sky was beginning to lighten. He glanced over at Eddie. "You look dead on your feet, soldier."

"Officially, I prob'ly died an hour ago," Eddie muttered. "Just don't tell my feet!"

Doc stopped suddenly. "Wait a minute—"

"What?"

"Look," he said, pointing up the road. "You see that truck? Just the front end, sticking out from that stand of trees?"

"Yeah! I see it. Damn, that can't be the truck unit, can it?"

"Not unless they only have one lousy truck in their whole unit," Doc said. "And not unless they shifted their position east by about twenty miles. I wonder if that's even one of ours. Maybe we ought'a get a closer look."

"Mighty quiet over there, Doc."

Doc raised his rifle and proceeded cautiously. "Come on."

After a few steps, they heard a man's voice from behind the truck.

"Whadda schmendrick!"

It appeared that he was talking to himself until a muffled voice answered from under the truck. "Kiss my ass, Morty!"

"I told you it's the goddamn valve, Marv!"

Doc grinned at Eddie and lowered his rifle. "Oh, yeah. It's definitely one of ours. New York, to be exact."

Eddie sighed. "Maybe they got some food. Damn, I'm starvin'."

"Good morning," Doc called.

A man leaned out from behind the truck and shaded his eyes as he peered over at Doc and Eddie. He was thin and white, and looked about thirty-eight. He was wearing dirty khaki pants and a greasy tee-shirt, and on his head was a beat-up camouflage cap. "Wait a minute, Marv," he said, tapping the side of the truck. "We got company."

"I heard him. If he ain't a Nazi, give him my regards. I'm busy under here!"

Eddie stepped forward stiffly and saluted. "Private First Class Edward James and Demetrius Calhoun reporting for duty, sir!" he barked in a crisp boot-camp voice.

Morty winced. "Take it easy, Private! And if ya salute me again, I'm gonna slap ya silly. So what was that name? Edwards?"

"James, sir. Edward James."

Doc chuckled. Eddie was still standing at attention.

Morty grinned at Eddie. "Would'ja relax already? I got one lousy more stripe than you, James, which I'm not even wearing at the moment, for chrissakes. And this is a *very* unofficial outfit here, in case ya hadn't noticed." He stuck out his hand. "Name's Morty. Morty Klein."

Eddie smiled and shook Morty's hand.

Then Morty turned his attention to Doc. "And what was *your* name again?"

"It's Calhoun, sir. We were headed to Algiers to deliver sup-plies—"

"Nah, nah, soldier," Morty said, grinning. "The *first* name. It was like some gladiator name or sump'm, wasn't it? Come on...."

Doc cut his eyes at Eddie. "It's just that no one calls me that, and—"

"His name's Demetrius," Eddie said, grinning at Doc. "Demetrius Octavius Calhoun."

"What?" The man working on the truck laughed and finally slid out from under it. "Hey! You're colored guys!"

Morty scowled at him. "Brilliant deduction, Sherlock Holmes. And by the way, they're colored *soldiers*, not just guys."

Marv stood up, brushed off his khakis, and walked over. "Hey, as long as one'a yuz can drive and one'a yuz knows his way around an engine, I don't care if you're green. All I wanna know is... which one'a yuz is Demetrius, and where the hell'd ya get a name like that anyway?"

Doc glared at Eddie, who was still cackling. "Same place you got a name like Marv, I guess. Our mothers."

"Fair enough." Marv peered over Doc's shoulder toward the road and his smile suddenly disappeared. "Wait a minute. You guys are on *foot*? Weren't you supposed to be bringin' us a truck? With my crankshaft in it?"

"Wait," Doc said, "You mean you guys are actually from the *real* truck unit? The one we've been trying to get to?"

"Yeah," Morty said. "We were with 'em till these trucks conked out, and the brass didn't want us leavin' 'em behind. So we got orders to stay and fix 'em. The real action is in Algiers, so they figured we'd be okay here doin' repairs. We're supposed to wait for further orders."

"Wait," Eddie said. "You said 'these trucks.' But all I see is this one."

"And you wouldn't have seen this one if you hadn't been on foot." He pointed into the dense brush. "Good cover, huh? Three Dodge supply trucks stashed back there. They ain't workin' yet, but Marv's nearly got this one rollin'. So what's the story on *your* truck, guys?"

Doc carefully dropped his overloaded backpack. "Well, we came under fire and the engine caught a bullet. I fed it some water from my canteen and it started up, but then drained right out. So we grabbed whatever supplies we could carry and pronounced the patient dead."

Marv opened the door to the truck he'd been working on, put his tool box inside, and wiped his hands on a rag. "There ain't an engine in this man's army I can't fix! Hop in and we'll go rescue your chariot, Private Demetrius."

"Thanks, Marv. But *please* call me Doc. It's the name everybody on earth calls me."

"Sounds like a name for a medic!"

"It's initials," Eddie said as Doc glared at him. "Demetrius Octavius Calhoun—D.O.C."

Marv climbed into the driver's seat. "Aw, 'Doc' don't sound like a guy who drives a chariot! If *my* name was Demetrius, I'd make everybody call me that. And ya know what else?"

"Hey!" Morty snapped. "Is the goddamn truck gonna run or what?"

"You're gonna see how she runs, ya sonofabitch."

It took two tries, but Marv got the engine started. After a series of groans and grinding of gears, the truck lurched forward, jerking all four men back in their seats. Marv turned to Morty and grinned triumphantly. "Purrs like a kitten, don't she, Morty?"

* * *

For the next two days, all four men worked together on truck repairs, and things remained pretty calm as they awaited orders. No air attacks; no land attacks.

They broke for supper at sundown every evening, eating K-rations, which was all they had. On the third night, Eddie nearly fell asleep over his food until Morty nudged him.

"Hey, soldier! Better hit that bedroll before that ground hits you!"

Eddie rubbed his face and stood up. "Ain't gotta tell me twice. Man, I'm tired. G'night, fellas."

"Ain't you tired, too, Doc?" Morty asked.

"I should be, I guess, but I'm not."

Marv stood up and stretched. "Well, I am," he said. "Any chance I get to sleep, I'm takin' it. You never know when you'll get another chance in this crazy war. G'night, guys."

Morty waved. "G'night, Marv. I'm gonna stay up awhile and get the lowdown on the gladiator here."

"Good night, Marv," Doc called.

Morty tapped out a cigarette and offered it to Doc.

"Thanks, Mort."

Morty grinned. "You been callin' me Mort for two days. Ya know, my wife calls me Mort. *Hates* Morty. So where ya from, Doc? I know it ain't the south. Not unless it's the south Bronx. I caught that New York in your voice, first day."

Doc laughed. "Born and raised in New York. Harlem, to be exact."

"Oh, yeah! Harlem! Hey, you ever been to that Cotton Club?"

"I've played it."

"Whadaya know about that! You're a musician?"

"I am."

"What instrument?"

"Trumpet."

"Whadaya know about that! Hey, I tell ya who I like. I like that Benny Goodman. Wonder if he ever played the Cotton Club?"

Doc took a pull on his cigarette and smiled as he exhaled. "I saw him at the Savoy once."

"You did? Man, I gotta get uptown when I get back. I'll come see you play that trumpet."

Doc nodded. "Sure, Mort. That'd be cool."

"So what about Eddie? He a musician too?"

"No. I met Eddie in boot camp."

"I bet he's from the south. That accent and all. Where's he from? Georgia? Texas?"

"Alabama."

Morty winced. "Whoo. Rough for you guys down in that part of the country, huh?"

"That's why I never go there. Closest I ever came to it was the plantation treatment from that drill sergeant at boot camp. I didn't think I was gonna make it, but Eddie took it like a champ. Told me he was used to it. So where are you from, Mort? The Bronx?"

"Brooklyn, my friend. And I sure miss it."

"Noplace like New York."

"Yeah. Sometimes I wonder if I'll ever see that beautiful green lady in the harbor again. It's gonna be tough gettin' out of this war in one piece. But I gotta stick it out. It's personal for me." He looked over at Doc. "I'm, uh, I'm Jewish, ya know."

Doc's eyes widened in mock surprise and he placed a palm on the side of his face. "No!"

That got a belly-laugh out of Morty. "I like you, gladiator! You're like *mishpucha*! Ya ever heard that word around New York?"

"Yes, I have. And thank you. But just the same, here we are with this big *mishegas*—"

"*Mishegas*, huh?" Morty laughed again and rolled his eyes. "He speaks the language, for chrissakes! So, gladiator, when you say *mishegas*, are you talkin' about that half-ass truck you were driving, or just this messy war in general?"

"Both," Doc laughed. "Okay, look. You might as well know two things about me now, Mort. One, don't get *too* fluent on me, because I only know beginner's Yiddish. And two, I've got lousy luck with trucks. The one we had to go back for—that's the second one I lost."

"Where'd you lose the first one?"

"Spain."

Morty's smile disappeared. "You were in *Spain*? You were one'a *those* guys?"

"Lincoln Brigade."

"The U.S. Army should'a been over there to help you guys," Mort said bitterly. "I was sayin' that from the beginning. We could'a stopped that goddamn Hitler back then!"

Doc took a deep pull on his cigarette and blew out the smoke slowly. "I know. And that's why I'm here now. To do whatever I can to help finish the job."

Morty gave him a long look. "You hear about those—camps? The ones all over Europe they been taking Jews to? Well, I heard there were some in Spain back in '38. But some'a the guys say it's just—rumors. Even the ones in Europe."

"Not rumors," Doc said, shaking his head. "I learned a lot over there from a very reliable Spaniard. There was a camp called *El Hecho* that my friend told me about, and he said Franco was sending people there—mostly Jewish—all the way back in '36. So he fit in nice and cozy with Mussolini and Hitler. An unholy trinity of murderers, all tuning up for this main event, Mort. A second goddamn world war."

Morty stared into the darkness. "And they called the first one the war to end all wars."

Doc sighed. "Too much hate in the world, Mort, too much hate."

After a long silence, Mort said, "I gotta make a confession to you."

Doc snorted. "I'm no priest, Mort. And you're *sure* no Catholic."

Mort shrugged. "But you're colored, and you're the only colored guy around here right now, and now is when I need to say it."

Doc gave him a curious look. "Okay. Let me guess... You feel bad that sometime in your life you've used words like uh, jungle bunny... shine... nig—"

"Wait a minute! Wait a minute!" Mort sputtered. "That ain't what I wanted to confess!... But, okay, since I'm tryin' to be completely honest here, and since you brought up those words... Okay. I never said the first two, but yeah, I gotta confess to that last one... back when I was a dumb kid." Mort shrugged uncomfortably. "Look, I grew up in a rough neighborhood with a lotta gangs. Some whites, some coloreds, some PRs. And all those guys called me a kike *daily*. So what about you, Doc? Can you honestly say you never called a guy a kike? A sheeny? A Hebe?"

Doc laughed. "Okay, okay. I gotta take the fifth on one or two of those myself, I guess. Same situation as you. My block was mostly Negroes and Puerto Ricans, but on any block in any direction, you knock on any door and there were Italians, Irish, Jewish, Catholic, Polish, West Indians... Different colors, different languages, different religions... All tough kids. But you *had* to be tough to survive."

Mort nodded. "And we fought and called each other names, thinkin' it made us tough."

"How 'bout that?" Doc said. "We had it backwards. It was the surviving that made us tough."

"That's right, my friend. Okay. So obviously we both grew up into better men than we started out as kids. So whadaya say? A truce and a pledge and we call it even?"

Doc nodded and smiled. "Okay, cool... So now maybe you'll tell me what you really wanted to confess."

"Oh, yeah... Okay, here's what's been buggin' me, Doc... Slavery."

"Slavery?"

"Yeah! I never gave much thought to slavery before. I mean, I heard things about it... in school and here and there, but... to be honest, it was all pretty vague stuff. No details, ya know?"

"So you're saying that *I* made you think about slavery?"

"No, not you. I just figured you might understand, that's all. It was a story I heard from some soldiers—guys who fought in Europe. They told me they discovered a—"

"What?"

"A... a grave. A mass grave...." He paused, and could barely get out the next words: "It was Jews. Kids... and women. Old folks. Naked and shot...."

Doc stared into the darkness. "I've seen... similar things. Gave me a real sick feeling."

"It did?"

"Sure, it did."

Morty stood up and started pacing. "See, that's what I'm talkin' about, Doc. I mean, it wasn't your people! But you still got a sick feeling when you heard about it. Why the hell didn't I get a sick feeling when I first heard about slavery?"

"Well, first of all, you didn't *see* slavery up close the way I saw... what I saw in Spain. You don't see color or religion or any of that. All you see are people. Blood and suffering."

"Yeah, but I never seen any of those Nazi camps either, Doc. Just heard about 'em. And I'm sick over it. So, it *is* the same thing as slavery! And the only thing that makes me feel less guilty is that I sure get a sick feeling about it now."

"Why do you think that is?"

"Because... now when I get pictures in my head about what's goin' on in those camps to *my* people, I'm gettin' pictures of what it was like in slavery for *your* people. And you're a good guy, Doc, a real *mensch*. I feel bad it took me so long to even think about it...."

"Ease up on yourself, Mort. Hey, better late than never."

Mort groaned. "Aw, come on, Doc! Late's bullshit and you know it."

"Well, if late's bullshit, then we might as well go home right now. 'Cause we're late to this mess too. We should'a stopped this back in '37. Or '36."

"Which brings us back to Spain," Mort said softly.

"And Ethiopia. What if we would've stopped Mussolini in '35? But look. No matter how many people died, there are a lot more that need us to be here, even if we *are* late."

Mort sat back down and sighed. "Okay... So late ain't bullshit. And ya know what else?"

"What?"

"I'm gonna use this sick feeling to get me through this war. Hitler and Mussolini have gotta be stopped."

Doc nodded slowly. "*No parasan.*"

"Huh?"

"It's Spanish. It means we draw the line with this war, Mort. This time we stop 'em."

~~~

Thessaloniki, Greece, July 11, 1942 — On this morning, Hitler's fist of terror struck the Jewish citizens of Thessaloniki, Greece. Eyewitness accounts of Nazi soldiers dragging families from their homes were soon confirmed when an estimated 50,000 Jews were loaded onto trains for transport to a labor camp located in Auschwitz, Poland. The community raised over 2 billion drachmas for their freedom, but to no avail.

Among the Jews who were seized was Dr. Alexander Moskos, together with his wife Renata and their two children, Abigail and Tad. The Moskos family has resided in Thessaloniki for two generations, and Dr. Moskos is a well-respected pediatrician who specialized in the treatment of childhood Polio.

Before the last train departed, Nazi soldiers had already begun the torching of synagogues and schools, along with a Jewish cemetery in the center of the city.

~~~

CHAPTER 8

Ronnie walked into the public library and made his way past an obstacle course of bundled newspapers and bins of loose rags. A heavy, dark-skinned gentleman with sparse black hair and horn-rimmed glasses stopped him. "Are you here to donate to the paper drive, young man?"

"No, sir."

"The rubber drive? Tires are collected in the back, you know."

Ronnie looked up and spotted a row of large posters that explained the man's questions:

Wanted for Victory!
Waste paper! Old rags! Scrap metals! Old rubber!
Put the lid on Hitler! Buy war bonds today!

"No, sir," Ronnie said. "My, uh… Mrs. Sayles sent me over about a job."

"Oh! You need to see the head librarian," the man said, pointing. "Last desk in the back."

"Thank you, sir."

When Ronnie got to the desk, the librarian looked up at him briefly, then waved him away. "Paper, metal, and rag collection is up front. Rubber outside in the back."

She was a plump Caucasian woman in her forties with steel gray hair pulled into a severe bun. Her plain face looked as though it had never learned to smile.

"I wish I could donate, ma'am, but I'm only here to apply for a job."

"Oh! You're Mrs. Sayles' little boy?"

Ronnie clenched his teeth and stared at her a moment before answering. "Yes, ma'am."

"I'm Miss Nichols," she said. She removed her glasses and began cleaning them. "And what is your name, young man? Your mother told me, but I'm afraid I've forgotten."

"Ronnie, ma'am."

"Do you know the Dewey Decimal system, Ronnie?"

"Yes, ma'am. Almost all the libraries use the Dewey Decimal system now. And—"

"And what?"

Ronnie looked down at his shoes. "Well, I just..." He stopped when his voice cracked. "Excuse me. It's just that I really love books, ma'am. So I really want this job."

"How old are you?"

"Thirteen, ma'am, but everybody tells me I'm old for my age."

She gave him a skeptical look. "What's your favorite book, young man?"

"Well... I just read *The Three Musketeers* and I really liked that one, ma'am."

"And who wrote *The Three Musketeers*, Ronnie?"

"Alexandre Dumas, ma'am."

Miss Nichols put on her glasses and peered up at him again. "I didn't realize you were so young, but your mother has recommended you highly. Perhaps, as you say, you *are* 'old for your age.' All right. You may consider yourself hired. Report here every day after school, starting tomorrow. I'll have your forms ready. Ten to five on Saturdays, and we're closed on Sundays."

Ronnie nodded. "Thank you, ma'am."

He left the library quickly and walked to the park to wait for Larry. He had planned his day carefully and part one had gone perfectly. The low-paying library job was only a cover—the perfect excuse for any extra time he'd need to be in the streets working the policy racket for Larry. That's where he'd make the real money. But after waiting for thirty minutes at the water fountain, which was their prearranged meeting place, Ronnie began to worry. Without Larry, part two would be ruined. And without part two, his whole master plan would collapse.

He continued waiting at the water fountain for another twenty minutes before Larry finally sauntered up. Ronnie composed his face to show no anxiety, no expression at all.

Larry was patting his glistening black hair, freshly conked with a little flip around the neckline, just like Duke Ellington's. He was wearing dark glasses, a cheap, shiny suit in a noisy shade of blue, and his usual smirk. Ronnie looked down at the shoes. They were suede, and trying hard to match the suit, but failing comically.

Ronnie barely kept his eyes from rolling. "I didn't think you were coming," he said.

"I told you I'd be here, didn't I? So, did you think about my offer or what?"

"Yeah," Ronnie said. "I can do it."

Larry gave him a skeptical once-over. "I don't know, man. I'm havin' second thoughts. You gotta be street-smart to run policy, ya know." He shrugged. "But, then again, you *do* got one thing goin' for you. Ain't no cops gonna suspect a skinny li'l four-eyed square like you."

"I said I can do it. I need the money."

Larry shook his head and laughed. "Nah... I still don't know if you got what it takes. Them streets is rough, man. And if them cops *do* catch you with them slips...."

Ronnie stared at him. "I'll memorize 'em. I've got a photographic memory."

"Yeah, you might think so."

"Look, I've got it all planned, Larry. I'll collect 'em ten at a time. Then I'll go home and write 'em down. Then I'll go out and get ten more. And go home and write those down too."

"Yeah, but the first time somebody thinks you ain't remembered right...."

Ronnie gulped in mock fear and pushed his glasses up on his nose. "Golly, sir, I, I, I can run right home and come back with my list."

"Shee-it! You can turn on that choir-boy act anytime you want to, huh? We'll see how long that works for you. If you lucky, you might get by without a beatin'— 'least for a while."

Taking off his glasses, Ronnie gave him a hard stare. He was already ten steps ahead of Larry and felt nothing but contempt for him. All he wanted from him were his connections.

"Don't let my baby face fool you," Ronnie said. "I'm smart, and I can make us both a lot of money. And I'm pretty goddamn adept at takin' a beatin', too, if it comes to that... So how long are you gonna stand there with your mouth open before we get started?"

1945

The United States bombs Hiroshima and Nagasaki, bringing an end to World War Two.

NAACP Secretary Walter White's *A Rising Wind* is published.

Dizzy Gillespie's "Salt Peanuts" puts Bebop on the Billboard charts.

~~~

Natchez, Mississippi, 1945 — A controversial fratricide trial ended today with the conviction of defendant Calvin Bailey. Bailey received a life sentence for the murder of his brother Joseph Bailey, whose body was never found.

The jury based their verdict on eye-witness testimony, blood evidence, and scraps of teeth and hair identified to be that of the victim.

The defendant refused to reveal the location of the body, and it was the testimony of his own mother that finally sealed his fate. Leah Bailey stated that her son Calvin came home covered in blood on the night Joseph was last seen alive.

Judge Lockhart stated at trial's end: "Calvin Bailey should be facing a date with the electric chair."

CHAPTER 9

Pearl walked slowly along State Street, looking up from her book every few seconds to keep from bumping into people or stepping off the curb. When she finally got to the bench at the bus stop, she sat down and turned the page, trying to read faster. "Oh, no," she murmured.

"Good book?" a deep male voice asked.

Pearl looked up at a young copper colored man wearing horn-rimmed glasses. "Uh, yes. It really is a good book. *Native Son*. Have you read it?"

The stranger slowly took off his glasses and smiled. "It's me, Pearl."

Pearl clasped her hands over her mouth, and the book slid off her lap. "Ronnie?"

He reached for her hands and pulled her to her feet.

Pearl hugged him tightly, sobbing. "Oh, Ronnie! You got away from him!"

"Yes, I did. Sorry it took me so long. Hey, is that your bus?"

Pearl turned and saw the approaching bus. "Yes, but—I can't go to work now!"

Ronnie picked up her book and handed it to her. "Sure you can. I don't want you to get fired. Tell me what time you come home from work, and I'll be right here waiting for you."

The bus doors opened. "You promise? You *promise*, Ronnie?"

He grinned. "I promise. Better wash your face when you get to work. You're a mess!"

"I will. Ronnie, you should go see Mama while I'm at work. It's her off day!"

"No, I'll wait till tonight."

"Well, okay. I'll be getting off the bus right here at 7:30, Ronnie. Don't forget."

"7:30. I won't forget."

She hugged him again. "Oh, my God! Ronnie! Wait'll Mama sees you!"

* * *

Pearl hurried off the bus that evening and looked around, but Ronnie wasn't there. Then he snuck up behind her, grabbed her shoulders, and laughed.

"Boy, I ought'a whup your behind! You're still a brat and you still got that silly laugh!"

"Tough day at work? Hey, where *do* you work anyway?"

"Williford's Drug Store. I work behind the lunch counter. Can't you tell by my glamorous uniform?" She spun around, twirling her skirt.

Ronnie peered at her over the top of his glasses. "Dazzling, darling," he said dryly. "You're ready for Hollywood."

"I also sing at a club for tips on Saturday nights, but don't tell Mama."

Ronnie lifted up his glasses. "What?"

"I'll tell you later. Oh! I nearly forgot!" She reached into her pocketbook and pulled out a small bundle wrapped in a brown paper bag and tied with a ribbon. "I have sump'm for you."

Ronnie tore off the ribbon and paper and laughed. "Baby Ruth! You remembered!"

Pearl grabbed his arm. "Come on, let's go show you to Mama! She won't recognize you."

"Do I look that different?"

"Not when I *really* look. You still have the same eyes when you take off those glasses, and you still have the dimples and that crazy laugh! It's just deeper. It's gonna take some time to get used to hearing that man's voice comin' out of you!"

"Your voice got deep too! You sure you're a girl? You know who you sound like?"

Pearl grinned. "Charles Boyer?"

Ronnie shoved her shoulder. "Not that deep! Have you seen that new Bogart movie?"

"You mean *Casablanca*? I sound like Bogart?"

"No, not that one, the *new* one. It's called *The Have Nots*. Something like that. Anyway, the actress has a deep voice, very sexy. Her name's Lauren something... Bacall! That's it. Lauren Bacall. You don't *look* like her—she's white, of course. But you sure sound like her."

"Okay, guess I'm a vamp now... Oh, Lord," Pearl said, rolling her eyes, "That sounded like sump'm Mama would say! What would they call a vamp nowadays?"

"Well, first of all, nobody says 'nowadays' *or* 'vamp' anymore, and I believe the term you're looking for is *femme fatale*." Suddenly, Ronnie snapped his fingers. "*To Have and Have Not*! That's the name of the movie. Let's go see it. We'll take Mama. I bet she'd love it."

"Ronnie... why didn't you go to the house this morning and see Mama?"

"Well, I started to, but I was kind of... afraid."

They walked along for a while in silence.

"It wasn't her fault, Ronnie," Pearl said quietly.

"I know. I never thought it was her fault."

"Well, I hope you're ready to see her now because we're almost there."

"Yeah, but you go in first. When she sees me after all these years, she might pass out!"

Pearl smiled. "No, she won't. But she sure will cry a lot."

"Yeah. I guess she will."

When they got to the top step, Pearl grinned back at him. "Ready?"

"Yeah, I'm ready."

Pearl opened the door. "I'm home, Mama," she called.

"In the kitchen, baby."

Ronnie grabbed Pearl's shoulder and lowered his head. "Wait...."

"What's the matter?" she whispered.

"It's... it's her voice... All these years, I didn't think I remembered her voice—"

Pearl pressed her handkerchief into Ronnie's hand, and he quickly wiped his eyes.

"What'cha doin' out there, Pearl?" Alva called. "I got your favorite! Spaghetti and garlic bread. Come on in here and eat while it's hot!"

"Comin', Mama!" Pearl smiled at Ronnie, then grabbed his hand and held it firmly as they walked into the kitchen. Alva was standing at the stove with her back to them.

Ronnie cleared his throat. "Hi, Mama."

Alva didn't move for a moment. Then, slowly, her head turned in a series of small, hesitant movements. The instant she saw his face, she dropped to her knees, and Ronnie and Pearl rushed over to help her up.

"Oh, my God," she sobbed as she stared up at him. "Oh, my God, oh... my God!"

Ronnie held her tightly. "Not God, Mama. It's only me—Ronnie."

After helping Alva into a chair, Pearl and Ronnie sat on either side of her, crying and holding her hands. "I'm dreamin', Pearl," she whispered. "I'm dreamin'."

"No, you're not, Mama," Pearl sniffled.

Alva shook her head. "I'm dreamin'. Don't wake me up."

"No, you're not, Mama," Ronnie said. "Touch me. I'm real."

Alva took Ronnie's face in her hands and examined every inch of it, from his eyes, to his ears, to his chin. Then he smiled broadly.

"Oh!" she cried. "Look at my baby's dimples!"

"I know, Mama," Pearl said. "That's how I knew it was him!"

Alva wiped her eyes, took a deep breath, and stood up. "Awright, now. Enough of this cryin'. I gotta feed you, boy! Look how skinny you done got!"

"Wait a minute, Mama," Ronnie said, reaching for her hands. "Not so fast."

Pulling her back in front of his chair, Ronnie grinned up at her, closed his eyes, and leaned his head back. "I want my special kiss."

"You were so little! You still remember that?"

"I sure do," he said, peeking out of one eye. "Come on now, Mama."

Alva wiped her eyes, looked at Pearl, and then leaned down. She gave him a shaky kiss on his lips, then kissed his left dimple, his right dimple, and then rubbed her nose against his.

Ronnie opened his eyes. "And *now* you can feed me! 'Cause I sure am hungry!"

* * *

The reunion lasted all through supper and late into the night, with laughter, overlapping conversation, and frequent outbursts of happy tears. In an easy, unspoken understanding, the subject of Victor Sayles never came up.

After Alva had gone to bed, Ronnie and Pearl washed the dishes and headed back to the bedroom they had shared when they were little.

"Wow," Ronnie said as he looked around. "It looks so small."

Pearl laughed. "That's because it *is* small. Hey, what'cha gonna sleep in, Ronnie?"

"My tee-shirt and pants, I guess. I'll go buy some clothes tomorrow."

"You didn't bring anything with you?"

"I didn't want anything from him. I have my own money and I was in a hurry."

Pearl nodded. "I'm glad we didn't talk about him with Mama tonight."

"Me too... Man, she was happy."

Pearl hugged him. "Me too! We've both been wishing for you to come back, Ronnie."

"I guess you're wondering what took me so long, but I'll explain all that to you later. Right now, I just want to keep enjoying this night."

"Okay... Oh, you're gonna need this," Pearl said, tossing him a key.

He caught it and smiled. "Oh, boy! My own house key. I was too little to get one of these last time I was here."

"You probably would'a lost it or sump'm," Pearl said, making a face at him.

"Did you have this made for me today?"

Pearl laughed. "Well… no… I just had a spare."

"And why was that a funny question?"

"Because I keep losing mine!"

Ronnie laughed. "Okay. Let's get organized. I'll sleep over here on the floor tonight."

Pearl hopped up on the bed, tucked her legs underneath her, and leaned back against the headboard. "Sit'cho butt down on this bed with me. I am not makin' you sleep on that cold, hard floor! We can squeeze in here just like we did when we were little. Tomorrow night I'll fix up the sofa in the front room for you. "

Ronnie took off his dress shirt and hung it on the door with his jacket. When he turned around, Pearl was lighting a cigarette. He lifted up his glasses. "You *smoke* now?"

"Sure. It relaxes me. Want one?"

"No, thanks… Does Mama know?"

"Sure, she knows. She was mad at first, but I told her it helped me relax when I was studying, and she finally got used to it. She doesn't mind, as long as I pay for 'em with my own money from my job and don't smoke at the table."

Ronnie took a seat at the other end of the bed, facing her. Then he broke into a wide grin. "Now you *really* remind me of Lauren Bacall. She smoked her head off in that movie!"

Pearl dropped her voice into its deepest register. "Maybe that's why I sound like her."

"You know what, Pearl? You could pass for a twenty-year-old! How old are you now?"

"Sixteen. But I'll be seventeen in four months, so that would make you about—"

"Still fifteen," Ronnie said with a shrug. "Going on fifteen-hundred."

"You sure don't look fifteen! So I look twenty and you look like a college man. Lord! Wonder how ancient we're gonna look when we're Mama's age?"

"So what grade are you in now?" Ronnie asked. "Are you a sophomore or a junior?"

"I just finished my senior year."

"How'd you do that? You didn't start school till you were seven."

"I caught up, and even skipped a grade. I took a test and they passed me up to a senior."

"I always knew you were smart, Pearl. But you're not the only one. I skipped a grade too, when they realized I was reading at college level. I bet I read every book in that library."

"Oh, reading!" Pearl said, jumping up suddenly. "That reminds me—" She ran over to the bureau and yanked open a drawer. Reaching into the back left corner, she pulled out a package wrapped in white paper with a limp, faded green ribbon tied around it.

She sat back down on the bed. "I used to write you letters, you know. All the time."

"So… those are the letters?"

"No. I tore 'em all up. I didn't know where to send 'em, and they were too depressing. You wouldn't want to read any of 'em, now that you're back and we're all happy again."

"Well, then what's in that package and when are you giving it to me?"

Pearl grinned and handed it to him. "It's a present."

"More Baby Ruths?"

"Nope. Open it!"

Ronnie ripped open the package and laughed. "*The Ugly Duckling*? I said college level, remember? I believe this is first grade stuff."

"I got it for you when you turned six," Pearl said softly.

Ronnie's smile faded. "The day I left."

"No," she said bitterly. "The day he *stole* you. He stole you away from me and Mama."

"Forget about him. I'm back now, so let's have my birthday party now."

"Tonight?"

"Right now. Tonight."

"But—no cake."

"I still got that Baby Ruth you gave me. Wanna split it?"

"That's a great idea!"

115

Ronnie opened the candy and tore it in half, giving Pearl the bigger piece. When she laughed, he said, "I know, I know. I always kept the big piece for myself when we were little."

Pearl had just taken a big a bite of the candy, but she laughed and answered with her mouth full. "Yuh sure did!"

"Grow up! And swallow, please!"

Pearl giggled and flashed a chocolate-toothed grin.

Ronnie grimaced. "Do you have any milk?"

"Yup. Be right back."

Pearl sprang from the bed and left the room. When she returned, she handed him a glass of milk. "Here ya go."

Ronnie held the glass up to the lamp. "You and Mama still drink this thin powder milk?"

"You drank it too, boy. Don't get up on your high horse."

"Tomorrow we're going to the store and I'm buying you and Mama some real milk."

"So... That's what you drank at Daddy's house?" Pearl asked carefully.

"Don't call him that. But yes, we drank real milk. It came with a hot, steaming plate of beatings. Remember that belt?"

"Vividly," Pearl said.

Ronnie clinked his glass against Pearl's. "A toast: I'll take this see-through milk and you and Mama over real milk and goddamn Victor Sayles and Trey and goddamn Loretta *any* day."

"Such language! And you were shocked at my smoking... So who are Loretta and Trey?"

"Loretta's his wife, and Trey is his son. Victor Sayles the third. So they call him Trey."

Pearl shook her head. "Wait a minute. When did he marry her?"

Ronnie shrugged. "Before I got there. That's all I know. I never cared to ask."

"That's impossible! He was still married to Mama."

"He told me he was never legally married to Mama. We, my beautiful big sister, are a couple of bastard children. Not that I give a damn."

Pearl got up. "Don't move. I'll be right back."

When she returned, she tossed him a document. "State of Illinois... Divorce Decree. See? Mama had to divorce him so she could get married."

After a stunned silence, Ronnie said, "Mama's *married*? To who? And where is he?"

"His name is David Sims. They got married last year when he was home on leave. Now that the war's over, he's coming home. He just wrote Mama that he'll be here later this week. Then we're moving in with him. And you too, Ronnie. His Mama left him a nice house."

Ronnie was shaking his head, still stunned. "No, Pearl...."

"Ronnie. He's not like Daddy. He does *not* beat her. He's thirty-six years old, and he's a real gentleman. Mama's been missin' him like crazy since he shipped out. Didn't you notice her tooth? David's the one who got her tooth fixed. You should'a seen her cry when she looked in the mirror at that dentist's office. All those years she felt so ugly. She used to call herself—"

"An ol' Halloween jack-o-lantern," Ronnie said softly. "I just remembered that."

"You'll like him, Ronnie."

Ronnie frowned and stared down at the divorce decree. "I wonder how Victor got away with bigamy? Shit, I didn't think he was that smart. Boy, I sure would love to walk into that beauty parlor Loretta goes to and announce that she's not married and her son's a bastard! Embarrass her right in front of all her bourgeois friends."

"Ronnie? Was Loretta horrible? Did she beat you too?"

"No, she was nice to me, actually. She probably saved my life, now that I think about it."

"Then why do you hate her so much?"

"Because he made me call her Mama. And I already had a Mama... I guess I was wrong to hate her for that, but... I just missed Mama so much."

"You weren't wrong, Ronnie. You were too little. Daddy was the one who was wrong."

"Stop calling him that, Pearl. I can't even stand to think I'm related to that barbarian."

"Hey, you got away from him, Ronnie. That's the main thing."

Ronnie gave her a long look. "You know he's gonna come here lookin' for me, Pearl."

Pearl finished her cigarette and crushed it in the ashtray. "No, Ronnie. I'll kill him before I ever let him take you again. I mean it."

"Pearl... I *can't* stay here. Don't worry about me. I have plenty of money."

"How much is plenty?"

Ronnie got up and reached for his jacket, then pulled out a large roll of money.

Pearl gasped. "Those are fifties, Ronnie!"

"I know. Fifties and twenties. They don't draw as much attention as hundreds."

"Hundreds? Ronnie, where did you get all that money?"

Ronnie patted her hand. "Policy, that's all. I didn't steal it. People *gave* me money to play their numbers. When they win, they're happy, and when they lose, they just play another number. So don't worry! Nobody's gonna come looking for me, Pearl. Well, except Victor."

"Do *not* let Mama see all that money, Ronnie."

"Do I look dumb?"

"No. But even with all that money, you can't leave us again."

"Pearl. You *know* I can't stay here. I will *not* bring all his hell back on you and Mama."

"You act like everything he did was your fault, Ronnie, and it wasn't!"

Ronnie smiled. "You grew up into a real beautiful girl, you know that?"

"Stop changing the subject! We just got you back! It'll kill Mama to lose you again!"

"We won't lose each other again. Look, I have a plan. Mama getting married changed things, but it could still work. I'm heading to Kansas City, Pearl. And you're going with me."

"What? Wait a minute, Ronnie—"

"Look, Pearl, before you say no, just listen to my plan...."

CHAPTER 10

After talking until morning, Pearl fell asleep, but Ronnie was wide awake. Slipping out quietly, he locked the door and walked up to the corner grocer.

When he got back, he heard Alva rattling around in the kitchen.

"It's only me, Mama," he called softly. "Pearl gave me a key."

"Where were you off to so early, baby?"

He walked into the kitchen and gazed at her smile. "Mama, you are so beautiful."

Alva laughed. "Oh, Lord! Me?"

Ronnie put down the groceries and wrapped his arms around her. "Pearl told me about Mr. Sims. I'm so glad he got your tooth fixed, Mama. You are the most beautiful woman in the whole world. I missed you so much."

Alva dabbed at her eyes and then patted his chest. "Look at'cha! You taller than me!"

Ronnie handed her his handkerchief. "Move over, Mama. I'm makin' breakfast today."

Alva hugged him again. "Well, let me go wake up your sister."

"It's Sunday! Let her sleep. She'll wake up when she smells the pancakes and coffee."

Alva and Ronnie chatted happily as he made breakfast. Then, just as he had predicted, Pearl appeared wearing a sleepy smile.

"So that wasn't a dream! We got Ronnie back, Mama!"

"We sho' did, Pearl! And he fixed pancakes! Feels like Christmas, don't it?"

Ronnie rolled his eyes. "I'm leavin' if you two start singing 'Jingle Bells' or sump'm."

Pearl sat down and began smearing butter on the pancakes. "Not me. I'm fixin' to eat about ten of these!"

* * *

Pearl and Ronnie spent the next two days making plans for their trip to Kansas City, shopping for supplies and packing. His constant habit of looking over his shoulder troubled her at first, but Pearl soon realized the wisdom of sharpening her own senses about her surroundings. Victor still loomed over their lives.

"So you're sure David's coming home this week?" Ronnie said as they walked up the steps to the apartment.

Pearl fished out her key and unlocked the door. "For the tenth time, yes. He's flying in on a military plane to New York, and then taking the train to Chicago. He should be here day after tomorrow. Mama's fixin' a big supper for him."

"That'll make it easier when we break the news, and I don't want Mama to be alone."

"I don't know, Ronnie. Mama is not gonna be happy with us both leaving like this."

"We'll just have to convince her. I gotta get out of Chicago, Pearl. You know that. And I'm still fifteen. If you go with me, we stand a better chance. I told you, you look twenty-five."

"You said twenty the other night," she laughed. "I'm aging by the minute! So what am I supposed to be? Your aunt or something?"

Ronnie grinned. "Aunt Pearl. Maybe I should practice calling you that."

* * *

Alva took the next day off from her housecleaning job across town to prepare for David's return. Pearl went to work as usual, mainly so that she could pick up her final pay envelope.

The hours dragged for Ronnie as he helped Alva clean the house and buy groceries for David's welcome-home supper. Listening to her talk about David's house and how happy they would be was increasing Ronnie's anxiety about breaking his news. He looked out the window every few minutes for any signs of Victor, and finally noticed that the sun was going down.

He sat at the kitchen table and stared at his mother's back as she chopped vegetables for a stew and continued her happy monologue.

"David's gonna be a real good Daddy to you, Ronnie. I wrote him about you comin' back, but you know, those letters take so long to get to the soldiers, he might not get it till—"

"Mama, you've got to stop thinking of me as a little boy who needs a new Daddy."

"But you *are* still a boy! Not a little boy, but—"

"Mama, *please!*"

Alva looked back at him. "What's wrong, son?"

"Sit down for a minute, Mama."

"Oh, baby, I got all this cookin' to do. I gotta get this stew done tonight, 'cause tomorrow I got pies to make and—"

"Please, Mama."

Alva dried her hands, then took a seat across from him. "What is it?"

Ronnie gazed at her worried face and took a deep breath. "I gotta leave Chicago, Mama."

"No, baby. David's comin' back and everything's—"

"Mama, Victor *will* come lookin' for me. I'm surprised he let this much time pass. You know he hates losing control over people. And I will *not* bring him down on you again."

Alva stood up and went back to the counter to continue chopping vegetables. "I'm not listenin' to this, Ronnie. I just got you back, and you ain't goin' noplace all by yourself! You only fifteen, baby! Now, n-now that's all I got to say on it. No."

"I won't be by myself, Mama... Look. I might as well tell you everything. I'm going to Kansas City. I knew I couldn't stay in Chicago, so I had it all planned to take you and Pearl with me, so we could be a family again. But I didn't know about your new husband. He can come too, Mama, and we can all still be together, but for now, I need Pearl to go with me."

Alva was staring at him with a shocked expression. "Kansas City? You and Pearl been plannin' this? You tryin' to break my heart? You my babies! No!"

"Mama, look. You and Mr. Sims need some time together and we need to leave—"

Alva stepped back to the table and slapped it hard with her palm. "I said no!"

She went back to her chopping, and Ronnie stared at her, realizing that he had handled the situation badly. After an uncomfortable silence, he stood up and walked out of the kitchen.

"Where you goin', Ronnie? Don't go, son!"

"I'm just goin' for a walk, Mama. I'll be back later. I promise."

* * *

Before leaving Williford's that night, Pearl cashed her paycheck and bought a few last-minute items for the trip. She fell asleep on the ride home, and by the time she stepped off the bus, it was dark. Walking down State Street, she began wondering what Kansas City was like and whether Ronnie had enough money for his grand plan. Suddenly, she had an uneasy feeling that someone was following her. She was about to look over her shoulder when she heard the familiar step-slide rhythm of Victor's footsteps behind her.

She broke into a run and didn't stop until she reached her building. Yanking open the main door, she ran down the hallway to the payphone to call the police. As she fumbled in her pocket for a nickel, she heard Victor's footsteps starting up the stairs outside. There was no time. She ran back to unlock her apartment door, ducked inside, and quickly relocked it. "Mama!"

"In the kitchen, baby."

Pearl ran into the kitchen. "Where's Ronnie?" she whispered.

"He went for a walk. We got into a fight, Pearl. He was tellin' me—"

"Shh. Listen, Mama. Somebody was just followin' me and I think it was—"

The sound of sudden hard knocking made Alva jump.

"Shh," Pearl said again. "Don't open it, Mama."

"But what if it's David? What if he just caught an earlier flight or sump'm?"

The knocking turned into hard fist-pounding, and then: "Open this goddamn door, Alva!"

Alva let out a terrified gasp. "Victor!"

Pearl shook her gently. "Come on now, Mama. We gotta think!"

"W-well, maybe somebody'll c-call the police."

"The only phone is down the hall. Nobody's goin' out there with him yelling like that!"

She frantically looked around the room as if it contained an answer to her greatest fear. Then she saw it. Running over to the kitchen sink, she leaned over it, opened the window, and climbed up, kneeling awkwardly on the counter. "Get some teaspoons out of the drawer, Mama."

"Teaspoons? You crazy, Pearl?"

"Just do it, Mama! And give 'em to me one at a time!"

Alva opened the drawer, gathered up a few teaspoons, and began handing them to Pearl.

Pearl flung the first spoon out, aiming at a window on the building across the alley. It clattered against the glass without breaking it. "Another one, Mama!"

As Alva handed her the second spoon, Victor continued yelling from outside the door.

"Don't listen to that, Mama! Keep those spoons comin'!"

After Pearl had tossed the third spoon, the window across the alley finally opened, and she saw the familiar face of Mr. Dundee.

"What the hell? Pearl? Is that you? Why in the world—?"

"Call the police, Mr. Dundee! Daddy's back and he's tryin' to break down the door!"

Mr. Dundee banged his fist on the windowsill. "Damn him! You hang on, honey. I'm callin' the police right now and then I'm on my way over there!"

Pearl climbed down from the sink and grabbed two butcher knives from a drawer, then handed one to Alva. Victor was still shouting threats as the door rattled violently on its hinges.

"He mad 'cause his old key don't work," Alva said bitterly.

Pearl gave her a hard look and held up her knife. "No more beatings, Mama. If he finds a way to break down that door, you and me—we are gonna fight him this time."

Alva looked at her with a deadly expression Pearl had never seen before. "Fight him? Shit, I'm gonna cut out his damn heart!" She tapped the blade of her knife against Pearl's and tightened her jaw. "Then I'm gonna fry it up and feed it to them alley cats, you hear me?"

Pearl looked at her mother with wide-eyed surprise and admiration. "Yes, ma'am."

The pounding suddenly stopped, followed by the sound of two men arguing loudly out in the hallway. Alva and Pearl exchanged a smile.

"Mr. Dundee sure got here fast, huh, Mama?"

Pearl's smile faded as the arguing rose to loud cursing. Then the walls began quaking with the heavy bumps of men's bodies falling and crashing in the hallway outside the door.

"Oh, Lawd," Alva whispered, "I hope Victor don't kill him."

"Wait! Shh, Mama, listen!"

The faint wail of a police car siren sounded in the distance.

Alva sighed loudly. "How'd they get here so fast?"

Everything became quiet outside the door as the sirens grew louder. When the police arrived, Pearl and Alva ran to look out the front window. In the flashing red lights, Mr. Dundee was pointing down the street as he stood talking with two bored looking police officers.

"Oh, no," she groaned.

"That devil got away," Alva said, sinking down onto the sofa.

"Maybe they'll catch him, Mama."

Alva closed her eyes. "How long you lived here, Pearl? You know they don't care about catchin' nobody in this neighborhood. Not unless they hurt some white folks."

Pearl fell onto the sofa next to her mother. "And we sure ain't white folks, huh, Mama?"

* * *

About an hour after the police had left, Pearl and Alva were cleaning up the kitchen when the front doorknob began to rattle. Without a word, Alva grabbed the knives and handed one to Pearl, and they went into the living room.

The door opened and Ronnie walked in. He shut the door, relocked it, and slipped the key into his pocket. When he looked their way and saw the knives, his eyes widened and he took a step back. Pearl and Alva immediately began to laugh.

"What in the world is goin' on?" Ronnie asked.

Alva was still laughing as she took the knives back to the kitchen. "You tell him, Pearl."

Pearl hugged Ronnie. "Victor was here."

"*That* is nothin' to laugh about, Pearl!" Ronnie pulled away angrily and strode into the kitchen. "Was he really here, Mama?"

"Not inside the house, son."

"He was bangin' on the door tryin' to get in," Pearl explained. "Mr. Dundee from across the alley called the police, and then he came over and fought him off till they got here. He lied and told 'em somebody attacked a white man so they hurried right over!"

"Why didn't they arrest him, goddammit?" Ronnie shouted.

"Calm down, son," Alva said softly. "And where'd you learn that kind'a language?"

"He heard the sirens, Ronnie," Pearl said, "and he got away before—"

"Well, why the hell didn't they go after him?"

Pearl rolled her eyes. " 'Cause Mr. Dundee isn't white! They barely scribbled a report."

The sudden sound of a knock at the front door caused Pearl to jump. Ronnie hurried into the front room and grabbed the doorknob.

"No, Ronnie!" Pearl yelled. She could see his chest heaving with angry breathing, and lowered her voice. "Please don't open that door. Ask who it is."

Ronnie stared at her for a long moment, then spoke in a deep, angry voice. "Who is it?"

"Uh, I was, uh, looking for Alva. I'm her husband—David."

Pearl pushed past Ronnie and opened the door. "Mr. Sims!"

A tall, dark-skinned man wearing an army uniform and a puzzled expression was standing in the doorway. He was holding a duffel bag in one hand and his cap in the other.

"I don't know what all the ruckus was about, Pearl, but—" He gazed over her shoulder and smiled broadly at Alva, who ran over and threw her arms around his neck. "There she is!"

"David! Why didn't you use your key?"

"I didn't want to just walk in and scare you after all this time."

"Welcome back, Mr. Sims!" Pearl said.

"It's good to see you again, Pearl. But how many times I gotta tell you to call me David?"

"Okay, David. Sorry. Listen, I want you to meet my brother."

David placed his duffel bag on the floor and reached for Ronnie's hand. "Alva! This tall fella is your little boy Ronnie? The one you told me about? After all these years?"

"Yes, this is him. This is my baby."

"Well, I sure am glad to meet you, young man. I know you made your mother happy when you walked in."

"I wrote you a letter about it," Alva said, sniffling. "I figured you'd get here before that letter got to you. He got away from Victor! Ain't that sump'm? And you got away from them damn Nazis! They didn't hurt you, did they?"

"Don't cry, baby," David said, kissing her forehead. "We took care of those Nazis once and for all, and I don't have a scratch on me. Now. Let's get to the important things. *What* is that good smell comin' out of that kitchen?"

"It's stew. But that's about all that's ready 'cause I didn't expect you till tomorrow! And I ain't had a chance to fix my hair or nothin'! Look at me! I'm a mess!"

David smiled at her. "Alva. You are a feast for my eyes. And I know that whatever that is cookin' in there will be a feast for my stomach!"

"But I ain't had time to make my pies or anything!"

Pearl nodded in the direction of the front door, and Ronnie went to check the lock. Then they followed David and Alva into the kitchen.

"I don't care about no pies, Alva," David said. "Whatever's in that pot, let me at it!"

* * *

After everyone had eaten their fill of Alva's stew, they remained at the table talking. Ronnie gave David a broad-stroke explanation of how he had escaped from Victor, and then laid out his plan to move to Kansas City.

"This is no little boy, Alva. After all he's been through, this is a man right here."

"But they just kids, David! They too young to be goin' off to Kansas City by theyselves."

"No, we're not, Mama," Ronnie interjected. "I have some connections out there, and besides, you and David have never even had a chance for a honeymoon."

David grinned. "The young man's right about that, Alva."

"They ain't got jobs, and they ain't got no place to live! And I just can't lose my kids."

"You won't lose us, Mama," Pearl said. "And besides—"

Alva opened her mouth to protest, but David placed his fingers gently over her lips.

"Everybody calm down," he said. "I think I have an idea that might work for all of us."

Pearl sighed. "I sure hope so! Let's hear it."

"Well, the one thing there's no argument about is that Ronnie has got to get someplace far away from his father. Now, if—"

Ronnie cut him off. "Please don't call him my father. He's just Mama's ex-husband."

Alva narrowed her eyes. "And I *know* you remember what I call him."

David grinned. "Devil. That's right. I forgot about that. Anyway, that devil has already been here once, which means he'll be here again. Now, Ronnie... I know you got your heart set on Kansas City, but would you be open to another suggestion?"

Ronnie looked at Pearl and then shrugged. "Where?"

"What about New York? I just happen to have a sister named Ruby who owns her own boardinghouse in the Bronx. All it takes is a phone call for her to have two rooms ready for you and Pearl. Ruby's a good woman, Alva. She'll look out for 'em. And then—"

"But David—"

"—And then," David continued, "I'll start making arrangements to sell my house out here. Ruby's been trying to get me to move to the Bronx since before the war. Last letter she wrote me was all about this nice little house she has her eye on for me. All we need is a little time

127

to get our business in order, and then we'll follow the kids right out there. And we'll all be together."

Pearl smiled. "Mama! Doesn't that sound like a great idea?"

Alva was still shaking her head. "But Ronnie's gotta go to school."

David patted her hand. "There's a good high school near Ruby's place and she can get him enrolled there. Now, listen, Alva. That devil won't leave you alone as long as you got Ronnie. I've known fools like that. In his mind, you took sump'm that belonged to him. Now we can press charges, but they can't arrest him if he ain't done nothin' but pound on the door. And it's been too many years to charge him with assault."

"We already have money for train tickets," Ronnie said.

"No, son," David said. "I'll buy the tickets under my name and Ruby's name so he can't track you. Then I'll personally put you two on the train for New York. Alva can move in with me just long enough for me to sell my house. That's when we'll head up to New York and I can start lookin' into buying that house Ruby's talkin' about."

"But I should go with the kids now, David," Alva said. "You could stay here by yourself and sell your house, couldn't you?"

"Mama!" Pearl said. "Did you forget that David just got back from that horrible war? You two need some time together, don't you?"

David smiled and kissed Alva's cheek. "Well?"

"I'm sorry, David. I guess it won't take too long to sell your house. And the kids sho' will be safer away from Chicago."

"Then it's all settled," Pearl said. "David, how fast can we get those train tickets?"

"I can go get 'em right now."

"Wait a minute," Ronnie said. "I don't want Mama to spend any more time sittin' in this apartment so he can come back and beat her up the second you aren't around to protect her."

"I can protect myself," Alva said firmly. "I'll kill that devil before I let him lay a hand on me again, you hear me? I would'a killed him tonight if he got through that door."

Pearl nodded. "We were ready for him."

"I think these ladies have toughened up since you've been away, Ronnie," David said.

"Okay, but I'd feel better if you and Mama could move out of here tonight."

"I can't wait to get out'a this ol' tenement," Alva said. "Whatever we can't carry out, we'll jus' leave it."

David grinned. "You heard the lady."

"But once me and Pearl are gone, and you and Mama move to your house, what if he figures out where you live?"

"I *told* you, son—" Alva said.

"Come on, Mama! I can't help worrying about you. David can't be with you every minute."

David put his hand on Ronnie's shoulder. "Son, I just got through fightin' a war. And there were a lot more of us colored men who saw action than you heard about. So I was able to bring back a few high-caliber souvenirs. Go on in that front room and bring me my duffel bag."

"Yes, sir." Ronnie went and got the bag, then set it on the table.

David stood up and unbuckled the bag, then pulled out an automatic pistol. "This is an Astra 400, Ronnie. It's a German gun, and I'll tell you the story about how I got it some other day. Right now, I'm just gonna show you how to load it and how to release the safety. Now we can't be firing it in here, but if that devil comes anywhere near this building while I'm gone gettin' those tickets, that's when you release this safety... Like this, see?"

"Yes, sir."

He gazed at Ronnie and handed him the gun. "And then what do you do?"

Ronnie turned the gun carefully in his hand and smiled. "I shoot him."

"But first, you teach *me* how to shoot him, David, you hear me?"

David took the gun from Ronnie's hand and gave it to Alva. "That's a great idea, baby."

"Wait a minute," Ronnie objected.

David shook his head. "No, son, she's right. Men have got to get over the notion that a woman can't defend herself, just like a man. What do you think all those women servin' in the war were doin'? Washin' dishes and knitting? Ronnie, I once saw a female medic blow a Nazi soldier's head clean off his shoulders, and then go right back to triage without blinking."

David positioned the Astra 400 in Alva's hand. "I'll take you out for target practice once we get the kids on their way. Safety's back on, so go on and point it at that picture on the wall to get a feel of the weight. Both hands." He stood behind her and positioned her arms. "Once you identify your target, do *not* hesitate. One in the chest, one in the head. That'll send him straight back to hell where he came from. Just like I will if he ever tries to hurt you again."

CHAPTER 11

Shortly after midnight, Ronnie and Pearl were pulling out of Union Station on a train headed for New York. They slept off and on until their arrival on Wednesday morning.

When they disembarked, a pleasant-faced woman was pacing alongside the train. Her complexion was dark, almost identical to David's coloring. She was short and plump, dressed in a stylish blue suit and hat, and she was holding a placard that read: "David Sims."

Ronnie nudged Pearl and pointed. "There's David's sister!"

"Hello," Pearl called.

The woman turned around and hurried over to them. "You must be Ronnie and Pearl! I got worried when your train was delayed. I'm Ruby Reynolds," she said, extending her hand.

"It's so nice to meet you, Mrs. Reynolds," Pearl said.

"Oh, you kids just call me Ruby. I bet you're tired! Lawd! Train travel wears me out! Let's get your bags and get you to your new home!"

"Thanks, Ruby," Ronnie said. "You don't know how much we appreciate this."

Ruby drove a 1934 Ford Woodie station wagon with a noisy engine. Pearl sat in the front seat next to Ruby, with Ronnie in the back, and they spent the whole ride taking in the horizontal and vertical scope of New York City. Ruby took a roundabout route to point out the Empire State Building, Broadway, Times Square, and Central Park. Then she took them through Harlem to show them Striver's Row, the Apollo Theater, the Lenox Lounge, and Minton's Playhouse. She talked all the way to the Bronx, but Pearl and Ronnie barely heard her.

Ronnie tapped Pearl on the shoulder. "Look! There's Yankee Stadium."

"I know! I see it. And look at all the people!"

After the car turned onto Jerome Avenue and pulled up in front of Ruby's boardinghouse, Pearl was sure they had made the right decision. It was a sprawling three-story house in need of a paint job, but otherwise in good condition. Victor would never find them here.

"Come on in, kids," Ruby said, leading the way up the steps. "Your rooms are all ready. I put you two next to each other on the third floor in the back so nobody'll bother you. We actually have some very nice boarders now. One fella just got back from the war like David, and there's a couple'a businessmen on the first floor." She turned around and held her finger up to her lips. "One fella's a gambler! But long as he pays his room and board on time, Ruby don't care!"

Grinning at Pearl, Ronnie mouthed the word "gambler."

Pearl elbowed him, then followed Ruby inside. "Wow!" she said. "Look at that staircase! That's twice as wide as our stairs in Chicago."

"Oh, there's plenty of room here, honey. Over here's the common area, great room, whatever you want to call it. Got a radio over by the window too."

The room was wide with a high beamed ceiling. There were large club chairs scattered in corners and near the windows, and arranged near a large fireplace were two sofas. None of the furniture looked new, but it was in good shape. Somehow, the room was both spacious and cozy.

"Everybody comes down when *Suspense* is on the radio, or *The Shadow*. We make big bowls of popcorn and have a real good time. You kids are welcome to join us."

"Where is everybody now?" Ronnie asked.

"Most folks are at work this time of the morning."

"Oh, yeah. That makes sense, I guess."

"Does the fireplace work?" Pearl asked.

"Sure does, honey."

"Great place to curl up with a book, huh?"

Ronnie nodded. "It sure is. It's a real nice house, Mrs.—I mean, Ruby."

As they trudged up the stairs, a light-skinned man in a pale gray suit passed them on the way down and nodded at Ruby. "Good morning," he said, offering a quick smile.

"Mornin', Mr. Harris," she said. "He's the gambler," she whispered. "That's why he ain't at work. Ain't exactly a respectable nine-to-five job, ya know."

Ronnie peered over his glasses at Pearl and grinned.

They continued up to the third floor and walked down a long hallway. "Now here are your rooms. The closet in that last one's a little bigger, so I made that one up for you, Pearl."

"Thank you, ma'am."

Ruby unlocked the door and Pearl looked around the small, neat room. There was a single bed with two fluffy pillows and a rose-print bedspread. Next to the bed was a small table with an alarm clock, and next to that was a chest of drawers. Over the bed was a framed picture of an angel guiding two children over a broken footbridge.

"That's a pretty picture, ma'am," Pearl said as she put her bag on the floor.

"Well, I hope it's not too Catholic for ya. I'm just partial to it, I guess, because me and David are Catholics. Angels and all that, ya know. But I'm not sure when David last saw the inside of a church! He told me he ain't been to Mass since before the war!"

"Well, it's a real pretty picture. I like it."

"Okay, well, here's your key then. Now let me show Ronnie his room."

When they stepped into the next room, Ronnie grinned. "Another Catholic angel, huh?"

Ruby laughed. "Told'ja I'm partial to it! I got five of 'em in different rooms, so when the other boarders get to jokin' about it, you ain't got to whisper. Ruby knows all about it!"

"Well, I like it too," Ronnie said.

"Okay, now what else?" Ruby said. "Oh! Guess I ought to tell you that lunch is at noon and supper's at seven every night. You're on your own at breakfast. Just go on in the kitchen and the cook'll show you where everything is. The cook is my daughter Ellen, and she's pretty good, if I do say so myself! I taught her everything she knows about cookin'. I just ain't got the time to do it anymore, what with runnin' this place and my other building, and bookkeepin' and all...."

Ronnie looked up. "Bookkeeping?"

"Mm-hmm. I sure can't afford no accountant."

"I can help you with that, ma'am," Ronnie said. "I'm real good with numbers."

Pearl looked at Ronnie curiously.

Ruby grinned and leaned against the door jamb. "I might just take you up on that, son! You come on down to lunch and we'll talk about it. Oh! I didn't show you the dining room!"

"That's okay, Ruby," Pearl said. "As soon as we put our things away, we'll find it."

* * *

Over the next few weeks Pearl applied for jobs all over the Bronx as Ronnie helped Ruby with her bookkeeping. The only time they saw each other was at breakfast and supper.

Pearl walked in on a Friday night feeling discouraged, but smiled when she saw Ronnie sitting alone at the dining room table. He was waiting for her.

"How did it go?" he said, pulling out a chair for her.

"You used to ask me, 'What'cha learn today, Pearl?' Remember that?"

"I sure do," Ronnie said, grinning. "So what *did* you learn today?"

Pearl sighed. "I learned that I need to know shorthand and how to operate a switchboard to get an office job. All I can do is type. Hey, is there any food left? And is it still warm?"

"Sure it is," Ronnie said, passing her a plate of meatloaf. "I just got it off the stove."

"Thanks," Pearl said as she began picking at her food. "I might have to go back to working at a drugstore, I guess. Or a coffee shop. At least I'll get tips. I gotta get a job, Ronnie."

"Pearl. I told you I have money."

"That money won't last forever, Ronnie."

"It'll last till Mama and David get out here. I thought you decided to move in with them."

"I still need my own money, Ronnie. And besides, I've been thinking about it, and I really like the idea of being on my own."

"Me too. And that was my plan from the beginning. You and me, on our own."

"But what about Mama and David?"

"I never planned to live with them. I like David and everything, but Mama still sees me as a little kid, and I just can't see myself in that picture... Isn't it past your bedtime, young man? Did you brush your teeth and do your homework? Damn, Pearl, I've been in those streets too long. I'm just *not* going back to school, and that's all there is to it."

"Ronnie! You *have* to go back to school when summer's over! That was part of the deal!"

Ronnie shook his head. "I'm *not* going back to school." Then, before she could say another word, he stood up. "I've got an idea."

"What?"

"Let's go to a movie. Didn't Ruby say there was a theater over on Tremont?"

"I think so. But Ronnie—"

"Oh, stop being such a mother hen and go to the movies with me. You'll feel better."

Pearl sighed and got up. "Okay. Let me eat two bites and wash up first."

* * *

After four hours of newsreels, Merrie Melodies cartoons, a fright feature, popcorn, and candy, Pearl's mood was considerably better. As they walked home from the theater, Ronnie kept making her laugh with his horrible impression of Bela Lugosi.

"*Return of the Vampire*, Ronnie? I can't believe you took me to see that! But what I *really* can't believe is that I actually sat through the whole thing!"

"I didn't take you to see *that*. I took you to see Bugs Bunny."

"Can't go wrong with Bugs. And thanks for cheering me up."

"You're welcome. So now, I want you to go take a bath, go to bed, stop worrying, and go straight to sleep. You must be exhausted."

"I am. I hope I can make it up all those stairs."

"Me too, 'cause I am *not* carrying you. Not after all that pop-corn and candy you ate tonight! You probably gained about twenty pounds!"

"Oh, hush."

The boardinghouse was dark and quiet as they climbed the stairs to the third floor.

"G'night," Pearl whispered when they got to the end of the hallway.

"G'night," Ronnie said.

As Pearl unlocked her door, she heard Ronnie muttering angri-ly, and walked back quickly. "What's wrong?"

"My door's open, but I know I locked it." He turned on the light. "Shit! Look at this!"

Pearl followed him into the room and gasped. The mattress was flipped over onto the floor; all the drawers in the bureau were pulled out and the contents scattered everywhere. Ronnie hurried across the room, yanked open the closet door, and fell to his knees over an open suitcase. Slipping his hand between the lining and the outer leather case, he frantically felt around and then groaned. "They got my money, Pearl! Somebody stole my money!"

* * *

When Pearl came down for breakfast the next morning, Ron-nie was slumped in a chair at the table, staring vacantly into his coffee cup.

She leaned down and hugged his shoulders from behind, then sat down next to him. "What are you doing up so early?"

"Couldn't sleep. I wish I knew who overheard us talking about that money. I *know* that's what happened. Damn, I should've been more careful."

"Ronnie, I've been thinking... Do you think there's any way it could've been Victor?"

"Nah. He would've torn *me* to pieces, not my room."

"I guess you're right. So did you tell Ruby what happened?"

"Yeah, and she was pretty upset. She said nothing like that has ever happened before."

"Well, don't worry. I'll get a job. If it takes me all day, I promise I'll get a job *today*."

Ronnie finally looked at her. "I can't be broke again, Pearl," he said bitterly. "I *won't*. That was *my* money! You don't know what I— You don't know how hard I worked for it."

They were the only ones left at the table, but Pearl looked over her shoulder and kept her voice low. "You can't go back to that policy stuff, Ronnie. You need to go back to school, 'cause Mama and David are *not* gonna like you being chased around by truant officers *or* the police!"

Ronnie groaned. "Come on, not that again, Pearl. What do I need with more school? I can get work, you know. I'm already working for Ruby."

"You mean she's paying you?"

"A little. But I talked to Mr. Harris this morning and—"

"Oh, hell, Ronnie!" Pearl snapped. "I knew you had your eye on that damn gambler!"

"From day one. But I just got a good opening this morning. I can read people, Pearl. When I told him how good I am with money and figures, his eyes lit up. So I told him a little about my hustle in Indianapolis. Omitting the skimming off the top part, of course."

"The skimming off the top—? Oh, Ronnie!"

"Never mind. Anyway, he agreed to give me a try and I'm gonna work for him. But it won't be enough. Meanwhile, don't mention any of this to Ruby. She doesn't know about Mr. Harris, and I'll need that money from him until I can get my other idea going."

"Oh, Ronnie! Mama will kill me if she knows you're doing something illegal."

Ronnie gave her a long, unreadable look. "Then don't let her know."

* * *

Two days later, Pearl was surprised to get a call from an insurance company where she had applied for work. The pay was low, but the office manager told her that she could learn the filing system while they trained her on the switchboard. Pearl immediately accepted the position.

Ronnie quietly went to work for Mr. Harris, who paid him generously in cash for his creative accounting. And he was still helping Ruby with bookkeeping chores for her two buildings. All Pearl could do was hope that whatever he was doing was legitimate.

Every Friday night Ronnie took her to dinner, letting her pick the restaurant. But on one particular Friday, he surprised her by picking her up at work in a taxicab.

"No subway?" she asked. "What's the occasion?"

"You'll see."

After a short ride, the taxi pulled up in front of a bar called "The Heights" on the Grand Concourse. Ronnie paid the driver and helped Pearl out. "This is it."

"Nice place," she said, eyeing the blue neon sign over the door. "How'd you find it?"

"Doing pick-ups and deliveries for Mr. Harris. It caught my eye for a special reason."

"Is the food good?"

"It's not special because of the food. It's something else. Come inside and you'll see."

Ronnie slipped some money to one of the waiters, who led them to a table near the small bandstand. The drummer counted off the intro to the first song, and the quartet began playing an up-tempo jazz arrangement of "Blue Moon."

Pearl lit a cigarette and Ronnie smiled at her. "You know that song, don't you?"

She nodded. "Sure."

"Okay, so...."

Pearl glanced over at him, and suddenly she understood. "What? I'm supposed to sing?"

"Yeah, Pearl. Mr. Harris set it up for you. It'll only be for tips at first, but—"

"Ronnie! I can't just jump up there and start singing!"

"Who said anything about jumping? Just sing! You said you sang in Chicago, right?"

"Sure, but—"

"Well, you *must* be better than you were when you used to make up those songs for me."

"For your information, yes. I *have* improved my skills since I was seven... sugar boy."

"And I trust that you've added some songs to your repertoire."

"Of course, wise guy. That little sugar boy song is only for you."

"Yeah. Let's keep it that way."

Pearl got up and tried to smack him on her way to the bandstand, but he ducked.

"Damn, you're slow!" he laughed.

The piano player smiled at her. "What's your name, baby? And what key?"

"Pearl Sayles," she answered. "And the key's fine where it is."

The band did a quick turnaround as the piano player introduced her:

"Ladies and gentlemen, give a nice welcome to tonight's singer, Miss Pearl Sayles!"

"Thank you," Pearl said. After a light smattering of applause, she eased into the song smoothly and laughed at the surprised expression on Ronnie's face.

When she finished "Blue Moon," the applause was much louder, and the piano player grinned at her. "Please tell me you know 'Stormy Weather.' I bet you could tear that one up!"

* * *

It didn't take long for Pearl to become a paid member of the band. Her only night off was Monday, which was a slow night at The Heights. After two months of singing by night and working by day at the insurance company, she was exhausted. But she kept her mind on moving out of Ruby's boardinghouse and into her own apartment. Sleep could wait.

Ronnie dropped by nearly every weekend. At first, he sat at the front table, but after a few weeks, she noticed that he had begun to sit at the bar. When she asked him about it, he assured her that he was only drinking ginger ale, but she was growing suspicious. One Sunday night during her break she walked over and sat beside him.

"What is that you're drinking, Ronnie?" she asked. "And don't make me ask Henry."

"Okay, it's scotch," he said, finishing his drink. "And don't start."

"You just turned sixteen!" she whispered.

"The bartender doesn't know that." He gestured for Henry, who came to refill his glass.

"Anything for you, Pearl?" Henry said.

Pearl smiled nervously. "No thanks, Henry. I gotta go back for the next set in a minute."

As soon as Henry was out of earshot, she whispered, "We're both lucky they're so loose about checking identification in this bar! You might look older than you are, but that's hard liquor, Ronnie. It'll make you sick!"

Ronnie nearly spit out the sip he'd just taken. "Pearl! I've been drinking since Indianapolis! Scotch is mother's milk to me."

"Oh, my God...."

Ronnie groaned. "Please stop babying me and let me enjoy my drink."

"Tell me what's wrong, Ronnie. You come in here and start drinking like an alcoholic, and you're in such a strange mood."

"You're right," he whispered. "Something *is* wrong. But if I tell you, *no* lectures! Deal?"

"Deal."

He sighed deeply. "I've gotta get out of that boardinghouse, Pearl. So I was saving up for this apartment I had my eye on."

"That's no secret. We're both saving up to move, Ronnie."

"Well, I've been making a lot more than you have, but it still wasn't enough. So I—"

"You what?"

"I gambled some of it. A lot of it. Mr. Harris gave me a tip on a horse. It went wrong."

"Oh… Well, that's really not so bad. We've been broke before."

"I'm *sick* of being broke, Pearl!"

"So you have to start saving again, that's all. And stop taking tips from Mr. Harris."

"Yeah. Anyway, Mike's waving at you from the bandstand. Must be time to sing."

"I'm going. But Ronnie. Please make that your last drink, okay?"

* * *

Ronnie didn't show up at The Heights for the next two weekends, and the only time Pearl could talk to him was over breakfast at the boardinghouse. He claimed he was fine, and promised that he'd drop by the following Saturday.

She was in the middle of "I Cover the Waterfront" when he walked in that night, and he took a seat at the far end of the bar. On her first break, she lit a cigarette and walked over to join him. She was happy to see that he was drinking a bottle of ginger ale and having a friendly chat with an older white man seated to his left.

Pearl took the seat to his right. "Where are your glasses, Ronnie?" she asked.

He ignored the question. "Monty, I want you to meet my sister Pearl. Pearl, meet Monty."

"Great to meet you, Pearl," Monty said. "I just love the way you sing."

"Thank you, Monty. It's nice to meet you too."

"Monty and I were just talking about books," Ronnie said.

"Oh, well, don't let me interrupt. I've got to go powder my nose before the last set anyway. See you later, right, Ronnie?"

"I'll be right here."

An hour later, Pearl was singing the last song of the night and looked over at the bar. No Ronnie. She waited until the band had packed their instruments, but he never came back.

Leonard, the bass player, tapped Pearl on the shoulder. "Your brother took off, huh? Need me to walk you to the subway again?"

"No, it's okay. He probably just went out for sump'm to eat. I'll wait a little longer."

"Okay. As for me, I gotta go see a man about a horse."

"Huh?"

Leonard patted her on the head and chuckled. "Nothin'. See you tomorrow, Pearl."

"G'night, Leonard."

After waiting until 3:00 a.m., Pearl gave up and headed for the door. "G'night, Henry."

"Oh, I thought you left," he said. "I already locked up. But I'll let you out the side door."

"Okay." Pearl followed him to the side door and he opened it.

"I got some more sweepin' up to do, but I'll walk you to the subway if you want to wait."

"No, it's okay, Henry. There's a light out there."

"Yeah, and all I ever see when I'm takin' out the garbage is those alley cats. Long as you don't mess with them, you'll be okay. See you tomorrow night, Pearl."

"Good night, Henry."

Pearl made her way along the side of the building until a metallic crash startled her. Telling herself it was just one of the alley cats, she continued toward the corner until she heard a voice that sounded like Ronnie's. Turning around quickly, she saw two shadowy figures near the row of trashcans in the corner next to the adjacent building. Then she heard Ronnie say: "Be patient! I'ma give you what you want. But you gotta stop being so rough."

Pearl had just turned back to get Henry to call the police, when she heard Ronnie's voice again. "That's more like it. Now you're bein' sweet...."

Before the meaning of those last words fully registered, Pearl began walking, then running toward her brother. Then she saw something that brought back a memory of Mr. Washington's hands groping her mother as he kissed the back of her neck. Only this time, it was Ronnie, and the hands belonged to Monty. She stopped running. "Oh, my God!"

Ronnie pulled away from Monty, and Pearl turned and ran as fast as she could to the main street. She could hear him calling her name, so she ran faster, but he finally caught her and pulled her into a doorway. She fought him as he tried to put his arms around her, and he was begging her to listen. When she heard the break in his voice, she stopped struggling.

"I'm sorry, Pearl," he moaned. "I'm really sorry you saw that."

"Ronnie... I—I thought somebody was robbing you, but you were— Oh, my God!"

"I *told* you I needed money."

"Money?" she sobbed. "You did that for *money*?"

"Okay," he said softly. "So now you know."

She stared at him, still stunned. "How could you let him— How could you *do* that?"

Ronnie tried to hand her his handkerchief, but she recoiled and refused to take it. "Oh, hell, Pearl! It's clean!" He stepped back and pulled out both pockets of his trousers. "No money, see? In-complete transaction, if you know what I mean."

Pearl pushed him away, but he stopped her. "*Please* let me ex-plain," he pleaded. "I want you to know everything, but I *really* need you to understand. Please try!"

"Okay... I'll try."

He stared at her and swallowed hard. "Okay, look. It wasn't the first time."

"What?"

"Oh, wise up, Pearl! How do you think I got out of Indianapo-lis? I would've done *anything* to get away from Victor. The policy racket was too slow, and even when I started skimming off the top of Larry's money, he would've caught me sooner or later. So I started taking advice from the hookers I knew—the women *and* the guys... *Don't* look at me like that, Pearl! They were my *friends*! They taught me there was one thing I could sell and still keep to sell again—over and over. And they were right. My cute little ass was a real good moneymaker."

"Oh, stop talking like that!" she cried.

"It's the only way I could get back home to you and Mama! And even with the way you're looking at me right now, I'm not sorry, you hear me? I'm *not* sorry!"

Pearl softened her tone. "Okay, okay... But... wasn't there *anything* else you could do?"

"I was fourteen and working in a library! I *had* to make some money! But it's okay now. Pearl—" He grabbed her shoulders. "Remember when I came back? And we walked into the kitchen and saw Mama's face? All those years, that was my *dream*! Every time Victor beat me! Every time I turned a trick! All I thought about was coming home to you and Mama. And it was even *better* than my dreams! I survived, Pearl! I got home! Doesn't that count for anything?"

Pearl threw her arms around his neck. "Don't cry. I'll try to understand. It's just that I *hate* thinking of men doing those things to you. Did they ever... Ronnie, did they ever... hurt you?"

"Not... not really."

"But *men*, Ronnie? Couldn't you be with women? Like a—a gigolo or sump'm?"

"That didn't exactly work for me, Pearl. And women aren't looking for that kind of action anyway. Not with a boy my age. But I'm *exactly* the right age for somebody like Monty. I spotted him right away—"

She put her hand over his mouth. "Please... Don't ever mention his name again."

"Okay. Pearl... please don't hate me."

"Oh, Ronnie, I could never hate you. But... just tell me one thing, and be *honest*. When you had to be with those men, did you ever... did you ever *like* it?"

Ronnie stared at her a long time before answering. "Let's just say I didn't like... *them*."

CHAPTER 12

After hoarding as much money as they could over the next month, Pearl and Ronnie had enough to move into a small two-bedroom apartment not too far from The Heights. The last detail was convincing Ruby not to mention it to Alva or David. Ronnie smooth-talked her by promising to continue working as her bookkeeper for free. Mr. Harris was paying him enough to live on.

After settling into the new apartment, Ronnie and Pearl agreed on two solid rules of the house: No more Monty incidents, and not a word about the apartment or Ronnie's love life to Alva and David, who would never understand. Everything else they could work out later.

For the first time in his life, Ronnie experienced the freedom to be his true self. Pearl accepted him as he was, and he knew that she would accept any special someone he might bring home for her to meet. The only thing missing now was meeting that special someone.

But then one afternoon, a man named William Levine walked into the New York Public Library and into Ronnie's life.

From the moment he met William, Ronnie was fascinated by him. He was nothing like the hardcore queens who had turned him out in Indianapolis, or the tricks whose money he had taken. In the sub-world of the streets, he had met all types of men—black, white, young, old, addicted, depressed, and more than a few were just bullies who had roughed him up. There were even two preachers who had used him and then prayed as they turned their sanctimonious self-hatred on him. Ronnie despised them the most. It wasn't his fault that they lived behind a mask, choosing to pay for their pleasures in secret.

William was white, wealthy, and Jewish, none of which mattered at all to Ronnie. Ronnie's interest in William existed outside the sphere of anything as dreary as race, class, or religion. Part of his appeal was that he was handsome and nearly twenty years older than Ronnie. He had a touch of gray at his temples and an abundance of life experience. Tall and elegant, William always walked into a room with high-headed pride. There was not a trace of shame in him. He was a true intellectual, well-read, and he had traveled all over the world. His tailor-made suits were made of silk in dark jewel tones—refined and never flashy. He had a way of looking at Ronnie that was attentive without being overt or smothering. It was an innate balancing act of attachment and autonomy.

Ronnie knew he was hooked when he realized he could talk to William about anything, from literature to the roughest times in his life. William listened intently as he sipped his brandy, sometimes offering insights, and sometimes only an understanding smile. But the thing Ronnie found most irresistible was William's musical ability. He was a virtuoso on the piano, and could coax music from a violin that would make a truck driver cry.

On the day they had first met at the library, William took Ronnie to a party at a private residence. It was Ronnie's introduction to a civilized homosexual culture he had never believed could exist. William referred to it as the "gay *demimonde*."

The minute they walked through the door, a middle-aged woman named Marilyn welcomed William with a smile and a kiss.

"And who is your lovely young man, William?"

"This is Ronnie, dear. Let's introduce him to everyone. It's time he knew that he's not alone in this god-awful, judgmental world."

"Hello, Ronnie," Marilyn said, kissing him on both cheeks. "I know, William! Let's celebrate your new friend. You know I love excuses to break out the champagne."

Across the room someone was playing a melodic ballad on a piano, and Ronnie craned his neck to see who it was.

William took him by the arm. "Ah, you've spotted Billy. Let me introduce you."

William led him over to a gleaming black grand piano on a raised pedestal near a huge window. Ronnie's eyes darted from the panoramic view to the crowd of guests surrounding the piano, and finally, to the pianist who had captivated them. He was a diminutive caramel-colored man, wearing a dark sports jacket and horn-rimmed glasses. William nudged his way in.

"Billy, I have someone I'd like you to meet. Ronnie Sayles, meet Billy Strayhorn."

Ronnie's mouth dropped open. "Billy Strayhorn?... Uh, it's very nice to meet you, Mr. Strayhorn. I love your music."

Billy smiled and made space on the piano bench. "Thanks, Ronnie. Have a seat and tell me what you'd like to hear. Any song, even if it's not one of mine."

"Don't steal him away from me now, Billy," William said, which made the guests laugh.

"Never!" Billy said. "Anybody can get a boyfriend. This young man just told me he loves my music! And Aaron would kill me anyway. Now what would you like to hear, Ronnie?"

Ronnie sat down next to Billy. "Surprise me," he said.

"Clever boy," Billy said, grinning at him. "All right. Here's a song I wrote a long time ago, when I was probably younger than you are. It's called 'Something to Live For.' "

"I have it!" Ronnie said. "I mean, I have the record! I love it!"

* * *

Hours later when Ronnie got home, he hurried into Pearl's room and turned on a lamp.

"Wake up, Pearl!"

She woke up with a gasp. "What's wrong?"

"Nothing's wrong. But wake up anyway."

Pearl squinted at the alarm clock and grumbled incoherently as she turned back over.

"Come on, Pearl," Ronnie laughed.

"No! It's four in the morning and I was asleep, boy!"

"Tomorrow's Sunday. You can sleep late. Come on, I brought you some *hors d'oeurves*."

"Some what?"

"Snacks! Wake up!"

Pearl rolled over and squinted at him. "*Why* are you so happy at four in the morning?"

"William," he said grinning. "William Levine."

"Oh, Lord," she groaned. "Go get me some milk."

147

She sat up and plumped her pillow against the headboard and closed her eyes until Ronnie returned with the milk. "This is as up as I'm gonna get, Ronnie."

"Here," he said, handing her the glass. "But first, open your mouth and taste this." He popped one of the *hors d'oeurves* into her mouth. "Good, huh?"

"Not bad."

"Come on, Pearl. Please tell me you've heard of *hors d'oeurves* before."

"Of course! I just never tasted one. Where'd you get 'em, anyway? Wait. William?"

Ronnie smiled. "You know that guy you told me about at your job that makes your heart flutter every time he walks past you?"

Pearl smiled and sighed. "Barry. Tall, handsome Barry."

"Well, that's exactly how William made me feel!"

"So how'd you meet him?"

"I met him at the library. I told you I was going to that Ralph Ellison signing, didn't I?"

"Oh, right," she said nibbling on another one of the *hors d'oeurves*. "Wait a minute. They had these things at the library?"

"Of course not. They were at the party William took me to."

"And where was that?"

Ronnie scrambled up onto the bed and crossed his legs. "I thought you'd never ask. Okay, it was at a penthouse! On Central Park West! The hostess's name was Marilyn—She's the one who gave me the *hors d'oeurves*. I think her husband's a doctor or something, and they both live there. Huge rooms. And the view!"

Pearl grinned at Ronnie's euphoric mood. "Really? What was the view like?"

"Central Park, of course! Aren't you listening? And believe me, you haven't seen it until you see it from a penthouse! And as soon as it got dark, you could see all the city lights of New York glittering everywhere! Oh! And guess who was there? Lena Horne!"

Pearl gasped. "Lena Horne?"

"Yes. And there was a huge—"

"Ronnie, you're lying! Was it *really* Lena Horne?"

"Yes, Pearl. And yes, she's gorgeous and very nice. But there was this huge grand piano over near the window. A Steinway! And you will never believe who was playing it...."

"Lemme guess... Count Basie? No, wait... Duke Ellington!"

"Now you're just being a wise ass. But you're close. It was Billy Strayhorn!"

Pearl shrugged. "Who's Billy Strayhorn?"

"Duke Ellington's composer, stupid! He wrote 'Take the A-Train,' for cryin' out loud!"

"Wow! And you met him?"

"I did. And he played me three songs. He is such a great musician and so cool. And William kept joking around, saying 'Don't you take Ronnie away from me.' It was so funny."

"So... Billy Strayhorn... likes men too?" Pearl said carefully.

"That's the best thing about this party, Pearl. Nearly everyone there was with someone of their own sex. Women too. But the host and hostess, Marilyn and Richard, are straight as an arrow. William said they just love having artistic people over, and when word got around, a lot of the Broadway crowd, and writers and singers and painters, just started coming to their parties. It was so wonderful. Nobody was hiding in corners. Nobody was depressed."

Pearl hugged him. "So why are you so gone on William and not Billy?"

Ronnie shrugged one shoulder. "Billy's wonderful, but he's not my type."

"I know what you mean. There's a guy at work who asked me out three times, but he just doesn't send me the way Barry does." She sighed. "But Barry won't give me the time of day."

"Stupid Barry," Ronnie said, frowning. "He doesn't deserve you."

Suddenly, Pearl rolled over on her side and began laughing uncontrollably.

"*What* is so funny?" he asked, smacking her leg.

"I just never thought I'd be sitting around talking about boyfriends with my brother!"

Ronnie laughed. "But you know what?"

"What?"

"I haven't had so much fun in my whole life!"

Pearl sat back up and reached for her glass. "Me either!"

Ronnie's laughter softened to a tearful smile. Then he leaned over and kissed her on the forehead. "You know what else?" he said softly. "You make me feel so... normal."

"Oh, Ronnie. You're so much better than normal... And William sounds like a real gentleman. Now gimme me some more *hors d'oeurves* and tell me all about him."

* * *

Alva and David had delayed their move from Illinois to New York because of repair problems on his Chicago property. In August, Alva began calling nearly every day pressuring Pearl to get Ruby to enroll Ronnie in school.

Ronnie flatly refused to go back to school, claiming that he was earning a decent living as a bookkeeper for Mr. Harris. Pearl begged and pleaded and argued with him, but nothing was working. She couldn't convince him of the importance of a high school diploma.

Then, by sheer accident, Ronnie stumbled over the perfect compromise. He was at Ruby's boardinghouse one afternoon working on her books when he overheard a conversation she was having with one of the new boarders—a returning war veteran.

"...and when I pass my G.E.D. test I'll be able to get that other job I was telling you about, Mrs. Reynolds."

"What in the world is a G.E.D. test?" Ruby asked.

"It stands for General Education Development. It's a test they came up with in '42," the boarder was saying. "Mainly for us soldiers who never had the chance to finish high school."

Ronnie's ears perked up, but he kept his eyes on his numbers.

"See, you go through a study program and then take the test. If you pass, you get your diploma. I mean, it ain't college, but there's a lot of jobs out there for a high school graduate."

Ronnie grinned and scribbled "General Education Development" on his scratch pad.

* * *

The next afternoon Ronnie and Pearl were standing with their heads together as he dialed Alva's number. "I'll do the talking," he said as the ringing began. "You know how you are."

"Hush, you! I just want to hear!"

"Shh...."

The phone rang twice before Alva picked up the receiver. "Hello?"

"Hi, Mama," Ronnie said. "I've got some great news."

"Did Pearl get you enrolled in a school? Please tell me that's it, baby. I been so worried."

"Better than that, Mama," he said. "I'm gonna get my diploma in a couple of months."

Alva sighed. "Oh, Lord, Ronnie, I thought you was serious."

"I *am* serious! Now listen, please. It's called the G.E.D. program. Ask David. I bet he's heard of it. I already looked at the study guide, Mama, and I can pass this thing easily."

After a long silence, Alva said, "But what's your hurry, son? You could be makin' friends at school and goin' to dances...."

Ronnie's eyeball roll was so exaggerated, Pearl had to stumble away from the telephone and cover her mouth. Ronnie glared at her and was barely able to choke out an answer without laughing. "Uh, I don't really like to go to dances, Mama."

"Well, what'll you do with your free time, son?"

"Work, Mama! I already have a job as a bookkeeper. Look, long distance is expensive, so I'll put it all in a letter. But don't worry. Everything's gonna be fine now."

* * *

When Ronnie and William weren't attending parties at Marilyn and Richard's home, they frequented a place called Café Society. Lena Horne, Billie Holiday, Hazel Scott, Johnny Hartman, Sarah Vaughan, and Art Tatum were among the artists regularly performing there. Even the audience was filled with celebrities. It was William's favorite place for a night out.

But Ronnie's favorite place was a cozy, welcoming apartment on Convent Avenue in Sugar Hill. Billy Strayhorn and Aaron Bridgers lived there, and parties were a frequent event. Aaron played host as

Billy held court in the kitchen. He would polish off entire bottles of wine as he created divine dishes and pots of stew. Their neighbors were a relaxed, multicultural mix of musicians, actors, businessmen, dancers, and writers. Some were homosexual and some were heterosexual. All that mattered at the Strayhorn/Bridgers home was a love of good conversation, the arts, food, and liquor. It didn't take long for Ronnie to become addicted to the atmosphere.

Pearl was about to leave for The Heights one evening when Ronnie hurried in, nearly bumping into her.

"Could this blur be my baby brother?" she laughed as he dashed into his room.

"Sorry, Pearl," he called. "But I gotta pack!"

She walked into his room and watched as he yanked out drawers and stuffed clothing into his suitcase. "Where are you going this time?"

He grinned. "We're going to Martha's Vineyard!"

"Wow. That sounds like fun."

"I'll be gone for the weekend, but when I get back—" He stopped and looked up. "You know, I've been wanting to talk to you about something, and I hope you're okay with this."

"Okay with what?"

"Well, William asked me to move into his apartment with him."

* * *

Pearl was so stunned by Ronnie's news that night that she actually forgot the lyrics to "God Bless the Child," a song she could have sung in her sleep. From the moment Ronnie had introduced her to William she had felt conflicted about him. She liked him; he was far too charming not to like. Her main concern was the age difference, though Ronnie had convinced everyone, including William, that he was twenty-one. William was so much more worldly and sophisticated than Ronnie, showering him with expensive gifts. He also drank heavily. Pearl feared that taken together, all these things would add up to a big heartbreak, sooner or later. And now they were moving in together.

On her first break at the club that night, she went into the kitchen and sat in the corner drinking coffee. Leonard walked in and headed straight to the sink. She watched him as he washed his hands. He was a large man in his mid-forties, and built like a slightly over-the-hill heavyweight boxer. But his kind, soft-spoken demeanor made Pearl think of him as a giant teddy-bear. He turned around and smiled at her.

"Faucet's broke in the men's room," he explained as he dried his hands. He gave her a curious look. "What's troublin' you, honey?"

"Oh, nothin' too bad, Leonard. Just some things on my mind."

Leonard smiled. "And coffee helps?"

"I don't drink, Leonard."

"Not even a little glass of wine to relax you?"

"No. I've seen what alcohol does to folks. I hate it."

"Oh... Well, I hope you work things out."

"Thanks, Leonard."

After he left, Pearl stayed in the kitchen until she heard the figure that signaled the end of her break. She stood up and rinsed out her coffee cup. As she headed to the bandstand, she heard Mike playing the long intro to "Mood Indigo" and wished that he'd picked anything else. Just as she made it to the steps, she heard Henry calling her from the bar.

"Hey, Pearl! Payphone! Some lady—says it's important."

Pearl hurried over and took the receiver from Henry. "Hello?"

"Pearl! Thank God I got you."

"Ruby? What's wrong?"

"Guess who showed up to surprise you?"

"Who—? Oh, my God... not Mama—"

"Yes. David and your mother are sittin' in the great room waitin' to surprise you kids! Lord, David's gonna skin me alive for lettin' you two move out'a here!"

"No, he won't, Ruby... Uh... listen, I'll be there as fast as I can."

"Well, what do I tell 'em in the meantime? And where's Ronnie?"

"Just stall, Ruby. Um, tell 'em we're at the movies or sump'm. And I'll figure this all out on the way. Let me go so I can get me a taxi."

* * *

By the time the taxi pulled up in front of the boardinghouse, Pearl had decided that it was time to come clean. At least semi-clean. She could never let her mother find out that Ronnie was living with William. She walked inside. Ruby was waiting for her by the door.

"Oh, Lord, Pearl! I thought you'd never get here!"

"Sorry, Ruby. But I'll take it from here."

When Pearl walked into the great room, she smiled at David and tried to hug her mother. Alva pushed her away, and neither of them were smiling.

"Where's my Ronnie?" Alva said stiffly.

Pearl took a seat in the chair facing them. "He's with some friends, Mama."

"It's pretty late," David said carefully.

"I know. But actually, I wanted to talk to you alone so I could explain."

David nodded gravely. "We're listening."

"Well, I ain't!" Alva snapped. "They's sump'm goin' on here, Pearl, and I want to know what it is! Ruby wouldn't tell us nothin'!"

"Okay, Mama. There is sump'm goin' on. You know Ronnie got his diploma, right?"

Alva nodded. "I'm glad he did, but where is he?"

"And you know he's working as a bookkeeper. It's freelance, but it's steady income."

"I *said* where is he?"

David narrowed his eyes, but said nothing.

Pearl swallowed hard. "Okay. Ronnie and I got our own apartment. We're roommates."

Alva nearly jumped to her feet, but David stopped her. "Calm down, honey. And before you start yellin', remember there's folks asleep upstairs."

"I won't calm down!" Alva shouted. "That boy's only sixteen, David!"

"Well, *you* were working a job at sixteen," Pearl said.

"But I was livin' with my Mama! And you ain't even eighteen yourself! How'd you get somebody to rent you an apartment?"

"That's what I was wondering," David said softly.

"Well, see... A friend helped me—a friend at my job." Pearl took a deep breath. "He's the owner, Mama. I'm singin' in a nightclub."

"Oh, Lord! Why don't you just stab me in the heart, Pearl? I raised you to be a lady!"

"It's a perfectly respectable place, Mama. And I'm making a lot more there than I ever made as a stenographer. I'll take you there so you can see the place."

Now Alva was sobbing on David's shoulder. "I knew I shouldn't have let these children come out here by theyselves, David. I *told* you that!"

"Mama, please don't blame David. We're okay. We're just working like adults. Isn't that why parents send kids to school in the first place?"

"But you both too young, Pearl!"

Pearl got up and sat next to her mother on the sofa. "I'm not too young, Mama," she said gently. "And neither is Ronnie. We take care of each other."

David sighed. "Alva, I don't mean to interfere, but the truth is, I saw a lot of boys not much older than Ronnie fightin' in the war. Now, I know you don't want to hear that, but sometimes life just makes it necessary for children to grow up fast. They've both been through a lot in their young lives."

Alva dabbed at her eyes. "I can't help worryin', baby."

David kissed her forehead. "There's one thing I learned about life a long time ago, Alva," he said softly. "You can't put the genie back in the bottle."

"What in the world does that mean?"

"It means that your children are not children anymore, no matter what the numbers say. They can't go back. They're both working, Alva. And Pearl made a good point about the reason we send kids to school. We want 'em to be independent, and I think you should be very proud of these two. They both got their diplomas, didn't they? And besides, we're all in the same town now, so if Ronnie and Pearl need us, they can just give us a call. I believe they'll be just fine."

Pearl smiled. "And Ronnie missed you so much all those years, he'll be over to see you all the time. Especially for supper! You know I can't cook like you, Mama. And I can't wait to see your new house."

"Well, it's real nice, but we ain't unpacked yet."

"Then we'll come help you with that—tomorrow, Mama. How's that?"

"I guess so," Alva said. "But you still gotta let me worry. Ain't that a Mama's job?"

Pearl smiled and hugged her. "You can worry, Mama. Just not too much."

CHAPTER 13

Ronnie was exhausted after a long day of juggling books and preparing for Mr. Harris's tax audit. Though he had convinced Mr. Harris that he was experienced with tax matters, the truth was that it had taken him days of studying regulations at the library before finally figuring it out.

The minute he finished, he called William to tell him he was on his way home, but there was no answer. He caught a taxi and napped until he felt the car stop in front of his building. After paying the driver, he got out and smiled at the doorman.

"Good evening, Jonathan," he said.

Jonathan seemed fidgety as he handed Ronnie an envelope. "Mr. Levine wanted me to give this to you personally, Mr. Sayles."

"Thanks," Ronnie said softly. He stared curiously at the envelope as he began walking toward the revolving door.

Then Jonathan stopped him. "I'm real sorry, Mr. Sayles, but I, uh, I got instructions to see that you read that note before we go inside."

Ronnie gave him a puzzled look. "We?"

"Yes, sir," Jonathan said, looking miserable. "I'm supposed to escort you. I'm sorry, Mr. Sayles. You're always so nice, but like I said, I got instructions."

Ronnie tore open the envelope. The first thing he noticed was that there was no date and no salutation. William had always begun his notes with "My Love." But this note was cold and impersonal. No date, no name. He closed his eyes and felt himself crumbling inside, but finally forced himself to begin reading:

I'm in a hurry to catch my boat, so I'll keep this brief. The doorman will let you into the apartment to pick up your things. I took the liberty of packing for you, and I want you to keep the gifts I've given you. So please take the suitcases near the door. If they are not removed today, I've instructed him to dispose of them in any way he sees fit. The lock will be changed immediately.

I will be gone for two to three months, at least. Perhaps longer. Do not try to contact me in any way or at any time in the future.

I'm sure you know what I've found out, and I'm sure you know that I have no intention of committing it to paper. All I will say is this: I had a friend look into your past. Do you realize the possible consequences of your deception?

You have broken my heart, but Paris is a good place to mend.

* * *

Pearl was in the kitchen when she heard a key turning in the lock. She hurried into the front room just as Ronnie stuck his head in.

"It's only me," he said softly.

Just as she was about to say hello, she saw him put two large blue suitcases on the floor.

"Don't ask me anything, Pearl. Just tell me I can stay here for a while."

"Of course, Ronnie. You know that."

He opened one of the suitcases, pulled out a sealed bottle of Napoleon Brandy, and placed it on the coffee table. "One of my gifts," he muttered. He sank heavily onto the sofa and handed her William's letter. "What the hell. You might as well read it."

Pearl unfolded the letter and read it, then sat down next to him. "But—why, Ronnie? What would make him think you were deceiving him? I know you weren't with anybody else."

Ronnie leaned back against the sofa cushion. "Didn't you read the part about the friend checking my past? He found out that I'm a minor, for chrissakes!"

"Oh, of course," Pearl whispered. "That's what he meant by consequences."

It wasn't until Ronnie began rummaging through the suitcases that he began to cry. "Look, Pearl! Silk shirts, ties, sapphire cuff links, Rolex watch… Pretty good payoff, huh?"

"I'm sure that's not how he meant it, Ronnie. He really wanted you to have those things."

"It was the *first* time I wasn't out for the money! Or the gifts! I never wanted *things* from him!" Ronnie shouted. "I told him that! And he said—he said, 'I know. That's why I love you.' "

"I'm sure he did love you, and I'm sure he still does. That's not why he ended things."

Ronnie stood up angrily and tossed a handful of silk ties into the air. "Guilt! That's why."

Pearl shook her head, crying quietly as she watched him.

After a long silence, he sat back down on the sofa and covered his face with his hands. "I never felt like this before, Pearl. I feel like—like I just want to die."

"Please don't say things like that."

"You don't know what it's like, Pearl! You're normal! You have all the choices you want when it comes to love, and you can meet men out in the open! But society decided that I'm *not* normal, so people like me have gotta go crawling around like goddamn shadows! Everybody's gotta wear the mask, so we can barely even find each other! You don't know how limited my choices are! And whenever I did manage to find somebody, they were never right for me. But I finally found William and now it's over. I'll never find anybody to love again."

"You will, Ronnie. I promise you'll find somebody."

"Not like William. He knew the *real* me, all but my age. I told him all about my dirty past and everything. And he said it didn't matter because it didn't have anything to do with love. It was just a tool to survive. And when he told me that, it made me feel so— clean. For the first time! But now it's all just pain! Every memory. How can that make sense?"

Pearl hugged him. "Unfortunately, pain always makes sense. But it still hurts… Oh, Ronnie, you'll meet somebody else and make new memories. The world is full of love."

He pulled away from her and laughed bitterly. "Bullshit! The world is full of *money*, Pearl. And money's the only thing that won't break your heart." He wiped his eyes roughly. "So stop smothering me and go get a couple'a glasses, would you? Please?"

"You know I don't drink, Ronnie."

He grinned and held up his hands. "They're both for me. I've got two hands, ya know."

* * *

Pearl did her best to show support for Ronnie without smothering him. After he had unpacked, he spent part of the next day in the apartment, but then he left for three days. When he finally returned, he was sullen and quiet, and barely ate the food Pearl cooked for him, preferring to drink alone in his room. When she tried to talk to him, his responses were short and dismissive, if he answered at all. Then he would leave again, complaining that he felt caged.

His absences stretched from days to weeks, and Pearl began to wonder if she would ever see her brother again. Finally, one night when she was in the middle of a set at The Heights, she spotted him sitting at the bar. As soon as the band took their next break, she hurried over to him.

"I've been worried about you, Ronnie. Are you okay?"

Ronnie stared into his glass and said nothing.

"Mama's been worried too...."

Again, no response.

"You look terrible, Ronnie. I know you're in a lot of pain, but please talk to me. I'm not the enemy, you know."

Ronnie laughed dryly and drained his glass. "Shit, right now you are."

"So you don't even care about Mama and me anymore, do you? You leave us to worry for weeks and... You know what, Ronnie? You know who your real enemy is?...You!"

After another long silence, Pearl stood up and called Henry. When he walked over, she said, "He's too young to drink. Ask him for his identification. Go on, ask him!"

Henry's eyes widened, but before he could say a word, Ronnie reached into his pocket, paid for his drink, and walked out.

* * *

In the two months since that night, Pearl had been vacillating between hating her brother and crying herself to sleep with worry. When she got to The Heights on the Saturday before Christmas, she realized that her two conflicting emotions had merged into one big depression. It was a feeling she and Alva had shared but never discussed after Victor had taken Ronnie away. Every Christmas they had swallowed their grief, pretending it didn't exist, only finding peace when he finally came home. But now he was gone again, and the old questions came back. *Where is he? What happened to him? Is he even still alive?* But as worried as she was, she couldn't avoid the streaks of anger blazing constantly through her mind.

As usual, she couldn't escape the ubiquitous holiday decorations and music. To make things worse, Alva and David had been planning a Christmas dinner at their new house, and kept asking why Ronnie had not been returning their calls about it. Pearl always covered for him, but when her mother asked her what Ronnie would like for Christmas, she fell into a long silence. *Liquor, Mama. All he wants is liquor...* She had nearly said it out loud, but finally managed to say, "Oh, a sweater or sump'm, Mama. You know he'll love anything you give him."

* * *

Christmas came with no word from Ronnie, and Alva cried all day. Unable to stand her mother's tears, Pearl left her in David's comforting arms.

Three nights later, Pearl was standing in the small spotlight on the bandstand, waiting for Mike's intro to remind her what song she was supposed to sing. But something David had said kept running through her brain: *You can't put the genie back in the bottle....*

At the end of the last set, she was about to leave when one of the patrons offered her a glass of red wine. He was an older well-dressed Italian man with white hair, and he had been sitting at the front table smiling at her all night. He pulled out a chair and she sat down.

"My name is Anthony, Miss Sayles," he said. "I took the liberty of ordering for you while you were singing. "I love your voice, and you seem like a classy, red-wine type of lady."

Pearl smiled sadly. "I don't drink," she said. "But I'll sit with you for a while."

She took a seat across from him and spent the time listening. As he talked about his love of jazz and his extensive record collection, Pearl stared at the sparkling garnet color of the wine, and nodded absently. *Where are you, Ronnie? Where are you right now?*

She suddenly realized that Anthony had stopped talking and was staring at her curiously. "I'm sorry, Anthony," she said. "I'm not very good company, am I? Anyway, it looks like everybody's gone, and I really need to get home."

"I'll be happy to give you a ride."

"Oh, no," Pearl said quickly. "That's not necessary. Uh, my friend Henry—he's the bartender—he always takes me home."

A flash of disappointment crossed Anthony's face. "Of course, I wasn't trying to—"

"Oh, of course not," Pearl said, backing away awkwardly. "But I better go let Henry know I'm ready now. He's probably in the kitchen. G'night, Anthony. And thank you."

"Good night," Anthony said. "And thank you for your lovely voice."

Pearl smiled and then hurried into the kitchen. "Henry? You back here?"

There was no answer, but she heard a rustling sound.

"Henry?"

"He ain't here," a muffled voice said.

The voice was coming from the back corner near the storage closet. Pearl stood there, not wanting to leave until she was sure that Anthony was gone. "Who's there?" she called softly.

Then she heard muffled laughter, followed by heavy breathing, and then a gasp. She hurried toward the sound and was surprised to see Leonard sitting all alone on a low step-stool.

"Leonard? What're you doin' back here?"

"Get out'a here, Pearl," he said in a choked whisper.

"What's wrong? You sound so strange—"

Then she saw it.

Leonard had just pulled a hypodermic needle from his arm, and his belt was slipping down from where he had tightened it just above the elbow. He looked at her, but his eyes didn't quite connect. Then a slow smile spread across his face, and his body jerked a little.

Pearl covered her mouth with her hand. "I'm sorry, Leonard," she said. "I should go."

"Wait, Pearl!" He gathered his paraphernalia into a bag. "It ain't—ain't whushu think."

"Yes, it is. It's heroin, Leonard. I'm not stupid."

"I–I–I only do a little… Look, you can't tell nobody, specially not Mike. He'll fire me."

"I won't, I promise. I won't tell anybody. I'd never get you fired. You can trust me."

"Thanks, honey. See, I jus' need it to feel better sometimes. And, and see, I–I wasn't feelin' good tonight, thassall."

"Come on, Leonard. People take it to get high. Like people take liquor to get drunk."

Leonard smiled sympathetically. "You had some bad 'sperience widdat liquor, huh?"

"I don't drink, Leonard. You know that."

"Not'chu, honey. Some folks in ya life though. Ya Mama? Ya Daddy?"

Pearl sighed. "My father. And my brother."

"Yeah… I seen him knockin' 'em back at the bar. Whuzzat young man runnin' from?"

Pearl stared at the angelic expression on Leonard's face. For some reason, she wanted to confide in him. "He had a bad life, that's all. I just hate what that alcohol does to him. He drinks so much. Does he have to get *so* drunk?"

"Seem like he tryin' to feel better, thassall."

"It turned my father into a monster," Pearl said bitterly.

"Alcohol duzzat to some folks. But seem like it just makes your brother sad. Leas' thass how he look when I shee him at the bar."

"That's exactly what it does to him, Leonard. It makes him more sad than he already is. Then he gets mean, and passes out or vomits. Why would anybody want to pass out and vomit?"

Leonard chuckled. "S'why I don't mess widdit."

"But you— "

"But I what?... Oh, this needle? Oh, this is real different."

Pearl stepped closer. "Why, Leonard? I mean, how is it different?"

"Well... it don't make me sick or pass out. Thash 'cause I never take too much."

"Oh. You mean if you only take a little, you just feel—happy? Not drunk or sad?"

"Thash right. But it a–a better kind'a happy. Like nooo kind'a happy you *ever* had."

"Well, you don't *sound* drunk," Pearl said. "At least not *very* drunk."

Leonard wheezed a soft chuckle. "Sometimes a li'l slur, huh?"

Pearl gave him a closer look. "Yeah, but you sure do look happy."

"See? Thass my reason. To be happy. But there's all kind'a other reasons cats take it."

"Like what?"

Leonard heaved a big sigh. "Different reasons for different cats, honey. Musicians say it makes 'em play better. Some folks use it to kill the blues... Hey! You like the way I play?"

"I love the way you play."

"See? Playin' better. Guess thass another reason."

"But what about that needle? Doesn't that hurt?"

"Ya ain't gotta stab all deep in ya arm. Jush a li'l stick is all. I'ont even feel it."

"But... how exactly does the happy feeling—feel?"

He closed his eyes. "Well, le'see... Right now, I'm feelin' like... like a li'l kid ridin' a rolly-coaster! But real gentle and slow. Sort'a like ridin' on a cloud... Waaaay up in the sky."

"That sounds nice," Pearl said, sniffling softly. "Maybe I should try it."

"Oh, no, honey! You ain't got no reason. You leave this stuff alone, you hear me?"

Pearl dabbed at her eyes with her handkerchief.

Out of a long silence, Leonard said, "Did I tell you it was my li'l boy's birthday today?"

Pearl tried to smile. "No, Leonard! I didn't even know you had a little boy."

"I don't," he said. "Anymore."

"Oh," Pearl whispered. "You mean he's—"

Leonard nodded. "Yeah. My li'l Lenny's dead. So I was feelin' sad tonight... But see? I took my li'l fix, juuus' enough, and I ain't sad no mo'. I feel fine now, Pearl. Reeeeal fine."

* * *

For the next two weeks, Pearl took notice of Leonard's moods. He was never unpleasant, but on the nights he seemed especially happy onstage, she always smiled, glad that he had found something in that needle to chase away his blues. It never seemed to affect his playing; if anything, he seemed to play more freely, in relaxed, colorful tones. Bonded by their shared secret, they became good friends. Pearl hadn't realized how much pain she had bottled up inside until it all flowed out in her talks with Leonard as he walked her to the subway each night.

"You're my best friend, Leonard. You're so wise, and you're the only one I can talk to."

"Aww, honey, I don't know about all that. I bet if you talked to your Mama, she'd understand more than you think she would. And I ain't so wise. I'm just an old fella that lived a little longer than you, that's all. You need to put them blues down and start spendin' time with some folks your own age."

Pearl shook her head. "I'm older than you think, Leonard. Lately, I really understand what old folks mean when they say they've lived too long."

Leonard gave her a curious look. "How old *are* you, honey?"

After a short pause, Pearl said, "Too old... Couple'a hundred years, at least."

Leonard chuckled. "Well, here comes your train, ol' lady. Get home safe now. G'night."

"Good night, Leonard."

* * *

When Pearl walked into her apartment that night, she heard a sound that flooded her with relief—Ronnie's voice. She stopped in the center of the living room and listened for a moment. He was muttering, the way he sometimes did when he talked in his sleep, especially when he was drunk. But he was safe, so she decided not to bother him. At least she could call her mother in the morning and tell her he was okay. She walked into her room and started unzipping her dress, but then stopped and sighed. "At least I better make sure he's in the bed and not on the floor."

Before she had a chance to turn around, she heard a loud thump, followed by a smack. Running to Ronnie's bedroom door, she yanked it open and turned on the light.

He was cringing on the floor next to his bed, with his hands over his head in a defensive position. Standing over him was a muscular, dark-skinned man, wearing trousers but no shirt.

Pearl shouted, "Stop it! Get out'a here right now! GET OUT!"

"Who's this goddamn bitch?" the man yelled, glancing quickly down at Ronnie.

Without waiting for an answer, he lunged at Pearl and took a swing at her, but she moved back just enough to deflect the punch. As she grabbed a ceramic lamp from the dresser, she saw Ronnie grab the man's ankle, which sent him crashing face down onto the floor. Holding the lamp high, Pearl brought it down hard, shattering it on the back of his head.

Someone was pounding on the door and yelling something about calling the police.

Holding his bleeding head, the man got to his knees and muttered as he reached for his shirt. Pearl saw his shoes and grabbed them, then ran to the front door and tossed them into the hallway. Stopping to pick up the living room lamp, she held it up threateningly as he staggered past her and out the front door.

Her stunned neighbor, an elderly Puerto Rican man, was standing in the hallway in his bathrobe staring at the whole scene with a horrified expression. "Sorry for the disturbance, Mr. Arroyo," she said. "He was tryin' to rob us."

He shook his head skeptically, then went back to his apartment, muttering in Spanish.

Pearl shut and locked the door, then placed the lamp back on the end table and headed back to Ronnie's room. She stopped in the doorway and stared at him.

He was sitting on the floor, leaning against the bed with his knees drawn up. He was holding his head in his hands, and wearing nothing but a pair of red underwear. When he looked up at her, there were tears in his eyes and bruises on the side of his face. His lip was swollen and bloody, but he grinned. "Oops! Another incomplete transaction."

Pearl pounded the wall with her fist. "I can't stand seeing you like this, Ronnie!" she screamed. "Just go! Get out!"

* * *

Ronnie disappeared again, and this time Pearl didn't bother with expectations. For the next two months, the ringing telephone never caused her to jump with hope; she knew that it was only Alva, fretting over her baby. Tired of covering for him, Pearl finally said, "You gotta stop doing this to yourself, Mama. Hell, it's just pain. Let's get used to it. We did it before. If he turns up, it'll be when he feels like it."

The Heights became Pearl's only sanctuary. Just walking into the club was both an escape and a comfort, like climbing under a warm blanket and drifting into the fictional world of a good book. Numbing herself to the pain, she began to realize that she was also numbing herself to the joy of singing. She stepped up to the microphone and stared at the audience.

Smile at 'em, Pearl... Tell a little joke... Sing some songs... Remind 'em to tip the waitresses... Just try to make it to the break and then we'll do it all over again....

"Good evening, ladies and gentlemen."

She looked back at Leonard, who was smiling his dreamy heroin smile. *Leonard ain't numb. Leonard's happy...* Before she knew it, she had finished the song.

That's applause, Pearl... Say thank you... And then just sing another damn song.

"Thank you, ladies and gentlemen. Right now, we're—"

She stopped when she spotted a blur of movement from the bar area. It was Henry. He was waving at her and holding up the phone receiver as he mouthed the word "Urgent."

Now what? Pearl looked over at Mike, who nodded and led the band into an instrumental number. Then she hurried over to the bar and grabbed the receiver. "Hello?"

She heard her mother sobbing and stammering. "Pearl! Oh, Lawd! I–I need you, Pearl!"

"Mama, what happened? Is it Ronnie?"

"No, it's David! He fell, and then... Pearl, them ambulance doctors told me it was, it was, it was a, a heart attack. But I, I told 'em he's too young to have a heart attack! I *told* 'em that!"

"When, Mama?"

"Hour... hour ago, Pearl... I told 'em—"

"Stop, Mama, listen to me. *Where* are you?"

"The—the V.A. Hospital, Pearl. Please hurry, baby. I, I need you! I need my babies...."

* * *

The next few days ran together in a blur of chaotic activity that never resolved. It went from the height of manic disorder to a sudden dull thud, followed by a soundless vacuum.

Alva had finally dozed off after taking two sleeping pills, and Pearl was sitting alone in the living room, staring at the front page of the *New York Times* lying on the coffee table:

*SENATOR BILBO URGES
MISSISSIPPI MEN TO EMPLOY
'ANY MEANS' TO BAR NEGROES
FROM VOTING*

The headline was depressing enough, but Pearl dreaded that newspaper because of something else—one last thing her mother had asked her to do. She wanted her clipping.

Pearl finally picked up the paper and turned the pages to the Obituaries section. She had never known anyone who had died before. Reaching for her handkerchief, she pressed it against her eyes and cried quietly for a long time before she could begin. Finally, she took the scissors and carefully clipped around the short paragraph that her mother so desperately wanted.

Lieutenant David Sims, World War Two veteran, was laid to rest today at Woodlawn Cemetery, Bronx, New York. In attendance were his beloved wife Alva Sims, his sister Ruby Reynolds, and his stepdaughter Pearl Sayles.

* * *

Pearl stayed with her mother for the next week and tried to comfort her. But it was an uphill battle. Compounding Alva's grief over losing David was the fact that, once again, her youngest child had vanished.

Once she was able to get out of bed and get through a day without breaking down, she told Pearl it was time for her to return to work. Pearl hesitated only slightly, realizing how much she needed the music and atmosphere of The Heights.

But this time The Heights offered no sanctuary. The pain followed her right through the front door, and she barely managed to get through the first set. The minute she looked back into Leonard's eyes, she came undone.

"Can I talk to you outside a minute, Leonard?" she said, wiping her eyes.

"Okay, honey, but please don't cry. I can't stand to see a sweet girl like you cry."

She led him out to the alley and gazed at him. "I have a reason now," she whispered.

He squeezed his eyes shut, and shook his head. "No, Pearl."

"Please," she sobbed. "The pain got me, Leonard! I can't sleep! I can't stand it!"

He put his arms around her gently and patted her back. "Okay, honey. Shh... Okay... I guess you been through a lotta sorrow lately."

"Leonard, please help me. I can't... I can't get numb anymore!"

"Okay, honey, okay," Leonard said softly. "There's a fella I know, and he's here tonight tryin' to put a band together. And he's the one... He can take you to meet the dealer, honey. I'll introduce you to him after the last set... but you're gonna need some money."

"How much?" she whispered.

"Ten."

She nodded and wiped her eyes. "I have ten."

The rest of the night dragged, but at the end of the last set Leonard kept his word. He led Pearl over to the bar and introduced her to a young, light-skinned man who was drinking a beer.

"Pearl, this is Melvin."

Melvin smiled at Pearl, but he didn't stand up. "Leonard told me you could sing, baby, but he didn't tell me you were so good lookin'! Sit down and let me buy you a drink."

"I don't—care for alcohol," she said softly.

Leonard looked at the floor. "I told her you could take her to... to meet that man."

Melvin's face suddenly lit up with understanding. "Oh! *That* man!... Okay, yeah. I was just about to head over there now. Come on baby. I'ma fix you riiight up."

PART TWO

CHAPTER 14

HARLEM

D oc Calhoun was feeling better than he had in months. For the first time since coming home from the war, he had no trouble climbing the 135th Street subway steps. The pain in his leg was diminishing. He was still troubled by nightmares, mostly about Spain, but he spent the sleepless hours studying charts, then practicing tenaciously during the day. His chops were back, sharper than ever. Gripping the handle of his horn case, he walked with a bounce that was almost his natural rhythm. He couldn't wait to get to the Red Regency.

As he approached the entrance, he saw a large sidewalk sign that had not been there the night before. When he read it, he rolled his eyes and laughed.

Stepping inside, he saw the other band members on the stage. Elton was tuning his floor tom; Alex was still working out chords on the piano for a new song that was supposed to kick off the first set; Sailor had his head down, clearly in his own world as he practiced a complicated figure on his bass; and Melvin, the bandleader and self-proclaimed sax master, was standing at center stage sucking away at a joint.

"Goddamn, Melvin!" Doc said when he got closer. "Get rid of that!"

Melvin grinned. "Why, man?"

Doc jerked his head in the direction of the bartender. "You *know* Eric's the manager's brother. And I've never met any managers who ain't scared of gettin' closed down because of some fool messin' with narcotics in their establishment."

Melvin scowled at him. "Yes, Mother." He quickly killed the joint with his fingertips and stuck it in his pocket. "Anything else you wanna nag me about?"

"Yeah, now that you mention it. I saw that sign outside. So who the hell came up with that corny name for the band?"

172

Melvin grinned and hooked his saxophone to his neck strap. "Up the River!" he shouted. "And for your information, muthafucka, I came up with the name. You wanna pick a name, get your own band."

Doc nodded. "Well, now that I think about it, that name might turn out to be perfect for us, if you keep up your public displays of dope-smokin'."

Melvin nudged him playfully with his shoulder. "You better meet me in that alley after the first set, man, for some *private* dope-smokin'. 'Cause this is some real good shit, Doc."

Doc laughed and sidestepped Melvin on his way to the piano. "My chart ready, maestro?"

Alex nodded without looking up and handed Doc his chart.

"Thanks, man." Doc walked over to an empty stool, opened his case and lifted out his trumpet. As he began studying the chart, he heard a wolf-whistle and glanced up to see who Sailor was admiring.

A tall Negro woman in a trench coat was walking slowly toward the stage. Even in the dark club, it was clear that she wasn't one of the regular B-girls who usually hung around hustling drinks at the bar. There was something very different about her. It was something in her walk—stately and smooth. It was in the curve of her neck and the high set of her head. Doc tried to look away and stop analyzing her, but couldn't. Smooth brown skin and soft black shoulder-length hair. A light shade of red lipstick. Hands in her pockets. No pocketbook. Cool and relaxed, even in a room filled with this rogue's gallery of lowlifes. He silently indulged himself by searching for a one-word description, but none of the regular adjectives seemed to fit. Then it hit him. *Elegant.* He smiled at his own foolishness and wondered what a woman like her would think if she could read a man's mind. Then she stepped up to the edge of the stage, and he finally got a close look at her eyes.

That's when everything changed.

Something about her eyes made him think of Spain. They were dark, very dark, and they seemed to be looking at something no one else could see. Like a vision. Or perhaps, like Enrique, into some painful past.

His thoughts were interrupted abruptly by Sailor's crass comment:

"Oooh! Sex on the hoof!"

Elton gave him a crazed look. "Hoof? She ain't a cow, man! Don't listen to him, baby. Let me take that coat for ya, so we can see what kind'a chassis ya got under there."

The woman's only response was a slight lift of her right eyebrow.

Doc lowered his head and smiled inwardly. *Now that's class....*

"Everybody shut the hell up," Melvin said as he helped her up the steps. " 'Specially you, Sailor, you nasty sonofabitch! Anyway, I told you fellas I had a surprise, and this is her."

Sailor rubbed his hands together. "For me? Aww, man, just what I always wanted!"

"Shut *up*, man," Melvin said, pushing him away. "This is Pearl. She's our new singer."

Everyone went stone silent. Even Sailor.

Doc closed his eyes and her name took up residence in his mind. *Pearl.*

Melvin started talking faster. "Okay, baby, let me introduce everybody. That's Elton on drums, and that's Alex at the piano. He helps me with some of the arrangements."

Doc shook his head and glanced at Alex, who rolled his eyes. Everybody in the band knew that Alex wrote *all* the arrangements. Melvin's forte was getting high.

"Now, Sailor's a hell of a bass man," Melvin was saying, "when he ain't talkin' all that mess. He was in the Navy—in the South Pacific during the war. That's why we call him Sailor."

Pearl nodded.

"And that's Doc over there hangin' onto his damn trumpet like he's scared somebody gon' steal it from him. He was in the war too. North Africa, right, Doc?"

Doc nodded, and felt the sudden need to check the valves on his horn. Pearl was looking directly at him.

"Caught a bullet in the leg, didn't you, Doc? That's why he's still a little gimpy."

"Just some shrapnel," Doc muttered.

Pearl's gaze drifted down to his legs, then back up to his eyes.

"It's nice to meet you fellas."

Her voice was even more startling than her looks. She spoke in a rich, deep contralto that made Doc's pulse race so fast he almost laughed at himself.

Melvin put his arm around her. "Uh, another thing I probably ought'a mention... She ain't just our new singer. She's my wife. So all you mugs lay off. Ya dig?"

Doc shrugged. "Cool."

He picked up his chart and turned around to hide the fact that this new singer, who also happened to be Melvin's wife, had left him feeling anything but cool.

* * *

With no time for a full rehearsal, Pearl sang only one song that night—"Lover Man." The song was popular, so the band had been playing it every night, but this was the first time they had played a vocal version. Doc accompanied her well, instinctively easing into her timing and filling the spaces without stepping on her vocal. He made up his mind to keep his eyes closed, even during his solo. Too many looks at another man's wife could be quite a hazardous distraction. But in the darkness behind his eyes, she was even more dangerous. Doc knew he was playing just for her and he wondered how it would all end—when he finally did open his eyes.

* * *

Over the next couple of weeks, Doc gave a lot of thought to Mr. and Mrs. Melvin Fulsome. Aside from the fact that he'd never seen a more mismatched couple, he couldn't help noticing an unusual pattern in their comings and goings. He tried not to jump to any conclusions about where Melvin might be taking her when they disappeared between sets. Sometimes he left without her, and Pearl would sit by herself at the bar, nursing a drink and chain smoking.

At the end of her third week with the band, Melvin did his disappearing act just before the last set. Pearl was sitting at the bar wearing the black sheath dress she always wore onstage. As Doc tried to decide whether or not to talk to her, he stared at that dress. It didn't have a plunging neckline and it wasn't too tight. Like

Pearl, it was sexy without trying too hard. It was the back of the dress that was provocative. It was cut low enough in the back that it showed the edges of her shoulder blades and just enough skin to drive a man crazy. After watching her for a few minutes, he finally walked over to the bar, ignoring the voice in his head telling him not to. He slid onto the empty stool to her left and ordered a neat Johnnie Walker Red.

"If you ever finish that Highball, I'll be happy to buy you another one," he said.

Pearl laughed in a deep rumble from her throat. As usual, the sound of it sent a chill down his spine.

"This ain't a Highball, sugah. It's just a Coke."

"Oh, you don't drink?"

"Not really. Maybe a glass of champagne on New Year's sometimes."

Eric walked over with Doc's drink.

"Thanks, Eric." Doc took a sip of his drink and tried to think of something to say to Pearl. Then he blurted out, "So, uh, where'd your husband go?"

Pearl narrowed her eyes at him. Then, instead of answering, she tilted her head back, tapped her cheek, and blew a series of soft, perfect smoke rings.

Doc raised his glass. "Hey! I been trying to figure out how to do smoke rings for years!"

"Patience, trumpet man. That's the trick."

"Okay. So, uh…."

Pearl eased into his broken sentence. "You born and raised in New York, sugah?"

Doc smiled, sensing that she was rescuing him from his awkwardness. "Born here and schooled here, but I wandered the world after that. What about you?"

"Born in Chicago, sugah. South Side."

Doc nodded. "Black Belt."

"I see you're familiar with the area."

"Is that where you met Melvin?"

"No, I didn't meet Melvin till I'd been in New York for a while."

"How long have you two been married?"

"Little over a year. Before that I was on my own—till Melvin rescued me."

For the first time Doc saw the needle marks on her arm. "So he... *rescued* you, huh?"

Pearl folded her arms and changed the subject. "You know, I just love New York. Only two places I've ever been are Chicago and New York. But you said you wandered around. Where did you wander to, trumpet man?"

"Oh, I spent a little time in Chicago myself, and Kansas City, New Orleans... anywhere jazz was. I didn't start seeing the rest of the world till '38."

Doc stopped when he saw Pearl's gaze shift toward something over his right shoulder. He turned around and saw two white men standing behind him. They were both wearing dark, conservative suits and stony facial expressions. He didn't know them, but he had a pretty good idea where they were from.

The man on the right had extremely white skin, which contrasted with his extremely black hair, which looked extremely Brylcreemed. There was nothing otherwise remarkable about him until Doc gazed into his eyes. He had seen pale blue eyes before, but this man's eyes were as colorless as ice.

The one on the left had a blond G.I.-style crew-cut and stared at Doc while unwrapping a stick of chewing gum and popping it into his mouth. Then he tossed the wrapper to the floor and grinned. Doc tried not to laugh at the man's jaws working so fiercely on that chewing gum.

Before he could speak, the man on the right flashed a badge and said, "Your name Demetrius Calhoun?"

"Depends on who's asking."

"Step outside with us, Mr. Calhoun."

Doc gazed at them over the top of his glass as he finished his drink. Then he pulled two singles from his pocket and placed them on the bar. "You have me at a disadvantage, gentlemen. You seem to know my name, but I don't know yours. Mind if I have another look at that badge?"

He read the badge and felt his teeth begin to grind. *Federal Bureau of Investigation.*

The man on the right smoothed his tie and gestured toward the door. "I'm Agent Adams," he said. "Outside. *Now.*"

When Doc stood up, Pearl touched his arm. "Wait, a minute. Maybe you shouldn't—"

Doc patted her hand and smiled. "It's okay. I'll be back in a few minutes."

As the two men walked Doc to the front door, Melvin was walking in.

"Hey, Doc," he said, eyeing the two agents curiously. "We, uh, we're about to start the last set in a few minutes."

"Play this one without me, Melvin. This might take a while."

When they stepped outside, Agent Adams led Doc to a black sedan parked directly under a "No Parking" sign. Opening the back door, he said, "In the car, Mr. Calhoun."

Doc sighed and slid into the back seat. Adams got in and sat to his right, and Crew-cut got in from the other side. A pair of dark eyes peered at him from the rear-view mirror.

"What can I do for you gentlemen?" Doc asked.

Adams got right to the point. "Do you know a man named James Turner?"

Doc turned his head slowly and stared at him. "Why?"

Adams grinned. "I'm asking the questions here. Do you know James Turner?"

"*Why* are you looking for this James Turner?" Doc asked pointedly.

Adams twitched slightly. "Didn't you hear what I said? *I'm* asking the questions here."

"Actually, your friend's gum-smackin' is making it hard to hear…" Before either of them could respond, he said, "Oh, yeah, James Turner. Guess that *might* be—"

He stopped. A blur of motion on the sidewalk caught his eye. It was Pearl. She was standing near the front right quarter panel of the car, casually smoking a cigarette.

"Guess that might be *what*, Mr. Calhoun? What were you saying?"

Doc looked at him, and then tapped his forehead. "I was just tryin' to remember sump'm. Lemme see..." He snuck another look at Pearl. Now she was pacing as she smoked, back and forth along the sidewalk.

"What I was thinking was that, uh, James Turner might have been Jimmy Turner. I knew a Jimmy Turner once, but I haven't seen him in years."

Adams showed his teeth in an unfriendly smile. "You're lying."

"Now why would I lie about that? I haven't seen Jimmy in years."

Doc had to concentrate hard to keep from grinning. Pearl was still strolling along the sidewalk, and had just lit a new cigarette off the end of the one she was finishing.

"We happen to know you were very close friends with Mr. Turner. And all of a sudden you lost complete touch with him? You expect us to believe that?"

Doc sighed. "Well, it was hard for me to believe too, till I heard he was dead."

Adams smiled tightly. "We talked to the family. They would've known if he was dead."

Doc stared straight ahead. The Party always handled breaking that kind of news to families, and he had notified them of Jimmy's death the day he returned from Spain. Had the family lied to the FBI? Or had the Party somehow failed to tell them what had happened to Jimmy? Doc felt a sudden wave of grief, knowing that he would have to visit Jimmy's mother—once he was out from under the scrutiny of the FBI.

Adams was still talking. "So you claim he's dead, huh? Did you see him die?"

"No, I *didn't* see him die. But I haven't seen him alive since—" Doc paused, as Jimmy's death replayed in his mind. *No, I didn't see him die, you sonofabitch. I don't know how long it took him to choke on his own blood—*

"Since when?" Adams said, shattering the terrible memory. "What year?"

Doc composed himself. "Oh, let's see... 1936. Maybe '37. Not exactly sure."

"Let me help you with that, Mr. Calhoun," Adams said, tapping the driver's shoulder.

The driver handed him an envelope. Adams opened it, pulled out a page, and looked at it.

"Says here you attended a meeting of the American Communist Party on May 9th, 1937. You were with James Turner. Don't deny it. Both your signatures are on the sign-in sheet."

Doc shrugged. "I'm not denying it. Yeah, I went to a meeting."

"With James Turner."

"If he was there, I didn't see him. We weren't Siamese twins, and it was a big hall."

"A big hall," Adams said contemptuously. "Who was there? Give me some names."

"Didn't you just say you had the sign-in sheet? I'm afraid you'll have to get your names from that, because honestly, my memory isn't what it used to be."

Doc snuck another look outside and was relieved to see Pearl going back inside the club.

"How long have you been a Communist, Mr. Calhoun?"

"I'm not a Communist, Mr. Adams."

"That's *Agent* Adams."

"Okay. I'm not a Communist, Agent Adams."

"You're a liar."

"A liar? Sure. All men are liars. Ask any woman. But I'm *not* a Communist."

"So you just decided to go to a meeting on a whim."

"Not on a whim. I attended a meeting that was about some local issues that concerned me. And that's not a crime."

"Jury's still out on that one, Mr. Calhoun. The FBI is looking closely into all subversive activities involving you Reds. The definition of 'crime' is changing every day."

"Evidently."

At last, Crew-cut spoke: "You're a real smart nigger, aren't you?"

Doc grinned at Adams. "Do I have to answer that one too?"

Crew-cut grabbed Doc's chin and yanked it in his direction. "Yeah, you do!"

Doc jerked away from him, but stayed calm. "Hmm. Sounds like a two-part question. Am I real smart *and* am I a nigger. And here's my answer... Yes to the first and no to the second."

"Stop wasting time, Vince," Adams snapped at his partner. "Now, Mr. Calhoun, how did you get back from Spain? ...Oh, I guess you figured we didn't know about you Reds sneaking over there and back. Well, we know all about it."

"I told you, I'm not a Red. I wasn't then, and I'm not now. I was a soldier."

"In Spain! Which was strictly prohibited by the United States Government!"

"In North Africa," Doc said, keeping his voice irritatingly calm. "I was a soldier in the United States Army, and I was stationed in North Africa. You can check it. And as far as Spain, I don't have any information for you."

"Let's get back to that Communist meeting you went to—"

"No, let's *not*. Let's get back to my job inside that club over there—unless I'm under arrest. Am I under arrest, Agent Adams?"

After a long silence, Adams opened the door and let Doc out.

"You know," Doc said, "you really ought'a take that chewing gum away from your partner. It's hard to take you guys seriously with all that juvenile smacking going on."

Adams smoothed his tie. "You'll be taking us seriously, Mr. Calhoun. Very soon."

* * *

By the time Doc got back inside, the last set had ended and the band was packing up.

"Sailor," he called.

Sailor looked up. "Hey, man, what the hell happened to you?"

"Unavoidable business I had to tend to. Where's Melvin?"

Sailor snorted. "Come on, man!"

Doc laughed. "Already?"

"Yeah," Sailor said. Then he jerked his chin in the direction of the bar, where Pearl was sitting alone. "I don't mind tellin' you,

Doc... If he keeps leavin' that Grade-A ass unattended, I might just have to steal it from him."

"Hey, man!" Doc snapped. "The last thing she needs is a shit-mouthed low-life like you! And if you don't roll your tongue back in your head, I'll go to work as her goddamn bodyguard!"

"Aww, lounge, man," Sailor groaned. "Goddamn... You boy-scout cats make me sick!"

Doc gathered his sheet music, placed his trumpet in its case, and walked over to the bar. Signaling the bartender, he took the seat next to Pearl. "You must'a missed most of the last set."

Pearl slid a pack of cigarettes toward him. "How do you figure?"

"All those cigarettes you were smoking on that long walk you took outside. Were you lookin' out for me?"

"I just wanted to make sure they didn't haul you off someplace with no witnesses. I got the plate number and you better believe I would'a raised some hell with *somebody*."

Doc smiled. "You little tiger!"

Pearl gave him a sidelong glance. "Little?"

"Correction. You *tall* tiger. But you *were* stalking. I was waitin' for you to take a bite out'a one of those guys. And what made you think they were gonna haul me off someplace?"

"I'm from Chicago, sugah. I've seen more than my share of Negroes gettin' hauled off by the cops."

The bartender walked over with a bottle of Johnnie Walker Red and yawned as he poured him a drink. "Awright, Doc, I'm warnin' you. After this one I'm closin' up the laboratory."

Doc grinned and pretended to flutter his eyelashes. "Eric! You remembered!"

"Yeah, yeah. Johnnie Red. That took a lotta guesswork. Hey, Pearl, you okay with that Coke? It's gotta be warm by now."

"It's fine, sugah."

"Awright, soon as I sweep up, I gotta throw both'a yuz out. 'Scuse me, Pearl. *You* I escort. Him I throws. And then I make like Santa Claus—to all a goodnight."

Doc laughed. "We'll be gone in five minutes, Eric."

Once Eric was out of earshot, Pearl said, "Okay, now tell me what those cops wanted."

"They weren't cops."

Pearl put out her cigarette and stood up. "Never mind. None of my business."

"Wait, Pearl. I'll tell you." He knocked back his drink and left two singles under the ashtray for Eric. "Let me walk you to the subway. Unless you're waiting for Melvin."

Pearl shook her head. "Let's go."

When they got outside, Doc said, "They were FBI agents."

Pearl looked at him with wide eyes. "FBI?"

"Mm-hmm. But look, Pearl, I'm not a criminal. Believe that, please. And since they already have all the information there is on me, there's no reason I can't tell you this. Hell, they investigated me inside out before they'd let me fight in World War Two. That's why this visit surprised me. You see, I was in Spain in '38. In the war."

Pearl tapped out a cigarette and Doc lit it for her. "So you fought in both wars?"

"I did. In Spain I was with the Lincoln Brigade."

"The Lincoln Brigade," she said, nodding. "I read about you fellas in the newspapers. So, are you a Communist? Is that what those FBI agents wanted to talk to you about?"

Doc smiled. Unlike most people, Pearl showed no horror at the word "Communist."

"No, I'm not a Communist, but a lotta the other Lincolns were. Those agents were askin' about one of my buddies."

"Oh. Is he in trouble with those fellas from Washington I been readin' about?"

Doc gazed at her for a moment, then lit a cigarette for himself. "He's dead."

"Oh, I'm sorry, sugah. Was he a close friend?"

"Yeah, he was. We grew up together and we learned a lot in Spain. All about the world, about people, about the *value* of people. Every single human life. He had a head start on me though, because he had joined the party. Sometimes I thought about joining, but I never did. It's hard to explain why so many folks joined up back then. But those were different times in the thirties. Hard times. Everybody was just lookin' for some justice."

Pearl nodded. "And some food. And some jobs. The Depression was... well, depressing."

"So was Spain. And it all led to World War Two."

"More folks dying," Pearl murmured. "Hitler and those damn concentration camps. I'm sure glad he's gone, and Mussolini too."

"Yeah," Doc said, "but everybody forgot about Franco. That sonofabitch is still in power over in Spain."

"I know, sugah. Nobody wins in a war."

Doc stared at her. "What did you say?"

"I just said nobody really wins a war. Everybody thinks they're right, that they're the only good guys. Everybody can't be right, so it seems to me that makes everybody wrong."

Doc was quiet for a moment. "Somebody told me that same thing once." He looked at her and shrugged. "Look, why don't we talk about something more pleasant."

Pearl shook her head. "No, sugah. If we don't talk about it, it gets forgotten. And we *better* not forget this war or Spain either. Maybe if folks talked about it more, then we could find some answers instead of killin' each other over and over again, in war after war. 'Cause as far as I'm concerned, there are no good guys in a war. Only bad guys and victims. That might not sound right, but I think a lot of soldiers are victims too, just like the folks they're tryin' to help."

"Well, all I know is that ever since we got back from Spain, what was left of us, the government's been making *us* out to be the bad guys. I don't feel like a victim myself, but I saw a lot of people who were. And we couldn't save 'em. So... I guess we failed."

"No, you didn't. The way I see it, you were a hero for just goin' over there to help."

Doc smiled. "Didn't you just say there are only bad guys and victims in a war? Anyway, whatever I was, I was too young and dumb to be a hero, believe me. All I did was follow orders."

"Well, doesn't that work out to be the same thing? At least sometimes?"

He gazed at her through the smoke. "Come to think of it, the closest I ever came to doing anything that felt heroic was *not* obeying orders."

"And what was that?"

"Well, I stopped to bury some... somebody when I should've been in... in Barcelona delivering—" Doc suddenly went cold and stopped talking.

"What? What were you supposed to deliver?"

"I just thought of sump'm... I was supposed to deliver a truckload of supplies, but I stopped to dig that grave. If I hadn't done that I probably would've made it to Barcelona just in time to get killed with the others. And I wouldn't have met Pablo and— My God, it's amazing how your whole life can turn on a dime."

"But you survived. All that means is you weren't supposed to die in Barcelona."

Doc stared at her. "Maybe. And I only survived because of a brave nurse from Harlem."

"A female nurse was in Spain? From Harlem?"

"Small world, huh? She told me she worked at Harlem Hospital before joining up with the Lincolns. She fixed up my shoulder at a triage unit on the way to Gerona. I sure hope she got back in one piece. She had an odd name... Sally-rce or sump'm like that."

Pearl gazed absently for a moment, seemingly lost in thought. "Tell me sump'm... Did you have to kill anybody in Spain?"

"More than I'd like to think about."

"That must be a hard thing to do, even in a war. 'Specially the first one."

"Not the first one," Doc said bitterly. "The first one I killed was the easiest. Actually, it was two of Franco's soldiers who'd just killed one of my buddies. I emptied my clip into both of 'em before they could reload. Didn't blink an eye."

"Lord! I don't know how any of you found the guts to go to war."

"You never know what kind'a guts you have until you face sump'm really evil or frightening. And Spain was all of that. That's why it kept botherin' me, I guess, so—"

"So you joined up for World War Two."

"Like I said, young and dumb. The FBI treated anybody who'd fought in Spain like we were the enemy. Interrogated us and made us jump through hoops before they'd *allow* us to serve in their segregated army! Imagine that. As bad as they needed soldiers! Anyway, next thing I knew, I was in North Africa gettin' my young, dumb ass shot at. But not for long."

"You were right on the front lines? Like—oh, what do they call that?"

"Infantry. But you don't have to be in the infantry to be on the front lines. All they let me do was drive a supply truck, and I *still* managed to catch two pieces of shrapnel—one in my back, and one in my thigh. I got hit in the shoulder in Spain, but that was nothin' compared to that thigh wound in North Africa. That's the one that hit a main artery."

Pearl's eyes widened. "Oh, Lord! Was it bad?"

"Pretty bad. I lost so much blood so fast, I passed out and woke up in a field hospital, with some medic givin' me the good-news-bad-news routine. 'You're goin' home, boy, and by the way, you'll never walk again.' But I made a liar out of him 'cause I walk pretty good now."

Doc dropped his cigarette on the sidewalk and crushed it with his shoe, then glanced over at Pearl. Her eyes looked ink-black and unreadable under the street lights. "I can't believe I'm talking about all this," he said. "I usually never do."

Pearl smiled. "I understand."

They fell into a long silence, then Doc said, "You know what you said before, about soldiers being victims? I have a very good book that talks about that. Real philosophical book."

"I don't read as much as I used to," Pearl said wistfully. "But what's the title?"

"It's called *Johnny Got His Gun*. I'll bring it to you at the club tomorrow night."

"Oh, no, sugah. Mama always taught me never to borrow books, except from the library. I'll find it... So, tell me about some other books you like."

Doc smiled. "You know, it's been a long time since I could talk to anybody about books. You're a mysterious lady, Pearl Fulsome. Lotta angles to you."

Pearl pointed at his pocket. "You got another cigarette, sugah? That was my last one."

Doc tapped out two cigarettes, lit them and grinned as he handed one to her. "I sure hope Melvin doesn't mind you callin' me that, 'cause I kind'a like it."

Pearl laughed. "Oh, he don't mind. I call everybody sugah. Sometimes I have trouble remembering folks' names. But stop changin' the subject. What happened after you got back from the war and figured out how to walk again?"

"Oh, yeah. Well, when I was released from the hospital, I came back to the States on the first plane I could get on. Soon as I got back to New York, I got my horn out of hock and limped on over to the Savoy to see if I still had my lip. And that's where I met Melvin. He was lookin' for a trumpet man and I was lookin' for a gig. So I joined the band and a couple'a weeks later he told us we had a singer, which turned out to be you. Since then, nobody's started any wars, we're working at a *glamorous* joint, and you and I are making beautiful music together."

Pearl exhaled a soft mist of smoke and laughed. "So we are, trumpet man... So we are."

CHAPTER 15

Doc kept his eyes on the front door the next night, half-expecting another visit from Agent Adams and his partner. But they never appeared, and the show went smoothly. He played a couple of innovative solos, which brought the audience to its feet, and he laughed when he heard a few of them shouting bravos at the end of the fourth set. But when he saw Pearl and Melvin duck out the door to the alley, his smile faded.

Forty-five minutes later, they returned together, both glassy-eyed. After the manager reprimanded them, they laughed like a couple of juvenile delinquents and hurried to the stage.

Doc scowled at them. "You're late," he said.

Pearl shrugged one shoulder carelessly as she reached for the microphone. "Thank you, ladies and gentlemen," she said with a slight slur. "Right now we' gon' slow things down an' do a special li'l number called 'Something to Live For.' An' Ronnie, ba-by, this one's for you...."

Doc turned away from her. As he played, he couldn't get his internal voice to shut up. *Okay, again with this Ronnie baby... Who the hell is he?... Goddamn... Listen to her... How does she sing with all that old-people pain?...How did she let somebody as trifling as Melvin get her hooked?...And how the hell did I get in so deep I can't even keep my mind on this song?*

As he followed each rise and fall of her voice, he realized that what he was hearing was the sound of trouble. She was drowning in it, and she didn't even know it. Or she didn't care.

At the end of the last set, Pearl and Melvin had a brief squabble, and she left by herself.

Doc approached Melvin, who was distractedly digging around in his pocket for something. "Melvin, why do you let your wife walk to the subway by herself?"

"Hell, there's ten cats staggerin' to the damn subway. She was mad so she went home."

Doc knew he was pushing, but he sensed an opening. "Yeah, I saw you two arguing. Thought it might be about that cat named Ronnie she always dedicates that song to."

Just then, Melvin fished out a battered joint from his pocket and kissed it. "Hah! There you are, baby! Hidin' from Daddy...."

"Melvin."

"Huh? Oh, yeah, yeah, yeah... Ronnie? Shit! That punk-sissy? That's her baby brother, that's all. Pearl loves that little faggot like kids love a goddamn crippled puppy."

"Oh, okay, cool. But she still shouldn't be walking to the sub-way by herself."

Melvin hopped off the bandstand in a silly pirouette and grinned up at Doc. "Better hurry up if you wanna hit this wit' me, man. I'll be the cat in the alley, howlin' at the moon."

Doc held up a hand. "Nah, man. My friend Johnnie Red's waitin' for me at the bar."

* * *

The next night, Doc decided to find out for himself why Pearl always dedicated that same song to her brother. He also wondered if he really was a homosexual, as Melvin had claimed. He waited to see if Melvin would leave without her, but they left together.

It wasn't until the following night that Doc got his chance. Just before the last set, Melvin walked Pearl over to the bar, whispered something to her, and hurried out the side door.

Doc made his way over to the bar and took a seat. "So when do we get to meet this mysterious brother of yours?" he asked, smiling.

Pearl did not smile back. "Who told you I had a brother?"

"Oh, Melvin mentioned it in passing. He said that's who you always dedicate that song to. So, is he here tonight?"

"He's only been here once. He comes around when he wants to. He has his own friends."

"But then he never hears you dedicate that song to him. He'd probably like that."

"Oh, he knows."

"But why is it always that same song? …I'm sorry. That's none of my business."

"Oh, it's okay, sugah. It's just a song Ronnie really loves. Billy Strayhorn wrote it. He based it on a poem he wrote when he was a teenager."

"Strayhorn, huh? I never knew that. I knew he worked for Ellington, but—"

"Oh, he doesn't work *for* Ellington. Billy's the creative engine behind a lot of what Ellington does."

Doc smiled. "How do you know so much about Ellington?"

"You ain't listenin', trumpet man. I don't know much at all about Ellington. I know a lot about Billy because Ronnie knows him. They talk sometimes, that's all. They're friendly."

"Well, your brother sounds real cool. I'd like to meet him sometime."

Pearl stood up and gave him a skeptical look. "I better go fix my hair before the last set."

* * *

Doc kept his mind on the music and managed to wait a whole week before attempting conversation with her again.

It was closing time and Melvin and Pearl were arguing near the ladies' room door. Doc heard him say something about her getting home on her own.

After Melvin left, Doc approached her. "Look, you shouldn't be walkin' to the subway by yourself and I'm goin' that way. I'm not makin' a pass at you. I just want you to be safe."

A slight hesitation, then: "Well, okay. Thanks, trumpet man."

As they walked along the sidewalk, the few small trees lining the street were dropping their autumn leaves in a colorful dance. She held out her hand, letting them brush her palm as they fluttered to the ground. She was smiling and Doc couldn't take his eyes off her.

A beautiful woman like that… strung out and wasted on Melvin….

He realized she was asking him something. "I'm sorry. What did you say?"

"I was askin' you what made you want to play trumpet? I mean, why didn't you pick piano or sax, or some other instrument?"

"Good question. When I was a kid, a friend of mine was crazy about Bix Beiderbecke. He had all his records and started playin' 'em for me. I'd listen to his solos and I thought he got such a cool tone out of his cornet. I really liked his phrasing too. Man, he had so much soul, I thought he was colored till I saw a picture of him. Probably because he hung out a lot with all those musicians on the South side. You're from Chicago. You probably know all about Bix."

"Oh, I heard about him, but he was a little before my time, sugah."

Doc grinned. "I keep forgetting how young you are. That's 'cause you're an old soul."

"That I am. But if you liked Bix and his cornet, how'd you end up blowin' that trumpet?"

"Oh, that was an accident," Doc laughed. "See, there was this old trumpet player on our block who made a little side money giving lessons. So I went to him and he got me a mouthpiece and put me to work on the trumpet. I saved up my money from after-school chores and bought my first trumpet from a pawn shop. I never thought about a cornet again. But I still catch Bix sneakin' into my music every now and then. Sidney Bechet too, and he didn't play trumpet either. I guess all musicians are influenced by other musicians, no matter how much they try to deny it. So, what about you? Where'd you learn to sing like that?"

"Like what?"

"Like... like... I don't know how to explain it. You just sing with so much feeling."

Pearl blew out a soft mist of smoke and smiled. "I never thought about it really. I didn't get it from records, I don't think. I guess I soaked up some'a what those blues musicians were doin' on the South Side. Sump'm about live music just got inside me. You can hear all the pain of the human voice, and all the tones of the horns and the bass. And the way a piano chord rings in the air for a long time after the song ends. You can't catch any of that listenin' to an old scratched-up record. When I'm singin', all I do is listen to what you fellas are playin'. You make me feel the song." She smiled. "Guess that makes me some kind'a translator or sump'm, huh?"

"I guess so."

They walked along for a while in a comfortable silence until Pearl leaned her head back and sighed deeply. "I sure do love autumn," she said.

"Me too. Most folks like spring the best, 'specially after one'a those hard New York winters, but I like all the colors—all those reds and yellows. Leaves sure are pretty when they're givin' up the ghost."

"Mm-hmm," Pearl agreed. "If you look close enough, nature's always teachin' us things. 'Cause when I really look close, I don't just see the reds and the yellows. I still see the green."

Doc stared at her face in profile. "I like the way you think. Even if it is a little cryptic."

Pearl smiled.

* * *

The Red Regency began doing turn-away business, especially after a disc jockey named Symphony Sid had been talking up the band and the club on his show. Symphony Sid was the most popular jazz and bebop disc jockey in New York, and he had reserved a front table for the following Saturday night. Melvin was convinced that this would lead to a big break for the band.

When everyone got to rehearsal that day, Alex was passing out charts for two fresh arrangements designed to knock the socks off Symphony Sid. "Where's Melvin?" he asked.

Doc nodded in the direction of the bar.

"Hey, Melvin!" Alex called. "Where's Pearl? I got her lead sheet here."

"Yeah, where is she?" Elton said. "We need to get rollin' with these new tunes, man."

"She ain't comin'," Melvin said, uncharacteristically sullen. "And she ain't gonna be here tonight either. She's sick. So let's get started without her."

Something about Melvin's mood disturbed Doc, but he decided to mind his own business, for the time being.

* * *

The show went well that night, and Symphony Sid hung around after the last set. He headed straight to the bandstand and reached for Doc's hand.

"Doc Calhoun!" he said, grinning. "Let me buy you a drink, man."

Doc placed his horn in its case. "I can't turn down a drink with Symphony Sid."

"After that virtuoso solo you laid down, you can call me Sid, baby!"

"Well, thanks, Sid."

When they got to the bar Doc sat at Sid's right and Melvin took the seat to Sid's left.

"What are you drinking, Doc?" Sid asked.

"He's a Johnnie Walker Red man," Melvin laughed. "All he ever drinks!"

"Well, then, that's what we're drinkin'. Rocks?"

"Neat," Doc replied.

As they waited for Eric to bring the drinks, Symphony Sid grinned at Doc. "I gotta tell you, man, I was skeptical when I first started hearing about you. But you have more than lived up to your reputation around New York!"

"Thanks, Sid. But we're still just chasin' the All Stars."

"Well, in my humble opinion, all you cats need is to put sump'm on wax."

Melvin sat up straight. "Matter of fact, I been savin' up to book a studio."

The drinks came just in time and Doc took a gulp to keep from laughing. All Melvin ever saved up for was reefer and heroin.

Sid nodded thoughtfully. "What if I was to book the studio? I wouldn't mind bein' the cat that introduced this band to the world."

Melvin grinned. "Shit, Sid, you find a joint tonight, and we're there!"

Sid shook his head and laughed. "Not so fast. I still need to hear the singer. I heard a lot about her. Where is she tonight?"

"Aww, she got a little cold is all," Melvin said. "I'll let you know the minute she's back and we'll put you right at the front table, baby."

* * *

When Pearl was still a no-show two nights later, Doc was really worried. Melvin craved this shot at recording with Symphony Sid like he craved his next fix, which meant that something must be very wrong with Pearl.

Melvin was silent and grim every night that week, and his quick departures led Doc to believe that his heroin use had escalated. Once he saw him rushing out the side door that Friday after the last set, Doc packed up his horn and looked at the other band members. "Anybody know where Melvin lives?" he asked pointedly.

"Hundred and eighteenth Street," Alex said, writing the address on a scrap of paper. He gave Doc a long look as he handed it to him. "Tell her we're worried about her. And be careful."

On the subway ride to Melvin's apartment building, Doc worked out the possibilities. If he was wrong, and Melvin had gone home instead of to the dealer's, he would tell him he'd lost a chart and needed a new one. Something like that. But if Pearl was alone....

His mind remained locked on that scenario for the rest of the ride and all the way up the stairs to her apartment. Before he knew it, he was knocking on her door.

Pearl opened it. As soon as she saw Doc's face, she lowered her head, but he had already seen what she was trying to hide. A swollen black eye.

That sonofabitch.

He nearly said it out loud, but smiled instead, pretending he hadn't noticed her eye. "So you feeling any better, Pearl?"

"Huh?"

"Well, Melvin said you were sick and that's why you haven't been to the club."

Pearl held her hand up to her forehead. "Oh, it's just a headache I couldn't get rid of. But a bad one though. It's one of those migraines, I think."

"I'm sorry to hear that, Pearl. I hope you feel better soon. Everybody misses you."

"Oh, I'll be back pretty soon. I'll be fine."

Doc felt his teeth grinding. She hadn't looked him in the eye once and she kept scratching her arm.

"Melvin here?"

"No, he's uh, out. But I'll tell him you stopped by." She moved back to shut the door.

"Wait just a second... You mind if I wait for him?"

"Oh, no... uh, I'd ask you in, but you know, Melvin really doesn't like... I mean—"

"Oh, it's okay, I understand," he said, forcing a smile. "Take care of that headache now."

"Mm-hmm. Bye, sugah."

She shut the door and Doc stood there staring at it. The hard pounding in his temples was telling him to wait for Melvin, but reason told him that beating Pearl's husband half to death right in front of her would surely be the wrong thing to do. Besides, he knew exactly where he was. Everybody in Harlem knew how to find Jude. He was the busiest heroin dealer around, and he lived in a walk-up right down the street. "How convenient for you, Melvin," Doc muttered.

After making the turn from Lenox Avenue, he walked a few blocks and felt his steps growing into angry strides until he found himself climbing the stairs to the third floor. When he got to the door at the end of the dark hallway, he began pounding on it with his fist.

The door flew open and Jude stood there for a moment glaring at Doc. "What the fuck you doin', fool? You want somebody to call the goddamn law?"

Doc pushed past him and began looking around the room for Melvin.

"Hey!" Jude said, closing the door quickly. "If you here to do some business then sit'cho ass down and hand over the goddamn money!"

"This ain't got nothin' to do you with you, Jude, so just get the hell out'a my way."

"Shit, you in my goddamn house, ain'tcha? That makes it my business!"

Doc ignored him and continued making his way through the foul-smelling apartment, kicking beer bottles and ashtrays out of the way, opening doors, and stepping over several customers who were seated, slumped, or lying on the floor. Jude was still following him and yelling, but Doc barely heard him. Then he yanked open the bathroom door and finally found Melvin. He was sprawled in a limp, semi-seated position on the toilet seat with his head back, eyes closed, and that stupid junkie smile—a pathetic picture of a mainliner who'd just hit.

Doc hauled him to his feet, and slammed him against the wall. Melvin's head rolled to one side and he let out a muffled laugh. "Saaay, babee!"

"Look at me," Doc said, grabbing Melvin's face with one hand. "I'm here to put you wise about sump'm right now, just so I can personally fuck up your high... HEY! Look at me, man!"

A barely perceptible scowl registered on Melvin's face. "Doc? Whushu doin' here, man? And, and whushu yellin' about?"

"Surprised to see me, Melvin? Huh? Well, then this shit ought'a *really* surprise you."

He stepped back and hit Melvin with a straight right that landed square on his left cheekbone. Then he watched him collapse to the floor like an old building that had just met the wrecking ball.

Leaning over him, Doc nudged his ribs with the toe of his shoe. "Your head hurt, Melvin?" he yelled. "Huh? ...*That's* for Pearl's eye, you sorry sack a'shit! You hit her again and I will take your whole fuckin' head off next time!"

He walked out of the bathroom and glared at Jude, who had finally shut up and was standing in the hallway. With the pleasing sound of Melvin's groaning in his ears, Doc stalked out of the apartment.

It wasn't until he was halfway to the subway that he thought about his next gig—if he could find one in time to pay his bills. "Shit."

* * *

When Doc woke up the next day it was just past 5:00 p.m. and his right hand was throbbing. Cradling it gently against his chest, he eased himself to a sitting position and blinked until his eyes focused. A close examination of the swelling and deep scrapes on his knuckles made him wonder just how hard he had hit Melvin. His gaze drifted to the floor and the Johnnie Walker Red bottle he had been talking to all night. It was empty. "Shut up," he muttered.

He stood up slowly and headed to the bathroom. "You are a lousy friend, Johnnie," he muttered over his shoulder. "But shit... a lousy friend is better than no friend at all."

He felt better after a shower, but he was alarmed at his reflection in the bathroom mirror. "Goddamn! Dorian Gray...."

After immersing his fist in a bowl of ice for a few minutes, he ate a sandwich. Then he puttered around aimlessly, tidied up his room, talked to himself, and finally got dressed. "Shit. Time to go face the music... so to speak."

By the time he arrived at the club, he had decided not to give Melvin the satisfaction of seeing him angry again. With the exception of Pearl, the whole band was there for rehearsal. When Melvin turned to see who they were all looking at, Doc was surprised at the damage he had done with only one punch. The left side of Melvin's face was swollen and lumpy, with a puffy slit where his left eye should have been. He was staring silently at Doc with his right.

"Just came for my charts, man," Doc said, meeting Melvin's one-eyed stare.

After a loaded silence, Melvin snapped, "Where's your horn, man?"

"Home. Why?" He tried to sound uninterested.

Melvin let out an impatient sigh. "Because."

"Because why, Melvin?"

"Because how the hell you gon' rehearse without a horn, muthafucka?"

They glared at each other in a teetering silence until the other band members began laughing. Melvin shrugged and held out his hands, palms up. "I had it comin', okay?" Then he stepped over and stuck out his hand. "Come on, man, let's shake hands and rehearse."

Doc thought about his rent payment and sighed, but he didn't shake Melvin's hand.

"Shit. Gimme the new charts and I don't need to rehearse. I'll be back for the first set."

* * *

They never discussed the fight until two weeks later when Pearl returned from a break with a red palm mark on her face and another questionable looking eye. Doc was scrutinizing her from the bandstand. As soon as she saw him, she walked out of the club and didn't return.

At the end of the night, Doc saw Melvin hurrying away from the bandstand. "Last call for alcohol, Melvin," he called. "And I *strongly* recommend you get yourself a drink."

Melvin didn't look back.

"Hey! Why are you in such a hurry, Melvin?"

Doc hopped off the bandstand a few beats too late. By the time he stepped into the alley, Melvin was nowhere to be seen. It didn't matter. It was time to have a talk with Pearl anyway.

On the subway ride, he thought up a list of different approaches, different things to say to her, but nothing felt right. He knew he was out of line, but he couldn't stop himself from stepping right into the middle of her misbegotten marriage.

He still hadn't thought of one definite word or phrase when he stepped off the elevator on Pearl's floor. But something kept his feet moving until he was standing at the door of her apartment. He knocked twice before she finally peeked out.

"The makeup's no good, Pearl," he heard himself say.

Shit. That wasn't on the goddamn list at all....

She looked up, startled. "What?"

"That eye. When the light hits it right, it's real visible. So he slaps you around in the alley and then here you are with your foolish ass, waitin' for him to work you over for missin' the last set. That about cover your night so far?"

"You best mind your business, trumpet man." She took a pull on her cigarette and jerked up her chin as she blew out the smoke in a show of careless defiance, but it was a bad acting job.

Doc felt his teeth grinding again. "He here?"

"Gone."

"Then why are *you* here?"

Pearl glared at him through a gust of cigarette smoke. "Good-bye, trumpet man."

Doc did an angry about-face and strode quickly to the stairs.

"Wait a minute," Pearl called.

"Wait a minute, my ass, Pearl!" He turned around and stared at her. "Aw, hell, don't worry. You seem to like this kind'a treatment and I need this gig too much to risk gettin' fired. So from now on I'm stayin' out of it. This is between you and Melvin—"

Pearl cut him off. "Thanks."

"—even if he kills you. But go on inside, Pearl. Maybe you'll get lucky and he'll be too high to beat you tonight."

As he walked away, he heard the door slam. He knew he had lied about staying out of it. He was already planning his next attack.

* * *

For the next few weeks, things blew pretty hot. Whenever Melvin mistreated Pearl, whether physically or verbally, Doc stepped in. Usually, it turned into a shoving match in the alley that sometimes escalated into a fistfight. One night Melvin surprised him by pulling a knife and cutting his right hand. But when the bandages hindered his ability to play his horn, the blade play ended. Melvin yelled and cursed and threatened to fire him, but he never followed through. Everyone in the band knew the reason. Aside from the need for Doc at the recording sessions with Symphony Sid, he had also become their big draw at the club. It was his growing reputation as one of New York's hottest new trumpet players that was keeping them all working.

Things would go along peacefully for short intervals, until the next brawl. The other band members griped about the fighting; Pearl gave both men the silent treatment; and Doc was miserable.

The only one who seemed to be unaffected was Melvin. Despite the occasional beatings, as long as he stayed high and the band stayed busy, he stayed happy. Doc made up his mind time and again to quit and leave all the melodrama behind. He had other offers from other bands, but he worried about what would happen to Pearl if he wasn't there to look out for her. So, like it or not, he was stuck like a phonograph needle on a badly scratched record.

Until Christmas night.

CHAPTER 16

The club was packed that night with Christmas revelers, most of whom were already thoroughly drunk, and the band was all set up and ready to play. But no one had seen Pearl or Melvin. The band members stalled as long as they could, and then Elton hit a loud rim-shot to get Doc's attention.

"Maybe we ought'a play sump'm, man, before our audience passes out cold!"

Doc nodded and brought his horn to his lips as Elton counted off the intro to "Body and Soul." Doc kept his solo brief, then did the same for the rest of the songs. In an unspoken round-robin of conversant looks, the band members caught on. It was going to be a very short set.

At the end of "Billie's Bounce," Doc leaned in to the microphone and said, "We're gonna take a pause for the cause. Meantime, drink up and don't forget to tip the waitresses!"

"Hey!" Eric yelled from the bar.

Doc quickly reached back for the mic. "And don't forget the bartender!"

He hurried out to grab the subway to Pearl's apartment, but there was a buzzing group of regulars blocking the front entrance. When he tried to push past them, he overheard a woman's voice: "Another damn O.D."

Doc stopped and turned around. "O.D.? Who?"

"Melvin, man. He's dead."

Doc froze for only a moment before running all the way to the subway.

When he reached Pearl's street, the whole block was chaos. The first thing he saw was the coroner's vehicle parked at the curb. Then, in the flashing red lights of three police cars, he saw Jude being led away in handcuffs.

Doc paused briefly to watch. "Somebody finally ratted you out, you sonofabitch," he muttered. Then he crossed the street to Pearl's building.

He managed to slip past the cop at the door and began asking the neighbors milling around in the hallway if they'd seen Pearl. Nobody had seen her, so he went back outside. He decided to head back to the club to see if she'd gone there, but just as he got to the subway entrance, he spotted her across the street huddled in a doorway. When she saw him, she turned quickly and hurried down an alley. Doc ran after her and caught her arm from behind.

"Pearl!"

She turned around and looked up at him. Her face looked gray and drawn, and her most recent shiner looked even worse than it had a week earlier when it was fresh. Her lips were split and dry, and she was staring at him with wild, red eyes.

She jerked away from him. "You got ten dollars, man?" she said in a hoarse baritone.

"Let me get you out of this alley, Pearl."

"I need to get right, man," she pleaded. "Please... You don't know what it's like...."

"I *do* know what it's like. But... Pearl—listen to me... Did you hear about Melvin?"

"Who the hell you think found him, man? Now *gimme* the damn ten or leave me alone!"

Doc was momentarily stunned by her callous response, but he just nodded and did a quick check of their surroundings. "Yeah," he said. "I got the money and I got the right connection. Come on. I'm gonna help you get right. This is some real good shit."

He took her arm and headed to his apartment. As soon as he unlocked the door, Pearl hurried in and yanked off her coat. Her eyes roved around the room as she rolled up her sleeve.

"Gimme sump'm to tie off with, man."

"Sit down," Doc said.

Pearl sat on the edge of the sofa and gestured impatiently at him. "Come on, man!"

Doc stood over her, giving her a hard stare, and then shook his head very slowly.

Pearl's eyes widened. "I'm sick, man! You said you were gonna help me!"

She tried to stand up, but Doc pushed her gently back onto the sofa. Her attempt at a scream was so dry and hoarse, he was certain his neighbors would never hear it. He grabbed her shoulders. "And I *am* gonna help you."

Pearl bared her teeth at him. "Then get me sump'm to tie off with, dammit! And go get me some stuff so I can get right!"

"Where's your works?" he asked calmly.

"In the—in the apartment. I–I couldn't go back in there."

"Then you must not've needed a fix as bad as you said you did."

"You—you promised!" She was panting the words at him in a dry rasp, licking her lips, and laboring with the mechanics of a gulp.

"No," he said firmly. "I said I was gonna *help* you. I'm gonna help you quit that needle, Pearl. Look at'cha. You can't even swallow."

"Oh, Jeeezus!" she croaked as she tried to pull away from him. "You said... You said you had some real good shit, you damn liar!"

She began ranting and kicking, but Doc managed to hold her down as he tried to work out the angles in his mind: *I know how it was for me... You'll be wantin' to jump out that window, but it sticks... I know you can't get it open... I gotta lock up all the knives and razor blades. Ain't no pills in the house... I gotta get some soup and some—* "Goddamn!" he yelled, jerking his arm away and staring wide-eyed at the curved row of bloody wounds Pearl's teeth had made on his wrist. He grabbed her hands and glared at her. "You bit me!"

"I'm gonna *kill* you, you liar!" she hissed. "I *hate* you!"

"You do now," he said firmly. "But when this is all over, you're gonna *love* me."

She was glaring pure evil at him and breathing in short gasps. Doc wondered how she would respond to the word "love." And then she showed him—with a hard knee to the groin.

Caught completely off-guard, he let out a howl and crumpled to the floor in a fetal position. As he was trying to remember how to breathe, Pearl made a lunge for the door. He barely managed to catch her by an ankle. She tumbled face down onto the floor and tried to crawl away, but then stopped suddenly, and began vomiting.

Doc made a grab for the wastepaper basket, placed it under her head, and somehow managed to get to his feet. Hobbling back to his bedroom, he pulled out a pair of pajamas from his bureau drawer and grabbed a towel from the bathroom rack.

"Here's a towel. Soon as you finish gettin' all that disgusting mess out of your system, you put these pajamas on. And then... and then I'm gonna lay down the score."

Taking a deep breath, he said, "And by the way... Vomiting. That's stage one."

* * *

Doc turned off his emotions and showed no mercy for the next two days as he watched Pearl suffer all the familiar horrors of heroin withdrawal. She was a wild stranger, who continued to fight him until she was too weak. Once her body had rid itself of every form of bodily waste, the dry heaves began. Then the cold sweats. The pounding, cracking headaches. The crying and begging for death. He force-fed her soup and water, but she could never keep it down. One minute she was freezing cold with convulsive teeth-chattering, and the next minute she was so feverish her pajamas were soaked with perspiration. Whenever she would lose consciousness, he would peel off the wet pajamas, sponge her off, and dress her in whatever tee-shirts and pants he could find. He was running out of clothing, but he didn't dare leave her alone to go to the basement to do laundry.

On the third day, the hallucinations began. The dry heaves were back, and she began spitting up blood and scratching her skin raw. Doc began to panic when he realized how much worse her sickness was than what he had been through when he cold-kicked.

"Oh, Pearl," he moaned, "what the hell kind'a poison was in those needles that sonofabitch was stickin' you with?" He realized that he was talking to himself when her eyes rolled back in her head. She had passed out cold. Again.

He stood over the bed, worried about her stillness. Taking her to a hospital was not an option; they would only turn her in to the police. He sat on the edge of the bed and pressed his fingers to a pulse point on her neck. It was weak, but steady. Leaning against the headboard, he surveyed the war zone that had once been his bedroom. Torn curtains, a broken chair lying on its side, a pile of books in a heap under an upended bookcase, a couple of holes in the wall, dirty clothes littering the floor, and the strong stench of sickness. Or death.

He got up, intending to pick up his only prized possessions, his books, but decided that he needed a breath of fresh air first. Struggling with the window, he had to jerk it open, which caused a loud scraping noise. He glanced back at Pearl, but she hadn't moved. Lowering himself to one knee near the window, he inhaled deeply, and felt mildly dizzy. The cold winter air smelled alpine clean, compared to what was passing for oxygen in his room.

He gazed sadly over at Pearl. "You don't deserve this... Hell, nobody does."

A narrow strip of light filtered through the torn, fluttering curtains and cast a gentle dance of blue shadows on the far wall and across the bed. He couldn't take his eyes off it, marveling at how something so beautiful could have found its way into this hellish room. His exhausted mind jerked and tilted at another image, then another, and another, each one beautifully incongruous to its setting: A golden sunrise in the middle of a bloody war; a young mother's face, angelic and peaceful, sleeping forever with her babies in a rushed, shallow grave; and the staggering beauty of this troubled young woman, who had wrecked his room and his life.

He shook his head to clear it. "Stop it."

Leaving the window slightly open, he righted the bookcase. As he began placing his books back on the shelves, he remembered her saying that she liked to read. Maybe reading to her might help. He reached for *Johnny Got His Gun*. But just looking at the title reminded him of their conversation about that book, and he felt a pang of hurt that nearly derailed his resolve. He placed it back on the shelf. "Not this one," he said, reaching for another book. "This one."

After closing the window, he walked back to the bed and checked her pulse. She was in a deep sleep, but her left arm jerked suddenly and landed in a streak of light from the window that clearly illuminated her inner arm. He ran his fingertips gently over the bruises and track marks that ran from her wrist all the way up past the bend in her elbow, feeling all the raised bumps of the scar tissue. Then he quickly pulled back his hand, reminding himself that the last thing she needed was tenderness. What she needed now was someone to lead the way out of hell.

"This is a different kind of war, Pearl," he whispered. "We gotta win this one. No bad guys, no victims, so pay attention. We're gonna take your mind off all that hurt."

He settled down on the bed beside her and turned on the reading lamp. Then he opened the book, turned a few pages, and began to read to her: "Chapter One... In the late summer of that year we lived in a house in a village that looked across the river...."

* * *

When Doc woke up, the book was lying on his chest and Pearl was still asleep. He squinted at the alarm clock on the floor. Two hours had passed.

He got up and went to the kitchen, heated up a can of soup, and brought it to her. When he shook her, she didn't move, so he shook her harder. He checked her pulse; it was so weak he could barely feel it. He squeezed her hand. "Pearl?"

No response.

He slapped her face lightly, and tried shouting. "Hey! Pearl! Wake up!...Come on now!"

After rubbing her hands vigorously, he squeezed them tightly. "All right, listen to me now. You can kick this goddamn habit! ...Pearl! Squeeze my hand if you believe you can kick."

Her eyelids fluttered, ever so slightly, but she didn't squeeze his hand.

"Shit!" Doc muttered. "Don't you die on me, Pearl! You hang on, you hear me?"

He grabbed the water glass and brought it to her lips. After a quick reflex swallow, she choked down a few sips.

"Good. Okay, now listen to me." He grabbed her chin and jiggled it. "Can you hear me?"

Her head rolled a little and she made a raspy sound.

"I'll take that as a yes. Okay, here's what I'm gonna do. I'm gonna make a deal with you. If you stay right here in this bed, I'm goin' out and gettin' you some'a that narcotic."

Pearl's eyes opened briefly, and Doc winced at how red they were. "Don't get excited now. It's only gonna be a weak taste— just enough to get you through. Then we're back on our mission again. You understand?"

Pearl barely nodded.

He grabbed her hand again. "Squeeze my hand, Pearl. Can't you hear me? If you believe you can kick, I want you to squeeze... my... *hand*. Right now!"

Her hand was so cold and limp it felt dead.

"Listen to me, Pearl! I'm only gonna be gone a few minutes. You hang on!"

Doc grabbed his jacket and put it on as he ran down the stairs. For the second time that night, the fresh winter air made him momentarily loopy. After a short subway ride, he took the stairs two at a time until he was standing on 116th Street. Since Jude had been arrested, there was only one other heroin dealer Doc could think of. As he hurried to the building in his old neighborhood, the weakness in his legs made him aware of his lack of sleep and nourishment. He took a deep breath to clean his lungs, then tried to expel whatever treacherous drug residue he had been breathing for the last few days.

"There it is," he muttered bitterly. "Hooper's friendly neighborhood drug store. I never thought I'd say this, but you better still be in business, goddammit."

He hurried up the stairs and down a dark hallway to number 612. Inside he could hear Hooper conversing with a woman. He knocked discreetly.

"Who is it?" the woman asked.

"Lookin' for Hooper."

"He ain't here."

"The hell he ain't. Tell him it's Doc."

After a short silence, he heard the chain move and the locks click. Then the door opened and he saw Hooper's familiar high-yellow face, with those half-mast eyelids and that gold-toothed smile.

"Shit, Hooper," Doc said, pushing his way in. "You still look like a crooked used-car salesman."

Hooper stumbled backwards and cackled. "Hey! If it ain't G.I. Joe! I heard you was back from the war! I *told*'ja you'd be back for some'a my good produck, brudda!"

"I ain't ever been your brother, Hooper, and I kicked your lousy product long before the war. I'm here to cop for somebody who's tryin' to kick. So I just need a little weak taste to get through the tough part. And if you hurry your slow ass up, I'll pay double your price, man."

Hooper's sleepy eyes popped open like Doc had just blown "Reveille."

"Oh, yeah, man," he said. "I can work wit'cha on that. You said double, right? 'Cause I can cut sump'm up for you that be juuus' right... So how you been, brudda? Now that you all upright an' straight an' shit."

"Stop all the bullshit and hurry up! And cut that shit weak, you understand me? Just to take the edge off. You give me sump'm stronger than what I'm asking you for, I will come back here and knock those ridiculous gold-plated teeth down your throat. And then I will kill you, Hooper. *Believe* that."

Hooper grinned and held up both hands. "Hey, man! I got'cha, baby! I got a reputation to proteck. I'm yo' friendly neighborhood drug sto', man. Don't want no parts of nobody gettin' killed. Shit. Specially not *me*!"

"Yeah, yeah... I need some works, too, man. I got a belt and a lighter, but that's all. And that hypo better be clean as a goddamn whistle, you understand?"

Hooper retrieved a box from the bottom drawer of a bureau and pulled out a thin hypodermic needle. "Hospital inventory," he said, grinning. "Friend of mine's one'a them orderlies." Then he reached into the box and pulled out a frayed red necktie and a small white packet. "Now this shit comes straight from—"

Doc cut him off. "I don't give a goddamn where it comes from. Long as it's not too strong. And I told you I got my own belt, man. I don't need that ratty tie."

"Okay, okay, man."

Once Hooper had cut the heroin, he placed it into a small envelope and folded it.

Doc took it, and then pulled out two twenties from his wallet. "That cover it?"

Hooper grinned and grabbed the money. "Nice doin' bidness wit'cha, brudda. Come on back anytime. Anytime at all. And tell a friend! I'll give ya a discount!"

* * *

When Doc returned to his apartment and put his key in the lock, he could hear the sound of Pearl moaning inside. As soon as he opened the door, he saw her slumped on the floor next to the bed. He shut the door quickly and hurried over to her.

"Did you fall?... Pearl! Did you fall?"

"Oh, God, Melvin," she gasped. "I sososossick... You got it, Melvin? You got my stuff?"

Doc flinched when she called him Melvin, but kept his focus. "I got it." He lifted her in his arms and placed her on the bed in a semi-sitting position. Placing a pillow behind her back, he took off his belt and laid it on the bedside table. Then he went to the kitchen for a spoon.

"Huuurry," Pearl called in a weak voice. "I finna die, I swear... Melvin?"

His hands were already shaking as he fished out his lighter and opened the heroin packet, but what really rattled him was the way she kept calling him Melvin. That, along with the slur in her voice, reminded him of a friend's death in Spain—how he kept calling him Esperanza over and over again until he finally bled to death. Doc squeezed his eyes shut to turn off the memory, then opened them again to focus on the flame under the spoon. "Hang on, baby. I'm comin'."

Dipping the tip of the needle into the mixture, he drew it up into the hypo and tapped out the bubbles. Then he hurried to the bed. "Pearl," he barked sharply. "Open your eyes."

Her head rolled slightly to one side.

Doc laid the needle carefully across the top of the water glass, then grabbed his belt and tightened it around Pearl's upper arm.

Then he turned on the bedside lamp and smacked her arm a few times until he finally found a serviceable vein. Picking up the hypo, he checked it for bubbles again, and then gazed down at her. "Okay, baby, here it comes...."

* * *

Doc woke from a deep sleep early the next afternoon. He was lying crossways at the end of the bed and couldn't seem to move. But the sound of running water made him sit up slowly. He looked to his right and panicked when he saw the empty bed. He stood up and the sound finally made sense. It was water filling the bathtub.

"Pearl!" he shouted.

The faucet squeaked and the water stopped. "I'm in here," she called softly.

Doc hurried to the bathroom and threw open the door.

Pearl blinked at him with red-rimmed eyes, and sank down in the water. "Do you mind? I'm tryin' to take a bath. But you ain't got any clean washrags or towels or anything."

Doc quickly turned his back. "Are you... are you okay?" he mumbled.

No answer.

"Pearl, listen, I'm sorry about the towels. I, uh, I'll see if my neighbor has one and—"

"I only got one thing to say to you, trumpet man."

"What's that?"

Her voice was so weak, he could barely hear her: "You were right... about everything."

* * *

Later that day, Doc helped Pearl downstairs to use the telephone to call her mother. As she talked, he strolled to the other end of the hallway to give her some privacy, but kept his eyes on her. He wondered what sort of a lie an addict might concoct for a worried mother, but he knew he would never ask her.

He spent the next two weeks weaning Pearl off the heroin, reading to her, and getting her to eat. Starting with soup and crackers, he was encouraged by the fact that her headaches and bouts of vomiting were less frequent. Soon she was eating scrambled eggs for breakfast and full meals for supper.

"You gonna make me fat, sugah! Where'd you learn to cook lasagna?"

"Picked it up from my uncle's Italian wife. She was one of my many Mamas."

"Really? Lord, I have a lot to learn about you, don't I?"

"That's a conversation for another day. Right now, I still have a lot to learn about you."

"Like what, sugah?"

"Like how you ended up with a sorry fool like Melvin."

Pearl stared at him blankly for a moment. "He took away my pain—for a while."

"But then he caused you pain! Why didn't you leave him then? God knows how many times he beat you up, and you just stayed."

Pearl slowly rolled up the sleeve of her sweater. "You see these needle scars?"

Doc nodded. "I have each one memorized. But Pearl, you didn't have to stay with him, even if you *were* hooked. There are pushers all over New York. At least you could've avoided the beatings."

"I didn't stay with him for the smack. I apparently have a problem with another kind of addiction. Melvin's kind of addiction."

Doc leaned back in his chair. "Oh."

"No, sugah, you took that wrong. I ain't talkin' about sex. Hell, Melvin was so high most of the time, sex was a memory I nearly forgot about. And to tell you the truth, it was never that good to begin with. I'm just talkin' about routines—things and people I'm familiar with, comfortable with. Or... I don't know. Maybe it has sump'm to do with the devil."

"The devil?"

Pearl flashed a cynical smile. "That's what Ronnie and I affectionately call our father."

"Oh, damn," Doc groaned. "He beat you too?"

Pearl gazed at him a long time before answering. "Savagely. Melvin could've taken lessons from him."

Doc lowered his head.

"Don't look all sad, sugah. It's just part of bein' a woman."

"No, Pearl—"

"Yes, it is. It's educational, sugah. Everything that happened to me as a little girl just prepared me for the reality of bein' a woman. I had to learn that when you're a woman, you really don't own your body. Guess that's why I always liked to read. My brain is the one part of me that no man can own. It's all mine."

"No, Pearl. Your whole body is yours. And so is your voice. And your soul... Pearl, it's your soul that sings."

"All right, but... a woman can't really own any of those things as long as the man's so much stronger. He can always do whatever he wants to with my body. He can beat it, rape it, hell, even kill it, if the notion strikes him."

Doc was shaking his head. "No, Pearl. No, no, no... Not all men are like that."

"Maybe not you, sugah. But there are plenty of men that are."

"And there are plenty of women that would cut a man's throat in his sleep if he tried to beat 'em."

Pearl laughed. "Well, maybe you're right after all. Remind me someday to tell you the story about how close me and Mama came to carving up that devil daddy of mine."

"I take it you changed your mind?"

"Oh, no. He just ran away before we got the chance. But Mama was *ready*. She was all set to feed his heart to some alley cats."

Doc laughed. "So where is your father—excuse me—that devil—now?"

"Oh, he died about a year ago, which puts him in hell, I imagine. When we heard the news, me and Ronnie got a couple'a bottles of wine, and took 'em home to Mama. She does *not* drink, but we celebrated so hard that night, Mama got cross-eyed, blind, and ossified! And didn't mind that hangover at all!"

Doc grinned. "I can't wait to meet your Mama."

"Everybody loves Alva."

"Well, now you're free from that devil and from Melvin, so your life's all up to you now. No obstacles. Even that low-life pusher Jude's out of your way."

"What happened to Jude?"

"Jail happened to Jude! I didn't hang around to get the details, but they arrested him the night of Melvin's overdose. You were right across the street. Didn't you see that?"

"My memory got pretty foggy after I found Melvin. And besides, I never met Jude. Melvin didn't want me around that place, probably because he had some junkie girlfriends layin' around there or sump'm. Who knows? So he just brought the stuff back to me. But sometimes he'd go off for days and leave me hurtin'. So I finally *did* get my own connection. I just couldn't find him for a few days, so I went back to Melvin, and—that's when everything happened."

Doc scowled. "Who?"

"Who what?"

"Who's that connection you got on your own?"

"Fella named Perry."

"Perry who? I gotta know so I can help you."

"You just said it was up to me. And I *don't* want you hurtin' Perry. He can't even talk."

"What is he? A deaf mute or sump'm?"

"Not deaf. He can hear; he just can't speak, so it's hard for him to find work. He just deals enough to get by. He's not a bad fella."

"Pearl. You *will* be tempted, trust me. So I'll ask you again... Perry *who*?"

"I don't even know his last name, sugah. Now look. You can't watch me every minute, so you're gonna have to trust me. I will *not* go back. No matter how much I'm tempted."

Doc sighed and shook his head.

Pearl smiled. "Give me your hand."

Doc gave her a puzzled look. When he clasped her hand, she squeezed it. "I can kick."

"I thought you were passed out. I didn't think you heard me say that."

"I heard it, I just couldn't squeeze your hand, sugah. But I can now."

* * *

Doc realized that Pearl was right. Staying off heroin was all up to her now. And besides, he was running out of money. He returned to the Red Regency that Friday night and received a welcoming ovation from the regulars. As he played his first solo, he felt the music flooding his senses like a cleansing river of sound. From his fingertips to his lips, from his heart to his brain, he felt resurrected. At the end of the first set, he walked over to the piano and smiled at Alex.

"Good to be back, man."

Alex handed him one of their old original charts for "Body and Soul."

"Thought we might start the next set with this one."

"Works for me," Doc said, eyeing the chart. "I always liked this arrangement."

"You know, it's not cool to speak ill of the dead," Alex said, "but it sure is peaceful without that goddamn Melvin around."

"I don't know how 'ill' that is, but it sure is a fact."

Alex grinned. "All those battles you two fought, and now you walk off into the sunset with the girl *and* the band!"

Doc shook his head. "No deal. We'd be nowhere without your arrangements. This band is all yours." Then he rubbed his hands together. "But I *will* take the girl! Now, if you'll excuse me, I'm about to go over to the bar and have a nice reunion with my old friend Johnnie Red."

As he stepped off the bandstand, Sailor was coming back his way. "There's some cat waitin' for you at the end of the bar, man," he said. "Asked for you by first *and* last name."

"Thanks, man."

When he got to the bar, Doc saw a slender man standing in the shadows. In the low light, all he could tell was that he was a fairly light-skinned Negro, at least six feet tall, and young. He looked clean-cut, but he did not look like a cop. "What can I do for you?"

"Your name Doc Calhoun?"

Doc nodded, and the man stepped into the light. There was a troubling look in his eyes, but it seemed to fade as soon as he smiled and extended his hand.

"I wanted to meet the man who saved my sister. I'm Ronnie Sayles."

* * *

When Doc returned to his apartment that night, he stopped in the bedroom doorway and stared at Pearl, who was sitting up in bed reading.

She looked up. "What's wrong? You have the strangest expression on your face."

"What in the hell did that man do to you and your brother?" he asked softly.

"Oh... you mean Victor? What would make you ask that all of a sudden, sugah?"

"I met Ronnie tonight, Pearl," he said. "How old did you say he was? Eighteen?"

"Mm-hmm."

"Eighteen... God*damn*, that boy's got fifty years' worth of scars. The kind you usually can't see... But I could see his."

Pearl nodded. "I know. He's got plenty of the visible kind too."

Doc took a seat on the edge of the bed and lit a cigarette, then stared at the wall. "Tell me about you and Ronnie, Pearl. Tell me everything."

* * *

Pearl spent the next two nights telling Doc about her life and the struggles with Ronnie and Alva, concentrating primarily on their time in Chicago. Doc listened closely to the stories and all the silences between them. Sometimes the words seemed to float away and he found himself listening only to the music of her voice. He listened with his eyes, interpreting every expression of her face, every gesture of her hands. And each time the shadows clouded her eyes, he heard whispers of Spain.

At around midnight, Pearl yawned. "There's a lot more, sugah, but my name ain't Scheherazade, and it'd take me a lot more than a thousand and one nights to tell you everything."

Doc was sitting next to her in bed with his head leaning against the headboard. "It was enough," he said, without opening his eyes.

She rested her head on his shoulder. "Any idea how long I've been here?"

"Little over a month."

"Mind if I ask you sump'm personal?"

He smiled. "I think we're way past personal. Ask me anything."

"Okay. Well… why haven't you made a pass at me? Ain't I your type?"

"I don't have a type."

After a short silence, she said, "I understand."

"No, you don't."

Pearl laughed softly as she reached for her cigarettes. "Want one?"

"Nah. I'll just steal a couple'a puffs off yours when you ain't lookin'."

She was quiet for a long stretch of time as she smoked.

Doc opened his eyes and reached for her cigarette. "You don't understand, Pearl."

"Yes, I do. Look, I don't remember everything about the last month, but I remember what a mess I was. It must'a been awful for you. Cleanin' me up, and me scratchin' and cursin'—"

"And let's not forget that mule kick to a certain region of my male anatomy," Doc chuckled as he handed the cigarette back to her. "I walked funny for a couple'a days after that."

"Sorry, sugah. I was pretty much out'a my head that night."

"Exactly. And none'a that had anything to do with me keeping my hands off you, Pearl."

She sighed. "Okay then… why?"

"Because we're not ready for that… Not yet. I think we'll both know when we are."

When she turned to look at him, he took the half-smoked cigarette from her hand, and reached over her to crush it in the ashtray. Then he smiled and turned off the lamp.

In the sudden darkness of the room, Pearl emitted a soft, deep laugh. "Guess we both knew we were ready to put out that cigarette, huh?"

Doc chuckled, and then drifted off so quickly, he was surprised when he opened his eyes and saw the morning light filtering in through the blinds. He could hear the distant sounds of the city waking up and the nearer sound of Pearl's breathing. She was lying next to him with her head on his shoulder, so he closed his eyes and tried not to disturb her. It wasn't until she moved that he realized she was awake. Then she said something he had been waiting to hear.

"You know what, sugah? I think I'm ready to sing again."

* * *

Doc had gone back to Pearl's building two weeks earlier to pick up her personal items from the superintendent. She spent the next few days washing clothes and practicing her singing as she ironed.

Late on the afternoon of the show, Doc left to run an errand. When he returned, Pearl was walking out of the bathroom wearing her black dress. She was still pinning up her hair as she turned her back to him. "Are my seams straight?"

When he didn't answer, she looked back at him over her shoulder. "What's the matter?"

"You're a real beautiful woman, Pearl."

She smiled. "But are my seams straight?"

"Yes, ma'am. Your seams are definitely straight. And I brought you a little something to wear with your dress."

Pearl turned around and took a long blue box from his hand. "Jewelry?"

Doc shrugged. "They're not real or anything. But the salesman told me they're pretty high-end for costume jewelry."

Pearl opened the box and smiled. Lying in a cushion of black velvet was a long string of pearls. "Oh, sugah, these are beautiful!"

He cleared his throat nervously. "They're not real," he repeated. "It's just that with a name like Pearl, I thought it was high time you had some around your neck."

Pearl nodded. "And they're perfect with this dress."

"Well, yeah... That too."

Pearl slipped the necklace on and fastened it so that a long section trailed down her bare back. "How's that for a final touch?"

"Oh, yeah, now," Doc said, grinning. "That looks *real* nice."

Pearl picked up her pocketbook. "Let's go to work, trumpet man. I believe we're late."

* * *

Doc held open the front door of the Red Regency, and Pearl walked in. As she made her way slowly through the club, she stopped to hug the regulars and chat with them for a while.

When she finally made it to the bandstand steps, Elton reached for her hand and smiled as he helped her up. "Glad to have you back, Pearl," he said.

Alex walked over and gave her a hug. "You look great, Pearl!"

Even Sailor kept it wholesome: "We been missin' you, baby!"

"Thanks, fellas. I missed you too. Hope I'm not too rusty."

"You'll do fine," Doc said as he handed her the song list.

As she took the list, she handed him a book.

He looked at it curiously. "What's this?"

"I went to that little book store around the corner one afternoon while you were takin' a nap. I didn't see this one on your shelf. It's all about that war you were in—the one in Spain."

Doc gazed at the title: *For Whom the Bell Tolls*. "You have no idea how much I wanted to read this, but I just wasn't ready." He smiled at her. "I think I'm ready now. Thanks."

Pearl shrugged. "I owed you one, sugah."

"Okay, then. We're even. Now, take a look at that list. What do you want to start with?"

Pearl stepped to the microphone and smiled at the patrons, which brought them to their feet. Doc had to shout over the applause. "Standing ovation! You better pick a show-stopper!"

Pearl took a quick look at the list and handed it back to Doc. "Number 5, sugah."

When Doc held up his hand and turned to show the other band members five fingers, Elton grinned. "Told'ja!" Then he counted off the intro to "Someone to Watch Over Me."

CHAPTER 17

Doc was more nervous about meeting Pearl's mother than he had expected to be. As soon as he walked into her house, it was clear from the smell of pot roast, potatoes, and gravy that Alva had been cooking all day. As Pearl led him through the living room, Doc swayed and let his eyes roll back in his head, pretending to swoon.

"Oh, stop it," Pearl said. "You act like you never smelled home cookin' before."

"Not like that!"

"We're here, Mama!" Pearl called.

"Be right out, baby."

When Alva appeared, Doc smiled. Alva Sims was a future version of her daughter. She was tall, with salt-and-pepper gray hair, a little heavier, but nicely put together. She wore a belted blue dress, and on her face were faint etchings of a hard life. But when she smiled, the beauty was still there. Her dimples were the only thing Pearl had not inherited from her mother. Alva had given her smile to Ronnie.

"It sho' is nice to meet you, Mr. Calhoun," she said softly.

"I've been looking forward to it, Mrs. Sims. But I would've talked Pearl into bringing me here sooner if I knew what a good cook you were."

"But you ain't even tasted nothin' yet!"

"My nose works just fine."

Alva laughed. "Well, come on in and let's eat then! Everything's ready."

"Where's Ronnie, Mama?" Pearl said.

"On the phone. I'll go get him."

They walked into the dining room and Doc sat next to Pearl and across from Alva. Ronnie took the chair next to his mother, and started the conversation.

"I'm tellin' you, Doc, you're gonna get spoiled eatin' Alva's cooking," he said, shaking his head. "Pearl's still in training, you know."

"Oh, hush! I can follow a recipe. I just don't have the patience like Mama. I never cook."

Ronnie threw up his hands. "You bring your date over to eat Alva's food, and then confess that you don't ever cook! We'll never get rid of her that way, will we, Alva? Doc was probably gonna propose after supper, but now—"

"Who says I'm not gonna propose?" Doc said. "Mrs. Sims, will you marry me?"

Alva and Ronnie laughed, but Pearl cut her eyes at him playfully. "Oh, don't encourage him, Mama. That was so corny. And you *know* you'd never say yes anyway. And even if you did, there is no way in hell I'm *ever* callin' him Daddy."

* * *

When supper was over Ronnie and Pearl made a big show of stacking up the dishes.

"We'll be in the kitchen for quite a long time, Mama," Pearl said.

"An hour, at least," Ronnie agreed. "All these dishes to wash, and we really ought'a clean up the whole kitchen, right, Pearl? Mop the floor and all that."

Pearl nodded as she and Ronnie began herding Doc and Alva into the living room. Doc took a seat in a large chair, and Alva sat on the sofa.

"Here's a fresh pot of coffee," Pearl said. "Now you two sit and talk."

"Get to know each other," Ronnie said, grinning.

When they had shut the door to the kitchen, Doc said, "Subtle, ain't they?"

Alva smiled. "They knew I wanted to talk to you is all. I been worried about Pearl ever since she married that Melvin. I know it ain't right to wish somebody dead, but I'm glad he's gone. But then, here you come! You seem a lot nicer than that fool, but you still a musician. Ronnie told me I'd like you, but I just wanted to see for myself, that's all."

"Ask me anything."

"Well, now I ain't got nothin' left to ask you! We talked about everything at supper."

"We did, didn't we? I hope I don't worry you anymore, Mrs. Sims. I really care about Pearl, but we're still gettin' to know each other."

"Well, there's one thing I already know about you, Mr. Calhoun—"

"Please call me Doc. And what is it you already know about me?"

"I can tell you was brought up right. You must'a had a good Mama and a good Daddy."

"Well, actually, my Mama died when I was thirteen, and my Daddy... Well, let's just say he wasn't around much. But I had friends who shared their parents with me. A Mama here, a Daddy there. I listened and learned. So I guess I sort'a pieced together my own upbringing."

Alva gave him a long look, then smiled. "Well, now, I think that's just fine. Sometimes folks gotta make they own family when the original pieces are missin'. And there ain't nothin' wrong with that. That's what me and my kids had to do. I was the Mama *and* the Daddy."

"And you did a great job. You taught them how to survive."

"I guess I did."

"Mrs. Sims, I want you to know that Pearl and I are takin' our time gettin' to know each other. I think we have pretty realistic views of each other. No pie-in-the-sky notions."

"Well, that's good. That damn Melvin was wrong as two left shoes! I knew he was rushin' her into marryin' him, and I *told* her not to marry that fool!"

Doc laughed. "You did?"

"I sho' did! I told her marriage ain't nothin' but a place where love affairs go to die."

"You really believe that?"

"I sho' do. That's what I told Pearl the day she got married. And you'll never believe what she said."

"What?"

Alva clasped her hands under her chin and batted her eyelashes comically. "She said, 'But Mama... I luuuv him.' "

Doc laughed, and that made Alva laugh.

"Can you believe my beautiful Pearl thought she loved that damn devil?"

Doc raised his coffee cup to Alva. "That was a mystery to me too, Mrs. Sims."

Alva clinked her cup against Doc's. "Oh, you go on ahead and call me Alva."

* * *

It was nearly ten when Pearl and Doc got back to his apartment.

"You tired?" he asked.

Pearl took a seat at the kitchen table. "No. But I could use a cigarette."

"And I could use a drink to knock that coffee jangle down a little," Doc said. He lit two cigarettes, handing one to her, and then turned on the radio next to the refrigerator. Frank Sinatra was singing the last verse of "You Go to My Head."

"Oh, turn that up a little, sugah," Pearl said. "I like that song... So what did you and Mama talk about? You were in there a long time."

Doc poured himself a short drink and grinned as he sat down. "Wasn't that the plan?"

"Yes, it was the plan. So how tough was the interrogation?"

Doc laughed. "No interrogation! She asked me a little about my 'upbringing' and I told her the truth about my many parents. What I *didn't* tell her was that I ran the streets with some pretty rough characters. It was actually my two best friends who set my course for me."

"How'd they do that?"

Doc took a sip of his drink. "Well, one of 'em got pinched for manslaughter and ended up in prison. His name's Rico."

"Manslaughter! Lord, he does sound like a rough character!"

"Actually, Rico's a good cat, deep inside. He was older than us, and he always tried to protect us. So there were some extenuating circumstances, but that's another story."

"Okay, so who was the other friend?"

"His name was Jimmy, and he was already easin' away from the streets before Rico was convicted. He decided to go back to school, and the next thing I knew, he was all involved with the NAACP and all these Negro rights issues. Jimmy was in Spain with me."

"Oh, he was your friend that died."

"He was one of 'em."

Doc took another sip, and continued. "Anyway, when we were still teenagers, I looked at the path Jimmy took, and then I saw where Rico ended up, and I got myself back to school."

Pearl smiled. "So it was really Jimmy who set your course."

"No. It was both of 'em. Rico made the case for 'don't let this happen to you.' See?"

"I see... So what was Mama talkin' about?"

"Oh, she told me all about how smart her kids were, how sorry she was that you suffered so much, and how proud she was of you. She told me what a good girl you were, never messed with boys, and always had your nose in a book."

Pearl rolled her eyes. "Oh, Lord."

"I bet you were cute."

"A cute little goodie-two-shoes... Till I met Melvin and turned into a train wreck."

Doc crushed his cigarette butt in the ashtray. "Yeah, but wrecks can be fixed, and you're put back together pretty good now... So let me ask *you* a question. Why does Ronnie call your mother Alva and you call her Mama?"

Pearl stared into the lazy curls of smoke drifting toward the ceiling. "He stopped calling her Mama after David died. That's when he started calling her Alva. I thought it was sort'a disrespectful till he explained it to me. See, Ronnie's still carryin' around a lot of guilt about—oh, a lot of things he put Mama through. And when David died, he decided to be somebody she could lean on. She took care of us through all those hard years, and Ronnie wants her to feel like he's takin' care of her now."

"That's nice."

"It really is. And I love him for it. So what else did you and Mama talk about anyway?"

"Well, let's see... She told me how she warned you about Melvin."

Pearl nodded. "She sure did."

"And she told me her theory about marriage being a place where love affairs go to die."

"Oh, yeah. She started drillin' that into me when I was a little girl and I first saw Victor beat her up. He made her so bitter. But when she met David, she started believin' in marriage again. He was so good to her. But when he died...."

Pearl fell silent for a moment. "Mama looked at me right after his funeral and her eyes were—dead, like two cold stones. And she said, 'I tried it again, Pearl. And there's my marriage right there in that coffin. Where my love affair went to die.' "

"Poor Alva," Doc whispered. "What a life."

Pearl blew out a soft mist of smoke. "So that's what my Mama taught me about marriage. And it turned out she was right. I learned it about a week after I got married. Melvin made me a bride, but he also made me a cynic. No more marriage for me, thank you."

Doc shook his head. "I think you and Alva are both wrong."

Pearl shrugged one shoulder. "Can't stop a man from thinkin' what he wants to."

"In that case, let me tell you what *else* I think."

"I'm about ready to change the subject, sugah, but okay. What else do you think?"

"I think I could make a believer out of you again."

Pearl put out her cigarette and gave him a hard look. "All right, now. This might sound presumptuous since you haven't even tried to kiss me or anything, but don't get any ideas about makin' a believer out of me when it comes to marriage. I am *not* interested."

Doc rubbed his chin and gave her a crooked smile. "Ouch."

Pearl tapped out another cigarette and Doc lit it. "You took it wrong, sugah," she said. "I'm very interested in *you*. I just ain't interested in takin' all these feelings you brought out in me to a place where they're just—" She stopped.

Doc leaned forward. "Where they're just... what?"

"Like Mama said—where they're just gonna... die."

When Sarah Vaughan's "Tenderly" began playing on the radio, Pearl looked at him and jerked up her chin. He wondered if that defiant expression was a silent challenge to the message of the song, or just love in general. Refusing to look away, Doc held her gaze in what felt like a life-or-death staring contest. And then he saw it again. That look. And for the first time he realized why her eyes always reminded him of Spain.

The evening breeze... caressed the trees...

Tenderly....

He slowly took the cigarette from her hand and laid it in the ashtray. Lifting her chin with his fingertips, he brushed his lips against her forehead, then kissed the corner of her mouth, and then her cheek. When he got to her ear, he whispered, "I am *not* Melvin."

After a long stillness, he heard her say one word: "Please...."

It was barely a whisper. All he could do was hope that he wasn't misreading her. Standing up slowly, he reached for her hand and she gave it to him. Then he pulled her to her feet, wrapped his arms around her, and began moving in a slow two-step.

The room was filled with the richness and dark sexuality of Sarah Vaughan's voice:

Your arms opened wide... and closed me inside...

You took my lips... You took my love... So tenderly....

Pearl's head was heavy on his shoulder, and Doc closed his eyes. After all they had been through, it was finally time. He could feel it rising in his body like a song that his mind and soul had already written. He lifted her chin and gazed at her eyes. They were soft and dark, very dark, and something in that darkness was reaching for him. Leaning his face down slowly, he brushed his lips over hers, and then took her mouth with more pressure, opening it and nuzzling her bottom lip. Then he lifted her in his arms and carried her into the bedroom.

As he put her down on the edge of the bed, Pearl closed her eyes. "I feel like I don't know you... all of a sudden."

Doc sat down next to her and kissed her palm. "Open your eyes, Pearl. You know me."

Pearl opened her eyes and smiled. Then she stood up and pulled the bedcovers down.

Doc got up and stood close to her. "Turn around."

When she turned, he unzipped her dress slowly and eased her out of it. Then he moved her hair out of the way and kissed the back of her neck. There was no hurry now, but he was still amazed at his patience. It seemed so important to memorize each second, each touch, each response. He moved the two silky straps off her shoulders until her slip slid to the floor. Turning her around, he kissed her as he finished undressing her, and then laid her in the center of the bed. He stared down at her as he undressed himself, and then lowered his body over hers.

Then, a flicker of hesitation. Her gaze had shifted to his left shoulder and he knew she was staring at the jagged scar from his old shrapnel wound. She touched it gently with her fingertips. "This one... this one's from Spain," she whispered.

"Yeah... Guess we both have our scars."

She smiled. "Seems like our scars are what brought us together."

There was such intensity in her closeness, Doc could only stare at her for a moment. But then all his senses took over and he couldn't hold back. Burying his face in her hair, he breathed in the smell of it, then kissed her mouth. Slowly, he ran his hands along the curves of her body to feel the smooth texture of her skin. From her shoulders to her hips and thighs, he touched every part of her, even the curves of her feet. Finally, he laid his head against her breasts and listened to her heartbeat. He wasn't sure whether it was the feather-light touch of her hands on his skin or the sound of her low moan that ran a shiver down his back. But as he moved inside her body, he could feel her moving inside a part of him that only pain and music had ever touched before.

* * *

He was lying on his back, gazing at the ceiling and trying to figure out how long he had been making love to Pearl. He could hear her breathing next to him, and he turned on his side to look at her. They hadn't said a word in a long time, and the silence was soft and serene.

Pearl turned on her side to face him and sighed deeply. "Once you kiss a girl you don't leave any stones unturned, do you?"

Doc's eyes followed the path of his fingertips as they slowly moved over the curve of her bare hip. "I can testify that there is nothing remotely resembling a stone anywhere on you."

"Just… just an expression, sugah… And that tickles."

Doc grinned. "Good… I told you we'd know when the time was right."

Pearl sighed again. "I never knew a man as patient as you, trumpet man."

Doc chuckled. "Not patience. Cold showers."

* * *

Doc spent the next two months proposing to Pearl, but each time, she smiled and said no. She seemed to treat it as a running joke, but he had never been more serious.

He tried long, philosophical discussions about how different he was from all the other men she had ever known, and how he had never loved any woman the way he loved her. A nod, and a soft "I'm sorry, sugah. Marriage just isn't for me."

He tried the down-on-one-knee approach one night after the last set, but all that got him was a barrage of wisecracks from the band.

He tried several times in bed when he knew he had brought her to the height of passion. A deep kiss that whispered the possibility of love, followed by another sweet but firm refusal.

Doc understood that she was not trying to drive him crazy. Telling himself that she was simply afraid, he decided to drop the subject for a while.

* * *

When the club shut down for two weeks of renovations, Doc surprised her with a trip to the Poconos for a romantic holiday. They rented a small bungalow and set up house for a week.

The mornings were chilly, but the afternoon sun lured them outdoors for long walks in the surrounding woods. He watched her closely as she pointed at the deer and scampering squirrels. Sometimes she would stand very still, just gazing upward into the tall pines. He had never seen her so relaxed.

At night, he built fires in the fireplace, and they cooked cozy meals on a hotplate. Her appetite for sex seemed more intense and passionate, and they spent long hours in bed together.

There was no moon on the last night of their holiday, and they were lying together talking in the extreme darkness of the room. The fire had gone out and Doc was too cozy to get up and restart it. Something about the way Pearl sighed sounded like a happy smile in all that darkness.

"I love you," she said. "I love you so much it scares me."

He closed his eyes and let those words sink in. It was the first time she had said it.

"Oh, Pearl, for God's sake, just marry me."

"Oh, Lord," she murmured.

"Pearl… I really need you to marry me."

She sighed. "Listen. I gotta know one thing from you… and *please* don't tell me anything but the absolute truth. Promise?"

"All right. I promise."

"*Why* do you want to marry me so much, Doc Calhoun? I'm right here in bed with you any time you want me. I already love you as much as… hell, more than I've ever loved a man in my life. I mean, most men would—"

He interrupted her softly. "I love your feet."

She laughed. "You love my *feet*?"

Doc felt around on the nightstand until he found his lighter. Then he propped himself up on one elbow and flicked up a flame so they could see each other in the dark room. "I love your feet," he began, "only because they walked upon the earth… and upon the wind… and upon the waters… until they found me."

Then, in what felt like a perfect harmony of sound and movement, he flipped the top of the lighter shut and settled back down against her body. He smiled at the sound of her sigh.

"Did you… did you just think that up… right now?"

"No. That came courtesy of a buddy of mine named Pablo. I didn't meet him till—well, he was my last friend in Spain. He used to carry this beat-up old notebook of handwritten poems by Pablo Neruda in his musette bag. I think he was proud that his name was Pablo too, 'cause he sure liked Neruda. Anyway, when we weren't gettin' shot at, I was teaching him English and he was *trying* to teach me Spanish. And he told me he was trying to memorize those poems so he could impress his girlfriend when he got back home to their town. Her name was… Esperanza. So every chance he got, he'd be practicing. In Spanish *and* English. But… he never made it home to Esperanza. Sometimes I still wonder about her. What kind of woman could inspire a shy, clumsy guy like Pablo… Anyway, I guess I was touched by how much he loved Esperanza, and I missed him a lot more than I thought I would. He made me think about what I'd learned from Jimmy and Enrique, and all those people in Spain—about the value of every single life. And I got it in my head that the only way I could value Pablo's life—you know, keep him alive in my mind—was to go back and remember those poems. But all I could remember was that one about feet, because I always liked it the best. So sometimes when things got bad, especially when I thought I might not ever walk again, I'd recite that poem. And I'd picture Pablo down on one knee reciting it to Esperanza… And I'd see her smile… And that'd make *me* smile."

Doc felt Pearl's palm touch his face, and he could feel her soft breath on his chin. He closed his eyes. "That poem's been on my mind ever since the first time I laid eyes on you, Pearl… That's why you always make me think of Spain… I guess you're my Esperanza."

After a long stretch of quiet, Pearl whispered, "Trumpet man?"

"Mm-hmm?"

"I sure do like Pablo. Thanks for keepin' him alive so I could meet him."

Doc was too choked up to answer. Then he felt Pearl's foot gliding slowly along his leg.

"Trumpet man?"

"Mm-hmm?"

"Will you marry me… and my feet?"

Doc smiled and exhaled a long sigh. "Let me think about it."

* * *

Two weeks later, Doc and Pearl were standing in the courthouse office of an ancient looking white judge named Julius Hammerly.

Pearl wore a drop-waist "After-Five" cocktail dress in a soft shade of lilac, and Doc wore a tailored navy-blue double-breasted suit that made Alva call him "George Raft" all day.

Ronnie and Alva served as two very happy witnesses.

As the judge shuffled through his papers, Pearl turned to Doc. "You got a cigarette?"

Doc laughed. "You plan to smoke through the ceremony? You nervous or sump'm?"

"No, wise guy. I just want a cigarette."

"I'll light you up as soon as we're married. It'll be my first official act as your husband."

The judge peered at them through his thick horn-rimmed glasses. "Ready?"

"Yes, Your Honor," Doc said.

"All right then, join hands... We are gathered here today...."

The judge hurried through the opening until he came to the vows: "Do you... Demetrius uh... Octavius Calhoun... take—"

Pearl tilted her head toward Doc and whispered, "Octavius?"

Leaning close to Pearl's ear, he whispered, "So?"

Judge Hammerly looked up, annoyed. "I'm trying to conduct a wedding here."

Doc held up his hand. "One moment, Your Honor."

Pearl cleared her throat to cover a laugh. "I knew about the Demetrius, but *Octavius*?"

Doc smiled and whispered to Pearl, "If you ever call me that I'll divorce you."

"No, you won't sugah. Not after all that beggin' you did."

Doc chuckled and turned his attention back to the judge. "We're ready now."

The judge scowled. "Are you *sure*?"

"Absolutely. You may proceed."

"All right... Do you, Demetrius Octavius Calhoun, take Pearl Marie Fulsome as your lawfully wedded wife?"

"I do. From her head to her feet."

CHAPTER 18

The recording sessions with Symphony Sid had produced two singles that were doing well on local radio, but not so well in other regions of the country. Sid recommended a booking agent, and Alex worked with him to arrange a three-month road trip. They decided that with all their equipment, the best method of travel would be by bus. Pooling their funds, the band members bought a second-hand Ford school bus that had been painted an eye-opening shade of ocean blue. The paint couldn't hide all the dings on the outside, but it had a rebuilt engine.

They spent the first two weeks on a string of one-nighters, which meant sleeping on the bus and taking turns at the wheel. The upside was no motel bills. The downside was a broken heater. It was an extremely cold February and everyone began grumbling, with the exception of Doc and Pearl, who always snuggled in the back corner of the bus under a blanket.

"Come on, Pearl," Doc whispered. "You said you'd teach me! What am I doin' wrong?"

"Shh! It's three in the mornin', sugah! Everybody's asleep. They'll hear us!"

"No, they won't. Now let me try it again...."

"Okay, go ahead," she whispered. "Wait, not like that... No, no, no! There's too much comin' out—and too soon!"

"Damn, you're bossy! Okay, let me try again."

"Wait, sugah. Let me get a fresh one."

"No, Pearl! There's only two left in the pack, and we're in the middle of Mars or someplace!" he whispered. "I'll just work with this... Okay... Wait... How's that?"

Pearl snorted a laugh. "That one was like a—oh, what do they call those big puffy clouds that don't look *anything* like a smoke ring?"

"Cumulus, wise ass," Doc whispered. "And it *was* a smoke ring! You just couldn't see it because it's twenty below zero in here and I was blowing frost out with it!"

"Shut up!" Sailor yelled from the front of the bus.

"We didn't make a sound!" Doc yelled back.

"I hear you two back there! You're necking! Again!"

"Jealous, sugah?" Pearl called.

Alex groaned loudly from the driver's seat. "Everybody shut up or one'a yuz get up here and drive!"

Doc grinned at Pearl. "Havin' a nice honeymoon, baby?"

She laid her head on his shoulder. "Oh, just dreamy… But I give up on you *ever* learnin' to blow a smoke ring."

* * *

When Melvin was alive, Doc had always forced himself not to look at Pearl when she was singing. So now he made a point of making up for it by posting himself to her left on the stage. Night after night, he openly watched her sing as he accompanied her. She would customarily sing to the audience; sometimes she'd close her eyes for the blues. But when she sang love songs, she never let her eyes leave his. It was something that always charmed the audience, not that Doc cared. He knew she was singing only for him, and it reminded him of the first time he had met her and looked into the mysterious world of her eyes.

One night, when they finally had the luxury of staying in a motel, he brought it up for discussion.

"That was a nice conversation we had onstage tonight," he said as he climbed into bed.

"Mm-hmm. I don't know how we get away with doin' that sort'a thing publicly."

"Well, now, *that* was an intriguing remark. Exactly what are we gettin' away with?"

"Musical intercourse, sugah."

Doc gently pulled her over onto his chest and smiled up at her. "That was *not* intriguing. That was just plain ol' provocative."

"Thank you, sugah. So now that we have this nice comfortable bed instead of a bus, why don't we get *real* provocative?"

* * *

They woke the next morning to the ringing of the telephone. Doc grabbed the receiver. "Hello?... Oh, yeah. We'll be ready."

Pearl covered up her head. "Please tell me that wasn't Alex."

Doc pulled the covers away from her face and grinned. "Okay, I won't. Guess it was just some cat who sounded exactly like Alex who told us we've gotta be ready to leave in an hour."

She groaned. "Kiss me so I won't feel the pain of leaving this heavenly bed."

He kissed her slowly, and was about to kiss her again, but then stopped. "Don't let me get started or we'll be late... Get up, lazybones."

Pearl sat up and stretched, then eased into her robe. "Quick shower. I'll be right out."

"Okay, I'll start packing our stuff. Oh! By the way, I wrote you a song last night."

Pearl stopped at the bathroom door and smiled back at him. "When?"

"After we finished being provocative and I put you to sleep."

"What's it about?"

"It's a surprise. I'll play it for you when we get to... Where's our next stop anyway?"

"Hell if I know."

"Well, we know it'll be a nightclub and it'll have a piano. So I'll play it for you when we get to the next piano, how's that?"

"Can't wait, sugah."

The next stop happened to be the Blue Bird Inn, arguably the most popular bebop club in Detroit. The bus arrived at the motel at 3:20 in the afternoon. Since it was located only a block from the club, Doc and Pearl quickly unpacked and walked over before rehearsal.

Doc looked around the empty club and then took a seat at the piano. "Good. Nobody's here to laugh at my barely passable singing."

Pearl pointed toward the bar. "Bartender's right over there. He might laugh at you."

"He's okay. He probably hears drunk singers all the time. I gotta sound at least a little better than them."

"Ya think so?"

"My wife, the wise guy." Opening his horn case, Doc pulled out a folded piece of sheet music, placed it on the stand, and began picking out the chords.

Pearl stood behind him and lit a cigarette as she peered at the sheet music.

"Okay," Doc murmured, "here's how it goes...."
Blue shadows—The wind blows
You are still the light
That fills my night....

He continued to play and sing for a moment, then finished with a soft sustained chord, and turned to look up at Pearl. She was smiling.

"That's beautiful, sugah! What's it called?"

He grabbed her cigarette. " 'Pearl's Blues.' Someday I'll tell you why I wrote it."

"Oh, no you don't. This ain't *Suspense Theater*, ya know. Tell me now."

"Well, it's a portrait... sort of a painting of a night we spent together a long time ago, that's all. Only I use music as my paint brushes. I started it a long time ago, and sump'm made me finish it last night. Maybe it was all that provocative stuff you were doin' to me."

Pearl leaned over and distracted him with a playful earlobe nibble, then reclaimed her cigarette. "But the blues is supposed to be sad and lowdown. That's too pretty to be the blues."

"Well, hell, it was a sad night! If you recall, *we* started out sad and lowdown. But we got through it, didn't we? And now *we're* pretty."

She gave him a long look that slowly turned into a smile. "Well, I have news for you, trumpet man. We're about to get even prettier. In about six months."

Doc's mouth fell open, and Pearl laughed.

"You mean... you...?"

"That's right. It's my own little portrait—a pretty little family of three. So hush up and kiss me. Then I'll sing the song and you smoke the damn cigarette."

Doc laughed and kissed her at the same time, then made space on the piano bench for her.

"That's right, Daddy," she said. "Shove over and let an expert do sump'm with this song… Lord! If I can read your artistic chicken-scratch, that is."

* * *

Pearl was able to finish the road trip, but as the band made its way back to New York, she stood up in the bus and made her announcement.

"I hope you fellas don't mind, but I won't be goin' back to work at the club with you when we get back. I hope you can find another singer, even though you really don't need one."

"What's the problem, Pearl?" Alex asked.

She reached for Doc's hand. "No problem, sugah. We're fixin' to have a baby, that's all."

A great cheer went up in the bus, and the band members took turns hugging Pearl.

"Are you sure you're ready?" Alex asked.

"Sugah, I have never been so ready or so happy in my life."

Sailor grinned. "I *knew* you two were foolin' around in that back seat!"

Elton smacked him on the back of the head. "Shut up, man!"

"So Doc's gonna be a Daddy," Alex said. "I can't realize it, man! I just can't realize it!"

"Well, I am, so get to realizin' it," Doc said. "Now everybody get your paws off my wife, so she can rest. And Alex, you better get to work on those instrumental arrangements."

* * *

Pearl breezed through the middle months of her pregnancy with hardly any discomfort. Doc had to part ways with Alex's band when they booked another road trip. It was an amicable split; everyone understood that he needed to stay close to home for the birth of the baby.

After a few days of auditions, he landed another gig with a hot local bebop band called "Red." The band leader's name was Rudy, and he was an accomplished saxophonist, as well as a hard-working manager. Rudy had gigs lined up for Red seven nights a week, mostly on 52nd Street, and Doc was happy to get the extra money.

"I hate bein' gone so much, baby," he explained to Pearl. "But I want you to have this baby in a hospital, and hospitals cost money."

"As long as you're in the city I'll be okay. Just leave me the numbers of these clubs in case I need you. Mama and Ronnie can keep me company at night. We can listen to the radio and play cards or sump'm. You know how Mama loves gin rummy."

* * *

Pearl was nearing the end of her eighth month when Ronnie and Alva came over, right on schedule, and fixed supper for her. After they ate, Ronnie cleaned up the kitchen and they all went into the front room to play gin rummy.

"You playin', Alva?" Ronnie said as he shuffled the cards.

Alva slipped off her shoes and curled up on the sofa. "Next hand, baby. I'm just gonna rest my eyes a minute first."

"That's right, Mama, you get some rest. You and Ronnie have been spoilin' me so much, I won't know how to boil water or wash out a coffee cup when this baby's born!"

"Well, I hope you can figure out how to change diapers," Ronnie said, "because that's where I draw the line."

Pearl laughed and turned to Alva. "Mama?"

"Oh, no you don't, Pearl," she said. "I did my share of changin' diapers with you two! I'll show you how it's done, but then you and Doc are gonna have to take turns and fight it out."

"Nighty-night, Alva," Ronnie said.

Alva yawned without opening her eyes. "I'm just... restin' my eyes, son...."

Ronnie began dealing the cards. "Pearl. *When* are you gonna tell us this baby's name?"

"Not till he or she is born, Ronnie. So stop buggin' me about it."

"Obstinate. Obstinate and round! Alva sure named you right. These last couple of weeks you look just like a big, round, giant-size pearl!"

Pearl cut her eyes at him. "Oh, you're so hilarious, Ronnie. You ought'a go on *Jack Benny* and give Rochester a run for his money." Then she laughed and pointed at Alva, who was snoring softly. "Look at that! Your comedy put Mama right to sleep."

"Good! Come on with me in the kitchen. Hurry! I got sump'm to tell you."

"Well, if you want me to hurry, then you are gonna have to help me up out of this chair and *roll* my big obstinate behind in there."

Ronnie pulled her to her feet and led her into the kitchen. As soon as they sat down, he scooted his chair close to hers and grinned.

"Oh, Lord," she said, rolling her eyes. "You met somebody."

"Not just somebody. I finally met the *right* somebody."

Pearl smiled and patted the side of his face. "Tell me all about him."

"His name is Walter. He's twenty-two, and he goes to Columbia."

"A college man! Where'd you meet him?"

"At a party. A friend of mine introduced us and we just hit it off right away. We started talking about books—he adores Russian literature! But I knew there was a spark when he told me to put my glasses back on. He'd caught me taking them off when he walked over. I told him I always felt awkward having to wear glasses and all that. And he just smiled and said it's more awkward to stumble around because you can't see. But he said it so nice… Anyway, his friends were leaving so he had to go, but when he stood up, he leaned down and said, 'All I know is… you're sure not awkward.' "

Pearl smiled. "Well, that was smooth."

"It sure was! Because when he was telling me how awkward I *wasn't*, he slipped me his telephone number! And I called him and we talked all night. He was telling me about this class he's taking on the ancient Greeks. Did you know that the great intellectual Greeks did not consider homosexuality abnormal, Pearl? It was just a normal part of their culture."

"No, I didn't know that."

"Walter's so smart and so easy to talk to. And Pearl, I haven't felt like this about anybody since William. This feels so *right*."

Pearl reached for his hand and gave him a long, meaningful look. "Ronnie, listen to me a minute, baby... Go slow this time."

"I will. But I need to ask you something, Pearl."

"What is it?"

"Well, do you think I should come clean about my past? I don't mean right away, but maybe if things go the way I hope they will?"

Pearl took a long time with her answer. "Ronnie, that's all in the past. Leave it there."

Ronnie hugged her tightly. "I was hoping you'd say that because I really feel like this is a fresh start for me. And it feels so good to be sort of... brand new."

* * *

Pearl gave birth to a baby boy at 12:55 p.m. on November 12, 1947. He weighed seven pounds and two ounces, with a dark, earth-red complexion and busy limbs. He hardly cried at all, but he kicked so much, Doc nick-named him "Jitterbug."

"You better stop callin' this child Jitterbug before we take him home," Pearl warned.

"Well, what *is* his name then?" Ronnie asked from the doorway.

"Ronnie!" Doc said. "It's about time! Come see your nephew. Hey, where's Alva?"

"Here I am," Alva said, already sniffling into her handkerchief as she hurried over to the bed. "My baby has a baby!" she sobbed.

Doc laughed. "And you know what that makes you, Alva. A granny!"

"Oh, hush, you! And Granny don't mind a bit! Take this and let me hold that angel."

Doc took the package from her hands and rattled it. "For me?"

"No. It's diapers. And believe me, you' gonna need 'em."

Pearl eased the baby into her mother's arms and gazed over at Ronnie. "So who's that hangin' back behind you, Ronnie?"

Ronnie stepped aside and a nervous looking young man walked in. He was about an inch shorter than Ronnie and well-built, with a smooth, milk-chocolate complexion and dark eyes.

"This is my friend Walter," Ronnie said, exchanging a smile with Pearl.

"How you doin', Walter?" Pearl said.

"I'm fine, thank you. It's so nice to finally meet you, Mrs. Calhoun. And congratulations on the new baby."

Doc walked over and reached for Walter's hand. "Good to meet you, Walter."

"Good to meet you, too, sir."

"Walter," Ronnie said, "this is my brother-in-law, Doc, and that baby Alva's holding is their new son who we *still* didn't get a name for."

"Tell him, sugah," Pearl said, smiling at Doc.

"His name is Edward Kennedy Ellington Calhoun."

"Four names?" Walter said. "Is that a family tradition or something?"

Pearl laughed. "No, sugah. If we were followin' any kind'a family tradition, the po' child would'a ended up with a name like Caligula or Tiberius or sump'm... Wouldn't he, Octavius?"

Doc shook his fist at her. "Divorce court, woman!"

Pearl grinned and blew him a kiss.

Doc rolled his eyes. "Pay no attention to that woman in the bed, Walter... Actually, my son is named after Duke Ellington, whose full name is Edward Kennedy Ellington."

Ronnie leaned down and kissed the baby. "Billy would like that name. Even though it is a long name for such a little fella... Oh, Pearl, I almost forgot. We brought you a gift."

"More diapers?"

"No, this is for you. Walter picked it out. Give it to her, Walter."

Walter handed Pearl a rectangular package wrapped with a green bow. "Ronnie told me you liked to read."

"It had your name written all over it," Ronnie cracked, nudging Walter.

Pearl unwrapped the package and smiled. "Oh! *The Pearl*! I read about this book in the newspaper just the other day. Thank you, fellas."

"Look at the title page," Walter said.

Pearl turned the page. "Oh, Lord! It's autographed! Look what he wrote, baby!"

Doc leaned down and read the inscription: " 'To a lovely Pearl of the World—May the song of your family live forever—John Steinbeck.' Wow! How did you get his autograph?"

Ronnie grinned. "It was Walter's idea. He read that Steinbeck was in New York for a signing, and he stood in line for hours and hours in the pouring rain to get that autograph."

Walter rolled his eyes, clearly embarrassed. "Does this guy always exaggerate like that? It wasn't hours and hours, and it wasn't even sprinkling! Maybe one hour, and he was very nice. He seemed to get a kick out of the fact that your name was Pearl. I'm just glad you like it."

"I love it! I never had an autographed book before. Give me a hug, Walter."

As Walter leaned down to hug Pearl, Ronnie frowned in mock outrage. "Hey! It's from me too, you know! Don't I get a hug?"

"Oh, you get plenty of hugs," Alva said, still cuddling the baby. "But that *is* a real nice gift. Guess I should'a got the lady at the store to autograph them diapers."

Pearl laughed. "The diapers are a great gift too, Mama. And thank you."

Doc patted Walter's shoulder. "Hey, man, you'll have to come over to the house for supper some night soon. I can cook up a storm."

"Thanks, Mr. Calhoun. I'd like that."

* * *

After leaving the hospital, Ronnie and Walter walked Alva to the subway and chatted with her as they all rode to her stop. When they reached the house, she said, "Ain't you and Walter comin' in? I fixed a real nice casserole for supper. I can warm that up for you."

"Well, we sort of planned to go to a party," Ronnie said.

Alva sighed. "Ever since you got that apartment, you ain't got time for me no more."

Ronnie hugged her. "How 'bout I come by in the morning and take you to breakfast?"

"That's more like it," Alva said. "But don't wake me up too early, 'cause I'm wore out!"

"It won't be too early, don't worry."

"And you come on by too, Walter. We'll make Ronnie buy us both breakfast!"

Walter smiled. "That's a date, Mrs. Sims! G'night."

"Okay, baby. You two be careful out in them streets now."

"We will."

Ronnie and Walter hurried down the steps, then slowed to a leisurely stroll. Ronnie stuck his hands in his pockets and smiled. He loved this time of night. They were the only ones on the street, and there was something reassuring in the clacking echo of their footsteps as they walked along the quiet avenue. The air was brisk, and a few leaves were still clinging to the trees. He lifted his glasses and peered over at Walter. "What are you grinning about?"

"Your family! I wish I had your family instead of mine."

Ronnie grinned. "Well, they're not perfect, but I'll share 'em with you. How's that?"

Walter shrugged and looked at the ground. "They just seem so warm. So relaxed."

"Well, I haven't met your family. Are they... tense or something?"

"That's a good word to describe 'em. Tense, as in concrete. Set in stone." He glanced quickly at Ronnie. "It's not their fault though. I–I love 'em and everything. It's just that—"

"What? Tell me."

"Well, I told you I'm an only child... So my father has all these expectations. He's *always* talking about me carrying on the family name. Always asking me if I've met a girl, and I keep stalling. But someday he's bound to find out the truth about me, and it's gonna destroy him."

"Oh," Ronnie said softly. "I understand."

Walter looked around, then pulled Ronnie into the shadows between two buildings. "Well, *I* don't understand, Ronnie. I don't even understand *me*! All I feel is pressure."

"I know. I guess it's just easier for me, Walter. I feel pressure too, but never about who I am. I've known who I am since I was thirteen. Some of it's good and some bad, but I understand myself. I just refuse to wear that mask. At least not *all* the time. It helps that Pearl knows about us. She knows we're not just buddies and she's fine with it. She just wants me to be happy. And I think Alva's beginning to catch on, too. So I'm gonna sit her down and tell her all about you."

"And you're not scared to tell her?"

Ronnie reached for his hand. "You've gotta get to know Alva. She's just like Pearl. If I'm happy with you, she'll be happy too."

Walter leaned his head on Ronnie's shoulder. "Now I *really* wish I had your family."

"I'm your family now, Walter. No pressure. And my family is your family."

Walter kissed him, and then gazed at him with such sorrow, Ronnie felt like crying.

"What is it, baby?" he whispered.

"My family will never be your family, Ronnie. They'd— they'd never accept you, I mean, as somebody I *love*. And that really breaks my heart."

He gripped Walter's hands. "Uh-uh. Nope. You can't have a broken heart as long as I'm around. I won't let you. We live for the moment. Forget tomorrow. Now, come on and smile."

Walter laughed. "I don't know how you do it, but you can always cheer me up. Okay, let's get to that party."

Just before stepping back out onto the lighted sidewalk, Ronnie let go of Walter's hands. As they walked along, separated by the physical distance mandated by society, Ronnie smiled, knowing that they had grown much closer. He nodded at something Walter was saying, just enjoying the lift in his voice. He had made him happy, and nothing else mattered.

CHAPTER 19

"You sure are gettin' good at that, sugah," Pearl laughed as she watched Doc bathing Edward in the kitchen sink.

"Seven months of practice," Doc said, tickling Edward under his arm.

Edward laughed and slapped the water, sending a high splash into Doc's face.

Doc grabbed the towel draped over his shoulder and dried his face. "Good shot, boy! Looks like I need dryin' off more than you do! Guess I got plenty of practice at that too, huh?"

He handed the towel to Pearl. "Okay, Mama, here comes the flyin' baby!"

Edward let out another shrieking laugh, and Doc gave him a playful growl as he swung him in the air and handed him to Pearl.

Edward continued to laugh as she bundled him up and rubbed him dry. Then she carried him into the bedroom for diapering and dressing. Doc got in the way by tickling him and making him squirm and kick his legs.

"No wonder he likes you to give him baths. All you do is play with him the whole time."

"Jealous? If you let me give *you* a bath, I promise to play with you the whole time too."

Pearl picked up the baby and laughed as she carried him to his playpen. "You tryin' to start a collection of these things, sugah?"

"That's a great idea," Doc said, grinning. "When do we get started?"

Pearl patted his chest and smiled. "Guess we already did... 'cause I'm pregnant again."

Doc laughed and danced her in a circle. "When?"

"When did I get pregnant or when does this new baby get here?"

"When does this new baby get here? And have you gone to the doctor?"

"I have an appointment tomorrow, sugah."

"Well, then, how do you know? I mean, are you sure?"

"I'm positive. And I'm thinkin' the date ought'a be around the end of January. But we'll find out tomorrow, won't we?"

"Guess we will. Wow, Pearl! Two kids! Guess this takes us out of the amateur ranks."

"Oh, yeah," she said dryly. "We're a couple'a seasoned professionals now. Which means another mouth to feed. Which means you better get to work, sugah."

"Oh, hell! What time is it?"

"Seven-thirty."

"Shit! Let me get dressed. And don't worry. We'll work things out."

* * *

Pearl was asleep when Doc returned from the club that night. He eased into bed next to her and wondered whether he should wake her or wait until morning to tell her his news.

Then she turned over and leaned into his arms. "Hi, trumpet man," she mumbled. "Did'ja knock 'em dead tonight?"

"Oh... I guess so. How do you feel?"

Pearl sat up and looked at him. "I'm fine and what's wrong?"

He sighed and reached for his cigarettes. "What're you? A mind reader? How do you always know?"

"I just know."

Doc lit two cigarettes and handed her one.

"Thanks. Now let's have it."

"Okay... Rudy booked us for a road trip, but I won't go if you don't want me to."

After a long silence she said, "How long will you be gone?"

"Three weeks."

"Well, three weeks isn't too long, I guess."

"But we have this new baby coming."

"That's a long way off, sugah."

"Yeah, but to tell you the truth, I really hate the road now. Especially the bus. It's not the same without you. You were a great bus snuggler."

Pearl laughed softly. "Those were some good times, weren't they?"

"They sure were, but these are better times. We have a family, so if these road trips get to be a habit with Rudy, I'll definitely find another gig."

Pearl leaned her head against his. "Let's face it, sugah. You just ain't hip anymore. You have turned into a square, married daddy."

Doc chuckled. "A square, married *professional* daddy. So you're okay with this?"

"Well, you *know* I hate it when you're gone, but I guess I can stand three weeks. As long as you drop me a love letter from every town."

"And I'll call you collect every night, and you—"

"I know. I refuse the call, but at least I'll know you're all right. And no charge."

"Wonder why the phone company ain't hip to that trick yet?"

"Shoot, those operators don't make enough money to care about folks sneakin' in a little signal call now and then."

"We can talk on Sundays. Rates are lower on Sundays."

"Okay, so where are you fellas heading on this road trip, and when do you leave?"

"We leave Wednesday. First stop is Trenton, and he booked sump'm in Harrisburg, I think, and a couple of towns in Delaware. Then it's a few stops on the way to Virginia."

"What part of Virginia? Rudy didn't book anything in the *deep* south, did he? They've been havin' a lot of race trouble down there lately."

"Nah. Just Arlington. That's as far south as we go."

* * *

The band's last stop turned out to be a considerably deeper dip into the south than Doc had originally been told. It was a weekend engagement at a club called "Delbert's" on the outskirts of Roanoke, Virginia. According to Rudy, it was the only club in the area with no race restriction, and several big-name bands had played there.

"Artie Shaw played the joint and he ended up extending his engagement," Rudy said, "and he's Jewish."

Doc smiled patiently. "You think folks in Roanoke know Artie Shaw's Jewish? All they see is his white face. As you can see, my face is far from white."

"Your call, Doc," Rudy said. "I just wanted to let you know that I checked on the joint. The owner claims that all he gets in there are hardcore jazz and swing fans. Not one visit from any of those Confederate-flag wavers. But you're the only Negro in the band, so, like I said, it's your call, a hundred percent. You want to pass on this club, we'll scratch it."

"Nah... It's already booked. I guess it'll be okay."

* * *

The first sign of trouble appeared the minute the band walked into Delbert's, but Doc was the only one who detected it. Rudy stopped at the entrance to talk to the owner as the rest of the musicians trudged past the bar on their way to the bandstand. Doc took note of the bartender, who was wiping down the bar and nodding at the musicians as they passed. He was a husky farm-boy type with a ruddy face and a dark crew-cut. When Doc passed him, the bar rag stopped moving. There was no nod from the bartender, only cold, staring green eyes filled with generations of carefully taught racial contempt. Doc kept walking.

When he stepped up onto the bandstand, he lit a cigarette and took out his horn. Then he leveled a hard, direct gaze at the bartender, who finally looked away.

Rudy had just made his way to the bandstand and turned to see what Doc was looking at.

"What's up, man?"

"The bartender just figured out I'm not Artie Shaw," Doc said.

Rudy scowled. "Screw him. That sonofabitch needs his job too much to start any trouble. Let's get set up and go over these charts. The owner said people start getting here around eight."

"In the meantime, I could use a drink," Doc said.

"I'll get it for you," Larry said quickly. "Johnnie Walker, red label, neat. Right?"

"Thanks, Larry, but I can get it myself."

Larry scowled at Rudy. "I told you we should've passed on Virginia, man. I just saw the way that bartender looked at Doc, and I don't like it."

"Relax," Rudy said. "I'll go get the goddamn drink. And while I'm over there I'll wise up Li'l Abner about a couple of things."

Doc reached for Rudy's arm. "Bad idea," he said. "Trust me on this. I'll just wait till we get to the motel tonight to have my drink. But I *will* let you buy me a bottle on the way out."

After a short hesitation, Rudy shrugged. "Okay, Doc. We'll play it your way."

As the club began to fill up, Doc did a quick scan of the crowd. Jazz had been attracting more and more white fans, so he was accustomed to playing before racially mixed audiences, but this group was a sea of white, without one dark face anywhere in the room.

He nudged Rudy. "So much for an integrated crowd."

Rudy shook his head. "I guess just because they got no official race restriction—"

Doc finished for him. "—doesn't mean local Negroes are fool enough to test it."

"But, hey, look at 'em, Doc. At least they're smiling. Well, everybody but the bartender."

"Why don't we start with 'Begin the Beguine'?" Doc cracked.

Rudy grinned. "Did you bring your clarinet, Mr. Shaw?"

Doc snapped his fingers. "Damn. Left it at home."

Rudy laughed and counted off the intro to " 'Round Midnight."

The first set went well, with the patrons cheering each number. But just as they began Sonny's show-stopping arrangement of "Night in Tunisia," three white men who looked like freshly unhooded Klan members walked into the club and pushed their way to the bandstand. Doc glanced over at the bartender. He wasn't surprised to see him grinning for the first time that night. Doc turned to look at Rudy, who was in the middle of his solo. Rudy kept playing, but nodded. He had seen the troublemakers.

Larry was already positioned at Doc's right flank, and Rudy moved over to Doc's left. They were standing almost shoulder to shoulder, staring at the trio. The finish of Rudy's solo dovetailed nicely into the beginning of Doc's, and he started on a high, hot note. Aiming the bell of his horn at the three white men, he blew a scorching solo with startling accuracy, and brought the patrons to their feet. Frank's drum solo could barely be heard over the cheers and stomping.

Rudy was laughing so hard, he had to turn his back to the audience. "Wonder how those three cats like being the minority?" he shouted.

When Frank finished his solo, Doc and Rudy came in together for the finish, and the stomping and cheering started up again. Doc took a small bow as Rudy continued laughing.

By the time Rudy announced that the band would be taking a break, Doc noticed that the three troublemakers had drifted away from the bandstand and were headed back to the entrance. As he followed them with his eyes, a waitress handed him a drink.

"That man sent you this," she said, pointing toward the front door.

He was about to hand it back to her when he saw a large card sticking out of the cocktail napkin. When he slipped it out, he nearly dropped it.

Larry looked over his shoulder. "What is it, Doc?"

"Just a friendly little postcard from our redneck friends who just left."

Larry looked toward the door. "They're gone?"

"They left the club but trust me, they're not gone," Doc said.

"Let me see that," Larry said.

Larry's eyes widened as he looked at the postcard. On the front was a photo of a white lynch mob gathered around a black man hanging from a tree. His neck was twisted at a sharp angle, and his trousers were around his ankles. A long bloody shirt was the only thing covering his private parts. The caption under the photo read: *The only good nigger is a dead nigger.*

As Larry handed it to Rudy, Frank and Sonny leaned in to have a look.

Doc lit a cigarette. "Turn it over."

Rudy turned the postcard over. There was a handwritten note on the back:

Cleaning up the South, one sassy nigger at a time.
—Ed and the Dixie Brigade

Doc took a seat on the corner of the piano bench and blew out a gust of cigarette smoke. "I take it from the looks on your faces that you've never seen any postcards like that before."

"You mean there's *more* of these?" Frank said.

"I've only seen a few, but I've heard they're real popular in this part of the country."

"Everybody pack up," Rudy said. "We're blowin' town right now."

Doc took the postcard. "Owner won't like us runnin' out after only playin' one set."

"Fuck the owner and fuck this town. We gotta get you out'a here."

"We might want to discuss this before—"

Sonny cut him off. "Yeah! What if they're out there waitin' for us? Like Doc said, they left, but they might not be *gone*."

Rudy turned his back to the room and unbuckled his equipment bag. Reaching inside, he pulled out a .38 caliber revolver and discreetly tucked it into his belt under his jacket. Then he turned the microphone back on, apologized to the audience, and hurried down to talk to the owner. As the talk escalated into an extended argument, the rest of the band members helped Frank break down his drum kit, and then finished packing their remaining equipment. They waited until Rudy signaled them, and then made a quick exodus to the door.

"You wait while we pack, okay, Doc? Limo service at the door in five. Be right back."

When Sonny was gone, Doc heard the bartender muttering, and turned around to look at him. The muttering stopped, but the stare-down intensified. Doc finally flipped the postcard high into the air and watched it until it hit the floor. Then he smiled at the bartender and walked out.

The station wagon was just pulling up. Larry opened the passenger door, but Doc looked around before getting in. To his left was a row of parked cars. One car was running, and the driver gunned the engine loudly.

"Come on," Rudy said.

Doc slid into the front seat next to Rudy, who was driving. Then Larry climbed in on his right. Frank and Sonny were crowded into the back seat, with Rudy's saxophone between them. The rest of the equipment was in the back of the wagon.

After a tire-squealing takeoff, they headed straight for the motel they had checked into that morning. There was only one way to get there—a two-lane farm-to-market road lined with a thick overgrowth of bushes and tall trees. It was considerably darker now than when they had driven it at sunset. All five men kept a lookout for any approaching headlights from the rear. No one appeared to be following them until a car suddenly swerved up onto the road behind them.

"Shit!" Larry hissed. "They're rollin' up on our right bumper, Rudy!"

Rudy hit the accelerator and the wagon lurched forward. "Where did they come from?"

"From behind those bushes on the side of the road," Doc said.

"Just waiting for us," Sonny said. "Come on, Rudy! Can't you floor it?"

"He is!" Frank yelled. "It's all this equipment! My goddamn drums, mostly."

"It's this old wagon," Rudy said. "This ain't no getaway car, man."

"Shit! They're right on our tail!" Sonny cried. "We gotta—"

A sudden crack of gunfire stopped Sonny cold, and everyone ducked but Rudy. He was working the steering wheel, fishtailing the wagon from one side of the road to the other. His leg was fully extended, jamming the accelerator to the floor. "Come on, baby, come on, baby!"

Two more shots rang out, cracking the glass of the back window, followed by a thudding echo that reverberated throughout the car.

"Hang on!" Rudy yelled. Then he ripped a right turn that near-ly sent the wagon up on two wheels. When they came out of the spin, the wagon squealed to a stop in the parking lot of their motel. The car that had been pursuing them continued down the dark road at top speed.

Rudy put the wagon in reverse and turned toward his room. He parked sideways in front of the door and handed his room key to Doc. "Everybody out. Go directly into my room."

"What about you?" Doc asked.

"I'm just turning the car around. I'm gonna back it up to the door." Then he pulled out his .38 and grinned. "Don't worry. I got company."

Once Rudy had parked the car and joined the others in his room, he locked the door. No one had turned on any lamps, so the only light came from the bathroom. In the semi-darkness, he unbuckled one of his suitcases and pulled out a box of bullets and a .45-caliber Colt.

"How long have you been carrying guns around, man?" Frank asked.

Rudy looked at Doc. "Not long. Just insurance for this trip. So who can handle this?"

Doc reached for the gun and the ammo and laughed when everyone stared at him. "Aw, lounge, man. I was a soldier, not a gangster."

"Well, I'd like to shoot all of 'em," Frank fumed. "They put a hole in my bass drum."

"You're lucky they didn't put a hole in your head, man," Sonny said. "And how do you know they hit your bass drum?"

"The shots that broke the back window, man! Ping, ping, bawooom! That was my bass!"

"Okay, let's calm down and get moving," Rudy said. "Everybody go get whatever stuff you left in your rooms. Go in twos. Then we pack the wagon and get the hell out of here."

Larry was standing at the window peering out through a slit in the curtains. "Hey, man," he said, "there's a car parked out there, and somebody's in it. I see two heads in the front seat."

"Same cats who were following us?" Rudy asked.

"Can't tell. It's too dark."

"And they're just sitting there?"

"Yeah. I can't tell if there's anybody in the back seat or not."

Sonny stood up. "Why the hell ain't we calling the sheriff or the police or somebody?"

"Yeah," Larry said. "I saw a payphone right outside the office when we checked in."

Doc shook his head and chuckled. "Very, very bad idea."

"Why?" Larry asked.

"You'd be surprised how many times the cats doing the chasing and shooting at Negroes in the south *are* the sheriff or the police. Sometimes their kids. Or at least some close buddies."

"You really think so?"

"Five'll get you ten."

No one spoke for nearly a minute.

Sonny sighed. "Goddamn, I'm feeling a real intense sitting-duck vibe right now, man."

"And whoever that is in that car is still out there," Larry said.

"All right," Rudy said. "We can't just sit here. I'll go with Frank to get his stuff, and when we get back, I'll take Sonny, and then Larry. Then we'll go get your stuff, Doc."

"This is not a good idea, man," Doc protested.

"You're the target, so you stay put. We'll get your stuff."

Once everything had been retrieved from the other rooms, Rudy picked up his bags and headed toward the door. "Everybody ready?"

Doc was sitting in a chair and didn't make a move to stand up. Lighting a fresh cigarette, he said, "I have a question. How many miles are we from the interstate? Anybody know?"

"About ten or fifteen," Rudy said. "But we have *got* to get out of here."

Doc took a pull on his cigarette and blew out the smoke slowly. "First, let me paint you a scenario... We begin driving ten or fifteen miles up a dark, isolated back road in dear old Dixie... with three crackers out for my blood lurking around out there somewhere. No, wait, let's not forget the bartender, who I'm sure was the one who called those cats to tell 'em about me. So that makes four crackers out for my blood. Now... What was the key word in that scenario?"

Rudy closed his eyes and sighed. "Okay, we get your point."

"No, you don't. Now what was the key word? Any guesses?"

"Blood?" Sonny murmured.

"Crackers," Larry said, taking another peek outside. "And by the way, they're still there."

Frank shrugged. "The word *blood* sort of jumped out at me, man."

Doc shook his head. "The word is *dark*. Cowards of all stripes and colors have a way of doing things in the dark of night that they wouldn't try in broad daylight."

Rudy nodded. "Okay, *now* we get your point. So I guess we wait till sunup to leave."

"Yeah," Sonny said, "and even if they try to start something with us in here, the last thing they'll be expecting is for us to shoot back."

Doc stood up and carried his chair over to the window. "We'll take turns on guard duty," he said, sitting down. "Somebody hand me that ashtray and I'll pull the first shift."

* * *

Pearl had just turned off the reading lamp when she heard the click of the front door lock and heard Doc's voice. "It's only me, Pearl."

Quietly placing his bag and horn case on the floor, he crossed the room and turned on the lamp. He gazed into her eyes for a moment, then wrapped his arms around her and pressed his face against her neck.

Pearl was rattled by the look in his eyes. She felt his chest rise and fall with a big sigh, and then he leaned away from her and smiled.

"I missed you—a lot."

"I missed you too, trumpet man. I read a whole book while you were gone and I couldn't tell you one thing about what was in it. How's that for a review? So, what happened? I wasn't expecting you till tomorrow."

"I came back early."

"I'm glad."

He stood up. "I'ma go check on Edward."

"If you wake him up I'll throw this book at you when you come back."

He didn't even smile at her playful threat. Something was definitely wrong.

When he returned, he stuck his head in and said, "I'm runnin' up to JJ's and get a bottle."

Pearl crossed her arms. "What happened?"

"I'm just wound up from that long drive, and it'll help me sleep. I'll be right back."

* * *

Pearl studied him for the next couple of days. He was drinking more than usual, and seemed distracted when she tried to make conversation. By the third evening, she was determined to find out what was disturbing him.

"Mood Indigo" was playing on the radio, and Doc was smoking a cigarette after barely touching his dinner.

"Sugah?" Pearl said softly.

She could tell by his blank stare that he hadn't heard her. It wasn't until she stood up with a startling scrape of her chair that he snapped out of it. She pulled Edward out of his highchair and took him to his bed, which brought on a loud wailing jag.

"Pearl?" Doc called.

Pearl closed the door on Edward's crying and walked back into the kitchen.

"Why'd you put him to bed so early?"

"Because you need to tell me what's wrong with you, Doc Calhoun."

"But he's cryin', Pearl."

"He'll stop in a minute. I need you to tell me what's wrong."

Doc stared at her for a long time, then put out his cigarette. "Wait right there."

He left the kitchen and went into the bedroom. When he returned, he leaned over and kissed her forehead, then sat back down. He was holding the postcard.

"Before you look at this I want you to keep one thing in mind. I'm okay. I'm here. Nothing happened to me."

Pearl reached for the postcard. As soon as she saw the image, she gasped. "Oh, my God!"

"We were in Virginia... Roanoke."

"Roanoke? You said you were only goin' as far as Arlington!"

"I know, and I'm sorry. Believe me, *that* will not happen again."

Pearl studied both sides of the postcard, then closed her eyes. "Tell me what happened."

"Well, we'd just finished a set and one of the waitresses brings me a drink with that postcard stuck into a cocktail napkin. By the time I looked at it, she was gone. But I knew who it was from—a few white locals, definitely not there for the jazz. I threw it on the floor, and I guess they didn't like that very much."

"Oh, Lord... Did they... did they put their hands on you? Or shoot at you or anything?"

Doc gazed at her a long time before answering. "No. And... I'm all right."

"Okay, then. Go ahead and tell me the rest."

"We packed up and left, that's all."

"But you said you threw the postcard away. How'd you get it back?"

"We decided to wait till morning to head back to New York. We spent the night at the motel, and when the sun came up, Rudy found the postcard tucked under the windshield wiper of the station wagon."

"And you plan on keepin' this... don't you?"

Doc exhaled and stared at her through the smoke. "It's a decision I've been wrestlin' with the past couple of days. Look, Pearl... I hope you understand what I'm about to ask of you."

Pearl nodded as she gazed sadly at the postcard. "You want to save it for Edward."

"How'd you know that?"

Pearl pulled a handkerchief from her pocket and wiped her eyes. "I know he's still so... so little, but someday he's gonna grow up into a full-grown man, with that same target on his back that you have—that *all* Negro men have in this *damn* mean world." She stood up and handed the postcard back to him. "And our son needs to be prepared for what's out there... Even this."

The separation of the races is not a disease of colored people, but a disease of white people. I do not intend to be quiet about it.
~ Albert Einstein

CHAPTER 20

Shay Elizabeth Calhoun was born at 5:33 a.m. on February 3, 1949. She weighed exactly seven pounds. According to her father, she was a perfect replica of her mother.

The following afternoon Doc and Pearl brought the baby home to meet her brother, who was uncharacteristically stunned into silence at the sight of her.

"Here's your sister, Edward," Doc said. "She's little, huh?"

Edward nodded wordlessly, and then ran into his room.

"Don't be scared, Edward," Ronnie called. "She's just a baby!"

"Po' little fella!" Alva laughed. "He been waitin' to meet his little sister all day, but I guess I never explained how little she was gonna be. He probably thought she'd be his size. I better go talk to him."

Pearl was seated on the sofa, and began to squirm uncomfortably. "Maybe I ought'a go on to bed," she said.

"You want me to call the doctor?" Doc said, handing the baby to Ronnie.

"No, sugah. I'm fine. Just that taxi ride and all. Too much sittin' up."

"Okay, let me get you to bed."

As he helped Pearl to her feet, he looked back at Ronnie. "I'll be right back for the baby. Then do me a favor and fill up that big pot on the stove with water and put it under a high flame. I'm making spaghetti for supper, and you and Alva are staying. And no argument."

"Hey, no argument from me, 'cause I'm starving. And that's real nice of you, Doc."

"No, it's not," he said, grinning. "Pearl's goin' to bed, and I need somebody to wash the damn dishes."

When supper was over, Doc and Ronnie cleaned up the kitchen. Then they all headed back into the living room. Within minutes, Alva was sound asleep.

Ronnie chuckled. "I better take Alva home. She's exhausted."

"Aw, hell," Doc groaned. "I thought we were gonna celebrate!"

"We are! Just let me put her on the subway and I'll be right back."

"All right, I'm countin' on you!" Doc reached into his pocket for his key and tossed it to Ronnie. "Here, use this so you don't have to knock and wake Pearl up. I'll be in there with her."

After Ronnie and Alva left, Doc tiptoed into the bedroom. Pearl opened one eye. "You men sure are noisy when you're washin' dishes."

"I'm sorry, baby. Did we keep you awake?"

She smiled. "It was a happy sound. I love hearin' you and Ronnie laughin' together."

"Yeah, he's in a pretty good mood tonight."

Doc fixed the blanket and plumped Pearl's pillow, then adjusted the two additional pillows along the side of the bed to keep the baby from rolling off.

"Pearl, are you sure she'll be all right in bed there with you?" he whispered.

"I won't have time to do anything but doze a little, sugah. She'll be wakin' me up in about an hour for some dinner. And I ain't movin' an inch. She'll be fine."

"Okay. I got you some water right over here on the nightstand, and here's a little towel in case the baby spits up or sump'm. Edward's knocked out, and Ronnie took your Mama to the subway, but he'll be right back. We're gonna run up the block for some cheap form of alcohol so we can celebrate. I'll come check on you the second we get back. Five, maybe seven minutes."

Pearl laughed softly. "Go! We'll be fine."

Doc was about to leave, but stopped. Something about the way his new baby girl was tucked into Pearl's arm was familiar. Without warning, an image from Spain flickered in his mind: Mama and her two babies lying in the dirt waiting to be buried. For years, he had carried the emotional burden of that memory. But now, for the first time, its heaviness had lifted, and all the sharp edges of its pain had softened. Pearl and their two babies had healed that wound in his soul, replacing it with new life. He felt privileged just to stand on the edge of that moment.

"Pearl?"

"Yes, sugah?"

He wasn't sure what he was going to say until he heard the words: "You saved me."

She smiled. "You saved me first."

He leaned down and kissed her forehead. "I love you."

"I love you too," she whispered. "But if you wake this baby up, I'm gonna conk you with that water glass."

Doc chuckled and left, closing the door softly.

When he walked back into the living room, Ronnie was just coming through the front door. "I got some bad news, Doc," he said as he tossed him the key.

"What?"

Ronnie emptied his pockets and scattered a pile of change on the coffee table.

"That all you got?" Doc laughed.

Ronnie shrugged. "Rough week. What about you?"

Doc rubbed his chin. "Well, you *know* I missed a few gigs this week." Stepping back, he pulled out his pants pockets, and a folded dollar bill fell to the floor. He picked it up and grinned at Ronnie. "I usually celebrate with Johnnie Red, but tonight it looks like Thunderbird for us."

"Long as it's alcohol," Ronnie said.

Doc opened the door and gestured with his arm. "After you, Uncle Ronnie."

Ronnie bowed slightly and stepped out.

As they walked up the block, Ronnie was in a great mood and did most of the talking. By the time they reached the liquor store, they were laughing so hard the proprietor asked them if they were already drunk. Ronnie gave him a solemn look, then methodically stacked all his coins on the counter for payment. Doc stood beside him grinning. It was going to be a fun night.

When they got back to the apartment, Ronnie took a seat on the sofa as Doc pulled the two bottles from the paper bag and set them on the coffee table. "Let me go check on Pearl."

Opening the bedroom door, he peeked in, then closed it softly. "They're asleep."

He went to the kitchen and brought back an ashtray and two large tea tumblers. As he pulled his lighter from his pocket and tapped out a cigarette, he scowled at Ronnie. "That's right, you don't smoke, do you?"

"Nope. Pearl smokes enough to meet the family quota. Me, I don't like 'em."

"Whadayou? Some kind'a Martian?"

Ronnie grinned and shrugged. "Probably."

Doc chuckled as he lit his cigarette. "It won't bother you if I smoke, will it?"

"Your house, man. I'm just here for the alcohol."

Doc made a big show of arranging the items on the coffee table: cigarettes, lighter and ashtray at the edge closest to his side, with the two Thunderbird bottles precisely in the center. He pretended to measure reaching distance for each item, and finally took a seat at Ronnie's left. Then he rubbed his hands together and reached for the first bottle.

"The only good thing about cheap wine, my young no-smoking Martian friend, is no corkscrew." He twisted off the cap and filled the tea tumblers until the first bottle was empty.

Ronnie laughed. "We goin' for a record?"

"Yup." Doc held up his glass and clinked it against Ronnie's.

"To my beautiful wife and our beautiful new baby girl."

"To Pearl and Shay!" Ronnie said.

Doc took a big swallow and suddenly started laughing.

"Shh! What's so funny?"

"I was just thinking about a story Pearl told me—about how you three celebrated when your father—oops—'scuse me... when the *devil* died."

"Woo! I had my hands full that night. Neither one of them knows how to drink. At *all*."

"All Pearl told me about was Alva gettin' blasted."

"Mm-hmm. Pearl never tells on herself. She was in worse shape than Alva!"

"Pearl got drunk?" Doc chuckled. "Wish I would'a seen that!"

"No, you don't," Ronnie said, shaking his head. "She got sick."

Doc grimaced. "Ooh... What about Alva?"

"Nope. Alva just stumbled around a little and fell asleep with a big smile on her face."

"Good!"

"I love those two ladies a lot."

"Me too." Doc reached over and unscrewed the second bottle, then laughed at Ronnie's reaction. "I'm just lettin' it breathe, man. Isn't that what you do with fine wine?"

Ronnie rolled his eyes. "Anyway... Pearl's special, but I'm sure you know that. She's the only one who's always been there for me, and I mean *always*. Alva too, but Pearl knows *everything* about me. And we both decided there was no use worryin' Alva with the past. I put 'em both through some tough times. They ought'a hate me."

Doc took a swallow from his glass. "Nah. They love you."

Ronnie stared into his glass. "I should've been there for Alva when David died. I didn't know he died, but that's no excuse... I was in the middle of a badly-timed disappearing act."

"Where'd you disappear to?"

"Well... can I trust you not to tell Pearl? This is one thing she *doesn't* know."

"I know how to keep a confidence. I won't tell her."

Ronnie took a deep breath. "Well, I went to one of those AA meetings, but—"

"Oh, shit," Doc muttered, reaching for the screw cap. "And I got you drinkin' goddamn Thunderbird!"

Ronnie laughed. "I'm not an alcoholic, man. Relax. This is actually the first liquor—if this shit even qualifies as liquor—that I've had in weeks."

Doc exhaled and took a gulp, then made a sour face. "Woo! This *is* some of the nastiest lighter fluid I've ever tasted! But not to worry... It'll start tastin' better by the time we get to that second bottle. Anyway, finish your story, man. You were at an AA meeting."

"Only one. I was just so miserable. I swear to God, I was just lost." He fell quiet for a moment, then looked at Doc. "I have a question for you."

"Fire away."

"Well… Have you ever felt like a shadow?"

Doc studied him carefully before answering. "Can't say that I have. Why, have you?"

"Shit. My whole life… See, I have a theory. I think we're *all* just shadows, only some people wear a mask. That gives other people sump'm to see. Some kind of fake substance so nobody can see what they're hiding. But me, I'd rather just drift around and not be seen at all, especially when I'm in that kind'a shape."

"You mean when you're miserable."

Ronnie nodded. "You don't know what it's like to know you're hurting everybody who loves you, but you just—keep doin' it. I started hating myself, so I went underground."

Doc put down his glass and turned to face Ronnie. "Okay, listen to me a minute. In the first place, I *do* know what it's like to hurt people who loved me. In the second place, we all do it, sooner or later. And in the third place, where was this 'underground' you drifted off to when you were a miserable shadow?"

"Well, this guy named Ed who was one of the sponsors at AA saw what a mess I was, and he just took me to his house. His *house*, man! I don't know why the hell he trusted me. Shit, I wouldn't have! I told him I wasn't AA material, and he said it was okay. He told me all I needed was somebody to talk to. So we talked—a lot, but mostly, he just listened. He was a real good listener. He made me eat right and go to bed early and even when I screwed up and drank, he didn't judge me. He was a good friend. Still is. But more like a big brother or a father—at least what I imagined a father should be like. I stayed there for over two months, but it wasn't until I left that I found out—something weird. Too weird to talk about."

"Come on, man. I'm not Alva. You don't need to protect me. I can take the weird parts."

"Well, he was—I mean he *is*… Okay. Ed is a homosexual."

Doc didn't flinch. He was sitting back against the sofa cushions smiling, with his cigarette clenched in his teeth. He extended his hands. "That's it? That's the weird part?"

Ronnie closed his eyes and nodded. "So Pearl told you about me."

"No, she didn't, Ronnie. All she told me about was your rough childhood. But whatever she knows about your adult life she has never shared with me. And I never asked her to."

"But you know... Don't you?"

Doc sighed. "That sorry sack a'shit Melvin mentioned it once. I didn't have any reason to believe him *or* disbelieve him. I just figured that your life was none of my business."

"Melvin, huh? Yeah, he saw me with somebody once. Back in my reckless days...."

Ronnie finally looked at Doc. "So, all this time you've been seeing me with Walter, you *had* to have put two and two together... but you never said anything."

Doc smiled. "Walter's a real nice cat."

"And it doesn't bother you?"

"I'm never bothered by things that aren't my business."

"Come on, Doc! It *really* doesn't bother you?"

Doc laughed softly. "Aww, hell, Ronnie! Do you have any idea how many homosexuals I've worked with in the music business? If it bothered me, I'd have to go get a job as a—a damn long-shoreman or sump'm. You know, one of those *manly* jobs."

Ronnie rolled his eyes and laughed. "Pearl always said you were unusual."

"Sure she didn't say I was *weird*? And that brings me to a very important question."

"Which is?"

"Well, why did you find it so weird that Ed was a homosexual?"

"Because I *told* him about me, man! And all that time I was staying with him he never even made a pass at me. Not once!"

"Ah-hah!" Doc said, grinning. "Caught yourself judgin' a book by its cover, huh?"

"What do you mean by that?"

"Well, just because you were both homosexuals, you assumed he'd make a pass at you. And you didn't base that judgment on good ol' brotherly Ed. Or Ed, the father figure. Or Ed, the friend and good listener. You judged him on the narrow basis of him bein' a homosexual."

"Wow," Ronnie said softly. "I guess I did."

"Well, don't feel bad. I'm guilty of a similar crime. See, I'm around a bunch of those *manly* heterosexuals every day, and I pretty much assume they're all worthless sons'a bitches. Only difference between my prejudice and yours is—I'm always right."

Ronnie laughed, then coughed on the gulp of wine he'd just taken, and Doc smacked him on the back. Then he reached for the second bottle. "Drink up, Martian! I think this bottle's been breathin' long enough!"

* * *

At the end of March, Doc landed a gig with a sizzling bebop band with the providential name "Nirvana." For the first time since returning from the war, he was with a predominately Negro band. The only white musician was a bass player named Nate. It was a group of single, young, energetic musicians, all devoted to the principles of the art form, and constantly reaching for new innovations, new ideas. After two weeks of rehearsal, Doc was lit with inspiration, especially after the news that they would be recording soon.

He couldn't imagine his life getting any better. He was married to a beautiful woman who loved him; their two children were happy and healthy; he was playing better than ever; and now, to top it all off, the band leader, whose name was Jerry, had booked them for a long engagement at one of the most popular jazz clubs in New York—the Onyx on 52nd Street.

As he was dressing for their opening night, he was struck with a brilliant idea and grinned at his reflection in the bathroom mirror. "Pearl," he called. "Come in here a minute."

She walked into the bathroom. "Yeah, sugah?"

"Why don't you come out to the club with me tonight?"

"Oh, that's a great idea, sugah," she said dryly. "I'll just strap the baby on my back like a papoose, and Edward can sit on my lap. Be ready in a minute."

Doc grinned. "Alva can be here in half an hour to watch the kids. Give her a call and get dressed. You already took a shower."

"And what do I wear? One of my sexy maternity dresses?"

"Can't you squeeze into that red dress I got you for Christmas last year?"

Pearl sighed. "I'll try."

By the time Doc walked into the bedroom, Pearl was hooking the last garter clip to her stockings. Smoothing the dress over her knees, she turned her back to him. "Zip me up, sugah, and let's see if I can actually sit down in this dress."

Doc reached for the zipper. "Okay, take a deeeep breath."

"Oh, hush. It ain't that tight."

Once he had zipped the dress, Pearl fastened her pearls and turned around. "Well?"

Doc was staring at her. "I sure wish I could give you some real pearls."

She smiled. "You did, sugah. Those two babies in there are my real pearls."

* * *

As they rode to the Onyx that night, Doc pleaded with Pearl to sing a few songs with the band. It wasn't until just before the band took the stage that she finally agreed.

They started with an up-tempo version of "How High the Moon," and Pearl came in like a regular member of the group. Three songs later, Doc turned to request a ballad, but Pearl was already saying something to the piano player. He nodded and played the intro to "Tenderly."

As she began her sultry interpretation of their song, Doc raised his trumpet to his lips and watched her. When she gazed over at him, he smiled with his eyes. As soon as the song ended, he leaned close to her and whispered, "Wait till I get you home tonight...."

Pearl laughed, and the set ended to loud applause. As Doc took her hand to lead her off the stage, he heard a shout from the audience that almost made him lose his footing.

"Gladiator!"

Doc shaded his eyes from the glare of the stage lights as he scanned the room. "Mort?" he called. Then he grinned at Pearl. "It's Mort!"

Pulling Pearl through the crowd of patrons and waitresses, he saw his old war buddy reaching out to shake his hand. Doc clapped his palm into Mort's with a brotherly smack, and then hugged him. "Man, it's good to see you! This is my wife Pearl. Pearl, this is—"

"Couldn't be Mort, could it?" Pearl said with a grin.

Mort stepped back and gave Doc a wide-eyed look. "Gladiator! How'd you get this gorgeous doll to marry you?"

Doc laughed. "I ain't sure, Mort. She might not be playin' with a full deck."

Mort pulled out a chair. "Have a seat, Mrs. Calhoun. It sure is good to meet you."

Pearl sat down and smiled. "Good to meet you too, Mort, but please call me Pearl."

"Okay! So Pearl, did this guy tell you anything about our adventures in the war?"

Pearl exhaled a soft mist of smoke. "He told me every single Mort story he could remember. I could probably recite 'em to you with all the details."

"Boy, I wish my wife was here tonight to meet you, Pearl. What a singer you are!"

"Let's have dinner, Mort," Doc said. "We'd love to meet your wife, wouldn't we, baby?"

"We sure would. But right now, if you two will excuse me, I've gotta run to the ladies room." She stood up and kissed Doc. "You fellas go ahead and get caught up. I'll be right back."

When Pearl was out of earshot, Mort grinned. "I hope I'm not out'a line here, Doc, but—va-va-va-voom! What a doll! Guess that's one of the perks of bein' a gladiator!"

Doc laughed. "I sure am glad you came by, Mort!"

"Me too! But I nearly didn't. To be honest, I was a little scared."

"Scared of what?"

"I was scared you'd be a lousy horn player and I'd have to smile and lie all night."

"Not too lousy, I hope."

"Are you kidding? You're great! So lemme buy you a drink. Name your poison."

Doc signaled the waitress. "Johnnie Red for me, and another round for my buddy."

"And put it on my tab, dear," Mort called.

"Nah, this one's on me," Doc said.

"Hah! We'll slug that out later, my friend."

"So how'd you find me, man?" Doc said. "Or did you just finally decide to come to 52nd Street to hear some jazz in general?"

"I saw your name in the newspaper. You're the featured guy in this band, ya know that?"

"The bandleader decided to run the ad that way. I'll enjoy it while it lasts."

"Have you got any records out?"

"Just some old stuff with another band, but I found out last week that we're goin' into the studio soon to record some new tunes. I'll let you know and you can come see how it's done."

"Aw, that'd be great! Let me write down our new number so you can call me. We moved out of that cramped apartment shortly after I got back. Got a nice little house in Brooklyn on that G.I. Bill. Did you apply?"

"Well, the G.I. Bill isn't working as well for a lot of uh, *us*, if you know what I mean."

"What?" Mort let out a frustrated sigh. "Aw, Doc, I'm sorry to hear that's goin' on. Hell, you go fight for your country and still get treated like shit when you come home? But why am I surprised with a segregated army! We still got a long way to go in this country, don't we?"

"Yeah, but let's not dwell on all that tonight, Mort. Tell me what you hear about the other guys. Have you talked to Marv since you got back?"

"Aw, hell, I hate to have to tell you this, but… Marv never made it home."

Doc closed his eyes. "I'm sorry, Mort. Marv was a great guy. Good soldier."

"And a hell of a mechanic," Mort said. "He was proud of that… So, what about Eddie?"

"Eddie made it home. I got a letter from him a few months ago. He got married to his high school sweetheart and got a good construction job."

"With all this building goin' on, he'll be a millionaire in no time! I'm glad he got back in one piece. I nearly didn't ask you. Any time I check on the other guys… it's always bad news."

The waitress brought the drinks and Mort smiled. "Thanks, dear!"

Doc raised his glass. "To all the guys who didn't make it."

Mort sighed and raised his glass. "And to all the guys who did."

"Like us," Doc said. "*Mishpucha*."

"That's right," Mort said. "Hey, how 'bout us? We can still talk like no time went by! Oh, here comes your wife." He stood up and pulled out her chair. "Here ya go, dear."

"Thanks, Mort," Pearl said as she settled into the chair. "So are you fellas all caught up?"

"Oh, it's gonna take a lot'a dinners and visiting to really catch up," Mort said.

Doc tapped out a cigarette and lit it for Pearl, then offered one to Mort. "Want one?"

"Sure, thanks… Oh, wait!" Mort rolled his eyes and smacked himself on the forehead. "What's the matter with me? I almost forgot to tell you my big news!"

"Well, let's hear it."

"My daughter Polly's expecting! I just found out yesterday I'm gonna be a grampaw! Howdaya like that?"

Doc laughed and held up his glass. "*Mazel tov*! Just so happens that Pearl and I have some news too. We just had our second baby in February. A little girl named Shay."

"Hey! *Mazel tov*! New babies in the world! Now *that's* sump'm to celebrate! Where's that waitress? We need champagne here!"

As Doc turned to look for the waitress, he caught a glimpse of a familiar face on the other side of the room. For a moment he thought he had imagined it, but he had to be sure. He stood up quickly. "Uh, let me go find that waitress. Be right back."

Making his way through the crowd, Doc saw him again. He was walking outside with a short, stocky Italian in a blue sharkskin suit. Hurrying to a front window, Doc found a good spot to watch them without being seen. They were standing on the sidewalk with their heads together, engaged in what looked like a highly confidential conversation. Then the Italian handed him a thick envelope, which he tucked inside his jacket. Without another word, they both walked away.

Doc's jaw tightened. *Agent Adams. What are you up to, you sonofabitch?*

He glanced quickly toward their table and saw Pearl laughing at something Mort was saying. Hurrying over to the bar, he finally spotted their waitress. He mouthed the words "house champagne" and pointed toward their table. The waitress nodded.

"Where'd you go?" Pearl asked when he finally returned.

"Oh, I thought I saw somebody I knew," he said. "Turned out to be nobody."

"Well, Mort was just teachin' me a few Yiddish words while you were gone. So I have now learned that my husband is a *mensch*—and that we're like family. And I like that one, but you're gonna have to tell me how to pronounce it again, Mort. "Mishmish-pooksa...?"

"Close enough. *Mishpucha.* That's a tricky one, Pearl. Oh! Here's the waitress."

After pouring the champagne, Mort raised his glass. "Here's to old friends and new babies! *Mazel tov!*"

CHAPTER 21

For days, Ronnie had been trying to ignore the feeling that something was wrong with Walter. Since they had met, Walter had called him at least twice a day and they had seen each other at least three times a week, usually spending entire weekends together. But recently, his calls had tapered off to once a day, and then he began missing days altogether.

Over the past week Ronnie had called him four times, leaving messages with his mother. But Walter didn't return the calls. And now, three days had gone by.

Ronnie bought a bottle of wine and sat staring at the telephone and drinking. As the afternoon dragged on, he wasn't sure whether he wanted it to ring or not. He thought about William's "Dear John" letter and knew he couldn't stand another rejection of that magnitude. After only two glasses of wine, he fell asleep.

When the phone rang, he thought it was a dream for a minute, but then grabbed the receiver. "Hello?"

"It's me, Ronnie."

As soon as he heard the tightness in Walter's voice, he went cold.

"If you're not busy, I'd like to come over," he said in a stiff, formal tone. And then he said the dreaded words: "We need to talk."

Ronnie kept his voice cheerful. "Cool. I'm here. Come on over."

"I'm just up the block. I'll be right there."

"Okay." Ronnie hung up and closed his eyes. Why was there never any time to prepare for heartbreak? *Not again. Please... Not again.*

When the doorbell rang, he stared at the door for a long time before walking over to open it. He finally managed a smile. "Hi, Walter."

"Hi."

Ronnie turned and took a seat on the sofa, his smile frozen in place. He gazed expectantly at Walter, who was still standing in the center of the room with his hands in his coat pockets.

"Have a seat," Ronnie said. "Come on and relax."

Walter swallowed hard. "Ronnie... We need to talk."

"You said that on the phone. So sit down and let's talk."

Walter shook his head and looked out the window. "I don't know how to say this...."

Ronnie crossed his arms over his chest and stared at the floor. "Oh, God... Just say it."

"Okay, I'm sorry... Do you remember the girl my father fixed me up with?"

"Emily? Wait... Don't tell me you—changed up on me?"

Walter sighed loudly. "No! Of course not. I mean, she's a nice girl, but this is all just what I told you—a front to keep my father happy. Only now, she's gotten serious. Real serious. She had a long talk with my father and told him how much she loves me."

"But, well, doesn't she wonder why... I mean, how can she be so gone in love with you when you never—" Ronnie's eyes widened. "Wait. You *told* me you never slept with her."

"What I *told* you was I never had *sex* with her. I slept with her once. I had to."

"You *had* to?"

"She was throwing herself at me! I couldn't get out of it. But you're gonna love this. I told her I was impotent—well, temporarily."

Ronnie laughed nervously. "I *know* better."

"It didn't take much of an acting job. I was completely cold and detached—physically, that is. Emotionally, I just felt like a rat. I mean, it's not her fault my father threw us together."

"And it's not her fault that you're so easy to fall in love with... Poor Emily."

"Emily's not the problem. It's my father, Ronnie. It's *always* been my father."

"Oh, not that again. I really don't want to hear about your father, Walter. I know he'd never understand, but—"

Walter continued as though he hadn't heard him. "He wants me to marry her and take advantage of her father's offer to join his firm."

Ronnie stopped breathing for a moment. "Marry? ... *Emily*?"

Walter finally slumped down on the sofa next to Ronnie. "Oh, man, that sounds horrible to hear you say it out loud."

"*You* just said it out loud. And believe me, it sounded horrible to me too!"

"You'll never understand, Ronnie! You don't know the kind of pressure he puts on me."

"But Walter—"

"I can't change things. They're already arranging the wedding."

After a long silence, Ronnie said, "Then get married, Walter. Do your duty and give him his grandchild! We can still see each other. You can just see me... on the side."

Walter shook his head, and Ronnie could see that he was crying. "I didn't tell you everything. After the wedding I have to move to L.A. That's where the opening is—at the firm."

Ronnie reached for his hand and gazed at him. "Then *don't* get married, Walter. Let's run away," he whispered. "Let's go away somewhere."

"Where?" Walter shouted. "There's no place for us! And even if there was a place, I can't just run away like that, Ronnie. I told you before, I can*not* do that!"

"Yes, you can. Don't you realize how much your father gives you the blues? You're only happy when you're with *me*. You tell me that all the time! Do you realize how miserable your life's gonna be? ...Look, Walter, we all wear the mask sometimes, but you'll be wearing the mask twenty-four hours a day!"

Walter covered his face with his hands. "You don't understand, Ronnie. I love you, but I love my father too. I just can't—I can't stand to disappoint him. I never could. And this! His big football hero son turns out to be a sissy? It'd break his heart in a million pieces."

Ronnie leaned back and stared at the ceiling. "I wonder how many pieces my heart's gonna break into?"

"Oh, God," Walter moaned. "I'm—I'm sorry. I'm so sorry for all this."

"Maybe you're right," Ronnie said bitterly. "Maybe I *can't* understand how you love your father. I *hated* Victor. Shit, I wouldn't have pissed on him if he was on fire."

Tentatively, Walter placed his hand on the side of Ronnie's face. "I know," he whispered. "I wish I could've made you forget the things he did to you. I—I wish I could've made it better."

Ronnie leaned his cheek into the warmth of Walter's palm and closed his eyes. "You did. You always made it so much better."

Walter slowly withdrew his hand and closed his eyes.

"I'm sorry, Walter. I didn't mean to get like this. Please look at me."

Walter opened his eyes and gazed at him. Ronnie's heart was pounding, but he kept his eyes locked on Walter's. "Please don't leave me."

Walter lowered his head for a moment, then wrapped his arms around Ronnie, kissed his forehead, and stood up to leave. When he got to the door he said, "It's not us, you know. We're not hurting anybody. It's *them*. It's the world that's hurting *us*, Ronnie! *They're* the ones who are wrong! If we didn't have to live in this damn judgmental world, we could just be... us."

Without looking back, he walked out the door and closed it softly behind him.

Ronnie stared at the door. *How many pieces?*

* * *

Doc woke up so abruptly, his feet were on the floor before he even knew what it was that had jerked him awake. Then he heard it again. Someone was knocking. He grabbed his robe and squinted at the alarm clock. "Four-thirty? Oh, goddamn, I'm about to break somebody's neck...."

Hurrying into the front room, he yanked open the door with a ripe selection of curse words ready to erupt from his mouth. But when he saw that it was Ronnie, he just shushed him softly, pulled him inside, and closed the door. Ronnie's face was streaked with tears, and Doc decided not to ask any questions. "She's in the bed."

"I'm sorry," Ronnie croaked.

"It's okay, man." Doc patted his shoulder and led him to the bedroom. "Pearl," he said. "Wake up, baby. Ronnie's here."

Pearl sat up as Ronnie sank down onto the edge of the bed and leaned into her arms.

Doc moved toward the door. "I'll be out on the sofa."

"It's too cold out there, baby," Pearl said.

Doc shook his head. "I'll take this extra blanket. I'll be fine. Take care of your brother."

* * *

Ronnie stayed until the next afternoon, promising Pearl that he'd be back for supper, but he never showed up that night. After two days of calling his number with no answer, Pearl began to panic. She was about to call Alva when the phone rang. She picked it up quickly and stared at Doc with dread in her eyes.

"Hi, Mama... No, we haven't seen him... But don't worry. He'll turn up... Now, Mama, don't think that way. I'm sure he's fine... Mm-hmm. I sure will. Good night, Mama. I love you."

She hung up and looked at Doc. "Where can he be?"

Doc put his arms around her. "He'll be okay," he whispered. "He's just gotta work out his own troubles, Pearl. We can't do it for him."

"I can't believe he's doing this again...."

* * *

After nearly a week with no word from Ronnie, Pearl's nerves were frayed. She was short-tempered with the children, and Doc gave up on trying to find the right thing to say. She was smoking over two packs of cigarettes a day and hardly sleeping at all.

One evening after supper, Doc put the children in their room to play and took a seat next to Pearl on the sofa. She was flipping the pages of the newspaper and didn't look at him.

"Want me to take the kids to Rose's?" he asked, wishing his tone hadn't been so sharp.

"I can take care of my kids," she snapped.

"I know that. I just mean... they seem to be gettin' on your nerves."

"No, right now *you're* gettin' on my damn nerves."

He stood up. "Okay, well, that's easy to remedy."

"So you're leaving, huh?"

"Yes, I am. I gotta get to the club."

"This early."

"Yeah. This early." Doc grabbed his jacket and his horn case and walked out.

* * *

When he got home that night, Pearl was in bed, but he could tell she wasn't asleep. He took a shower and got into bed facing away from her. He had been trying to figure out how to tell her that Nirvana was going on another road trip, the third in the last six months. To make things more difficult, she wrapped her arm around his waist and kissed the back of his neck.

"I'm sorry, sugah."

Doc closed his eyes and rolled over. "I'm sorry too, Pearl. I'm really sorry."

As he held her against his chest, he wondered if his apology was for what had happened earlier that evening or for what he was about to spring on her. "Any word from Ronnie?"

"No."

"Oh. I'm sorry to hear that, Pearl... Uh, listen... there's something I need to tell you. I just found out tonight. I know it's bad timing, but we're goin' back on the road."

She pulled away from him. "When?"

"This weekend. I'm really sorry. Jerry's been workin' out the logistics, but he just let us in on it tonight."

"How long?"

Doc shivered inwardly at her icy tone. "About a month."

After a short silence, she threw off the covers and stood up. Without a word, she pulled on her robe and walked out of the bedroom.

Doc didn't follow her. He knew it was pointless.

* * *

Pearl didn't speak a word to him the next day. He went to the club that night and came straight home. When he saw that his bedroom door was shut, he went into the kitchen and rummaged in the refrigerator until he found some leftover chicken legs. He plopped three of them onto a plate and sat down. The kitchen clock read 2:45. He had just taken a bite when Pearl walked in. Her arms were crossed and her eyes were angry.

"A month," she snapped. "Right now. With Ronnie missing and everything."

Doc dropped the chicken leg back onto the plate and looked at her. "First of all, Ronnie is missing by *choice*. At least I'll let you know where I am. Look. You didn't want me goin' back out with Rudy's band after what happened in Virginia, and all I could get were a bunch of pick-up gigs before I finally joined Nirvana. So we're still tryin' to catch up on the bills. If I say no to this road trip, they *will* replace me. And it's back to ones and twos."

"There was that house-band gig you could'a taken. But no! You passed on that 'cause it wasn't that hard bop shit!"

"That is not why I passed on it!"

"The hell it wasn't! And now you tell me you are just gonna leave us for a whole month and you expect me to be happy about that?"

"Look, Pearl. I'm tired and I'm hungry. Can't you just let me eat and then we can talk about this in the morning?"

"Nobody's stopping you from eating. But I just wanted to let you know that I understand a lot more than you think I do. You don't *have* to go on the road. You *want* to go on the road 'cause you got your nose open for this damn bebop and some new band!"

Doc shoved his plate aside and glared at her. "I'm goin' on the road to make money, goddammit! Whenever I go on the road, I bring the money back home to you, don't I?"

"To *me*?" she shouted. "No, man, you're bringin' it home to these *babies*! When was the last time I had a new dress? No. When was the last time I even *asked* for a new dress?"

Doc sighed. "So I'm not providing for you and the kids, is that it? Then why don't you just leave me if I'm such a sorry husband and father?"

Pearl narrowed her eyes at him. "I hate it when you do that."

Doc pounded his fist on the table. "When I do *what*?"

"Twist it around till *I'm* the bad guy. I could be the one goin' out on the road, ya know. I can still sing."

"And leave the kids with Rose, huh?"

"No. I'd leave the kids with you! Their *father*. See how *you* like bein' all alone in that bed every night after the kids are asleep."

Doc felt a remark bubbling up that he knew would cut her to the quick, but he swallowed it back and shook his head.

Pearl leaned close to his face. "I *know* that look! Go on and say what's on your mind!"

"You want to go on the road," he said. "That's all I was thinking."

"And I could do a lot of smack on the road too. That's what you were *really* thinking."

Doc knew that they had drifted into dangerous territory, so he softened his tone.

"Pearl, if I thought you'd go back to the needle after all this time, I would never leave you with our kids. Now please sit down and listen for a minute."

Pearl yanked out a chair and sat down across from him, then lit a cigarette.

"Okay," he began, "let's talk about this trip—this goddamn trip that started this whole argument. I'll skip it, if that's what you want. I'll stay here and audition for some local gigs that may or may not last past the first week. And then, what do we eat in the meantime? But if I go on this trip, it's a whole month of guaranteed money. We can pay a lot of bills when I get back."

Pearl exhaled, gazed at him through the smoke, and shrugged one shoulder. "So go."

* * *

The next three weeks were a silent form of warfare unlike anything Doc had ever experienced. He called from each town the band played, but mostly spoke to the children. When Pearl got on the line, she was short and to the point, asking when she could expect checks for food, bills, and rent. When he asked about Ronnie, all she said was, "He turned up."

"Well, that's good news! How is he?"

"How do you think he is?"

On the final week of the road trip, Jerry made an announcement that he had booked another trip for the next month. Doc knew he had no choice but to quit.

The night before their last engagement in Hartford, he went to Jerry's room to tell him.

"Shit, Jerry, I hate to leave. I love playin' with this band, man. I'll never find a band in New York that plays the shit we've been playin'."

"Aw, man, it's cool. I knew the road was gon' be rough for you, bein' married and all, but I couldn't pass on it. Bebop's burnin' up the radio and New York's crawlin' with competition. Shit! I'd be a fool not to take some of that money these out-of-town clubs are payin'. But first gig we book in the city, you're my first call. Meanwhile, let's smoke this joint. You won't feel so pinched up between that rock and that hard place Pearl just stuck your ass in."

"Thanks for understanding, man."

Jerry shook his head as he lit the joint. "Wives, man... A husband's curse."

"No, Jerry, don't get me wrong. I mean, I hate her at the moment, but I really love my wife. That's what makes this so hard. She's never been like this before, and I can't really blame her. A month is a long time to be away from your family."

Jerry hit the joint and laughed as he passed it to Doc. "Guess that's true. My marriage was a casualty of the road, so now it's uncomplicated one-night stands with chicks who understand that my only wife is the music."

Doc sighed. "Well, I hope you're serious about giggin' in New York. I'd love to play 52nd Street again, man. But, shit, till then...."

"Long as you hang with us through this extra Saturday in Hartford. This joint's packed on Saturdays, and don't forget we get a cut of the door. You better not miss that big payday."

"I'll be here Saturday. I need that big payday for a peace offering when I get home."

* * *

Doc hurried back to the motel to call Pearl. He was working on what to say as he dialed the number. He was sure that the good news about him quitting the band would soften the bad news about his delayed return. The phone rang three times before she answered.

"H-huullo?"

"Why's your voice—What's wrong with your voice, Pearl?"

"Had me a li'l damn drink, sugah. Zat okay?"

"You don't drink. And a little damn drink wouldn't put that junkie slur in your voice, now would it?" As soon as the words left his mouth, he squeezed his eyes shut and clenched his teeth. *Shit! Why the hell did I say that?*

Pearl was presiding over a long silence that he knew would never end unless he ended it.

"Pearl. I know you wouldn't go back to that stuff... I just meant...."

Pearl's voice was suddenly crystal clear and sharp. "Sure, sugah," she snapped. "I went out and scored while the kids took a nap, and then shot up in the alley. That's okay, isn't it?"

"That wasn't funny, Pearl."

"You really thought I'd leave my kids and go right back to the needle 'cause I'm missin' my trumpet maaan?" Her voice was laced with sarcasm.

"Look, I know you're still worried about Ronnie. That's the only reason my mind jumped to that conclusion. And why the hell did you answer the phone that way? That was a dirty little trick and it doesn't help things."

Pearl slurred her voice again. "I be okaaay, sugah... in a li'l bitty whiiile."

"Goddammit! Knock it off!"

After another long silence, Doc sighed. "What the hell are we gonna do, Pearl?"

"We?" Pearl chuckled. "Well, *you* are gonna go play your li'l horn in that li'l ol' club in Hartford. What the hell did you say it was called? Oh, yeah. Call of the Wild, wasn't it? Sounds like a real glamorous joint. So that's what *you're* gonna do. And me, I'ma be home like a good little obedient wife, baking you a birthday cake. Edward's been planning a little party for your birthday on Saturday. He even helped Shay scribble some pictures for you an' everything—"

"Pearl... Okay, look, Pearl, I'm sorry, but I won't be home till Sunday. I'm really sorry."

She laughed dryly. "Oh, that sounded reeeal sincere, sugah."

"Look. Can't the party wait till Sunday—evening?"

"Of course, the party can wait. And the kids can wait and I can wait. Don't we always?"

"Pearl, listen. This is the last road trip. I already quit the band. That's what I called to tell you. But I just can't pass up Saturday. This club gives us a cut of the door, and it's always packed on Saturdays. I want to be able to pay those damn bills when I get home so I can start looking for another gig. I'm sorry about Saturday."

"Mm-hmm, I know. You're *always* sorry, aren'tcha, sugah?"

"We're *both* pretty damn sorry, aren't we?" Doc said bitterly.

He could hear her angry breathing just before the loud bang of the receiver. He sat there for a long moment listening to the dial tone and wondering if she had broken the telephone. Then he hung up and headed out to find a liquor store.

* * *

Jerry was right about the packed house that Saturday, and the money was even better than Doc had expected. But by 3:00 a.m. he was standing under the spray of the shower hating himself. Technically, it wasn't his birthday anymore. It was Sunday morning.

He knew he should have been home hours ago, eating birthday cake and gushing over all the drawings Shay and Edward had made for him. He should have been kissing his wife and trying to make her happy again. But instead, he was trying to sober up with a cold shower after a long night with his friend-turned-assassin, Johnnie Walker. And to make things worse, he had to figure out a way to get rid of the B-girl he had picked up earlier, who was waiting for him in that sagging bed in this crummy roadside motel with the dubious name "Dick's Hideaway."

He grabbed the shower curtain and yanked it open, cringing at the metallic screech the hooks made on the curtain rod. "Congratulations, ya goddamn drunk," he muttered. "You have performed the unheard-of feat of bein' hungover and plastered at the same damn time."

He splashed his face with another dose of cold water and dried off. Then he slipped on his underwear and opened the bathroom door to let out some of the steam. When he looked out, he saw the girl, stretched out in the middle of the bed, as naked as the day she was born. He closed his eyes, partly to shut out her image, and partly to wade through the alcoholic cobwebs of his memory for her name. And now, someone was knocking on the door.

"Man, get lost!" he yelled irritably.

The girl giggled, causing several of her more voluptuous body parts to jiggle. Doc closed his eyes again, trying to think of something to say that would make her leave. She had a pretty face, but wore a lot of makeup in a much lighter shade than the saddle-brown color of the rest of her proudly exposed skin. Her hair was bleached blonde— or was it a wig? Didn't matter. The total effect screamed "cheap hooker." He was about to slip on his pants when he heard another knock. Louder this time.

"Goddammit!" he yelled as he strode to the door. "Jerry, if that's you—"

The second he yanked open the door, his eyes were fixed on a cake wrapped in wax paper, and then he saw Pearl's face. She was wearing the sweet smile that always melted his heart. This was her way of apologizing.

"Who is it, baby?" the girl crooned from the bed.

Doc had to close his eyes when he saw the change in Pearl's expression.

His slow reaction to the sudden blur of movement let him know just how drunk he still was. Pearl was suddenly in the room advancing toward the girl. The girl had pulled herself up to a kneeling position in the center of the bed, which naturally made the whole scenario even more lewd than it already was.

Before he could stop her, Pearl shifted the cake to her right hand, cocked her arm back, and launched it at the girl, smacking her squarely on the side of her head. In his drunken state, it seemed somehow notable to Doc that the mystery was solved regarding the girl's hair. It had twisted around and was now covered with frosting. Definitely a wig.

He snapped out of it when he saw Pearl lunge at her. He grabbed her from behind, pinned her arms to her sides, and yelled at the girl to get out. Then he tried a few softer words on Pearl:

"Calm down now, baby."

"Calm down?!" she bellowed. "I'm fixin' to *kill* that bitch! And *then* I'ma kill *you!*"

The girl's eyes widened and Doc nearly laughed. Pearl rarely raised her voice, but when she did, it was not a run-of-the-mill scream. It was a deep, bone-chilling roar.

As the girl dressed frantically, Doc continued to hold Pearl, even when she connected with a couple of sharp elbows to his mid-section.

Grabbing her pocketbook, the girl spewed a string of curse words Doc had never heard come out of a woman's mouth before. Then she took a wide, safe path around Pearl and left, slamming the door so hard the walls of the cheap room shook.

After all the noise and tumult, the sudden silence was nerve-wracking. Doc could feel Pearl's hard breathing. He relaxed his grip on her arms and stepped back to brace for an attack. A slap, an acid-laced condemnation to hell, a kick to the groin. Something. But she only stood there for what seemed like an eternity, breathing hard and refusing to turn around and look at him.

It was only when she sank in a slow meltdown to the floor that he realized the hard breathing had been silent, wracking sobs.

He knelt down and tentatively laid his palm on her back. "Oh, my God, Pearl... Oh, God, what have I done to you?"

As he moaned those words, he was at last mercilessly sober.

* * *

The bus ride from Hartford was an eternity of torture. After Doc followed Pearl to the back seat, she turned her face to the window and didn't speak a word until they got to New York.

On the way to the apartment, she stopped in front of a neighborhood bakery and finally spoke to him, strictly out of necessity.

"You better go on in and buy a new cake since your *friend* left wearin' the old one. And hurry up. The kids are waitin' to surprise you with your birthday party. I'll be out here."

When they got home, Pearl took the cake from his hands. "You go in first," she said.

He nodded, opened the door, and walked in. Rose was standing in the middle of the living room holding Shay in her arms, and Edward was jumping up and down. They were all smiling and wearing pointed paper hats and yelling happy birthday.

Doc reached deep for a smile, then rushed over to them. After swinging Edward high in the air, he took Shay from Rose's arms, and began covering them both with kisses. Then he carried them into the kitchen, watching Pearl for any sign of a truce.

Pearl plopped the cake on the table, then yanked out a drawer. Ripping open a box of birthday candles, she jabbed a few of them haphazardly into the cake.

"Got your lighter?" she said to Doc without looking at him.

Doc fished out his lighter and grinned at the children as he lit the candles. "One, two, three, four, aaaand five… Guess Daddy's five today!"

Shay and Edward laughed hysterically at their father's joke. Pearl did not.

Rose cleared her throat. "Uh, I need to get home, Pearl. I got… uh, so much to do."

Pearl's protest was unconvincing. "No, Rose. Stay and have some birthday cake with us."

Rose was already backing into the living room. "Oh, you can just save me a piece. I really gotta go…."

"Thanks for everything, Rose," Doc said. Then he busied himself cutting the cake and chatting with the children, sneaking occasional looks at Pearl. She was standing in front of the refrigerator staring inside as if taking a careful, protracted inventory of its contents.

"So when do I get my presents?" he asked the children.

"Right now!" Edward scrambled from his chair and ran back to the living room.

Shay broke into loud sobbing, clearly upset that she was trapped in her high chair and unable to follow her brother. Doc lifted her out and quieted her just as Pearl slammed the refrigerator door and ran out of the kitchen.

He carried Shay into the living room, but all he saw of Pearl was a partial view of her back as their bedroom door banged shut.

* * *

After bathing the children and putting them to bed, Doc cleaned up the kitchen and took a long, miserable shower. Leaning both palms on the tile, he shut his eyes and hung his head, letting the spray sting the back of his neck. When he opened his eyes, he stared at the water swirling down the drain, and wondered if his marriage was doing the same.

When he finally eased into bed next to Pearl, he knew that he had to tell her the absolute truth. He also knew that she wouldn't believe a word he said.

Reaching for his cigarettes, he lit one and stared at the dark ceiling as he smoked. Every time he thought of something to say, the moment seemed wrong. He felt as nervous and out of sync as he had on his first professional gig when he was trying to ease in for his first solo. He sighed, then crushed the cigarette in the ash-tray.

"I know you're awake, Pearl. And we have *got* to talk about this."

She didn't respond.

"Okay, look, I know you can hear me, so I'm gonna go ahead and tell you everything and I will not lie to you… First, *nothing* happened with that tramp. I was wrong as hell to even have her there in the first place, but all it took was thirty seconds in that cold shower to know that I wasn't gonna touch her. You got there before I had the chance to throw her out."

Without a word, Pearl got up and walked out of the bedroom. Doc closed his eyes and waited. He heard the sound of the kitchen faucet filling a glass with water and watched her as she walked back into the room. She returned to the bed without looking at him or speaking.

"Pearl, I know you don't believe me," he said softly. "And that's okay. I don't deserve to be believed."

Again, no response.

"Pearl, if I had a gun I'd give it to you so you could shoot me with it."

He rolled his eyes at himself. That foolish "gun" line was clear proof that he had run out of words. All he could do now was light another cigarette and smoke it.

As he was riding the razor's edge of all that silence, the telephone jangled, and his body jerked. "Goddamn..." He grabbed the receiver, but before he could even get it to his ear he heard Ronnie sobbing. "What's wrong, Ronnie? What happened?"

Pearl grabbed the receiver. Doc quickly turned on the lamp and put out his cigarette.

"Ronnie? Calm down, sugah. Tell me what's wrong. Is it—"

For the first time in twenty-four hours, Pearl stared directly into Doc's eyes. She was already crying. "No... oh, no... Not Mama...."

Doc got up and began dressing, keeping his eyes on Pearl.

"You stay with her, Ronnie," Pearl said. "D-don't let anybody touch her, you hear me?"

Doc took the receiver from her hand and hung up. Then he gathered Pearl in his arms and finally thought of something right to say. "Get dressed. We gotta go help Ronnie."

* * *

Due to the late hour, there was no traffic on the way to the Bronx. As Doc was paying the cab driver, Pearl ran up the steps of her mother's house. By the time he reached her, she was pounding on the door and screaming for Ronnie to open it.

Doc knew better than to mention anything about waking the neighbors, and instead just reached into her pocketbook and handed her the key. Pearl unlocked the door, and ran to the kitchen. Doc stayed right behind her.

The kitchen was empty, but the light was on and the back door was open. Outside was a courtyard just large enough for a clothes-linc and the small maple tree that Alva and David had planted when they bought the house. Pearl hurried out and Doc turned on the back porch light.

As he looked over her shoulder, he caught his breath. Ronnie was sitting in the grass leaning against the clothesline pole, holding Alva's lifeless body across his lap. Her face-up position in her son's arms reminded him of an image he'd once seen in a book—a sculpture by Michelangelo. Doc closed his eyes for a moment. When he opened them again, he saw the overturned laundry basket and its contents spilled in the grass.

Pearl slowly began walking down the steps.

Ronnie stared up at her with a lost look. "Shh… She's asleep, Pearl."

Pearl nodded and knelt beside him, then put her arms around them both.

Doc remained on the porch. His gaze drifted up to the clothes-line, where a man's white shirt was dangling by one clothespin. Alva had never let Ronnie wash his own clothes. Any time he tried, it always ended with one of their playful squabbles. An echo of Alva's voice ran through his mind, and Doc realized how much he would miss her.

Don'tchu argue with me, boy! My David's gone, but I still got my baby to do things for! So you just gimme them dirty shirts and get on away from here!

He leaned heavily against the porch post. All he could do was watch Pearl and Ronnie holding their mother for the last time. Then Ronnie said, "Mama's asleep, Pearl."

A light wind blew through the courtyard, gently rustling the leaves on the maple tree. Pearl closed her eyes and turned her face upward, as if in prayer. Doc lowered his head, hating the useless tears on his face. It was the first time he had heard Ronnie call Alva "Mama."

CHAPTER 22

Doc took a week off to take care of the children and handle the funeral arrangements. Pearl was carrying enough of a load trying to comfort Ronnie, who had fallen into a deep depression. When he was at the apartment, he upset the children with his crying, and when he was away, he rang the phone at all hours. Pearl was barely hanging on.

On the night before the funeral, Doc had just gotten the children to sleep when he found Pearl dozing on the sofa. She had hardly slept in days, so he was careful not to wake her. After covering her with a blanket, he went to the bedroom and stretched out on the bed. But the second his eyes closed, the phone rang. He snatched the receiver quickly, but it was too late. Shay was wailing, and he could hear the sofa springs squeak as Pearl got up.

"Ronnie!" Doc said firmly. "This has gotta stop, man."

At that moment he saw Pearl run past the bedroom door and into the bathroom.

"Wait a minute, Ronnie. Hold on."

Doc ran to the bathroom door and knocked. He could hear her vomiting. "Are you okay?"

Instead of answering, she continued to retch, and Doc opened the door. "Let me help you, Pearl," he said, wetting a towel.

"Go talk to Ronnie," she gasped, grabbing the towel. "I'm okay... Go! Go talk to him!"

As Doc stepped into the hallway, he saw Edward standing there crying.

"Everything's okay, son. Go back to bed. I'll come in there in just a minute."

When Edward didn't move, Doc yelled, "I *said* go back to bed, boy!"

Edward ran back into his room, sobbing, and Doc headed back to the phone. He could still hear Ronnie crying through the receiver.

"Okay, Ronnie, enough is enough! Listen to me now. Hey! Listen to me! You have got to stop calling, you understand? I know you're upset, but you ain't the only one who lost your mother, you know. Pearl's fallin' apart, and you've got her so worried she's in there throwin' up, man! Can't you think of her for once in your life?"

"Pearl's all I have now!" Ronnie yelled. "I'm sorry, Doc, but I really need to tell her something... Please let me talk to her!"

"I just told you she's in there sick, man! Now, we'll see you tomorrow, Ronnie."

He hung up and went straight to the bathroom door just as Pearl opened it. She was glaring at him. "Why were you yellin' at Ronnie?"

"He's okay, Pearl. We both yelled a little, but he understands that we'll see him tomorrow." Doc smiled to cover his lie. "He said he's sorry, and he said he's okay now."

Pearl pushed past him and headed straight to the phone. Doc shook his head and went into the children's room to get them settled.

When he returned to his room, Pearl was sitting on the edge of the bed gripping the receiver. "Now he won't even answer," she said. "Why'd you have to yell at him like that?"

Doc sank down on the bed next to her. "I didn't mean to yell... I'm sorry."

Once he realized that Pearl was too angry to respond to any form of comfort, he retreated to the living room sofa. He checked his watch. It was only 9:15.

He managed to sleep in short, troubled stretches. But then something woke him in a jerk of consciousness that put his feet on the floor and set his heart racing. He hurried in to check on the children, and then went into his own bedroom to check on Pearl. Everyone was asleep.

He squinted at his watch again. It was 1:40. If he hurried, he could make it to the corner in time to buy a bottle at JJ's before they closed.

As he slipped out the front door, he absolved himself before his own guilt could rat him out. "Goddammit, I deserve a drink."

Hurrying down the street, Doc went into JJ's and was glad to see Howard tending bar. Selling by the bottle was against JJ's policy, but Howard didn't mind bending the rules for Doc.

Doc thanked him, gave the bottle of Johnnie Walker a grateful pat as he stuck it in his pocket, and then walked back to the apartment. Pearl would never know he'd been gone.

But as soon as he got back and headed up the stairs, he heard disturbing sounds floating down from an upper floor: Children crying, and the unmistakable deep timbre of Pearl's voice. He bolted up the stairs.

When he reached his floor, Pearl and Edward were standing in the hallway with Rose, who was holding Shay. Pearl was wearing her coat, but the children were still in their pajamas. They were all crying. The other neighbors were standing in their doorways whispering.

Doc walked over and gently took Shay out of Rose's arms. Then he grabbed Edward's hand. "We're goin' home, kids," he said.

Rose shook her head firmly and pulled Edward away from him. "You better go get her, Doc," she said, nodding in Pearl's direction. "Look."

Doc handed Shay back to Rose and hurried over to Pearl who was walking blindly toward the stairs. He reached for her arm and stepped in front of her.

"Wait, Pearl... Look, I just ran up to JJ's for a bottle, that's all. I came right back."

There were tear streaks on her face and she was staring at him with an eerie expression he had never seen before—a flat unconnected gaze that ran a chill down the back of his neck.

"Why'd you have to yell at Ronnie?" she whispered.

"Listen to me, baby," he said gently. "I know your brother's in a lot of pain, so here's what I'll do. I'll go pick him up and bring him over here. How's that? I'll go right now."

She slipped out of his grasp, placed both palms on his chest, and gave him a feeble push.

"Pearl... Listen to me...."

Rose had taken the children inside her apartment, but she stepped out into the hallway and called to him before he could say another word. "He's dead, Doc."

Those words had such a concussive effect that Doc stepped back without even realizing he had done it. He turned awkwardly to look at Rose. She nodded firmly, went back into her apartment, and closed the door. He finally pulled himself together and reached for Pearl, pressing her head to his shoulder. "I'm so sorry, baby," he whispered.

Pearl didn't move or speak to him.

"Where were you... trying to go?" he asked carefully.

"Harlem... Harlem Hospital. They... they want me to come claim him."

"Okay," he said, guiding her toward the stairs. "Hold onto me."

* * *

For the next five days Doc turned off his emotions. Pearl's pit of suffering was a hazard he had to sidestep if he were to remain focused on the mountain of duties he had never attempted before. The postponement of one funeral to arrange for two. A side-by-side burial. The nearly forgotten call to Jerry, who had booked some local gigs that Doc was supposed to play. Swallowing his pride when the band took up a collection to help with expenses. Cooking, tending to the children, and keeping the landlord off his back. But the toughest job was trying to comfort Pearl and get her to sleep.

It wasn't until the day of the funeral that Doc realized there were no more tasks, duties, or arrangements to hide behind. The children were with Rose, so the house was quiet as he and Pearl got dressed. They had only spoken a few words to each other when the driver from the funeral home arrived to pick them up.

When the car pulled away from the curb, Pearl rested her head on Doc's shoulder. It was the most intimate gesture she had offered him since Hartford, and it elicited a sensory memory of the band bus. It took him back to the old days when they were so happy and he was reeling from the idea that it was actually possible to fall in love with a woman, not once, but over and over again. But that was before all this pain. Before she had lost Ronnie and Alva. Before he had broken her heart with that tramp. That was the first wound, and the one that had left him powerless to diminish even the slightest degree of her suffering.

In the silence of the car, all the chaos of the past few days ran through Doc's mind. No matter how hard he tried to turn it off, the manic series of sounds and images would not leave him alone. It was a suicide. That much was clear. But there was one lingering question that disturbed him more than anything else. What were those mysterious cuts on Ronnie's lips?

* * *

The minute the service was over, Pearl began watching Doc and plotting her escape. As he was talking to mourners, she gradually moved away from him, using the hugs of her mother's church friends as cover. Each sobbing embrace, each offer of condolence was a stepping stone to the side door of the church. At last, she saw her opening. Doc was talking with the preacher, and his back was turned. But before she could slip out, he spotted her and walked over.

"I know you want to go home," he whispered. "But we still have to go to the cemetery."

Pearl stared at him. "I can't do it."

"We don't have to stay all the way till—the last part. And I'll be right beside you."

Pearl held his hand tightly as he led her out to the waiting car.

By the time they got to the cemetery, the caskets were already placed over their side-by-side graves, ready for burial. The image filled Pearl's eyes, and she felt her body growing rigid with horror. She could see the preacher's mouth moving, but all she heard was a shrill ringing in her ears. Then the preacher looked directly at her and said something. Doc nudged her. She could feel, more than hear, his deep voice in her ear. "He wants to know if you have anything to say."

She closed her eyes. "Yeah... Tell him... tell him I said this is a damn mean world."

* * *

When they got home, Rose brought the children back to the apartment and Doc fixed supper for everyone. Pearl picked at her food and didn't say much at the table.

"Pearl?" Doc said. "Why don't you try to sleep for a while. Rose said she'd be happy to take the kids again so you can have some quiet."

She nodded and kissed the children. "You kids be good for Miss Rose."

After Doc walked the children across the hall to Rose's apartment, Pearl went into the bedroom and closed the door. She was wide awake, but every time Doc came in to check on her, she pretended to be asleep. Each time she heard the door close, her eyes would open and she'd spend the next eternity staring at the ceiling. *Why can't I cry now?*

Suddenly, she sat up, slipped on her shoes, and peeked out the bedroom door. Doc was sitting on the sofa smoking and studying a music chart. The radio was playing softly in the kitchen: *No matter where you go… a flower is a lovesome thing….*

Pearl stood there clenching her teeth for a moment as that sweet, ominous song scratched at her nerves like a harpy. She tried to look composed and stepped into the living room.

Doc looked up, and then hurried over to her. "What is it, Pearl? What do you need?"

"I need you to go back to work, that's all. I know you got a gig tonight, and you're skippin' it to stay here babysittin' me. But I'm okay."

"No, Pearl. I'm not leaving you here all by yourself. Not tonight."

"I know you mean well, but everybody's been smothering me with sympathy all day. I'm gonna go take a bath and then I'm gonna go across to Rose's and soak up some'a that music my babies make when they laugh. I need that more than anything right now."

Doc was shaking his head, and Pearl laid a hand on his shoulder and smiled. "We need the money, don't we?"

Doc sighed uncomfortably. "I don't know, Pearl… Are you sure?"

"I'm sure."

"Well, we are pretty broke. Let me call Jerry. I got just enough time to get dressed."

Pearl went to the bathroom and filled the tub, then eased into the water and waited.

Doc tapped on the bathroom door, then stuck his head in.

"If you need anything—*anything*—call me. I left the number of the club under the phone where you can see it. And I'll be home right after the last set… Pearl. Are you *sure* you're okay?"

"I'll be fine."

"I love you, Pearl."

She smiled at him, and waited for the sound of the front door closing. After drying off and getting dressed, she waited twenty minutes before stepping outside.

As she hurried down the alley, she felt free for the first time in days. The night air was cool and her mind was such a blank that she was shocked when she felt tears trailing down her face. She made the turn onto Amsterdam Avenue, and felt a strong compulsion to run.

Then she saw it—the sign for 143rd Street. Halfway down the block, she entered the foyer of an old run-down apartment building and hurried up the stairs to the second floor. She knocked on the door marked 2F and wrapped her coat tightly around herself. The door opened and she saw the dark, round face of her old friend Perry. He seemed to be alone.

He moved back as Pearl walked inside. "Hello, Perry."

Perry nodded, then shut the door behind her and locked it. Then he crossed the room and opened the top bureau drawer where he kept his supply. Holding up a packet, he gave her a questioning look, and she nodded.

Taking a seat on the sofa, she took off her coat and rolled up the sleeve of her dress. She watched as Perry methodically prepared her dose. It had been years since she'd been in this room. Glancing around, she realized that not much had changed. Perry's hair had a little more gray in it, but his expression was still placid and childlike. And there was still that strange calmness inside his silence, as if all sins were forgiven in this quiet room.

He handed her a rough-woven necktie to tie off with, and waited as she found a good vein. Then he handed her the needle and walked back over to his chair next to the bureau.

The sorrow was gone the instant Pearl's fingers touched the hypo. Deliverance was only seconds away, and even the sharp stab of the needle was intense pleasure. She welcomed the tingling burn of the narcotic like an old friend as it danced through her vein. And she smiled at the sweet suspense just before the impact. When it finally hit, her whole body convulsed, and she laughed softly. As she felt the waves of pleasure rolling through her body and mind, she began to sing in a slow, breathy slur: "Flower'za... lovesome thiiiing... Shhh... Hush, Ronnie... Don'tchu tell Mama...."

Her head rolled to one side and she smiled at Perry, wondering why he looked so sad over there watching her from his chair next to the bureau.

* * *

Pearl didn't know what to expect when she unlocked the door to the apartment. A beam of morning sunlight was shining through the small living room window. It was half past ten, but everything was quiet and there was no sign of Doc or the children. Her throat was dry, so she went to the kitchen for a glass of water, but when she got to the doorway, she stopped.

Doc was sitting at the table staring at her. She waited for him to say something, but he was as still and silent as a granite statue. She took a seat in the chair across from him and stared at her hands, wishing she could keep them still.

"Say sump'm, sugah... Tell me to go to hell or sump'm."

Doc lowered his eyes and then covered his face with his hands. He sat like that for a few more seconds before his shoulders began to shake with soundless crying.

"I'm sorry, sugah," Pearl whispered. "I saw the newspaper this mornin'... I didn't even know... I been gone three days, huh?"

There was so much pain in his silence, Pearl had to look away. "I'm sorry, sugah."

After a long moment, he stood up stiffly, and Pearl wondered how long he had been sitting at that table worrying about her. She watched him walk slowly over to the sink for a dish towel to wipe his eyes. Then he filled a glass with water and brought it to her. Easing back down onto his chair, he folded his hands and gazed at her. He still hadn't said a word.

Pearl gulped down the water until the glass was empty. "How'd you know I was thirsty?"

"I know you're thirsty, Pearl."

"I wouldn't blame you if you left me," she said miserably.

"I'm not leaving you, Pearl. And you're not leaving me."

"Then—you think maybe this makes us—even?"

He shook his head slowly. "It's not about gettin' even, Pearl. This is about—I love you."

She stared at him through a long, tense silence before finally breaking down. "Where are my babies?" she sobbed.

"With Rose. They're fine."

"What'd you tell 'em?"

"Nothin' bad. I wouldn't do that."

Pearl gulped a deep breath and looked down. "Thank you."

Doc reached for her arm and she didn't resist. As he rolled up her sleeve and ran his fingers along the inside of her arm, she knew that he was counting the fresh needle wounds. She squeezed her eyes shut, but couldn't stop the continuous flood of tears. "See, I—I never hurt this bad before, sugah. Guess I—guess I'm hooked again. I'm sorry...."

She felt his palm slide down from her arm until it clasped her hand firmly. It was warm and reassuring. Then she heard his voice, calm and steady, as though nothing had happened. "We're finished being sorry, Pearl. We're all finished with that."

* * *

A week went by before Pearl learned the details of Ronnie's death. Doc was in the kitchen when someone knocked on the door. Pearl opened it and stared at a white man wearing a tan sports jacket and hat. The knot in his tie was loosened as though he'd worked a hard day.

"Mrs. Calhoun?" he said, taking off his hat.

"Yes?"

"I have the report on your brother," he said, reaching into his inside jacket pocket. "I think you were expecting it?"

Pearl stared at him, unable to answer for a moment. The radio was on in the kitchen, and she could hear Billie Holiday crooning sadly.

Hush now... don't explain... You're my joy and pain....

Doc walked up behind her and put his arm around her shoulder.

Pearl continued to stare at the white man. "Your name's not—Gallo, is it?"

"No, ma'am. I'm Detective Greely. I'm sorry it took so long, but we had to wait until we finished our paperwork and everything."

Pearl nodded, and reached for the two brown envelopes in the detective's hands.

"What's this other envelope?" Doc asked.

Pearl stared at the word "Evidence" stamped on the second envelope. "Is it the letter?" she asked softly. "They told me he wrote me a letter…."

"Yes, ma'am," the officer said. "It's addressed to you."

"But—but, that Sergeant Gallo told me it was unreadable."

Greely cleared his throat. "Well, we uh, we cleaned it up for you—the best we could."

Tears were streaming down her face, but Pearl kept her voice calm. "Thank you."

Greely nodded. "It might comfort you to know that he didn't even have a record."

Doc glared at him. "But you sure checked, didn't you!"

Greely stared at him a moment, then put on his hat and walked away.

Pearl drifted aimlessly to the center of the room, clutching the envelopes to her chest.

Doc closed the front door and hurried over to her. "You sure you're ready to read that?"

She nodded and he walked her into the bedroom.

"You want me to sit with you?"

Pearl shook her head and sat on the edge of the bed.

Doc touched her shoulder. "If you need me, I'll be right outside the door."

When the door was shut, Pearl opened the first envelope and took out the only page. She stared at Ronnie's uncharacteristically sloppy handwriting, and then ran her fingers lightly over the ink smears and some faded brownish stains. She said a prayer for strength and began to read:

Dear Pearl—

I'd say I'm sorry, but I'd be lying. I'm not sorry. It's just that I'm so beat up and tired. So I guess I'm only writing to ask you to forgive me. Saying you're sorry and asking for forgiveness are two different things, at least I think they are.

Ronnie is my sugar boy. Ha ha! Remember that? Sorry I'm a little drunk. Sure wish I had a baby ruth instead of all this. Now what was I saying? Oh yes. I always meant to tell you something, Pearl. You were my North Star. When I got lost I always looked for you to guide me back and you always did. I know we both took broken roads in our lives. Not broken really—just roads all those so-called respectable folks would never take. And our broken roads took us into a big dry desert and our only sin was that we got too thirsty. So I reached for a drink. And you reached for the wrong thing too. But then you reached for Doc. And I reached for Walter, but he was my poison. He didn't mean to be and I don't blame him but see, I just can't wear that mask no matter how much people hate my real face.

The last two lines at the bottom of the page were blurred too badly to read. Pearl wiped her eyes and frantically turned it over. There was more:

...and Mama was beat up and tired too, Pearl, that's all. That's why she fell that day and let her heart go to sleep. Too much sorrow. She worked so hard all her life to protect us from Victor. From ourselves. And then she lost David. Poor Mama. So now it's my turn to go hold her in my arms forever so she can be safe from this damn mean world.

Pearl, I want to thank you for loving the real me. You never made me wear a mask and I love you

*for that. So please forgive me and <u>please</u> don't go
back to that poison. I want you to take all that love
you gave to me and give it to Doc and the kids.*

*I only have one thing I can give you in return.
You can finally stop worrying about me. I'm not sad
anymore, Pearl! I'm going to Mama now.*

Pearl saw the page shaking in her hand, but she couldn't put it
down. She read it again, hearing Ronnie's voice in each line.

She jumped when she heard Doc's voice from outside the
door. "Pearl? You okay?"

"Yes... I'm okay. Give me—a few more minutes."

She took a deep breath before opening the second envelope,
then pulled out the official document titled "Death Certificate." Her
eyes moved quickly over the vital statistics: name, height, weight,
date of birth, date of death, but froze on the section she feared most.

Cause of Death: Suicide.

She squeezed her eyes shut and began breathing in a quick,
shallow rhythm. It took several seconds before she could force herself to read the rest:

Secondary conditions leading to death:
(1) extremely high blood alcohol level;
(2) consumption of 20 Nembutal capsules
(100 mgs).
Primary condition leading to death:
*Massive internal bleeding resulting from
consumption of fifteen...*

The final two words blazed into her eyes:

...razor blades.

She didn't even realize she was screaming until she felt Doc
grabbing her, rocking her in his arms, holding her, shaking her, and
shouting repeatedly into her ear.

"Pearl! I'm here! Look at me... I'm right here!...Pearl?...Pearl?
I'm right here, Pearl!"

PART THREE

1949 - 1952

Nine of the Hollywood Ten are sent to Federal Prison for refusal to implicate friends and associates when questioned by the House Un-American Activities Committee.

Protesters disrupt a Paul Robeson concert in Peekskill, New York, spewing racial epithets and attacking attendees, including Woodie Guthrie, Pete Seeger, and World War One veteran Eugene Bullard.

Ralph Bunche becomes the first Negro recipient of the Nobel Peace Prize.

Birdland opens in New York City.

CHAPTER 23

Pearl opened the apartment door and stuck her head out. "Edward! Where are you? Supper's ready. Come in here and wash your hands, baby."

"He's in here," Rose called from across the hall.

"Hi, Rose," Pearl said. "He ain't botherin' you, is he?"

Both women were standing in their doorways laughing as Edward scampered across the hall from one apartment to the other.

"Oh, no, honey," Rose said. "He was helpin' me fold clothes."

Pearl laughed. "Oh, Lord. Big help, huh?"

"He ain't no trouble, girl. Go ahead and tend to your supper 'fore it gets cold."

"Come on over, Rose. I made spaghetti."

"Ain't you got enough mouths to feed?"

"I made garlic bread, your favorite."

"Oh, Lord, Pearl. You know I can't resist your garlic bread. I'll be over in five minutes."

Pearl chuckled and went back inside. "You washin' those hands, Edward?"

"They ain't dirty!" he called.

"Hey!" Doc barked from the bedroom. "You do what your Mama tells you, boy!"

The bathroom faucet squeaked on.

"Yes, sir!" Edward called. "I'm washin' 'em... But they ain't dirty!"

"They're always dirty! And stop saying ain't!"

Pearl walked into the bedroom to wake Shay, who was sprawled in the middle of her parents' bed sound asleep. "Wake up, baby. Time for supper."

Shay squirmed, but didn't open her eyes.

Doc grinned at her from the mirror. When he finished adjusting the knot in his necktie, he tiptoed to the bed and began tickling her.

"No, Daddy!" she screeched.

Pearl sighed. "Well, there went my left eardrum."

Doc hoisted Shay up over his head and carried her into the kitchen, then stopped and glanced at Pearl. "She need to wash her hands too?"

"No, sugah. I gave her a bath before her nap."

Doc made a loud airplane noise as he swung Shay into the high chair. Edward ran in and grabbed his legs. "Me too! I wanna be a hair-pane!"

"Not a hair-pane, boy," Doc laughed. "I told you it's called an airplane!"

"Pick me up!" Edward yelled.

"Say it first. Airplane."

"Hair-pane!"

Doc flipped him up over his shoulder, barely missing the overhead light fixture.

Pearl shook her head as she sidestepped the acrobatics, and then began filling the first bowl. "You got time to eat sump'm before you go, baby?"

"Naw, I'm late."

"But you got time to romp around with these two little miscreants, huh?"

"I ain't no miss-grunt, Mama!" Edward laughed. "I'm a hair-pane!"

Doc slid Edward into his chair. "Aaaand a perfect landing at LaGuardia Hair-port!"

"Okay, now, settle down and eat your supper," Pearl said.

Doc straightened his tie and glanced at his watch. "Oh, hell, I really *am* late. Everybody give Daddy a kiss before he goes out into the wicked streets of New York."

After the kissing was done, Pearl walked him to the door. "You sure you got this gig?"

Doc grinned. "These cats think I'm the most! The glory-hallelujah second coming!"

"That's right, Superman," she said dryly. "Keep 'em in the dark about your true identity."

* * *

After supper, Rose stood up and stretched. "I bet I gained ten pounds tonight, Pearl. I wish I didn't like your garlic bread so much."

"It's the cheese sprinkles," Pearl said as she wiped spaghetti sauce from Shay's face.

Shay giggled and Pearl nuzzled her cheek. "Look at you, little messy girl! I don't know what I was thinkin' givin' you a bath before supper. Especially spaghetti! Now you got an orange face and orange arms and I'm gonna have to give you another bath! And you're lookin' pretty orange too, Edward. Come on in the bathroom. I'm throwin' you both in the tub. Hey, Rose? I'll be back in a few minutes to make the coffee."

"Need some help in there?"

"No, I can handle 'em."

Rose started stacking the plates. "I'll start washin' these dishes then."

"No argument from me," Pearl called over her shoulder.

Rose was nearly finished rinsing the last plate when someone knocked on the door. "You expectin' company, Pearl?" she called.

"No, but whoever it is, tell 'em I'll be right there."

Rose opened the door to a tall, well-built man who looked Puerto Rican. He was wearing black trousers and a dark gray shirt, with no necktie. He looked hard, but youthful, despite the gray streaks in his straight, black hair. His face was smooth and brown, and his eyes were black.

Rose was staring at him wordlessly as Pearl walked up behind her.

"Oh, hi, sugah! Rose, this is Rico. Rico, this is our neighbor Rose."

Rico nodded his head. "Hello, ma'am."

"Nice to meet'cha, uh, Rico," Rose stammered.

Pearl opened the door wider. "Doc's at the club tonight, Rico, but you're welcome to come in and have some coffee with me and Rose."

Rico shook his head and took a step back. "I'll come back to-morrow. But thank you."

"I'll tell Doc you dropped by."

"Thank you. Good night."

Pearl shut the door and went to the kitchen. "Let me get this coffee started, Rose."

Rose hurried after her. "The hell with some coffee, Pearl! *Who* in the world was that scary lookin' fella?"

Pearl smiled. "I told you. His name's Rico and he's a good friend of Doc's."

"He looks dangerous. Is he a musician?"

"No, they grew up together. They're like brothers."

"If you say so. But I don't mind tellin' you, he scared the livin' daylights out'a me!"

Pearl pulled a strand of hair away from her face and turned on the burner under the coffee pot. "Rico got into some trouble when he was a teenager and he ended up in prison. He just got out a few weeks ago, and he's still tryin' to adjust. But he'd lay down his life for Doc."

Rose's eyes widened. "Prison! Lord, no wonder he looked so scary."

"Well, I guess fifteen years in prison does things to a man. I imagine it's still hard for him to remember to smile."

"Fifteen years? Any idea what he did?"

Pearl sighed. "Okay, Rose. I know I can trust you not to repeat this... He killed a man, okay? But from what Doc told me, he was protecting somebody and it was justified. He said that the man needed killing. There were a lot of other details, but the judge didn't want to hear 'em, and all Rico had was a Public Defender. He had a juvenile record for assault, but fighting was the only way to survive in those streets. It could'a been Doc that ended up in prison if he hadn't gone back to school and started playin' music. He told me a lot more, but you get the general idea."

Rose sat down as Pearl put the cups on the table. "Has he ever been in the apartment?"

"Of course! Doc finally got him to come to supper last week. I knocked on your door, but I think you had choir practice that night or sump'm."

"Well, don't get me wrong, Pearl. You know my husband was on the wrong side of the law sometimes, but there's just sump'm real scary about this fella. And he *is* a killer."

Pearl lit a cigarette and sighed. "Rico doesn't scare me, Rose. I watch people, and all I saw that night was how nervous he was.

That's why he wouldn't come in tonight to have coffee. He wouldn't know what in the world to say to you and me, 'specially without Doc around. But you should'a seen him playin' with the kids—"

"He played with the kids?"

"He sure did. As a matter of fact, that's the only time I saw him smile that night. And he was so gentle with Shay, you would'a thought she was made of glass."

Rose sighed. "Well, maybe he'll settle down with some nice girl and have some kids of his own. I guess he'd be a good-lookin' fella—if he wasn't so doggone scary."

Pearl laughed. "Coffee's ready, Rose."

* * *

Pearl was in the tub when Doc got home that night. He tapped on the bathroom door.

"I'm home, baby."

"Come in, sugah. You're just in time to scrub my back."

Doc walked in and grinned as he began rolling up his sleeves. "With pleasure."

Pearl handed him a soapy washcloth and leaned forward. "So how did it go?"

Doc knelt on one knee and made slow circles on her back with the washcloth. "These are some very good musicians, Pearl. Good groove—right from note one."

"Okay, so let's get the comedy questions out of the way. How many of 'em are crazy?"

Doc chuckled. "All of 'em. Zoot-suits, porkpie hats, and everybody slingin' the latest, silliest slang. They all want to be Dizzy Gillespie."

"Lord...."

"Hey, they're younger than me. Hell, everybody's younger than me these days."

"Especially me," Pearl said, leaning back in the tub. "Okay, so gimme a cigarette and tell me some more about these Zoot-suit-wearin' characters."

Doc dried off his hands and lit two cigarettes, placing one in her mouth. "That'd take all night. But there's one kid, the singer.

He's one'a those country boys from the south, tryin' to act hip with no success whatsoever. There's sump'm strange about him."

"Strange, huh? Thought we covered that part."

"Guess we did."

"Is it another white band?"

"Well, semi-white. The drummer's Italian, there's a couple'a Jewish cats, and the sax player's a Mexican from East L.A. He's got a *real* nice style with that Latin jazz."

"So you're the only colored fella in the whole band?"

After a long pause Doc said, "Yeah... I guess so."

"Well, now, that's a strange answer, but I'll let it stand 'cause I want to get to my last question. And you know this is always my favorite part. *What* is the name of this band?"

"They didn't have a name, but by the end of the night I came up with one. And they loved it. It has sump'm to do with this sopping wet shirt and my jacket which is hanging on a kitchen chair, by the way. The rehearsal hall these cats use is a goddamn incinerator!"

Pearl laughed out a puff of smoke. "So your name for the band is Incinerator? Or *The* Incinerators?"

Doc scooped up a handful of water and splashed her. "No, wise-ass. It's Beat the Heat."

Pearl rolled her eyes. "The Incinerators would'a been better... Oh! I nearly forgot to tell you. Rico came by lookin' for you."

"Did he say why?"

"Of course not. I asked him in for coffee with Rose and me, but you know he wouldn't."

Doc chuckled. "Rose was here? What did she think of him?"

"He scared the hell out of her!"

"I didn't think anything could scare Rose! Hey, when are you gettin' out of that tub? I'd like to discuss some possibilities for the rest of the evening."

"Hand me a towel, sugah. And when I get dried off, I will meet you in the bedroom and consider your offer."

* * *

Beat the Heat landed a limited engagement at a club called Café Nocturne. After a few weeks, they had begun to draw such a good following that the manager hired them as a house band. Doc called Pearl to tell her that he was bringing everyone over to celebrate.

"I thought it was just gonna be a little jam session, sugah," Pearl said. "All I made was enchiladas and pie. I don't even have any beer. All I got in the house is Kool-Aid."

"Don't worry. We took up a collection and we'll be bringing some beer."

Pearl laughed. "What about your friend, Johnnie Red?"

"You know I try not to drink hard liquor at home anymore around the kids. I'll drink beer with the amateurs."

"Okay, sugah. But don't forget to bring ice. Nothin' worse than hot beer."

"Yes, ma'am... Hey, Pearl?"

"Yes?"

"A house-band gig, baby! What you always wanted! And the club owner loves us."

"I will give you a proper thank-you the minute you get here."

"I like the sound of that! But not in front of the fellas."

"No. That would be an *improper* thank-you."

Doc laughed. "We'll be there in about an hour. Keep everything hot. Especially that improper thank-you."

By the time Doc arrived with the band and opened the front door, the house smelled delicious. When Pearl walked over to meet everyone, he smiled at the band members' reactions.

"Hi, baby," she said, reaching up for a kiss.

"This is my wife Pearl."

"Hi, fellas," Pearl said.

A tall man with longish dark-hair and a wide smile reached for her hand. "Nice to meet you, Pearl. I'm King. I'm the drummer."

"Hey," Doc said, "this is your usual duty anyway, so go ahead and introduce the band!"

Without hesitation, King went into his stage routine and began pulling each man into the room. "On piano—the cat who writes the most frantic charts on planet earth—Zig Ziegler! Applause, applause,

applause! And on bass—diggin' down to the deepest depths and gracing us with the greatest grooves—Reet Ritenour! Applause, applause, applause! On sax—straight out'a East L.A., bringin' the latest Latin jazz to the Nocturne—Oliver Mendoza, the Mexican sax master! Hey! Where the hell's Oliver, man?... Oh, well. Anyway, applause, applause, applause! On vocals—luring the ladies with all those lascivious lyrics —our resident crooner Joe Bluestone! Applause, applause, applause. And swoon, swoon, swoon... Aaaaand, here's where I do a real long drumroll... Last but not least—on trumpet—"

"Aww, lounge, man," Doc said dryly. "Me she's met. And gimme a nail."

Pearl chuckled. "Applause, applause, applause."

As the room filled with people, Edward ran over and Shay toddled up behind him.

Pearl picked her up and glanced back at someone coming through the door carrying two heavy looking grocery bags.

"Is that the beer?" she asked.

"Sure is. I'm Oliver, by the way. As usual, nobody introduced the Mexican!" he called.

"Yes, he did," Doc shouted back. "The whole damn Mexican sax master routine."

"Hi, Oliver," Pearl said. "I'll show you where the kitchen is. Wait right here a second while I put this baby in her playpen."

By the time Oliver and Pearl had all the beer on ice, a din of loud conversation had erupted in the living room, and someone was pounding on the old upright piano.

"*¡Hijolé!*" Oliver groaned. "I sure hope that's not Zig playin' in there! If it is, he ain't gettin' none'a this beer, 'cause he's drunk enough!"

Pearl laughed. "That's my son playin' that solo. I'm sure Zig plays much better."

Oliver shrugged. "He has his moments."

Pearl gave Oliver a friendly push toward the kitchen door. "Then *please* go recruit him, and when you get back, I'll have a plate ready for you."

Oliver grinned. "I smelled those enchiladas. I'll be *right* back!"

As Pearl took the enchiladas out of the oven, Rose stepped into the kitchen. "Need help?"

"Oh, Lord, yes, girl!" Pearl said.

"You feelin' okay, honey?" Rose said. "You lookin' a little tired."

"I'm fine, sugah." Pearl said, then quickly changed the subject. "Girl, I thought Doc said there were only six band members, but that sounds like about ninety-six out there!"

"Well, Marion and her husband are here, and a couple'a folks from downstairs. Even old Mr. Sanders is out there havin' a good time. Oh, and I just saw Doc's friend Rico. He's standin' by the front door, not talkin' to nobody."

"I told you he doesn't talk much, Rose."

"Maybe I ought'a take him a beer or sump'm," Rose said.

"Rico doesn't drink. Why don't you take him a plate, Rose? He's probably gonna be standin' right by that door all night."

Rose reached for a plate. "Guess I ought'a make friends with him."

As she carried Rico's plate down the hallway, the sound of the piano changed suddenly. Edward had been replaced by a much more skilled pianist. Oliver walked in, followed by a line of hungry looking musicians, and Pearl began serving the enchiladas.

"Thank you, Mrs. Calhoun," Oliver said.

"You just call me Pearl. And that was my friend Rose you just passed. When she gets back, she's in charge of the beer."

Doc walked in and grinned. "Manfred just got here with his drums," he shouted.

"Oh, Lord. Somebody's gonna call the law!"

"No, they won't, 'cause I'm pretty sure the whole block's in our living room. Hey! Any of those enchiladas for me?"

Pearl smiled and handed him a plate and a fork.

"Thanks, baby," he said, leaning down for a kiss.

Pearl leaned her head back and Doc gave her a long kiss on the neck.

She closed her eyes, and when she opened them she saw the white singer staring intently at her. It took her a moment to remember his name. Joe something. Some strange last name.

Oliver let out an ecstatic yelp. "Hey, Pearl! You sure you ain't from Guadalajara, baby? These enchiladas are the most!"

At that moment, a chaotic clash of instruments began to develop into a sparse version of " 'Round Midnight."

"Goddamn!" Doc called. "Help is on the way!"

All the musicians in the kitchen abandoned their enchiladas and filed down the hallway for their instruments. The jam session had officially begun.

The rest of the night was a continuation of music, noisy conversation, eating, and drinking. Pearl managed to slip away to put the children to sleep, and then found her way over to Doc's side in the living room doorway. "Baby, why does that singer keep starin' at me?"

Doc grinned and nuzzled her ear. "He's got eyes for you, baby, that's all."

"Well, his girlfriend's givin' me a very different kind'a look. That *is* his girlfriend, isn't it? That terrified lookin' dishwater blonde sittin' over there by herself?"

Doc chuckled. "Her name's Elsie. Be nice."

"Sorry, sugah. I just don't like it, that's all."

"If Joe's gettin' out'a line I'll take his youngster ass outside."

"Oh, he's not botherin' me as much as her. She acts like somebody dragged her up here against her will and forced her to socialize with Negroes."

Doc kissed Pearl's head. "I'll get Joe straightened out next time I get him alone."

Pearl settled against his chest for a moment, and then he nudged her toward the piano. "Hey. Why don't you sing tonight, Pearl? Just this once."

She hesitated for a moment, but finally walked over to the piano. As she sang "God Bless the Child," she gazed at Doc and tried to ignore that vague, ominous vision that sometimes flickered in the back corner of her mind.

CHAPTER 24

Pearl had not visited Perry for a week, and she knew that Rose was aware of it. This long abstinence from heroin could be the beginning of a full withdrawal, but Pearl was not ready to go through the horror that Doc had put her through after Melvin's death. She was already sick every morning, and she could no longer sleep at night.

She couldn't leave the apartment without Rose questioning her, and she couldn't leave the children alone. Her only chance was to wait for Doc to come home very tired one night. Once he was asleep, she could slip out. But she had let two nights pass without making the decision.

Her usual routine was to wait up for him in bed, reading a book. On Tuesday night, she took her bath, got into bed, and opened an old Raymond Chandler mystery. She licked her lips and took a swallow of water from the glass on the bedside table, then dabbed at the perspiration on her forehead. For several minutes her eyes followed the words without reading them. One line. Then the same line again. A paragraph. A page. Then, slowly, the book closed itself. She watched her hand shake as she turned off the lamp. In the darkness of the room, and the deeper darkness of her mind, she saw that formless, flickering image that she could never quite identify.

When she heard the click of the front door unlocking, she felt her eyes close.

Doc was moving quietly through the room, trying not to wake her. She waited for him to go into the bathroom and start his shower. The decision was making itself.

* * *

It was cold outside, and no one was around at half-past three in the morning. Pearl felt like a ghost drifting along 125th Street to the subway. She hurried down the steps for a short ride. When she got to her stop, it was only a two-block walk to 143rd Street. It seemed endless, and she couldn't stop licking her chapped lips in anticipation.

Finally, she reached Perry's building and counted the stairs as she climbed. She felt no guilt. The decision was making itself.

When she got to Perry's apartment, she watched her hand knock on the door. He didn't answer right away so she knocked again. It was late. He was probably asleep.

It wasn't until she felt the soreness of her knuckles that she realized how long and hard she had been knocking. Then she heard a door opening across the hall, and saw one of Perry's neighbors scowling at her over the chain lock.

"He don't live there no more. So get on away from here!"

"Wait! Can you—can you please tell me where he went?"

"Jail! Where you ought'a be!"

Pearl stood there for a long time after the man relocked his door. A small internal voice told her to go back home, but she knew she couldn't.

She walked downstairs and stared out into the street. If she waited, something would happen. Something had to happen. A car passed, stirring up a blast of cold wind. She waited.

Then she felt a hand touch her shoulder.

"Hey, pretty lady," a man's voice said. "You been up there lookin' for Perry?"

"Yes, I need to—talk to him." She took a step back. The man was standing too close.

He rubbed his chin. "Yeah... Shee-it... Some shumbish informed on him, tryin' to get his own damn self out some hot water. Perry gon' be in jail... long time—leas' five years."

Pearl felt the wetness of tears on her face and wondered if they were for Perry or herself.

"Ya know what, lady? You need to go where I jush been."

Pearl looked up at him. He was brown and burly, like a big bear, and his gray shaggy hair was sticking out the bottom of his battered knit cap. His happy heroin smile made her think of Leonard until she looked at his eyes. They looked hungry, in a sexual way, and they were roaming up and down her body. She took another step back.

"Where?" she whispered.

He reached for her hand. "Lemme take ya, baby."

Pearl recoiled from his touch. "Can you just point? I—I can find it."

The man shrugged. "See dat diner on'a corner?" he said pointing down the street. "Ain't no street sign, so jush turn left at dat diner. Ish'a only yella buildin'. Ash for Margaret. But'cha better hurry. She was fixin' to leave when I finished up."

Pearl was already walking toward the street with no sign. "Thanks," she called over her shoulder. Then she began to run. The decision had made itself.

A dim yellow bulb was burning in the tight entryway of number 441¼. Pearl watched her hand knock on the yellow door. The night wind had turned icy, but she could feel perspiration rolling down her back. The door opened and a brown-skinned woman of indeterminate age gazed at her with a perceptive smile. "Come on in, baby," she said in a slow legato. "I'm Margaret. Take off your coat."

Pearl walked into the narrow segment of the fourplex. Her eyes darted around at the confined space, and she knew that this building, like so many other Harlem properties, had once been a duplex before the property owners had subdivided it. As she took off her coat, she gazed at the tattered maroon rug on the floor and the long curved sofa with faded green upholstery. On the opposite wall was a long sideboard with no dishes on it. The whole room was bathed in a dim pink light that glowed from an old chipped Victorian lamp. At the far end of the room was a door that led into darkness. She stared at that dark doorway until Margaret's voice made her jump.

"Who told you 'bout the quarter house, baby?"

Pearl was shivering and scratching her arm. "The... 'scuse me... the what?"

Margaret laughed dryly. "That's what they call my place. On account'a the address."

Pearl wanted to scream at her to hurry up, but she just crossed her arms and bit her lip.

Margaret smiled and handed her a length of hot-water-bottle hose. "You sick, baby?"

"Yeah."

"Sit down right there on the sofa, baby."

Pearl sat down and tied off her left arm. "Do you—do you call everybody baby?"

"Mm-hmm. 'Cause ain't no names here."

She went to the sideboard and began preparing Pearl's dose. "You got twenty, baby?"

"Twenty? Perry only asked for ten…."

Margaret laughed again. "This is the Hydra, baby. It's worth it. You'll see."

Pearl felt like crying as she rummaged through her pocketbook. "I only got fifteen…."

"Well, since you a new customer, Margaret'll give ya a little discount."

She took the money and stuffed it down the front of her blouse. Then she sat next to Pearl and held up the needle. "You want me to do you, baby? Or you want to do yourself?"

Pearl wondered why Margaret's smile frightened her, but only said, "I can do it myself."

An artful look of concern crossed Margaret's face. "You shakin', baby. You sure you don't want Margaret to do you?"

Pearl licked her lips and reached for the hypo. "No… S'okay."

Margaret pulled it back and smiled. "This be a might stronger than most of the stuff out there, so I cut it just a little. Here ya go, baby."

Pearl grabbed it, unable to wait another second. Leaning her head down, she fought to keep her hand from shaking. After a couple of unsuccessful sticks, she found a cooperative vein and the needle slipped in. When she felt the hit, she looked up at Margaret and gasped.

Margaret smiled.

Pearl barely managed to tug off the hot-water-bottle hose before she felt herself falling. It was not the gentle fall she'd always experienced with Perry's heroin. This was a high-velocity drop into an endless abyss. And all the way down were convulsions of sexual pleasure twisted by an undercurrent of terror. Pearl felt her head hit the sofa, and her back arched involuntarily. Her eyes snapped open and she heard herself moan. One second, she saw Margaret sitting next to her. Then, in an eye-blink, she saw her standing in that dark doorway across the room. She was saying something, but her words sounded like scratchy radio static or fingernails on a chalkboard.

"How you like it, baby?"

As Pearl's body continued to convulse, all she could do was curl into a tight fetal position and ride out each tremor surging through her body, one after another, after another, over and over and over again. Her eyes rolled back in her head until she saw that flicker in the back corner of her mind. And the flicker became sound. It was laughter.

* * *

"Daddy?"

Doc heard the distant voice, but couldn't lift his head from the table for a moment. Then he felt a small hand touching his shoulder. His eyes opened and he blinked until Edward's face came into view. He sat up quickly. "Oh, hi, son," he mumbled.

"Where's Mama?" Edward asked softly.

"Oh, she probably just ran downstairs for a minute."

"How come you sleepin' in the kitchen, Daddy?"

Doc stood up and patted Edward's head. "Well, I didn't plan to. I was, uh, havin' a snack and I guess I just fell asleep." He quickly snatched his empty scotch bottle from the table and tossed it into the trash. "You want some breakfast?"

Edward nodded. "Cereal, please!"

"Okay, cereal. Comin' up."

"Shay wants some cereal too, Daddy. She's still in bed though."

Doc walked into the children's room and saw Shay sitting quietly in the center of her bed, wide awake and smiling at him.

"There's my baby girl!" he said as he lifted her out. "Uh-oh... Somebody wet the bed. Guess I should've put a diaper on you last night, huh?"

"Nuh-uh. I go potty now. I big girl."

"I know. Okay, big girl. Let's get you a bath and put some clean clothes on you."

"I go potty first, Daddy."

"By all means." Then he gave her several growling nuzzles until she giggled. As he carried her into the bathroom, he heard the front door open. He placed Shay on her training toilet. "Okay, you potty and Daddy's gonna be right back to give you a bath."

When he walked into the front room, Pearl was leaning against the door, staring at him. The circles under her eyes were so deep and pronounced, she looked as though she'd been beaten. "What happened to you, Pearl?"

"Been almost a week, sugah," she mumbled. "Couldn't wait no more... You mad?"

Doc hesitated briefly, then walked over and put his arms around her. "I was worried."

"M'sorry. I didn't mean to worry you. I—I fell asleep or sump'm. Woke up on the floor."

"Where was Perry?"

"In his room, I guess. Nobody wuzh there but me. I guess—I guess he went to bed."

"Look at me, Pearl. You promised me you'd always come home after. You need to quit."

She looked up and smiled weakly "I was tryin', sugah. It was almos'—almos' a week...."

"Pearl. I woke up and you were gone. You can't just... You should've told me, at least."

"I know. But I knew you'd try to talk me out of it."

"We were supposed to go to Joe's wedding today."

"Oh... M'sorry. Must'a forgot. When we need to be there?"

Doc gazed into her glassy eyes. "In about an hour. And you're not in any shape to go. I'll just call and tell him we can't make it."

"No, sugah. You go on ahead. Joe really wants you there."

Edward ran into the room and hugged Pearl around the legs. "Hi, Mama!"

"Hiiii, sugah!"

"We'll talk about it later," Doc said softly. "Can you fix him some cereal while I give Shay a bath? She wet the bed."

As Edward pulled her by the hand into the kitchen, Pearl smiled crookedly at Doc over her shoulder. "M'okay now, sugah. M'straight."

Doc stood there until they disappeared into the kitchen. Then he slipped out the front door and hurried across the hall to Rose's apartment.

There was something about Rose Norwood that was both comforting and empowering. She was a full-figured woman with a strong bearing, and she was nearly as tall as Doc. Her skin was the color and texture of dark chocolate, and her eyes were a lighter shade of brown. She was in her late forties, with gray-streaked hair that was usually wrapped around a headful of curlers, and she had a great sense of humor. It was her smile that made her beautiful; it was a "Mama" smile. Over the years Doc had learned that Rose was loyal, did not gossip about anyone, and was a quiet, considerate listener. She was the only one who knew about Pearl's off-and-on struggle with heroin addiction, and gladly took on the dual role of supporter and lecturer. Rose had lost her husband to heroin years earlier, so she knew all the pitfalls and all the signs. Through it all, she defended Pearl like a lioness, and Doc adored her. And now he needed her again. Just as he was about to knock, he felt a pang of guilt. The truth was that he didn't need her; he needed to escape for a while. He hated seeing Pearl in the condition she was in.

He knocked softly and felt better the instant she opened the door. He tried to smile at her, knowing that she would see right through it, which she did.

"What's wrong, Doc?"

"Rose, I'm really sorry to bother you with this, but could you—"

Rose nodded. "How bad is she?"

"Not too bad now. I just don't want to leave her alone with the kids. We were supposed to go to a wedding today."

"That's right. She told me about that weddin'."

"Well, she can't go in the shape she's in. Look, maybe I should just stay home."

Rose sighed. "We done talked about this. I'm here for those kids anytime you need me."

"I know, Rose, but I get tired of always asking for your help. Especially after that last long road trip—"

"I know. That was tough, and she got away from me more than a couple'a times while you were gone. But I got her right back on track, and those kids didn't miss a meal or a bath. You gotta remember, she's fightin' a battle she can't fight by herself. And she's gonna be fightin' it for her whole life. That's why she needs us. We are a team. Don't you forget that."

"I won't forget. And thank you, Rose."

"Oh, please. I love Pearl. Ain't no judgment here. I'll just stop by for some coffee and stay till she's okay. I ain't got a thing to do today, 'cept clean the house. And I can sho' drag myself away from that! Now you go on back and I'll be there in a minute."

Doc pulled her into his arms for a hug. "Rose—"

"Aw, hush now! Go on! I'll be there in a minute."

When he got back to the apartment, Pearl was standing in the kitchen doorway smoking a cigarette and staring at him. "I can take care of my kids, Doc Calhoun. You ain't got to run to Rose every time."

"Rose is family, Pearl. Just let her help, okay?"

Before Pearl could answer, Shay came running into the living room squealing, "Daddee!" She had managed to pull off every stitch of clothing, and was peeking out from under a towel she had draped over her head. "I nekkid for my bath, Daddy!"

Doc laughed. "I see that!" He wrapped her up in the towel and carried her to the bathroom door, but stopped to look back at Pearl. "What's it gonna take for you to quit?"

She gazed at him with a weak smile. "I'm cuttin' back. I really am... Now you g'on get ready for that wedding, sugah. Tell 'em I'm sorry, and... I really want to meet Magda. Be sure and tell her that, okay? And t-tell Joe m'glad he didn't marry that uppity blond girl... Well, ya ain't gotta tell him that, I guess."

* * *

Pearl did not meet Magda for nearly a month. Since Joe had left Beat the Heat to begin recording as a solo act, the band had begun to work on a project of their own. Doc was gone nearly every day for recording sessions, and performed five nights a week at Rhythm Nocturne.

During that time Rose was a constant visitor, so Pearl only managed to slip out twice to visit Margaret at the quarter house. When she returned, she was flying so high that Rose's lectures were nothing more than comedic side-shows. Pearl always apologized and promised never to go back, and did her best not to laugh in her friend's face.

The daily radio coverage of the HUAC hearings kept her mind occupied until the need for a fix came back with its usual torture. She couldn't keep from scratching her skin raw, and she perspired heavily and felt sick when she drank coffee with Rose. All the shouting and gavel pounding began swirling in her ears like a windstorm, and she jumped to her feet.

"Rose! Can't we listen to some music… or sump'm else?"

Rose looked up at her. "Sure, honey. I'll change the station."

"It's okay. I'm up. I'll do it."

She turned the radio dial until she found a jazz station. Sarah Vaughan's voice filled the kitchen:…*but that lucky old sun got nothin' to do… but roll around heaven all day….*

Then the phone jangled in the bedroom, and the sound ran a jolt through her body. She glanced quickly at Rose to see if she had noticed.

"Why are you so jumpy, Pearl?"

"I'm not jumpy," Pearl snapped. "The phone just startled me. So get off my back."

She hurried into the bedroom and picked up the receiver. "Hello?"

"Hi, baby."

"Oh… Hi, sugah. You on your way home?"

"Yeah, I'll be home soon. But I was callin' to see if you want to go with me to a little get-together at Joe's apartment tomorrow afternoon. Ever since they got back from their honeymoon, Joe's been talking about having a poker party. Just us and the band. So it's tomorrow, and I really want you to meet Magda. She's a sweet girl. Oh! Don't say anything about her leg brace. She had Polio when she was a kid or sump'm."

"I wouldn't do that, sugah. And I'd love to go. It sounds like fun."

When she hung up, she licked her lips and tried to swallow. Then she held out her hand and looked at it. She was getting the shakes.

* * *

Late the next afternoon, Pearl was still smiling from the spine-tingling aftereffects of her fix. She was standing on the sidewalk squinting up at a building when a man she didn't know stopped and asked her if she was all right.

"I'm fine, thank you," she said, trying to look sober. "Why?"

"It's just that you were standing there for quite a long time, ma'am."

"Well, I'm fine, sugah... I mean, sir."

She looked at the matchbook cover Doc had thrown at her after their fight that morning. He had scribbled Joe's address on it. She sighed and began climbing the stairs. "I don't wanna hear no lectures today, Doc Calhoun," she muttered. "I held on—long as I could, dammit."

When she reached the apartment, the door was open so she walked in. "Anybody home?"

Everyone welcomed her but Doc, who was sitting at the poker table glaring at her.

King pulled out a chair for her, and she sat down. "Hello, everybody. Hiii, Beatriz! How you been, sugah?"

Before Beatriz could answer, Doc cut in sharply, "Who's watchin' the kids, Pearl?"

The room fell silent. "The kids are okay. They been with Rose all afternoon."

"*All* afternoon?"

Pearl took her time tapping out a cigarette, and Joe quickly lit it. Without taking her eyes off Doc, she inhaled and blew out a slow mist of smoke. "All afternoon, sugah."

As everyone went back to talking and playing poker, Pearl continued to gaze defiantly at Doc. She always felt a little invincible a few hours after a fix. She relaxed into her own untouchable world until an unusual voice broke through:

"You are hungry to eat? Or you are playing da throat-cut cards with dese bums too?"

Pearl looked over at a petite girl with a sweet smile and raven-colored hair. Despite the ill-fitting apron and flour smudges on her face, she was the prettiest white girl Pearl had ever seen. She had a guileless bearing, as though she were completely unaware of her beauty. And there was something sad about her pale blue eyes. Pearl couldn't help smiling at her.

She stood up. "Oh, you must be Magda. I heard some wonderful things about you, sugah. Let's go to the kitchen and I'll help you clean up."

"Oh, no! You are guest!" Magda said.

After a few seconds of Magda's protests, Pearl managed to nudge her into the kitchen. "Lord, sugah, I sure do love the way you talk. Where are you from anyway?"

"Thessaloniki I am from."

"Thessa-Thessa... Say that again for me, sugah. I want to say it right."

"Thess-ah-low-nee-kee. Is village in Greece. I am immigrant, you see."

Pearl smiled. "I sort'a figured that, sugah. Listen, I'm sorry I missed your wedding."

"Oh, is all right, Pearl. I may call you Pearl, no?"

" 'Course you may, sugah." Pearl turned on the faucet. "I'll wash and you dry. How's that?... So tell me. How'd you meet Joe anyway?"

Magda smiled and handed Pearl the dish liquid. "In da studio. I play da violin, you see."

"That's right. Doc told me you play with one of those big studio orchestras."

"Yes. On Paul Ballantine's orchestra I play. Is very busy time for me. For Joe too."

"The life of musicians, huh, sugah? Doesn't leave much free time to run around and shop with your girlfriends, does it?"

"Run?" Magda asked with a puzzled expression. "No. I must wear dis brace from dat Polio, I'm afraid. I now walk okay, but no running for me. So… dat is what girlfriends do in New York? Run together around? For to shop?"

Pearl smiled. "I'm sorry, sugah. That didn't translate right, did it? Running around means, well, going places. Shopping with your girlfriends and things."

"Oh," Magda said, then shook her head. "No. All da time I must work, work, work. And Joe all da time is busy. When I sleep, he is awake. When he sleeps, I am awake. No girlfriends for me, I'm afraid."

"It can sure get lonely sometimes, sugah. I know."

Magda gazed at Pearl in a long silence, then looked away self-consciously. Pearl reached for a dish towel and dried her hands. "You got a pencil, sugah?"

Magda found a pencil and Pearl wrote down her phone number. "You call me anytime."

Magda smiled up at her. "For to… run around? And shop?"

"We can do all that too, but you need a girlfriend to talk to. 'Cause some things men just don't understand."

CHAPTER 25

Pearl pushed through the next week in a tense state of mental isolation. For the first time, she was truly terrified of heroin. When Melvin had injected her with her first dose, she had welcomed it as a panacea to her pain and worry. Then Perry came along.

She had been tempted to go back to Perry many times over the years, even before Ronnie and Alva had died. Even as the preacher droned his ineffectual platitudes at their funeral, it was Perry's quiet, illegal healing that she was craving.

For years it had been an off-and-on battle of need vs. guilt, until the drug danced through her veins with its reassuring rapture. But she had never been afraid—until she met Margaret.

The water was boiling on the stove, and Pearl watched her hands shaking as she dropped in the pasta. The burning pain in her abdomen was something well beyond the intense nausea she had experienced when Doc had helped her quit heroin the first time. She clutched at the pain with both fists and then ran into the bathroom and slammed the door. After she emptied the contents of her stomach, she heard Edward's voice. "Mama?"

It took her nearly a minute to stop gasping for breath. "Be out in a minute, son."

She quickly washed her face and opened the door. Edward was standing there holding his fists under his chin, and his dark eyes were round with dread. "You sick, Mama?"

Pearl stared down at him. *Oh, God. I'm scarin' my little boy to death*....

She managed a smile and ran her hand over his wooly hair. "Mamas get sick sometimes, too, sugah, that's all. I'm okay now. Come on in the kitchen and talk to me while I cook, okay?"

Edward reached for her hand and walked with her to the stove. Just as Pearl took the lid off the sauce to check it, the phone rang, startling her. She dropped the lid and gasped sharply.

"Mama?"

Pearl looked down at him and kissed his head. "It's okay, sugah. The phone just scared me. Come on with me and we'll go answer it."

Hurrying into the bedroom, Pearl picked up the receiver and sat down. Edward scrambled up and snuggled tightly against her.

"Hello?"

"Hello, Pearl. Is me, Magda."

"How are you, sugah?"

"You are okay, Pearl? You sound so terrible."

"No, I'm okay. Just rushin' from the kitchen. What—what can I do for you?"

"Well, I will come to Harlem tomorrow for to Christmas shop, if dat is okay for you?"

Pearl clutched at her midsection and nearly cried out, but smiled for Edward. "That's fine, sugah. I nearly forgot we were gonna go to Macy's. You come on by—about ten, okay?"

"I will be there, Pearl. Goodnight."

"G-night, sugah." Pearl hung up the receiver and gave Edward a shaky hug. "Magda's comin' over tomorrow, baby! Won't that be nice? She's goin' shoppin' with me, and when we get back we'll all play some games and draw pictures or sump'm. Won't that be fun?"

Edward nodded and looked up at her. "I like Magda."

"Me too, sugah." Pearl kissed the top of his head. *Oh, Lord, please help me quit....*

She spent the rest of the night riding out waves of sickness as she watched the clock.

When Doc finally got home, she was in bed, fully dressed, pretending to be asleep. Remaining still under the covers took all her effort. Her senses and every one of her nerves seemed to have turned against her, torturing her from the inside out. She had to listen closely for her opening, but listening was the worst torture of all. The sounds from the kitchen curled her hands into tight fists until she felt her fingernails cutting into her palms. The oven door squealed open as he took out the plate she'd kept warm for him. The chair scraped with an abrasive echo as he sat down to eat. The pages of the newspaper turning were like slow-motion whips whistling. A memory of her father flew through her mind.

But she hung on. She waited. And waited. And clutched her abdomen. And jerked with each loud tick of the alarm clock.

At last, Doc came into the room, quietly undressed, and headed to the bathroom. The second she heard the squeak of the faucet, Pearl threw off the covers, put on her shoes, and grabbed her pocketbook. Then she hurried out the front door.

* * *

It was nearly five in the morning when Pearl returned. She had tried to wait for the wild effects of the heroin to calm down, but a tiny sliver of reason kept urging her to go home.

When she walked into the bedroom, the lamp was on and Doc was lying on top of the covers, fully dressed. She knew what that meant. He had fallen asleep while waiting up to have it out with her. She also knew that waking him was a bad idea, but a strong physical compulsion pulled her to the bed. She quickly stripped off all her clothing and climbed in next to him.

"Make love to me, baby," she whispered, rubbing her body against his.

Doc jerked awake and pushed her away. "What the hell—?"

"Please," she moaned as she fumbled with his belt.

Doc grabbed her face and glared at her. "What kind'a shit are you on now?"

"Please, sugah… right now…."

Doc got up, snatched Pearl's robe from the back of the door, and threw it at her. "Go take a goddamn shower. A cold one! But put on your robe first in case the kids wake up."

* * *

The next morning Doc was home working on an arrangement at the piano and the children were playing in their room. Edward had been whining about being punished for rough-housing with his little sister, and Doc had not said a word to Pearl.

Once again, she found herself clock-watching, hoping that something would ease the tension. She had forgotten all about Magda's visit until she heard the sound of her heavy, uneven clomping out in the hallway. She smiled and opened the door. "Hey, sugah!"

"Good morning," Magda said, handing her a small basket of flowers.

"Thank you, sugah! Hey, no smile? Let me get you some coffee, and we'll talk about it."

Edward made a dash for the door, but Pearl intercepted him and sent him back to his room. Then she headed into the kitchen. "I just made coffee, Doc. You want some?"

"None for me, thanks. How are you doin', Magda?"

Magda shrugged and stared at the floor. "I guess I am fine."

Pearl poured the coffee and brought it in. She knew that a confrontation with Doc was coming, but Magda's visit had postponed it. Suddenly, he began playing a crazy boogie-woogie piece on the piano, apparently to cheer up Magda, and it worked. She laughed, and Pearl retreated into her own thoughts. She was still feeling the after-effects of the Hydra.

After a few minutes, she realized that Doc was saying something to her.

"Hmm? What did you say, sugah?"

"I said I'm takin' the kids out for a soda pop. You and Magda have a good time at Macy's."

"We will." Pearl walked them to the door and kissed the children, then kissed Doc. "We'll be back from Macy's in a couple'a hours or so. You kids be good for Daddy."

* * *

Doc knew that Pearl was dreading the subject of her recent strange behavior, but he wondered if she had any idea how much he dreaded bringing it up. After hours of trying to figure out a way to have a constructive conversation that didn't end in an argument, he decided to wait.

Instead, he spent the next morning at home playing with the children and talking to Pearl as though it had never happened.

Rose knocked on the door and stuck her head in. "Mornin', Pearl. Oh, hi, Doc."

Doc was giving Shay a pony ride on his shoulders, and Edward was pleading for his turn. "Hi, Rose! Hey, is that today's paper?"

"Mm-hmm. I'm finished with it and I thought Pearl might want to read the latest on those hearings we been listenin' to."

Pearl reached for the paper and Doc put Shay on the floor.

"My turn, Daddy!" Edward yelled.

"Hey! Lounge, boy! Take Shay in your room and play while grown folks visit, ya dig?"

"Yes, sir. I dig," Edward mumbled as he stomped out of the room.

"And stop pokin' out that lip, boy! Be a man."

"Yes, sir."

Shay stomped awkwardly behind Edward. "I be a man too!"

Doc laughed. "When did she start doin' that?"

"Oh, just lately," Pearl said as she gazed at the newspaper. "She watches him and then tries to copy everything he does. Po' Edward. I think she's drivin' him crazy."

"Well, that's what baby sisters are for. Someday he'll be beatin' up any boy who comes near her." Doc sighed as he settled onto the sofa next to Pearl. The newspaper was spread out on her lap, and he shook his head at the headline:

PRISON FOR DALTON TRUMBO

"Damn," he said. "There went the Constitution."

"We've seen some of his movies, sugah. There wasn't anything subversive or unpatriotic about 'em. What do you think, Rose?"

Rose sniffed contemptuously. "I think that Committee's a bunch'a devils, and I think I ought'a take the kids for a while so you two can read the paper in peace. That's what I think."

"You don't have to do that, Rose," Pearl objected.

Rose waved her hand. "Nonsense... Hey, kids," she called. "Y'all want some ice cream?"

"Rose! They just had breakfast."

Edward galloped into the room at top speed, and Shay was right behind him, hopping up and down and squealing.

"Aw, hell, it won't kill 'em," Doc laughed. "Okay, Li'l Miss Screech Horn! Kiss Daddy goodbye. You too, Edward!"

Edward was already at the front door, and had to do a speedy U-turn to run over for the kissing. Shay hopped over to the side of the sofa and kissed Doc, then Pearl.

Rose opened the door and smiled. "I'll bring 'em back in a couple of hours. But if you two get to missin' all their noise, you can come get 'em."

"No chance of that happenin', Rose," Doc laughed. "And thanks."

When the door shut, Doc watched Pearl's face as she read the front page. Her brow was furrowed and she shook her head sadly. Easing the paper out of her hand, he said, "No frowning. We got two hours to ourselves, and that depressing article can wait till later."

Pearl smiled. "We gonna have a two-hour honeymoon or sump'm?"

"Yup." He pounced on her, ravishing her neck with kisses until she laughed softly.

"Wait a minute, buster." She leaned away from him and dropped her voice to its deepest register. "All that ticklin' is fine for the kids. But you're out'a practice when it comes to a full grown woman. So all I want to know is... are you tryin' to make me giggle... or submit?"

Doc fanned his face comically. "Woo! Got warm in here, huh? But you're right. I *am* out of practice, I guess. Let me start over. Get you in the mood with some smooth conversation."

Pearl leaned back and stretched provocatively. "So what's on your mind, Casanova?"

Doc leaned so close to her face their lips nearly touched. Then he grinned. "Did you and Magda have a good time at Macy's?"

Pearl snorted a loud laugh. "*That's* your smooth conversation?"

"That's what you get for laughin' at me. But seriously, and this is only a *brief* interruption to our date... I *did* notice that Magda seemed real sad when she got here yesterday and I meant to ask you about that."

Pearl sat up and lit a cigarette. "She's havin' trouble with Joe. Po' baby."

"Already? Damn. How much trouble?"

"Let's see... He doesn't talk to her, he's gone all the time... and he's messin' around."

Doc groaned and shook his head. "Damn. Joe Bluestone is his own worst enemy."

"I was tryin' to take her mind off things, but then sump'm happened right after you and the kids left that really upset her. That's why we were gone so long. I was tryin' to cheer her up."

"What happened?"

"Well, she was helpin' me fold clothes so we could get goin' faster, and she found that lynching postcard in your bottom drawer."

"Oh, damn. I'm sure she didn't understand that at all."

"I explained it to her and tried to tell her a little about segregation, which she couldn't understand *or* pronounce. But she started catchin' on after what happened at Macy's."

"What the hell happened at Macy's?"

"Well, some of it was pretty funny, actually. There were these two white women in the elevator skinnin' up their noses at us, and—" Pearl stopped and smiled.

Doc gave her a curious look. "And?"

Pearl stood up. "Hold my cigarette, sugah. And don't smoke up the whole damn thing. Okay, I'ma have to act this out for you to get the full effect... Now, I'm Magda, see? She started mean-muggin' those heifahs." Pearl narrowed her eyes in an exaggerated scowl. "Then she says, 'I am Christmas shopping in da Macy's with my friend Pearl—who is *not* my maid, of course.' "

Doc laughed and coughed out a rush of smoke. "Where'd she get that 'maid' jazz from?"

"Oh, I was tellin' her how that's probably what they were thinkin'—that I was her maid. Lord, that really set her off! 'Is seg-gru-ration elevator or something? You never before see two friends together in da Macy's?' Sugah, I didn't know she could move so fast with that leg brace! She was hot on those heifahs' tails and hollerin'! 'You must make frowning and whispering?' "

Doc laughed. "Please tell me she caught 'em and put that brace in somebody's ass."

"No, but you're gonna love this... You ever go to Macy's and see those models they got walkin' around advertising the newest dresses and all that? Well, this one was wearin' this long evening gown, doin' the whole spiel about who the designer was, and what kind'a damn silk it is, and how you've just *got* to have one. So then—" Pearl began laughing again and couldn't finish.

"Come on, Pearl! So then what? What happened?"

"Well, she was still chasin' those heifahs and I—I guess she didn't see the model, and—"

Doc grinned and stretched out his arms. "And what?"

"And she tackled her!"

"Tackled who? The heifah or the model?"

"The model! Pow! Sugah, that model was about to hit the floor, but I caught her just in time. So I'm laughin' and trying to apologize, and what do you think Magda was doin'?"

"What?"

"Starin' at the model's damn dress, talkin' 'bout, 'I must buy dat dress, Pearl!'...Lord! I ain't laughed so much in my whole life, I don't think."

Pearl fell onto the sofa next to Doc and reclaimed her cigarette.

He smiled. "It sure is good to see you laughin'. I always knew you were good for Magda, but I think she's good for you, too... And gimme back my damn cigarette."

"It's *my* damn cigarette!" Pearl smiled and rested her head on his shoulder for a quiet moment. "I sure hope Joe and Magda can work things out. She's such a sweet girl, and she really loves him. I don't why, but she does."

"Hey!" Doc said, standing up suddenly and checking his watch. "Let Joe and Magda work out their own problems. We only have about an hour and a half before our little devils get back. *Why* aren't we in the bedroom?"

Pearl crushed the cigarette in the ashtray. "Because *you* changed the subject."

Doc grinned and lifted her in his arms. "Well, I'm changin' it back."

* * *

One night at the end of April, Pearl was smoking in the dark when Doc came home from the club. He took a seat on the edge of the bed. "No book? What's wrong? The kids okay?"

"They're fine. I was just lyin' here thinkin', that's all. There's a few cigarettes left."

"Thanks," he said, reaching for the pack on the nightstand. He lit up and smiled. "I have some good news about Magda and Joe. I think their troubles are over."

"And what would make you think that?"

"Because Joe came by the club tonight to tell us Magda's expecting a baby. He was passin' out cigars like the baby was already born! I think this might be just what he needs to settle his dumb ass down. I have a feeling they'll be okay now."

Pearl reached over him to put out her cigarette in the ashtray. "Don't be so sure," she said softly. "Magda called me today with the news about the baby too, but she sure wasn't happy about it. As a matter of fact, she was cryin' her eyes out."

1954-1956

Journalist Edward R. Murrow dedicates multiple segments of his top-rated television show *See It Now* to making the case against Senator Joseph McCarthy and the House Un-American Activities Committee.

The U.S. Supreme Court overturns the doctrine of "separate but equal" in *Brown v. Board of Education*, leading to the desegregation of America's public school system.

Emmett Till is lynched at the age of fourteen, allegedly for whistling at a white woman in Mississippi.

Singer Nat King Cole is attacked and beaten by local KKK members while performing at a theater in Birmingham, Alabama.

Paul Robeson testifies before the House Un-American Activities Committee in Washington.

We must not confuse dissent with disloyalty.
We must remember always that accusation
is not proof, and that conviction depends
upon evidence and due process of law. We
will not walk in fear, one of another.
                    ~ Edward R. Murrow

CHAPTER 26

Pearl lived for nights like this. The house was quiet and she
had a little time to herself. Rose had gone home exhausted
two hours earlier, and Doc was still at the club. She checked
on the children; they were asleep. It had been one day since her last
fix and she was feeling so close to normal that she could almost
put Margaret and the Hydra out of her mind.

After brewing a cup of tea, Pearl gathered the scattered pages of
the newspaper from the coffee table and put them back in order. Then
she curled up on the sofa and began reading page one. There were
two articles on the HUAC hearings, which she read quickly. She
smiled at the news about *Brown v. Board of Education*. A Negro lawyer named Thurgood Marshall had made a convincing case to the Supreme Court that "separate but equal" was unconstitutional. The only
thing left to do was wait for the court's decision. Then she saw an article that caused her to frown. Immigration Commissioner Joseph
Swing had implemented a massive undertaking that had rounded up
over a million Mexican migrant workers and sent them back to Mexi-
co. After reading the details of inhuman treatment and divisions of
families, the final line nearly brought her to tears: *Swing's odious
name for the action? Operation Wetback.*

She turned the pages quickly until she got to the movie page.
Her eyes froze on one of the titles. *When Worlds Collide*—an old
science fiction movie playing at the Harlem Theater.

When Worlds Collide. Reading those words took her back to a day she had tried to put out of her mind. She could hear the rain pounding on the kitchen window as she sat with Magda trying to calm her hysteria about the baby she was expecting. She was telling her that fatherhood would change Joe and make him a better man. She could still see Magda's reaction, and it still sent a rattle down her spine. There was such pain in her eyes and such loneliness in her silence, it was as though, in that moment, Magda had seen everything that would happen to her.

Pearl wiped the tears from her eyes and forced herself to stop dwelling on all the bad times and focus on her blessings. Above all, she still had her husband and her children, which now included a little boy named Nick.

She stood up and tiptoed into the children's room. Standing over Nick's bed, she could see his face in the beam of light from the hallway. He was the color of smooth milk chocolate, and the tightly-curled texture of his hair reminded her of Ronnie when he was a toddler. She leaned down and kissed him softly, then kissed Shay and Edward, and snuck back out.

She went to the kitchen and turned on the radio. The clock read 10:35 and Ella Fitzgerald was singing "Angel Eyes." Pearl sang along softly as she rolled up her sleeves to wash dishes.

She thought she heard a knock at the front door, but she wasn't expecting anyone. Then she heard it again. Drying her hands, she turned off the radio and went to the door. She left the chain lock on and opened it just enough to see who was there. A white man in a dark suit was staring at her. She recognized him, but couldn't place where or when she had met him. Then he flashed his badge, and she remembered. He was one of the FBI agents from the Red Regency. She stared at him silently, trying to remember the year. *Right after the war...1946.*

"I'm Agent Adams, Mrs. Calhoun. May I come in?"

"Why are you here?" she said in a flat tone.

"I have business with your husband. Is he home?"

"No." Pearl moved to shut the door, but Agent Adams stopped it with his hand.

"You have no business with me and I just told you my husband isn't here."

"I also have a few questions for you, Mrs. Calhoun."

"I can't imagine what questions you want to ask me."

Adams smiled. "I can ask them here, or we can go downtown. Your choice."

Pearl hesitated, but then let him in. She lit a cigarette without offering him one.

Adams walked to the center of the room and looked at her. "Have you been reading about the hearings in Washington, Mrs. Calhoun?"

Pearl saw him staring at her left arm and quickly yanked down her sleeves, hoping that he hadn't seen her track marks. "Yeah, I've been reading about 'em," she snapped. "Who hasn't?"

Adams gave her a hard, penetrating stare. "Well, then you know that the HUAC Committee isn't finished with Commie Reds like your husband just yet."

"My husband is not a Communist, so if that's your question, then I answered it. Now I'd appreciate it if you'd leave."

Agent Adams smiled. "Just give your husband a message, and this is coming straight from the top. Don't leave town."

Pearl stared at him with expressionless eyes and blew a mist of smoke directly into his face. "*Now* will you leave?"

Agent Adams leaned so close to her face his chin nearly touched her forehead. He whispered, "Tell him he's on the list." He pulled a folded booklet from his pocket and dropped it on the coffee table, then walked out.

* * *

When Pearl heard the front door opening late that night, she sat up quickly in bed. In the pale glow of the nightlight, she saw that it was Doc, and turned on the bedside lamp. She reached for her cigarettes. "You'll never believe who dropped by earlier."

Doc yawned and began unbuttoning his shirt. "Who?"

"Remember those two FBI fellas that gave you the third degree at the Red Regency?"

Doc stopped unbuttoning and stared at her. "What the hell did they want?"

"It wasn't both of 'em. Just the one with the black hair. Adams."

"You didn't let him in, did you?"

"He told me he'd take me downtown unless I let him in and answered some questions."

"Goddammit!" Doc hurried into the living room and began looking around. "Did the sonofabitch touch anything?"

Pearl pulled on her robe and followed him, then handed him the booklet. "No, but he left this for you."

Doc looked at the cover of the booklet. "*Red Channels*. Fascist propaganda rag."

"I know it. He had it folded open to a page with two names underlined—Lena Horne and Paul Robeson. Guess it's his way of lettin' you know they're targeting Negroes now."

Doc threw it across the room. "Sonofabitch! Where exactly was he standing?"

"Right about where you are now, sugah."

"Did he sit down at all?"

"No, he didn't. As a matter of fact, he was here less than five minutes."

Doc yanked open the front door and examined it, running his hand completely around the door jamb, top and sides, inside and out. Then he shut it and inspected the living room lamp.

"He didn't touch the lamp, sugah," Pearl said. "I watched his hands. He didn't plant anything. And we ain't got a thing to hide anyway."

Doc began pacing angrily. "That's not the point, Pearl," he said. "We're both United States citizens! I fought for this goddamn country, for cryin' out loud! This is our home, and that belly-crawlin' snake has got *no* right to walk through that door and treat us like criminals!"

"What do you figure he wants after all this time?" Pearl asked.

Doc stopped pacing suddenly and closed his eyes.

"What's wrong, sugah?"

"Nothin'. I was just thinking about Spain. That's all he questioned me about that night at the Regency. And he was real interested in Jimmy too... Aw, shit! He's still after Jimmy!"

"But Jimmy's dead."

"That's what I told him, but he kept pushin' it." Doc sighed and rubbed his face, then looked up. "Wait a minute. It can't be that simple...."

"What?"

"What if Adams is just one of those low-level cats angling for a promotion? He knows Jimmy was a card-carrying member of the Party. And with all this blacklist news everywhere, he *wants* to believe Jimmy's alive so he can drag him to the Committee like a trophy."

"He accused you of bein' a Communist. Maybe *you're* the trophy he's after."

Doc sighed and dropped onto the sofa. "You got another cigarette? I ran out."

Pearl sat next to him and tapped out a cigarette, lighting it off the end of her own.

Doc gazed absently into the smoke. "You know what? I brought this shit on myself."

"How you figure that, baby?"

"I visited Jimmy's mother a couple of months after Adams questioned me. I had a feeling the Party never notified her about Jimmy's death and I didn't want her wondering whether he was dead or alive for the rest of her life. So I broke the news to her. Man, that was almost as hard as watchin' him die… Anyway, after she finished crying, all she wanted to know was when it happened and how much he suffered. I told her the date and I told her he was a hero. Then I looked her right in the eyes and told her he didn't suffer. I lied about that, but I had to."

"I know," Pearl said softly. "But if they knew you visited her, why'd they wait all these years to bother you about it?"

"Because I visited her again last month. Stupid mistake."

"That's not a stupid mistake. How could you know they were still watching you?"

Doc seemed not to have heard the question. "War is not a time to feel," he said softly.

Pearl touched his hand. "What does that mean?"

He finally looked at her. "It means I shouldn't have let my guard down by gettin' emotional. But it was the anniversary of the day Jimmy died, and I'd given her that date to mourn on. She only had two sons, Jimmy and Robert, and her husband died when they were kids. Robert died in World War Two, so I knew she was all alone, and I just didn't want her to spend that day by herself."

"Well, I'm glad you went, sugah. And... that might not even be what Adams wants."

Doc shrugged. "So how long was he here? And what else did he say?"

"I told you, sugah, he was only here a few minutes. Just long enough to call you a Red and let me know you were on the *list*. And then he said you shouldn't leave town."

Doc stood up and picked up the *Red Channels* booklet from the floor. Then he took it to the kitchen and held it over the sink. Flicking up a flame on his lighter, he lit it from the bottom corner. As he and Pearl watched it burn, Doc smiled slowly. "This ain't nothin' but a game of Three-Card Monte... I've seen this trick before."

* * *

Doc had to clear his mind. He realized that he had been deluding himself about the extent of Pearl's heroin use. Lately she had been sneaking out at night, leaving him to worry, and returning in worse shape than he had ever seen her. And now he had to stay a step ahead of Agent Adams. The last thing he needed was for Adams to find out about Pearl's addiction.

After several nights of thought, Doc came to a decision. He had always felt responsible for Pearl getting hooked again, but it was time for her to quit. He had to cut off her supply, and all roads led to Perry. He considered paying him a visit with Rico to scare him, but he had no idea how to find Perry, and even if he did, Rico's temper could be a problem. Perry would definitely end up badly hurt, possibly even dead, and Rico would end up back in prison.

But there was one other possibility—a friend who occasionally ventured from lawful society into the shallow end of the drug world.

On the following Saturday night at the end of the last set, he made his decision. After placing his horn in its case and gathering his sheet music, he turned around and looked at King. "Let me buy you a drink, man," he said quietly. "Not here."

King squinted at him curiously. "Cool. Let me get my stick bag, man."

"Hey!" Oliver shouted from the bar. "Where are you *vatos* headed?"

"Home," Doc called.

"Date," King said, grinning.

"*You* got a date?" Oliver laughed. "*¡Hijolé!* The circus must be in town!"

"Hey, Oliver," Zig called from the door. "I'm headin' over to the automat. Come on. We can go over my new chart and I'll buy you a slice of that lemon pie you like, man."

"What about Reet?"

"Shit! Reet had one foot off the bandstand before we even finished the last tune, man! He's probably already home snoring. So if you're coming, come on! I'm hungry."

"G'night, you worthless *vatos*," Oliver called over his shoulder.

"I hope you choke on your pie, Oliver!" King shouted.

As soon as they were gone, he turned back to Doc. "So where to?"

"Let's jump on the subway and see where it takes us."

After a short ride, they walked around and found an after-hours bar on 43rd Street. It was quiet inside and nearly empty. King headed for the bar, but Doc caught him by the sleeve and nodded in the direction of a corner booth.

King slid into the booth across from Doc and grinned. "Okay, dig, man. I'm gonna give it to you straight. You ain't my type."

Doc scowled. "Knock it off, man. I have something serious to talk to you about."

"Okay, nix on the jokes. I had a feeling sump'm was buggin' you. You've been a little too quiet the last couple of weeks. So what's up?"

The bartender walked over. "What'll it be, guys?"

"Regular?" Doc asked King.

King nodded. "Cool."

"Pint bottle of Johnnie Red and two glasses," Doc said to the bartender. "No ice."

"Comin' up."

When the bartender came back with the bottle, Doc paid him. "Thanks, buddy."

"Okay," King said, "so what's goin' on?"

"All right. I know you clown around a lot and all, but my instincts tell me that you can keep a confidence. I hope I'm right."

King's whole expression changed. "You can trust your instincts. So talk."

Doc tapped out a cigarette and tossed it to him. "You know a dealer named Perry?"

King pulled out his lighter and lit the cigarette. "Yup. Negro cat from Harlem. Heroin dealer. Deaf mute or sump'm."

"Mute, not deaf. But that's the cat. Do you know where he lives?"

"Last I heard, he got pinched, man. About a year ago."

"Naw, that can't be right...."

"I'm tellin' you, man. He's in jail. Cat I know at one of the opium dens messes with smack sometimes—you *know* I don't. He was broadcasting the news about Perry about a year ago. That cat's still upstate doin' a nickel."

Doc lit a cigarette for himself and stared into the smoke.

After a long silence, King said, "Hey... You ain't usin', are you?"

Doc closed his eyes and shook his head slowly. "Not me... A friend."

"So, what's this about? Your friend get hold of some bad shit or sump'm?"

"You sure I can trust you?"

"Come on, Doc. Even if you weren't the greatest horn player on earth, which I think you *are*, you're also one of the most forthright cats I know. I'd take a bullet for you, man."

Doc smiled. "Not necessary, but thanks. All right... It's Pearl. Pearl's hooked, and I gotta find a way to help her."

King leaned back in the booth and let out a hard sigh. "Aw, shit, not Pearl. Aw, man... Look, whatever I can do, you just name it. Have you tried following her?"

"Of course I have. But she can be real devious when that jones hits her. She never goes when I'm around. She knows I'll stop her."

"So she knows that *you* know... Damn." King drummed his fingers on the table and stared at Doc for a moment. "What about a doctor? They got a treatment that weans 'em off."

"Yeah, I already looked into that. But you know how the city's been cracking down on doctors doin' that sort of thing. Three cats I know tried to sneak off to one of those clinics and ended up in prison hospitals."

"Well, then, what's the answer?"

"First thing I gotta do is cut off her supply. Then I've got to help her kick."

"Do you think she *can*?"

Doc took a drink and swallowed it slowly. "She did once... long time ago, but she nearly died. I didn't know what the hell I was doin', man, and I tried to get her to cold-kick. Maybe this time—we can try a more gradual approach."

After a long silence, King said, "Doc, *what* can I do to help? Name it. I'll do anything."

"Well, I thought you might be able to help me find Perry, but since he's in jail, that changes everything. If Pearl's not gettin' fixed up at Perry's, then she's got a new best friend."

"Goddamn, man, I hope she's not buyin' from those Sicilian dealers. Those cats scare the shit out'a me, and I'm Italian!"

Doc stared at the table. "You ever heard of a dealer named Hooper?"

King shook his head. "Don't know that name."

"Never mind," Doc said. "She'd never go to his hell-hole. As least I *hope* she wouldn't."

"Look, Doc, if it'll help Pearl, I'll follow her for you."

"No, just ask your friend at the den if he knows who's been pickin' up Perry's strays."

King nodded. "I read you, man. 'Cause Pearl sure wasn't Perry's only customer."

"Exactly."

"Okay, Let me talk to Rocky. That's my buddy at the den. Nice cat, but he does everything—opium, heroin, reefer, Bennies... I'll tell him I'm lookin' to score for a friend—see what I can find out for you."

"Thanks, man. And just—"

King held up one hand. "Stop, man. We never had this conversation."

~~~

Washington, D.C., June 12, 1956 — Controversial Negro entertainer Paul Robeson appeared before the House Un-American Activities Committee today. Mr. Robeson's disdain for the Committee was on full display, exceeding all expectations for gavel-pounding fireworks.

In an early exchange, Chief Counsel Richard Arens asked Robeson why he hadn't simply remained in the Soviet Union after a recent visit. Robeson replied, "Because my father was a slave, and my people died to build this country, and I am going to stay here, and have a part of it just like you. And no Fascist-minded people will drive me from it. Is that clear?"

Later in his testimony, Robeson accused the committee with more incendiary words: "You are responsible, and your forebears, for sixty million to one hundred million black people dying in the slave ships and on the plantations."

When asked about his association with known Communist Ben Davis, Robeson said, "I say that he is as patriotic an American as there can be, and you gentlemen belong with the Alien and Sedition Acts, and you are the non-patriots, and you are the un-Americans, and you ought to be ashamed of yourselves."

Chairman Francis E. Walter, clearly disgusted, refused to allow Robeson to read a statement he had prepared, and announced that the hearing was adjourned.

In addition to his work in the entertainment industry, Mr. Robeson was an All-American football player from Rutgers University, and holds a law degree from Columbia University.

~~~

CHAPTER 27

Each morning when Pearl looked in the mirror she could see the redness in her eyes and the dark, hollow circles under them. She tried makeup, but each time she caught Rose scrutinizing her face, she knew she wasn't fooling her. And when she came over for coffee, it turned into a pep talk or a lecture. But what annoyed Pearl the most was the timing of her visits—no more than five minutes after Doc left for rehearsal.

One Saturday when she opened the door, she did not invite Rose in, as she usually did, but remained in the doorway. "Right on time, huh, Rose? Doc just left and here you come. Look, I love you, but I do *not* need a babysitter."

She didn't realize that she was scratching her fingers and tugging at her wedding band until she saw Rose staring at her hands. She quickly folded her arms.

"Pearl, I'm tryin' to help you," Rose said quietly. "You got three kids now, two of 'em in school. How much longer you think you can keep this from 'em?"

"I'm tryin' to quit, Rose. And I can quit on my own."

Rose stared at her for a long time, and then smiled. "Okay, honey. But anyway, today I came over for another reason."

"And what might that be?"

"My son finally bought me a TV set! Took him long enough to get the hint! So I came over to bring you and the kids to see it."

Pearl sighed and smiled. She couldn't stay mad at Rose. "Kids! Come on out here. We're goin' to Miss Rose's to see her new—"

Before she could finish, Edward and Shay raced past her. Nick tried to keep up, but tripped and began wailing. Pearl picked him up.

"Don't cry, sugah. Don't you want to go see Miss Rose's TV?"

Nick swallowed back a sob and nodded. "Mm-hmm...."

Once everyone was in Rose's living room, she found a channel with cartoons.

"Okay," Pearl said. "You kids sit right here and be good while you watch your cartoons. Me and Miss Rose'll be watchin' you from the kitchen."

Rose laughed. "I don't think they heard a word you said."

Pearl sat down at the table and Rose began making a pot of coffee. "How you been feelin', honey?"

"I'm all right, Rose. I got a headache is all. Not too bad."

"Well, I hope you like my coffee. It ain't as good as yours, but I try."

Pearl's laugh gave way to a pained expression. "Well, I think I drank too much this morning. I'm startin' to feel a little queasy too."

Rose gave her a skeptical look. "Now Pearl...."

"I'm all right, Rose."

"Well, let me make you some tea. That'll be better than coffee. And maybe you can stay away from that stuff. At least a little longer, ya know?"

Pearl managed a weak smile. "That's what I've been tryin' to do."

Two hours later, the children had fallen asleep on the floor in front of the television set, and Pearl was feeling a little better. She and Rose were sitting on the sofa watching the HUAC Committee questioning a Negro woman named Annie Lee Moss.

"Lord, Rose, how long you think these hearings are gonna drag on?"

"I don't know, but I know folks are gettin' sick and tired of those bullies. I don't think that woman did a damn thing wrong. Not after hearin' her answers."

"Me neither. Lord, with all that talk from that senator, I was expectin' Mata Hari!"

Just then, Edward sat up and blinked at the television set. "What happened to Bugs Bunny?" he whined. "Can we watch Bugs Bunny again?"

Pearl laughed and rubbed his head. "It's 'may we' and no, we may not. Bugs Bunny's over for today. And besides, I gotta go home and start supper."

She reached down and shook Shay's shoulder. "Wake up, baby. We're goin' home now."

"You sure you can't stay a few more minutes?" Rose asked.

"No, Doc'll be home soon, and he only gets a couple'a hours to eat and shower before he's got to go back to the club." Then she turned around and grinned at Rose. "But then, you knew that, didn't you, Mata Hari?"

Rose laughed. "Tell Doc to drop by so I can show him the TV, Pearl. Maybe I can talk him into gettin' one for you and the kids."

"Yeah, Mama!" Edward shouted.

"Oh, please. You know we can't afford a TV. But let me know how that Annie Lee woman does, Rose. And thanks for lettin' us watch your set."

"Thanks, Miss Rose," Edward said.

"You're welcome, honey. And I tell you what I'm gonna do. I'm gonna figure out what time that ol' Bugs Bunny comes on tomorrow, and I'll come get you kids so you can come watch him, how's that?"

Shay hugged her. "Thanks, Miss Rose!"

"Pearl, come back later, if you want to watch some more of these hearings," Rose called.

"I will."

"I'm hungry," Nick mumbled as they trudged across the hall.

"I'll give you a cookie. That'll keep you till supper."

"How 'bout two?" he said, grinning.

Pearl laughed. "Oh, a wise guy, huh? You're gettin' too big and way too smart."

* * *

The minute Doc got to the club that evening, he spotted King sitting on the barstool nearest the door. He walked over to join him, and King called the bartender over.

"You know what this cat wants, right?"

The bartender nodded and held up the bottle as he brought it over. He set it down in front of Doc with a glass. "Drink up, fellas!"

"Thanks, Lloyd," Doc said. He poured himself a short drink and waited for Lloyd to walk away before he looked at King. "Well?"

King tapped out a cigarette for Doc and lit it. "It's just like you said, man. Soon as Perry got pinched, there was a dealer who picked up his strays. A woman."

Doc felt his teeth grinding as he stared into his drink. "Name."

"Rocky didn't know her name."

Doc let out an annoyed sigh. "How high was this cat when you talked to him?"

"He was actually pretty sober for a change. But this woman's not his direct connection so all he's got is second-hand information. All he knows is that her business is booming. I asked him to keep his eyes and ears open."

Doc nodded. "So she's in Harlem."

"All Rocky knows for sure is that she deals out of a place the addicts call the quarter house. No street, no address."

"The quarter house? Shit, that could be anywhere."

"Exactly. But it's probably in Harlem, near Perry's place. Junkies are a tight-knit bunch."

Doc drained his glass and stood up. "Well... thanks for trying. Let me know if Rocky can find out anything else. Otherwise, I might have to—"

"Wait a minute, Doc. There's sump'm else you should know."

Doc sat back down. "What?"

"Okay, dig this... Rocky's friend said this woman is dealin' a real potent product called Hydra. Very addictive."

"Addictive?" Doc snapped. "Shit, it's all addictive! What's your point, man?"

"Well... He said he heard that four people—at least four people—died from it."

After a short hesitation, Doc grabbed his horn case and stood up again. "Shit, man. That's it. I gotta go home and get Pearl straightened out *to*-night."

"Wait a minute, Doc," King said.

"Wait a minute, my ass!"

"Doc, sit *down*, man!" King shouted.

Lloyd looked over at them. "Hey! Everything cool, fellas?"

"Yeah," King laughed. "We're just messin' around, man. Ignore us."

His smile disappeared as soon as Lloyd turned around. "You didn't let me finish," he whispered. "Now *listen* to me, Doc. If you're still talkin' about cutting off her supply, you better understand one thing. Those four people did *not* O.D., man."

"Come on, King! Make sense! What the hell are you sayin'?"

"Doc... it's the withdrawal that killed 'em."

"Well, hell, it's always the withdrawal! And if the shit's that strong, they—they shouldn't have tried to cold-kick."

"Would you *please* listen to me? Three of 'em died tryin' to do it slowly, like you were talkin' about. Doc, this shit is *different*, man."

Doc tried to ignore the sudden death rattle he felt inside. "What did you say that shit was called again?"

"They call it... Hydra."

* * *

The house was quiet when Doc got home that night. He peeked into the children's room and went in to cover Shay with the blanket she had kicked off. Then he walked into his bedroom and gazed down at Pearl. She was asleep, but her right arm jerked, and her breathing was uneven. He walked out quickly and headed to the bathroom.

Standing under the shower, he tried to force his brain to work, but it seemed to have malfunctioned. All he could think of was that word—Hydra. The mythological monster with multiple heads. If you fought it and chopped off one of the heads, two more would grow in its place. As the water rained down over his shoulders, he felt all his anger at Pearl melting away. In its place was a cold, lonesome fear.

When he finally eased into bed, he tried not to wake her, but when he felt her stir, he moved against her and pulled her into his arms. "Pearl...."

"What's wrong?" she whispered.

"I love you... That's what's wrong."

She pressed her forehead gently against his shoulder. "I know, sugah... I know."

After she fell asleep, Doc stared at the ceiling until the room slowly lightened from darkness to varying shades of gray, and finally, to the soft colors of morning.

When Pearl woke next to him, he held her close for a long time.

"No more fights, Pearl," he whispered.

She smiled up at him. "Okay. No more fights."

"No, I mean, I still want you to try to cut back. You know, keep it under control. But I want you to know that I understand. Just don't ever bring it into the house again."

"I *told* you I'd never do that again. I can kick, sugah. I just need to do it at the right time."

"I know you can," Doc said patiently. "But I don't want you to get—too sick."

"Okay. Just enough to keep me straight. But right now I need to get up and fix breakfast."

* * *

Whenever Doc was troubled, he turned to his old friend Johnnie Walker. And he was troubled now. To make things worse, the coverage of the HUAC hearings had been pounding non-stop into his ears for weeks, like some additional form of torture. The only time he could shut it all off was on the stage of the Nocturne.

With one set left to go, he was alone at the bar with his drink. Then he heard King's double rim-shot, signaling the end of his fifteen-minute break. Taking one last pull on his cigarette, he crushed the butt in the ashtray, then drained his glass and headed to the stage. As he picked up his trumpet, Oliver gave him a brotherly pat on the back.

"Whatever's buggin' you, blow it out'a that horn, *hermano*. Put it in the music."

Doc gazed at him. "What did you just call me?"

"*Hermano*. It means—"

Doc smiled. "I know what it means. And thanks, brother."

King counted off the intro to "Autumn in New York." Doc closed his eyes and began to play the harmonic figure he and Oliver had worked out. Pearl crossed his mind as he waited for his solo, and through his half-closed eyes he could see several couples dancing. Just as Reet's bass solo resolved, Doc felt a nice melodic line rising in his chest. As he inhaled to begin, he opened his eyes and saw a familiar white face at a front table. Agent Adams.

The melodic line vanished, abruptly replaced by a rapid succession of shrill notes that stopped the band cold. Turning to King, he said, " 'Tempus Fugit.' Follow me."

King immediately changed the tempo with a press roll on his high-hat. Zig and Reet followed, and Oliver grinned. "Work it out, *hermano!*" he shouted. "Make 'em realize it!"

Doc stared directly into Adams's water-colored eyes and led the band into the most feverish rendition of "Tempus Fugit" they had ever played. He could feel rivulets of sweat pouring down his face as he murdered Agent Adams with a series of stabbing red notes. By the time he hit the finish, the audience was already on its feet, stomping, whistling, and roaring adoration. Only Agent Adams remained seated.

King jabbed Doc lightly with his drumstick. "Dig, man!" he shouted. "I hope you're ready for a long set. These cats might not ever let us split!"

Doc turned around. "Sorry, man, but we're gonna have to make this a short set. I've got some serious business sittin' out there. And it cannot wait."

"Two more songs?"

Doc nodded. "Count it off."

Fifteen minutes later, King did his standard goodnight shtick, which elicited groans of disappointment from the patrons, but once the band members started packing up their instruments, the club slowly emptied out. Only Agent Adams remained.

King gazed suspiciously at Adams, then looked at Doc. "Need me to hang around?"

"Thanks, man," Doc said, "but this is personal."

King shrugged and grabbed his stick bag, then headed for the door. Doc stepped off the stage and walked directly to Adams's table. He looked down at him and waited until Adams opened his mouth to say something just so he could cut him off.

"I'm walking out of this club, man. If you have something to say to me, come on."

Adams closed his mouth with a stiff smile, smoothed his tie, and stood up.

The tie gesture reminded Doc of that first interrogation. As he led Adams outside, it was all coming back to him. Spain had been the fundamental point of all his questions, even the questions about Jimmy. So if Adams wanted to engage him in a psychological war, with Spain as the central issue, Doc was happy to take him on. In Spain he had learned that war was no game, but a serious matter of life and death. No matter which version of history prevailed, war had no winners, only survivors. And survival depended on staying two steps ahead of the enemy.

He walked all the way to the corner before he turned around to face Adams. He saw a minor twitch in his smile, but his colorless eyes didn't blink. Doc knew he was probing for a crack in his armor, but Enrique had taught him well. He kept his eyes deceptively empty.

It was all coming back to him.

"What do you want, Agent Adams?"

"I don't *want* anything. The Bureau *requires* that you answer some questions. And not out here on the street."

"Okay," Doc said calmly as he extended his hand. "Where's your subpoena?"

Adams gave him a contemptuous look. "You're drunk."

"I'm a drinker. I rarely get drunk."

"This is all the subpoena I need," Adams snapped, handing him a business card.

Without looking at it, Doc reached over to stick it back into Adams's jacket pocket.

Adams slapped his hand away. "You be at that address tomorrow morning at nine a.m."

"I'll be busy tomorrow."

"Then I'll be—"

Doc cut him off. "Dropping by my house again?"

Adams smiled tightly. "That's exactly right."

Doc pocketed the card. "I'll think about it."

"Don't be late, Mr. Calhoun."

* * *

After another sleepless night, Doc got up early and slipped out before Pearl was awake. Stopping at a diner, he ate a leisurely breakfast, drank three cups of coffee, and smoked four cigarettes as he read the newspaper. A conflicting article about the HUAC hearings jumped out at him. The first paragraph stated that the Committee had overstepped its power and was self-destructing. But the second paragraph mentioned a new round of interrogations "designed to burn more terrified witnesses with the brand 'Un-American.' "

Doc read the article to the end, searching for any concrete statement of the Committee's demise, but all he found was a wishful sentiment in the final line: "The end is near."

"Shit," he muttered. "Can't come soon enough for me." He paid for his breakfast and headed to midtown.

Once he arrived at the address written on the card, he checked his watch and took a walk around the block. Just for spite, he waited until 9:35 before entering the building.

He took the elevator to the fourth floor and found the door marked 406. It was open, so he went in. There was a small reception area with a middle-aged white woman seated at a desk.

She peered at him skeptically over the top of her glasses. "May I help you?"

"I'm here to see Agent Adams."

"Your name?"

"Mr. Calhoun."

"One moment."

After briefly disappearing into an inner office, she returned. "You may go in."

Doc walked into the office and looked around. Adams was staring at him from behind a large, plain desk. There was an empty chair in front of the desk, and two stone-faced white men in suits were seated in chairs near the window. On the desk was a telephone and two thick files. No plants or books. No pictures on the wall. The entire room looked like a temporary setup.

Doc took a seat, angling the chair so that he could keep an eye on the door.

"I told you not to be late," Adams said.

Doc stood up. "Oh, well, I can leave if you have another appointment."

"Sit down."

Doc shot Adams a cynical grin and nodded in the direction of the other two agents. "Who are these guys? The second-string HUAC Committee?"

One of the men near the window moved to get out of his chair, but the other one restrained him. Doc gazed at their faces. They were not nearly as adept at masking their hatred as Adams was. Adams's smile was deceptively sweet.

"I'd like to question Mr. Calhoun alone for a while, if you gentlemen don't mind. My secretary will let you know when we're ready for you."

As soon as the two men were gone, Doc said, "So let me guess... if I don't name names and sign a confession, those two scary guys are gonna come in here with the handcuffs? Or are they gonna bring a blindfold and a cigarette and drag me in front of a firing squad?" He chuckled. "You and your buddies have been watching too many detective movies, man."

"You address me as Agent Adams."

Doc nodded politely. "Agent Adams. Okay, you said you had some questions."

"Yes, Mr. Calhoun. Let's get to business. Now, as you know, the HUAC Committee is closing in on all the names on the blacklist. Many of them are serving prison terms."

Doc held out his hands, palms up. "I'm sorry... I'm not hearing a question."

"Do you know a Communist named Paul Robeson?"

"Do I—" Doc swallowed back a laugh. "So *that's* what this is all about? The Committee couldn't break Robeson so you come after *me*? A small-time trumpet player? Why, because I went to some meeting? Man, that's pitiful! But I'll answer your question. No, I never had the pleasure of meeting Mr. Robeson, so it follows that I have no idea what his party affiliation is."

Adams leaned forward. "I know you were in contact with James Turner's mother."

Doc kept his expression blank. He'd seen these interrogation tactics before. Ask an unexpected question, then shift gears to the real subject, and then back to something else. *Deflect, distract, deceive… Three-Card Monte.*

"*What* do you want, Agent Adams?"

"I want a statement of facts as you know them." He flashed a smug smile. "It's for the Committee."

"Then ask me your questions, Agent Adams."

"Where is James Turner?"

"Dead. Next question."

"No, he isn't. We know you've been sending him messages through his mother."

Doc smiled. "Do you just make this stuff up at night when you can't sleep or sump'm?"

"I'm asking the questions, Mr. Calhoun."

"Then ask one."

"Are you a left-leaning Communist, Mr. Calhoun?"

"Are you a right-leaning fascist, Agent Adams?"

Adams narrowed his eyes at Doc. "Is Eleanor Turner a Communist?"

"I don't know."

"Yes or no, Mr. Calhoun. Answer the question."

"I answered it. I don't know. That's my answer."

"Do you know a Communist named Enrique Suárez?"

"I don't know the name Suárez."

Adams smiled. "We've been keeping an eye on your wife, Mr. Calhoun."

Direct hit.

Doc didn't flinch, but he felt his fists tightening and briefly considered breaking a few bones in Adams's face. Instead, he smiled calmly and lit a cigarette. "I see the game's afoot."

Adams sighed. "I'm not impressed by a little knowledge of Shakespeare, Mr. Calhoun, and I'd really appreciate it if you'd stop smoking in my office."

Doc leaned his head back and blew out a large gust of smoke. "And I'd really appreciate it if you'd stop asking me these unconstitutional questions. But we don't always get what we want, do we, Agent Adams?... By the way, have you got an ashtray?"

"I do not."

"Too bad. I'd hate to mess up your carpet."

Adams stood up. After a short pause, he slid an empty wastepaper basket over to Doc, and then smoothed his necktie as he sat back down.

"Thanks," Doc said, tapping his ashes into the wastepaper basket. "Any more questions?"

"Where is James Turner?"

"One more time, Agent Adams. He's still dead."

"Then why did you visit his mother?"

"What do you *really* want?"

"I told you, Mr. Calhoun. I want a statement of facts from you."

Doc narrowed his eyes, trying to read Adams's next move. Then he remembered a trick of intimidation an old pimp had taught him. Keeping his eyes on Adams, he held up his cigarette, crushed the burning end slowly between his fingers, and dropped it into the wastepaper basket. It hurt like hell, but he didn't show it, and Adams actually looked rattled—but only mildly.

"Okay, let's stop dancin' around this, Agent Adams. You know I fought in Spain. You also know that I was cleared to serve in World War Two. You say you want a statement of facts out of me. Okay, here goes... Fact: Jimmy Turner is dead. Fact: I do *not* know whether Eleanor Turner is a Communist, although I doubt it. Fact: I never met Robeson. Fact: You don't really want a statement of facts, Agent Adams. What you've been doing is trying to intimidate me with that spineless visit to frighten my wife when you knew I wasn't home, and then showing up at my place of work. The *real* fact is that public opinion is turning against your Committee, so you cats are desperate for a card-carrying Red boogie-man to justify your fascist tactics—even if he's dead! So you come after me, but you have nothing on me. Because if you did, I'd be in Washington right now answering to McCarthy or Cohn or somebody with at least a *little* political muscle left, instead of a B-flat errand boy like you."

Adams slipped and let a quick flash of anger show. "Stop right there, Mr. Calhoun!"

"I'll stop when I'm finished, Agent Adams. You have no evidence of any wrongdoing on my part. None whatsoever." Doc leaned back in his chair. "*Now* I'm finished."

Adams's smile slowly returned. "We *have* no evidence? You are naïve, Mr. Calhoun. We are quite capable of *having* any evidence we need... anytime we need it."

A long silence fell over the room as the two men stared at each other.

Finally, Doc leaned forward in his chair and folded his hands. "Agent Adams... As a veteran who fought and bled for this country, I've been tolerating you out of respect for your badge. But you just sat there and threatened to manufacture false evidence against me. That makes you a criminal with a worthless badge that I'm no longer willing to respect."

Doc stood up slowly. "I'm leaving now."

Adams leaned back in his chair and smiled. "I have a proposition for you, Mr. Calhoun."

"Not interested."

Pulling out a drawer, Adams took out a small white packet and tossed it onto the desk.

Doc eyed the packet. Was this the manufactured evidence Adams planned to use? Was it some sort of bait? Or was he actually involved in the heroin trade?

"As I said, Agent Adams... not interested."

"I can make your wife very happy, or very miserable, Mr. Calhoun. In any case, I'll be around. I'll pay her another visit real soon."

Doc smiled calmly. "No, you won't. Because then I'll have to introduce you to some cats in Harlem that will take your heroin and whatever other manufactured evidence you come up with and shove it up your ass, Agent Adams."

Adams managed a composed smile. "Is that a threat, Mr. Calhoun?"

Doc laughed as he turned to leave, unable to believe that Adams had left him such an obvious opening. "*That* was your statement of facts, Agent Adams," he called over his shoulder.

* * *

Doc was late to work the next night, missing nearly the entire first set. When the band took their break, King nudged him and pointed to the bar.

"Hey, man," Doc said. "I'm sorry I was late. Did Zig raise hell or sump'm?"

King shook his head. "I need to talk to you."

Doc took a seat on the barstool and lit a cigarette. "What's goin' on, man?"

King gestured for the bartender, who came over with the Johnnie Red and poured two short drinks. He waited for him to walk away, and then said, "I talked to Rocky again last night. It was too late to come over, and I didn't want to call you."

"Why not?"

"Your phone might be tapped, man."

Doc took a sip of his scotch and then set the glass down without saying anything for a long moment. Then he looked at King. "Tell me what he said."

"Okay, dig this… First, he starts broadcastin' all the shit everybody already knows—namin' names like a sellout HUAC witness! The Sicilians supplying the heroin in Harlem, the colored pushers they got workin' for 'em, first and last names of four or five cops on the take… Like I said, the shit everybody already knows. But he seemed real nervous about sump'm, so I let him talk it out till he finally got to the point."

"Which was?"

"Okay, dig… Rocky always hangs out with me whenever I'm at the den, but he's got this chick he's friendly with too. He told me he overheard her talking to a suit out in the alley two nights ago. And the suit dropped your name, man."

Doc stared vacantly into the layer of smoke floating in the club. "What's this woman's name? And how did Rocky know *my* name?"

"He wouldn't give me the chick's name, and as for *your* name, come on, Doc! I'd never talk about your private business! All I ever talk about is how you play that horn, man."

Doc nodded. "So this suit you keep talkin' about—I'm assuming he's a white cat?"

King looked away. "White as the FBI."

That got Doc's attention. "Did Rocky say that? Did he say the cat was FBI?"

"He did. And dig this... When Rocky heard your name he looked over, and the woman caught it. So Rocky wised up and slid down the wall, pretending to pass out. But they moved around the corner of the building so he couldn't hear any more of their conversation. But *then*, a few minutes later the woman came back and took Rocky for a ride."

Doc looked up. "A *ride*?"

King chuckled. "Not *that* kind'a ride, man. She just had to get him out of the vicinity."

"Okay, so get to the point, man."

"I am. But there's so much twisted shit in this... Okay, bottom line is this: Rocky is an *informant*, man! And the woman's an undercover cop."

Doc groaned. "A female undercover cop smokin' opium at the dens?"

King took a gulp of his scotch and smiled. "You'd be amazed at the characters I've met in the opium dens of New York City."

"Get serious, man!" Doc said, irritated.

"Okay, look. Rocky's the genuine article—a cokey, smoky drug addict, but the woman cop just makes appearances, doin' a little half-ass dope smokin' so she can hang out with Rocky and pick up information. I mean, think about it, man. Nobody would suspect a woman, especially one that attached herself to a cat like Rocky. Anyway, here's the important part... The FBI agent in the alley is *dirty*—on the wrong side of some real illegal shit. The undercover cop worked him so sweet, she's got him thinkin' that she's *his* informant. She's been feedin' him fake information. But when Rocky overheard their conversation—"

Doc cut him off. "This all sounds pretty implausible, man. And besides, informant or not, *why* would she trust Rocky with some confidential shit like that?"

"She *had* to! When she saw Rocky react to hearing your name, the FBI cat saw it too, and he mentioned it to her. She's sure he'll be back to question Rocky, so she put him wise about how to answer and everything. Damn, I hope he can handle it. She was kind'a rough on him and threatened to send him to jail if he told a soul, so we gotta keep this on ice."

"Then why the hell did Rocky risk tellin' you?"

"He's scared, Doc. I guess I'm his best friend, as sad as that is."

They fell into a long silence. Then King looked at Doc and said softly, "There's sump'm else I figured you need to know. Turns out the dirty FBI cat has been working with the Sicilian suppliers. For a price, he sort of leaves the door open for 'em and looks the other way."

Doc stopped listening. He could see King's mouth moving, but all he could think of was that night he had seen Agent Adams at the Onyx Club talking to that Italian in the sharkskin suit. And then there was that heroin packet he had tossed onto the desk in his office that day. But if his game was dealing, then why all the questions about Jimmy and his mother?

Then it hit him. Cover. He felt stupid for not figuring it out sooner. Everything made sense now.

King was nudging his arm. "Did you hear what I said, man?"

"Sorry, man. Repeat that last part."

"I said, the product he's helping them deal is that goddamn Hydra!"

Doc looked up, and King nodded sadly.

"That's right, man. The sonofabitch is linin' his pockets every time Pearl gets high on that deadly shit."

* * *

Since his conversation with King, Doc spent every waking moment reliving his time in Spain. Digging through his memory, he embraced the lessons of each death, no matter how painful, each loss, no matter how devastating, and each victory, no matter how small. In Spain he had learned the true meaning of war. The fight does not begin with one major attack or some political sea-change. It takes many small cuts over a long period of time, and the slow death of a country and its people, their bodies, souls, and ideals, to spark a full-blown war.

He slept very little over the next few days, but when he finally did fall into a deep sleep, he dreamed that Pearl was Spain, and another war was on the horizon. He woke up drenched in sweat, with his heart pounding a message to his brain.

Agent Adams had committed an act of war.

Gradually I came to realize that people will more readily swallow lies than truth, as if the taste of lies was homey, appetizing: a habit.

~ Martha Gellhorn

CHAPTER 28

A fter meeting with Agent Adams, Doc had nearly thrown away that business card with the office address. But at the last second he had changed his mind, thinking it might be useful someday. That someday had come.

After rummaging through the closet, he found the jacket he'd worn on the day he'd met with Adams. He searched through the pockets, still trying to remember whether the card had a telephone number or only an address on it. When he found it, he smiled. There was a telephone number after all. "My office this time," he muttered.

When he got to Café Nocturne that night, each set seemed to last an eternity. All he could think about was Agent Adams. The second he got home and discovered that Pearl was gone again, he was more determined than ever.

After checking on the children, he went back to the bedroom and into the closet. In the back left corner, he had loosened a floor board and hidden a box there. It was the only thing he had kept after cleaning out Ronnie's apartment following his suicide.

He looked at the alarm clock next to the bed. It was 2:45. In less than seven hours someone would be answering that office phone. After arranging everything he would need, he slipped the business card into his shirt pocket and kicked off his shoes. He thought about going to the kitchen for the bottle of Johnnie Red he kept in the high cupboard, but stopped himself before the temptation took hold. War was a time for clear-minded sobriety. Stretching out his legs in the bed, he sat up against a pillow and waited for Pearl to come home.

* * *

When he felt Pearl shaking his shoulder, he cursed himself for falling asleep. Before she could begin her slurry apologies or her desperate attempts to kiss him, he got up and went to the kitchen. The wall clock read 6:05. "Goddamn. What the hell am I gonna do for three hours?"

Then he heard Pearl go into the bathroom and turn on the faucet. He hurried into the bedroom, gathered everything he needed, then changed his clothes and headed for the front door. He hated to wake Rose, but didn't hesitate to knock firmly on her door.

She answered, looking half-asleep. When she saw his face, she nodded. "I got my key. Lemme get dressed and I'll go right over."

"Thanks, Rose. I uh, I'll be pretty late. If you could stay till I get back, I'd appreciate it."

Rose scrutinized him with worried eyes, but then nodded and didn't say another word.

Doc hurried downstairs and headed to East Harlem. By the time he reached his old block, his shirt was sticky and damp from the morning's humidity. He looked up at the dense, gray sky. The cloud cover had a strange, low-slung appearance over the old tenement buildings, as though trying to cover the shame of their existence in the shadow of American affluence.

He had grown up here with Jimmy and Rico, and memories jumped out at him from every corner. Jimmy was dead now, but after Rico's release from prison, he'd had no place to go but the place he'd been born. His mother still lived there, and the building was only two blocks up the street. Doc thought about paying them a visit while he waited to make his call, but decided to keep his mind on the mission at hand.

He found a diner on 3rd Avenue that was open. A little bell jingled as he walked in and he went to the counter to order breakfast. A thin, dark-skinned waitress wearing cat-eye glasses smiled at him and took his order. As she filled his coffee cup, he said, "Just leave the pot."

"Sure, Mista."

"Wait. Is that today's newspaper over there?"

"The boy just dropped 'em a while ago. I'll get you one."

When she handed it to him, Doc stared at the headline:

'REFUSE TO TESTIFY,' EINSTEIN
ADVISES INTELLECTUALS
CALLED IN BY CONGRESS

After reading the accompanying article about Einstein's condemnation of the House Un-American Activities Committee, Doc found little else in the paper to occupy his attention. The time dragged slowly as people on their way to work came in, ate, and left.

When the clock behind the counter finally read 9:05, he got up, paid for his breakfast, and left the waitress a generous tip.

The waitress smiled as she pocketed the tip. "Thanks, Mista!"

"You're welcome. And thanks for letting me take up your space for so long. Is there a phone booth someplace?"

"Yes, sir," the waitress said, pointing to the far right corner of the diner.

Doc walked over to the narrow phone booth, squeezed inside, and shut the door. Slipping a dime into the slot, he dialed the number on the business card. After four rings, he was about to hang up, but then someone answered.

"Agent Adams."

Doc got right to the point. He didn't say hello or identify himself, just laid out the bait.

"I have a counter–proposition for you."

After a short silence, Adams said, "I'm listening, Mr. Calhoun."

"You leave my wife alone, and I mean *completely* alone, and I'll give you some information on that person you were interested in."

"What information?"

"I'll only discuss this in person. And you gotta come to me this time. Ever since I went to your office I've got people following me."

"What people?"

"I'm not answering questions over the phone. Now, there's a neighborhood I know like the back of my hand. Come to the corner of 116th and 3rd Avenue at midnight tonight. When I'm sure nobody followed you, you'll see me. Not until."

"I know the area," Adams said.

"Good," Doc said. "All you have to do is wait for my signal."

"What kind of signal?"

"Nothin' elaborate. I'll just whistle. Be there at midnight tonight and you *better* come alone. And no recording devices, you understand?

It'll lead you to some major players."

"I'll be there."

"Good. And just so we're clear, you get your information and you leave my wife alone. Do we have a deal?"

"If your information is good like you say it is, yeah, we have a deal."

Doc hung up and stared at the receiver. "He knows the area... Shit, I *bet* he does. Probably right where he does his dirty deals."

It took Doc a minute to swallow back the bitterness and compose himself. Then he stepped out of the phone booth and headed for the door. As he turned to wave at the waitress, he nearly bumped into Rico, who was walking in.

Rico smiled. "Hey, Doc! What'chu doin' in the old neighborhood?"

Doc stared at him for a moment. "Let me talk to you a minute, man—outside."

He led Rico away from the door. "Listen, man, it might be a good thing I ran into you today. I might need a place to lay my head later tonight. It might be pretty late though."

"Sure, brother. What's up?"

"I just had a fight with Pearl and I might need a little time to clear my head. I got some things to do today, but I'll call you later. Just stay near your phone if you can, that's all."

"I'll keep the line clear, man."

* * *

With two wars under his belt, Doc had learned patience for the drag of the minutes. As he stood in the dark alley between the two abandoned tenement buildings, he went over the details. He had planned everything carefully, even waiting for a moonless night. There were two working lights—a streetlamp on 8th Avenue and a light fixture at the top of a rusty fire escape on a building deep in the alley. That was the one that would be most useful. The only uncertainty was whether something might scare Adams away. Only time would tell.

When he saw the headlights slowly approaching, he waited until Adams turned off the engine and got out of the car. Adams appeared hesitant as he looked around at the dark windows of the surrounding buildings.

Without showing himself, Doc whistled.

Adams looked over and walked slowly in his direction. Doc backed deeper into the alley until he was standing in the shadows next to a tall, dilapidated fence. Then he whistled again.

Adams's head snapped to his right in reaction to the whistle, but then he stopped and shook his head. "This is as far as I go."

Doc was ready for that. "Forget it, man," he called. "I changed my mind."

"Wait!" Adams said impatiently.

"I don't have all night, man," Doc said. "You either come back here where I feel safe, or I leave. Your choice."

Adams walked slowly toward him until he was standing in the pale sliver of light from the fire escape. As Doc approached him, he wondered whether Adams was really this gullible or just arrogant to the point of self-destruction. Then he stopped. There was just enough light for him to see Adams's face.

"What information do you have for me?" Adams said.

"I'm sorry, Agent Adams, but I've gotta pat you down first."

Adams looked amused. "Absolutely not."

"Then I can't give you this information. I've gotta make sure you're not wearing some kind'a listening device."

Adams chuckled. "*Now* who's been watching too many detective movies?"

Doc shrugged. "No pat-down, no information."

Adams hesitated a moment, then rolled his eyes and took his gun out of his shoulder holster. Then he held out his arms. "Hurry up. And don't come near my weapon."

"I won't touch your weapon," Doc said as he frisked him. "All I care about are listening devices. You FBI cats are famous for that sort'a thing."

When Doc finished, Adams reholstered his gun. "Do I pass inspection, Officer Calhoun?"

Instead of responding to the quip, Doc stepped back and stared at him silently.

"Okay," Adams said. "So what's this information you have for me? And it better be something I can take to the Committee."

Doc smiled ironically. "Oh, you can definitely take this to the Committee. But first, I have a question, Agent Adams… If someone came onto American soil and started murdering American citizens, would you consider that an act of war?"

"Get to the point."

"Answer the question and I'll get to the point. Would it be an act of war?"

"Of course. *What* has that got to do with Eleanor Turner?"

"Look around you. This is Harlem. Not very glamorous, but it's my little piece of America. And you, Agent Adams, have come onto Harlem soil and murdered Harlem citizens."

Adams scowled impatiently. "You don't know what you're talking about."

"Oh, I *do* know what I'm talking about. You need a shiny object to distract and deflect the attention away from your dirty activities. And Eleanor Turner would make a nice shiny object, now wouldn't she? Especially if she was a Communist, which she's *not*, by the way."

Adams started to say something, but Doc cut him off.

"And I know why you roam around here like a lone wolf. Dirty cops can't trust a partner. I was counting on that, by the way. But the main thing I know is that you're directly involved in flooding these streets with heroin."

Adams shifted, ever so slightly. "You're crazy."

"I'm *not* crazy. I'm right. You know all about this shit they call Hydra."

"I don't know what you're talking about."

"One last lie," Doc said calmly. "But you can't have a war without lies." He pulled the Astra 400 from under his jacket and pointed it at Adams. "I don't care about your badge. That Hydra is killin' my people, man. And *that* is an act of war."

Adams tried to interrupt, but again, Doc cut him off.

"One of those people is my wife. And *that* makes this particular war very personal."

Adams raised his hand to reach for his gun, and Doc took aim at his head. "If you move that hand another millimeter, I'll shoot you where you stand."

Adams flashed a defiant grin. "No, you won't. You'll *never* kill an FBI agent."

"But I will," a deep voice said.

Something caught the light in a bright glimmer just beside Adams's head. Doc wasn't even sure what was happening until Adams fell back against Rico, who lowered him silently to the ground. For the first time, he saw the large blade as Rico wiped it clean on Adams's pants leg. "Let's go, man," Rico said softly as he pocketed the knife. "*Now.*"

Doc took a quick look down at Agent Adams. His throat was cut wide open, from ear to ear, and he was drenched in blood. It had all happened in under ten seconds.

"Come on!" Rico said, tapping Doc's arm.

As they ran through the narrow alley toward Lexington, Rico pulled off his blood-spattered jacket, turned it inside out, and put it back on without missing a step. Doc stayed close behind him, intently focused, until a sudden mental flash took him back to Spain. He was trying to keep up with Enrique, who was leading him over the Pyrenees Mountains. He could feel Jimmy running behind him. He could even hear his breathing, rapid from the exertion of the climb. Doc glanced over his shoulder, surprised to see nothing but the darkness of the alley.

He shook his head hard and blinked, and he was back, hurrying down the 116th Street subway stairs behind Rico. There was a train about to leave, and they slipped inside just before the doors closed. With the exception of one old white man snoring over his newspaper, the car was empty. Doc followed Rico to the opposite end, then stood in front of him to block the old man's view in case he woke up. Rico discreetly wiped his hands on a handkerchief to remove any remaining traces of blood, then stuffed it into his jacket pocket.

"I couldn't let you get in that kind of trouble, brother," Rico said without looking at him.

"How did you know?"

Rico finally looked up with an impatient scowl. "Shit, the way you were acting this morning? *You* not going home to Pearl and the kids? Come on, man! I been followin' you all day."

Doc tried to interrupt, but Rico stopped him. "Doc! You don't belong where I been. You already did your time in two wars, man."

"You've gotta let me explain, Rico...."

"No, man. I heard everything you said to him. And I had to keep you from usin' that gun. What were you thinkin', man? A Fed? And what about shells? They can trace shells—"

"That gun was untraceable. Pearl's stepfather took it off a Nazi he killed in Germany. I found it when I packed up her brother's apartment after he died. She never knew I had it."

Rico stared at him with a vaguely sad expression, but then nodded. The train was slowing to a stop, and he leaned down to peer out the window. "We better get off here."

Just then, the old man with the newspaper opened his eyes and scrambled toward the door. Rico grabbed Doc's sleeve. "Let's wait a couple more stops just to be safe," he whispered.

No one boarded at the stop and the doors shut quickly. As the train picked up speed, Doc fell into a long silence and stared into the darkness that seemed to be moving outside the window. "Time," he murmured absently.

"Hey, you look weird, man," Rico said softly. "You okay?"

Doc heard him, but didn't answer. He was still trying to reel himself back from Spain.

Rico nudged him. "Hey, man. You feel okay?"

Doc smiled at him. "War is not a time to feel."

* * *

It was half-past two when Doc got home. The front room was dark, but he could see the pale glow from the small nightlight in the hallway. Without turning on any other lights, he moved quietly toward the children's room to check on them. Then he went to his bedroom and stared down at Pearl for a long time. She was completely still, with a serene expression on her face. Usually, her jumpy nerves tortured her all through the night in her manic pursuit of sleep. She had told him once that she could only sleep soundly on the second night after a fix. He left the room quietly.

Stretching out on the sofa, he stared up at the dark ceiling. For days, his mind had been busy with the detailed planning and execution of his war. Now his mind was occupied by something Pearl had said when he told her about Spain—about life turning on a dime:

You weren't supposed to die in Barcelona....

Why had he run into Rico that morning? Killing Adams would have been a justified response to an act of war, but Rico had appeared like an avenging angel and done the job for him. What would Pearl say about *that* dime turning?

You weren't supposed to kill that man....

This thought settled deeply into his consciousness until he completely dismissed the idea of sleep. Again. For hours, he reached back for Enrique's voice, all of his words, turning and turning, until he finally found the ones that would let him rest:

To have all power, a man would have to kill everyone. Pray that you are not that man....

* * *

Doc's body ached when he got up the next morning, and he knew that days of tension had been the cause. As he sat on the edge of the sofa, he whispered a few words that were as close to praying as he'd ever come. He decided that if there was a God in heaven, Adams's murder would prompt a deeper investigation that would lead to some arrests of more heroin traffickers in Harlem. And if that God was merciful, maybe there would be a cure for Pearl.

He stood up, suddenly remembering something that Rico's mother had often said when they were kids: *God helps those who help themselves.*

Quietly, he slipped out the front door, and hurried downstairs before he could change his mind. Walking swiftly to the corner phone booth, he dropped a dime into the slot and dialed Rico's number. After four rings, he heard his groggy voice.

"Yeah?"

"I forgot to tell you sump'm last night, man."

"What?"

"Thank you."

Doc hung up and fished out another dime from his pocket. Then he dialed the operator and asked for the police department. When the call connected, a gruff voice answered.

"This is Sergeant Sims."

"I want to report a heroin dealer in my neighborhood. Can you send somebody to arrest him?"

"Name?"

"His name is Edward Hooper."

"Not *his* name, your name."

"Anonymous tip, man. I'm just a citizen who's sick of dope dealers killin' my people."

After a short silence, the sergeant said, "What's his address?"

"Corner of 116th and 2nd. The shittiest tenement on that block. Apartment 612."

Doc hung up and stared at the receiver. "Sorry, Hooper, but the war's not over yet."

* * *

Every morning, Doc listened to the radio news and checked the papers for any report on Adams's death, but there was nothing. At the end of the second week, he figured that the FBI had kept it quiet because of what that undercover cop had found out about Adams.

He hadn't mentioned anything about Adam's death to King, but then realized that it would look suspicious if he never asked for any updates about Rocky. He made a few token inquiries, and one night King delivered some information.

Doc was sitting at the bar before the first set, and King took a seat next to him. "Got a report for you, man. Rocky told me the undercover cop came back to the den last night. She told him they were about to shut down a big heroin ring in Harlem. Guess that's a start."

Doc closed his eyes. *Hello, God.*

"The weird part is that when Rocky asked about the FBI cat, the undercover cop got sore. All she told him was that they were finished with him, and not to ask any questions about him."

Doc took a swallow from his glass. "That *is* weird."

"I guess no matter how dirty you are, if you're FBI, you're above the law."

"Depends on whose law you're talkin' about," Doc said cryptically. He could feel King scrutinizing him.

"Doc, I gotta ask you something... Do you know this FBI cat?"

Doc took a long pull on his cigarette and took his time answering. "We've met."

"He was the one at the club that night," King said. "That business you had to attend to."

Doc nodded.

Out of a long silence, King said, "Seems like the cat just—disappeared."

Doc blew a high, billowing smoke ring. "Seems like it."

King turned and faced Doc squarely. "Look... I know this is gonna sound like some far-fetched shit 'cause I know you're not the type, but you didn't—*kill* him, did you?"

Doc reached for the bottle of Johnnie Red and poured a generous amount into King's glass. Then he smiled. "I did not kill him. And that's the truth."

"Well, I hope somebody killed that snake. At least he's not on the scene anymore spreadin' that death all over Harlem. That renegade was a killer and he needed to die."

Doc smiled and took a sip. "He wasn't the first snake spreadin' death in Harlem. And sadly, he won't be the last. And what makes you so sure he was a renegade?"

King was about to take a sip of his drink, but his hand froze before the glass reached his mouth. He set it back down. "Goddamn, Doc. There's so much shit we don't know."

Doc drained his glass. "Welcome to the war."

1963

Civil Rights Leader Mcdgar Evers is assassinated outside his home in Jackson, Mississippi.

Dr. Martin Luther King delivers his "I Have a Dream" speech at the Lincoln Memorial.

Four little girls named Addie Mae Collins, Cynthia Wesley, Denise McNair, and Carole Robertson are murdered by Ku Klux Klan members in the bombing of the 16th Street Baptist Church in Birmingham, Alabama.

President John F. Kennedy is assassinated in Dallas, Texas.

CHAPTER 29

*D*ay two.
It was morning. Pearl stepped out of the shower and smiled at her reflection in the mirror. The intense aftereffects of the previous day's fix were leveling off.

On day one, she was a stranger to herself. She was not a loving mother, not a devoted wife. She was not the Pearl that Alva had raised. On day one, she was a slave, debased and owned by an all-consuming master named Hydra.

But on the morning of day two, her mind and spirit emerged from that orgasmic fog, that false euphoria. The second day after a fix was the closest thing to normal she could hope for anymore. She could function as herself, a wife and mother, a friend, an intelligent woman who could and would kick her addiction. Pearl reached for day two with all her might, despite that flickering image in the back of her mind that mocked her: *That smile ain't nothin' but the last little kick of your high, sugah.*

But she didn't care. There was none of the terrible sickness on day two, other than mild nausea and light-headedness, and a little swelling in her fingers. She twisted and pulled her wedding ring until it came off and then laid it on the side of the bathroom sink. As she ran the soothing cold water over her ring finger, she jiggled her right bicuspid with her tongue. She had lost one of her back teeth a few months earlier, and now this one was so loose she was afraid it would fall out at supper. There was no money for a dentist, but she didn't care. Not today.

After combing her wet hair, she got dressed and walked into the living room, where Shay was helping Nick with his reading.

Nick was bent over his school book, tracing his finger under each line as he read softly. "The... people of the t-town noc... noc—"

"Don't stop, Nick!" Shay said, sighing impatiently.

"Okay, what's that word?"

"Sound it out, stupid!"

"Shay!" Pearl said. "I don't ever want to hear you call Nick stupid again, you hear me?"

"Yes, ma'am," Shay said meekly. "Sorry, Nick."

Nick stood up and picked up his orange kitten. "Time for breakfast anyway," he said. "Me and Sylvester are hungry."

"See, that's why he's havin' trouble with his reading, Mama," Shay said. "He gives up too easily. He's not stupid, but is it okay to call him lazy?"

Pearl shook her head at Shay and wrapped her arm around Nick. "Bring your book into the kitchen, Nicky. I'll help you while I fix breakfast."

"Can Sylvester come too?"

"Not at the table. He can sit by your feet on the floor though."

Nick ran back for the book and returned to the kitchen. After putting Sylvester on the floor, he sat down and opened the book.

"Now what's givin' you so much trouble, sugah?" she asked.

"Well, I keep gettin' all the words backwards."

"Backwards?"

"Well, not all the way backwards, just… okay, what's that word right there?"

"Try to sound it out, Nicky."

"Noc… I mean, onc… Okay, wait. The… p-people of the town… noc—"

"No, it's con. Congregated. It's a hard word. Just say it piece by piece. Con-gre-gated."

"Con-gre-gated. Yes, ma'am."

"It means the people all got together, like at church. Keep reading. I'm listening."

"Okay. The people of the town con-gre-gated at… th-their… chone… chosen—"

Pearl moved to the counter to start breakfast as Nick continued reading. Then he stopped. When she turned around, he was grinning at her and Sylvester was stretched out in the center of the table, belly up. "Nicky! Get the kitten off the damn table!"

Nick grabbed the kitten. "Sylvester! You're gonna get us in trouble! Daddy would'a—"

"Daddy would'a what?" Doc said as he walked into the kitchen.

"I was tryin' to let you sleep, sugah," Pearl said.

"Daddy would'a what, Nick?" he repeated.

Nick was holding the kitten and grinning. "You would'a whupped Sylvester's butt!"

"Whose butt? *You're* responsible for Sylvester. What did you let him do?"

"He was uh… he was on the table." Nick was trying not to laugh.

"And what was he doin' on the table?"

Nick grinned. "He was, uh, sort'a… layin' on it?"

"Right in the middle," Pearl said, "rollin' around on his back." She held out a soapy dishcloth, and Doc reached for it.

As he wiped off the table, he said, "You're wrong, boy. Daddy would'a whupped *your* butt. And then I would'a put some salt and pepper on Sylvester and eaten him for breakfast."

"Nuh-uh!" Nick cackled.

"Hair and all."

"Yuck, Daddy!" Just then, Sylvester jumped out of his arms and Nick ran after him. "Run for your life, Sylvester!" he yelled.

Pearl laughed, and bumped Doc with her hip. "You and that boy."

"Me and that boy are hungry! What's for breakfast?"

"Eggs and toast. Ran out'a bacon."

"That's okay. Just throw in an extra egg for me. And what's the plan for supper?"

"Leftover chicken stew."

"Good. I love leftover chicken stew. Hey, how's Rose feeling?"

"Still got a fever. I'll check on her through the day and take her some stew for supper."

Doc shook his head. "How long has she been sick?"

"Let's see… About a week after the President got killed. We were all over there watchin' the funeral and she had to go lay down. Remember?"

"That's right. I thought she was just upset, but she did complain about stomach pains. Does her son know she's been sick this long?"

"I called him and he sent a doctor over to check on her. The doctor says it's a bad flu, but she'll be okay if she stays in bed and rests. Don't worry, sugah. I'm takin' good care of her."

* * *

That night after supper, Doc walked out with Pearl and Shay as they crossed the hall to visit Rose. "Give her my best," Doc said.

Edward walked out into the hallway with Nick right behind him carrying Sylvester.

"I thought you guys had homework," Doc said.

Edward grinned. "Mama gave us a temporary reprieve! One TV show at Miss Rose's."

Doc grabbed the top of Nick's head. "You and Sylvester better not tear the joint up now!"

Nick rolled his eyes and laughed. "We won't, Daddy!"

Doc headed for the stairs as Pearl unlocked the door to Rose's apartment. "Okay, you kids can watch television, but turn it down low. I'm goin' in to check on Miss Rose."

"Could I read my paper to Miss Rose?" Shay asked. "She likes it when I read to her."

"That'd be real nice, sugah. Come on in with me. You boys keep it down out here."

Edward turned on the set and then flopped onto the sofa. "Cool. *Rawhide.*"

Nick frowned. "No! Me and Sylvester wanna watch *The Beverly Hillbillies.*"

"That's not even on tonight, knucklehead. We're watchin' *Rawhide.*"

"Hey! No fighting," Pearl called softly from the hallway. "Flip a coin or sump'm."

"*Rawhide's* okay, I guess," Nick said. "Sylvester likes cows."

Edward gave Nick a wide-eyed double–take. "Maaan, you belong on *Looney Tunes.*"

Pearl tiptoed into the small bedroom and turned on the lamp. "Shh. She's asleep."

"No, I'm not," Rose said. "Just restin' my eyes. They been achin' a little."

Pearl laid her palm on Rose's forehead. "You feel cooler, Rose! Still need aspirins?"

Rose opened her eyes and smiled weakly. "That stew sure smells good, Pearl."

"That sounds like hunger talkin', and that's a good sign. Let me set up this tray for you."

Pearl and Shay helped Rose to a sitting position, and placed the bowl of chicken stew in front of her. "I'll feed myself, Pearl."

"Oh, you *are* feelin' better, huh?"

"Mm-hmm. But let me take them aspirins anyway."

"Here you go. And here's some water to wash 'em down."

"Thanks, Pearl." Rose smiled at Shay. "What'cha gonna read me tonight, honey?"

"Well, it's a paper for my history class, Miss Rose. We been studying World War Two, and so I decided to interview Daddy. He was a soldier, you know. And Mama told me what she remembers, and so I wondered if you could tell me what you remember about the war, and then I can finish my paper. But only if you feel like it, Miss Rose."

"Sure, honey. Read me what you have so far."

Pearl and Shay settled onto two kitchen chairs next to the bed. As Shay read her paper, Rose listened and ate. When she finished, Pearl helped her to the bathroom, then back to bed.

"That was a... a real good paper, honey," Rose said. "I'm a little tired now, but if you come over tomorrow, I'll tell you what I remember about the war too, okay?"

"Thanks, Miss Rose. Here, let me help you fix your pillows."

Once Rose was settled, she said, "Too bad she can't talk to your little friend Magda."

Pearl nodded. "Yes, Magda remembered a lot about the war."

Shay looked up. "She did?"

"Tell her that story about the doctor, Pearl."

"What doctor? Tell me, Mama!"

"Well, remember I told you about where Magda grew up when she was a little girl?"

Shay nodded. "In Thessaloniki. It's in Greece. I looked it up."

"That's right. And she had Polio. That's why she had to wear a brace on her leg."

"Poor Magda. I know a boy at school who had Polio. He wears a brace too."

"Well, anyway, when she first got sick, her parents took her to see Dr. Moskos. And he started comin' to her house and gave her therapy, like exercises for her muscles. But the worst part was when he wrapped up her leg in steaming hot towels. That was painful for a little girl. But Dr. Moskos would talk to her and tell her funny stories, and he made her smile. He made her feel brave and he told her every day that she'd walk again... Oh, Lord, she loved Dr. Moskos."

"And he *did* help her walk again, huh, Mama? With a brace, but she walked."

"That's right, sugah."

Shay smiled and began writing. "I'm putting Dr. Moskos in my paper, Mama. So after he helped Magda walk again, what happened to him? Did he join the Greek army or something?"

Rose had fallen asleep, and Pearl tucked the blanket around her shoulders. Then she gave Shay a long look. "No, sugah, he didn't. And I think you're old enough to know this now. Remember when you studied about Hitler and those awful concentration camps?"

Shay's eyes widened. "No, Mama! Dr. Moskos was Jewish?"

"Yes, he was. And the Nazis took him and his whole family to one of those camps. When Magda found out, she was so sad she almost gave up. But then her Mama told her that wherever Dr. Moskos was, he wouldn't want her to give up. So she kept doing her therapy, and when she finally got out of that bed, she went back to her music lessons and became a great violinist. I played you some of those records she was on, didn't I?"

"Yes, ma'am. She played so beautiful... You know what, Mama? I'm gonna put Magda *and* Dr. Moskos in my paper. I think my class is old enough to know about it too."

"That's a good idea, sugah."

"Mama, do you think Magda will ever wake up and come home from that hospital?"

Pearl laid her palm on Shay's cheek. "I don't know, sugah."

"Nick says she will."

Pearl nodded. "I know."

CHAPTER 30

D *ay three.*

Pearl pulled herself up from the bathroom floor and did her best to clean up the trail of watery vomit. Something caught her eye and she held on to the sink as she leaned down to pick it up. When she saw that it was her tooth, she let out a soft sob. Then she held it against her chest for a moment before throwing it into the trash. After washing her face and drying it, she pulled her lip back and stared at the space the tooth had once occupied. "At least it's not in the front." She closed her eyes with a sad memory of her mother.

She reached for the doorknob and composed herself. Walking into the kitchen, she stared at the radio. Johnny Hartman was singing "Lush Life," accompanied by the soulful, blue tones of John Coltrane's tenor sax. As it ended, the disc jockey began reading off the list of personnel playing on the date, and then gushing over the composer. Pearl closed her eyes and saw a flash of Ronnie at age fifteen, sitting cross-legged on the end of her bed, so excited about meeting the great Billy Strayhorn.

She opened her eyes and turned off the radio. A low rumble of thunder sounded, and she saw the rain beating against the kitchen window. She headed into the living room, where Shay was curled up on the sofa reading a book. "Shay?"

"Yes, Mama?" she murmured without looking up.

"Where's Nick?"

"In the room with Sylvester. He's a nut, Mama! He's showing the cat his baseball cards!"

Pearl sat down next to her. "Shay, I have to go out for a little while."

Shay looked up with a worried expression. "But it's raining real hard outside, Mama! Where do you have to go?"

"Just a little business I gotta tend to. Now, Shay, listen to me. You and Nick stay inside till Edward gets home. He ought'a be here in a few minutes, and I won't be gone long."

Shay put her book down and wrapped her sweater tightly around herself. "But... where are you goin', Mama?"

"Oh, I'm just gonna run out and get me some... medicine. I'm not feelin' good, baby."

"Then let me make you some tea."

Pearl stared at Shay's eyes and tried to smile. "I won't be gone long, baby. Now just stay right here and read your book till Edward comes home."

She stepped out into the hallway, making sure the door was locked, and hurried toward the stairwell. Her head was down and she nearly bumped into Edward, who was bounding up, two steps at a time. He was soaking wet.

"Hi, Mama," he said. But his smile faded when he saw her face. "Where are you going?"

"I gotta run an errand is all. I'll be back in an hour or so."

As she hurried down the stairs, she could hear his voice behind her. "Mama, it's pouring out there! ...Come on, Mama! Just... just stay home!"

The tears welled up in her eyes, but she couldn't turn back.

* * *

The next morning Doc woke up alone in his bed. From the kitchen, he heard a soft exchange of voices. He couldn't hear the words, just the tonal music of the conversation and its tempo. Shay's voice had a happy, rapid rhythm, like a song from a Disney movie. Pearl's voice always reminded him of a sensual bolero, deep, unrushed, and undulating. It still ran a shiver through his body, even after all these years. He sat up slowly and put his feet on the floor, telling himself to get up, but his mind was preoccupied with one thought: *She went there again....*

He closed his eyes and reflected on an early-morning conversation from the day before.

The kids are gettin' big. I gotta stop, sugah. Edward's sixteen now, and sometimes he looks at me like he knows.

381

Pearl, you cannot cold-kick. We can't let you get that sick again. We need you too much. So just... cut back some. Keep it under control. When the time's right, we'll get you straight.

When he had come home from the club later that night, Pearl was sprawled across the bed, still in her street clothes. Without saying a word, he helped her undress and put her to bed. After a long shower, he stretched out next to her. Edward had been sleeping on the sofa for months now, so there was no escaping Pearl's incoherent murmurings and low laughter. He closed his eyes, but couldn't sleep.

Night was always tougher for him than day. At night all the fears and anxieties swirled in his brain, with no solutions to chase them away. Edward was sixteen, and a city college was all he could hope for. Every month some new bill needed paying. And Pearl was on a runaway train that he couldn't stop for fear of killing her. He realized that Johnny Red wasn't such a good friend, after all. His true best friend was exhaustion. It was the only thing that let him sleep.

But somehow, morning brought hope, even if it was only illusory. Morning was the time he and Pearl played their roles and pretended there was no such place as the quarter house. He sat on the edge of the bed holding his head in his hands and tried to summon that hope again, and it came. The sound of Pearl's low laughter from the kitchen reminded him of how much he loved her. Taking a deep breath, he stood up. Then he put on a clean shirt and his morning smile.

When he reached the kitchen, Pearl was standing at the stove and Shay was helping her. They had their backs to him, so he stopped in the doorway and watched them for a minute. The radio was playing "I'll Be Home for Christmas" and Shay was telling her all about a book she was reading. As she talked, she wrapped her arms around Pearl's waist and smiled up at her. Then Pearl leaned down and kissed the top of her head. There was something so sweet and intimate about the moment, Doc felt his ornamental smile warm into something real.

"Good morning, beautiful ladies," he said.

"G'morning, Daddy!" Shay chirped. "I'm helpin' Mama make breakfast. You want waffles or toast with your eggs?"

"Waffles, please."

"Me too!" Edward called from the bathroom.

Doc laughed softly. "Man, the walls in this place are thin. No privacy whatsoever."

When Edward walked into the kitchen, Doc realized that he was staring right into his eyes, which would make him at least six feet, two inches tall. He saw his son every day, but was suddenly stunned by this man standing in his kitchen. What had happened to that scrawny, lanky adolescent, and when had he developed this muscular physique? All the roundness of his face had been replaced by manly angles. His black hair was bushy and he was already shaving. Doc felt a pang of loss. His baby boy had grown up too fast. Then Edward flashed his handsome grin and Doc chuckled. No wonder girls were always calling the house.

"Privacy?" Edward was saying. "Try sleepin' on the sofa, Daddy. Privacy's not even on my vocabulary list. All I want is for these two little brats you call my siblings to stop climbing all over me in the morning when I'm tryin' to sleep late!"

"Good morning, son," Doc said dryly. "And you're welcome for the groceries, the heat, running water, roof over your head, clothes on your back...."

Edward groaned and leaned his forehead against Doc's shoulder. "Oh, maaan... I walked right into that one, didn't I?"

"You always do. And by the way, you need a haircut."

"You sure do," Pearl said, smiling.

Doc saw the eerie shine in her eyes, but at least she wasn't slurring her words. He smiled at her. "All right, Edward," he said, "sit down and let's talk about your grades."

"Oh, boy," Shay cackled. "I really want to hear this!"

Doc pulled out a chair for Edward, then took a seat across from him. Folding his hands on the table, he narrowed his eyes at him. "It was literature, wasn't it, Mama?"

"C-minus in literature, that's right, Daddy."

Edward hung his head and tried not to smile. "I *hate* it when you call each other Mama and Daddy."

"What book are they making you read?" Shay asked.

"Do I have to answer the peanut gallery's questions, ya honah?" Edward asked.

"No," Doc said solemnly. "Only mine. So what book are they making you read?"

Pearl was chuckling continuously as she set the breakfast on the table. "Tell him, son. And eat your eggs before they get cold."

Edward took a quick bite of his eggs, then said, "It's by some crazy guy named Dante, and I do *not* get it!"

Doc's eyes widened and he laughed. "They've got you reading *Dante's Inferno*? Hey, Mama, that *is* a little advanced for a sixteen-year-old, don't you think?"

Pearl nodded and sat down next to him. "Seems a little advanced, but the rest of the class is reading it. He's gotta keep up."

"That's right," Doc said. "Because you've got to get ready for college. You can get a good education at city college. So what part of the book don't you understand?"

Edward shot him a look of disbelief. "Uh, all of it! Right now, we're in the fourth chapter of hell— Uh, 'scuse me. The fourth *canto* of hell."

"Edward said hell twice, Daddy! At the table!" Nick was standing in the kitchen doorway holding Sylvester and grinning. "That's a bad word! Want me to get your belt?"

"Put the cat down and come eat your breakfast, boy," Doc said.

The only empty chair was next to Edward. Nick scrambled onto it and grinned up at him triumphantly.

Edward bumped him with his shoulder. "Punk. I can say hell at the table when I'm talking about lit'tra'chure," he said with a prim expression.

Nick smirked. "Oh, yeah? How 'bout when you're in the alley shootin' them dice?"

Shay let out a snorting laugh. "Mr. Edward Kennedy Ellington's sho' gonna get it now!"

Before Doc could react, someone knocked on the front door.

"That'll be Rose," Pearl said.

Doc got up. "I'll get it. But you and I are gonna have a serious talk about you shootin' dice," he said pointing at Edward. *"And* college. Later."

When he opened the door, Doc smiled broadly. "Hey, Rose! You must be feelin' better. You look great!"

"I sure am feelin' better!" she said. "I just brought the mornin' paper over. Thought I'd trade it in for a cup of Pearl's coffee. She in the kitchen?"

"She sure is."

"Hey, sugah," Pearl called. "Come on in. I just made a fresh pot. You want some eggs?"

Doc carried in the extra chair from the living room and Rose squeezed in at the corner of the table next to Shay.

"No, thanks, Pearl. I already had breakfast. I'm just moochin' coffee, as usual."

Pearl brought the pot over and filled a cup for Rose. "Look at you! Just rarin' to go!"

"I don't know if I'm rarin' yet, but I'm a whole lot better than I was. Girl, you just don't appreciate your health till you get sick. And I ain't been that sick in my whole life, I don't think. Pearl, I want to thank you for takin' such good care of me."

"After all you've done for us? Girl, it was my pleasure, believe me."

"Well, we sure are glad to see you up and around again," Doc said, "Just in time for Christmas. Your son comin' to get you again this year?"

"He's comin' next week. And I will *not* miss this freezin' cold weather, Doc Calhoun!"

"But Florida's always hot, Miss Rose," Shay said. "That doesn't seem very Christmasy."

"Listen, honey, I'ma take Christmas to Miami with me! I'll decorate me a palm tree, and put on my sunglasses and some'a them Bermuda shorts, and sing the heck out'a 'Jingle Bells'!"

"Bring back lots of pictures, Miss Rose!" Shay laughed.

"You know, jonesin' for Florida is a sign of old age sneakin' up on you, Rose," Doc teased. "Old folks in New York *always* end up in Florida."

Rose smacked him on the back of the head. "You mind your manners, young man!"

"Ouch!" Doc rubbed his head. "You're definitely well now. You hit like Sonny Liston!"

"And don't you forget it! Come on, Pearl. Let's go shoppin'. I gotta pick up a few Christmas presents before I start packin' for my trip."

* * *

Doc got to rehearsal early that afternoon, and was sitting at the bar watching the new television set Mr. Ramsay had bought. He was gazing absently at the news until Malcolm X appeared on the screen.

"Turn that up a little, will you, Lloyd?"

"Sure, Doc," the bartender said, reaching up to twist the volume knob.

As several images of Malcolm X scrolled across the screen, Walter Cronkite's familiar voice droned in the background:

Today the Nation of Islam suspended its controversial spokesman Malcolm X for recent inflammatory comments on the assassination of President Kennedy. The former spokesman stated that the violence Kennedy had allegedly failed to prevent had come back to claim the President, calling it a case of "the chickens coming home to roost."

Doc heard a whistle, and saw King slide onto the stool next to him. "That guy really speaks his mind, doesn't he?"

"That he does. And don't be patronizing."

"I'm not. The guy might be harsh in the way he says things, but there's a lot of logic in self-defense. I don't think he's as bad as a lot of whites think he is."

"And maybe Kennedy wasn't as bad as a lot of blacks thought *he* was. Meanwhile, the rich get richer, the poor get poorer, and America's still kissin' Jim Crow on the lips."

King shook his head and sighed. "Hey, at least we got jazz. The great integrator."

Doc nodded. "It's the harmony. Musical *and* racial."

"Amen. Black or white, jazz musicians are like the United Nations, man. So why the hell can't the squares get hip to that?"

"Meanwhile, how 'bout you let me buy you a drink. Johnnie Red okay?"

"It always is!"

Doc nodded at Lloyd, and he brought over the bottle and a glass for King.

"Thanks, Lloyd. You can just leave the bottle."

"You're here early today, Doc," King said. "The other guys won't be here for an hour."

Doc emptied his glass, then leveled a direct stare at King. "I came early to drink. And before you ask, that was only my second. He grinned and poured himself another drink. "*Now* I'm on my third. You may commence your praying and hand-wringing."

Four students were arrested today outside Southern Christian Leadership Conference headquarters for disseminating pamphlets accusing Civil Rights leader Martin Luther King of consorting with Communists. When questioned by a reporter on the scene, one of the students claimed that the FBI and the HUAC Committee had evidence against King that would "put him behind bars where he belongs."

Doc scowled at the television. "The HUAC Committee? Aren't they dead yet?"

"Practically," King said. "But Hoover's still alive and kicking. And he might be worse."

"Hey, Lloyd?" Doc called. "This news is depressing, man! Anything else on?"

"Sure, Doc! My favorite show. You'll like this." He reached up and turned off the set.

Doc chuckled and held up his glass. "I like it already. How 'bout some music?"

Lloyd grinned and stuck out his hand. "Gimme some change. I'll plug in the jukebox."

King and Doc dug in their pockets for some change and handed it to Lloyd.

"So how's Pearl doing?" King asked softly.

"Well... some days are better than others."

"Maybe she'll make it, Doc."

The jukebox sprang to life with Sinatra's "In the Wee Small Hours of the Morning."

Doc lit a cigarette and shook his head slowly. "You don't believe that. But as long as I don't pressure her to quit completely, I've gotta believe she has a chance. She told me she's taking smaller doses and trying to space out her visits to that—place. She gets sick sometimes, but she hides it from the kids the best she can."

"Yeah, well, maybe if she cuts back very, *very* gradually, it might work."

Doc nodded. "All I know is...."

"What?"

Doc shrugged. "All I know is nothin', I guess. 'Cause I don't even know where I was goin' with that remark."

After a long silence, King said, "I'm worried about you, man. You're drinking a lot more than usual."

"And you're smokin' a lot more opium than usual."

"Nah. For a while I was, but I don't go to the dens that often anymore. And when I do, I usually just smoke the mild stuff."

Doc laughed and held up his glass. "Johnnie's mild... in an eighty proof kind'a way."

King sighed. "Everything's a joke, huh? Look, Doc. I hope I'm not out'a line here, but you've gotta think about how all this is affecting *you*. I know you're tryin' to save her, and I know how you love her, but it's still tough on you and the kids."

Doc put his glass down and glared at him. "You don't know shit, man! And you *are* out'a line! You act like Pearl's some kind'a goddamn… liability or sump'm!"

King held up his hands. "No, man. That's not what I meant—"

"I know what you meant, but you *clearly* don't know shit about Pearl and me. You said… What did you just say? You *know* how I love her? Man, you don't have *any* idea how I love her! You think I'm trying to save *her*? Man, she saved *me*!"

After a long silence, Doc knocked back what was left of his drink and then stared into the empty glass. "She's my heartbeat, man."

CHAPTER 31

Day four.

Or was it day five? Pearl wasn't sure. All she knew was that it was too soon to be feeling this sick again. From what seemed like a great distance, she heard Shay calling her.

"Mama, where are you?"

"In the kitchen, sugah."

Shay ran up from behind and hugged her. "I finished my book, Mama. You were right! It was so good!"

Pearl turned down the flame under the gravy and cleared her throat. It was so dry she could hardly swallow. "Which book was that again, baby?"

"*To Kill a Mockingbird*, Mama! You picked it out for me, remember?"

"That's right. Let me get a glass of water and you can tell me all about it, okay?"

"Yes, ma'am... Oh, Mama, I just felt so sorry for poor Tom Robinson and his family."

Pearl sat down and Shay slid into the chair next to her. After draining her glass, Pearl gazed into her expectant eyes and then kissed her head. "You know what, baby?"

"What, Mama?"

"You look just like your Grandmother Alva."

Shay grinned. "Daddy says I look like you."

"I look like her too, but I didn't get her dimples. You did."

"But I'm so skinny, Mama. My legs look like they belong on a chicken!"

Pearl laughed softly. "That might be my fault, sugah. They used to call me 'Chicken-Legs' when I was thirteen."

"They did? Good! There's hope for me then! Maybe my legs'll get pretty like yours!"

"Oh, they'll be prettier than mine. I told you, you take after my Mama, and she had much prettier legs than I do."

"I sure wish she was still alive. I love all the stories you tell me about her."

"She *is* alive, baby. She lives in those stories. Your Daddy taught me that. He introduced me to a lotta folks in his stories who had passed."

"Like Jimmy, huh, Mama! I love the story about how Daddy climbed that mountain with Enrique and Jimmy!"

"See? That's how he kept 'em alive."

Shay sighed. "Wonder if they ever met Alva? In heaven, I mean."

"I wouldn't be at all surprised." Pearl felt a sharp stab in her midsection, but managed a smile. "I love you so much, baby. I hope you know how much."

"I love you too, Mama... Hey, you're sweating! Are you hot?"

"Been cookin' over that hot stove is all. But let's get back to your book."

"Oh, yes. Well, all I wanted to know is why couldn't the people believe all the evidence? Tom Robinson was innocent, Mama! And why couldn't the book have a happy ending?"

"Well, sugah... some stories have happy endings, and that's the point. Other stories have sad endings, and that's the point too. This book was makin' a point about injustice."

Shay stared out the window. "But... how come white folks get justice and colored folks keep on gettin' *in*justice, Mama?"

"That, my lovely young lady, is a much longer discussion. And it all begins with history. So let's go to the library and find you some books that explain all that."

Shay grinned. "We can't go to the library on Christmas Eve, Mama."

Pearl stood up and headed back to the stove. "I meant... after the Christmas holidays."

"Yes, ma'am. I want to show you the new fashion magazines too! I want to be a dress designer! But you know what? Lately, I been thinkin' I might want to write books, Mama. I bet I could write a book with a happy ending for colored folks. Get us some justice for a change."

Pearl swallowed hard. "Well, that sounds like a book I'd sure like to read! But I thought you told your Daddy you wanted him to teach you how to play the trumpet?"

"Can't I do all three things?"

"Sure you can, sugah, for a while. But those are big goals and each one takes a lot'a dedication. So there's gonna come a time when you'll have to choose."

"Okay, Mama. But right now I want to try a few things and see which one I like best."

"That sounds like a very mature attitude, sugah. It's always better to have a few goals to choose from than no goals at all."

Shay smiled. "So when we go to the library, I'll show you the new fashion magazines and then you help me find some good history books, okay?"

"I sure will. But right now, I need you to help me find Nick."

"Nick's right on the couch takin' a nap with Sylvester."

"Nuh-uh. I'm right here," Nick mumbled as he shuffled into the kitchen. The cat was sound asleep on his left shoulder. "I gotta feed Sylvester. He's hungry."

Pearl smiled and rubbed Nick's head. "He doesn't look hungry. He looks unconscious!"

Shay laughed. "You should give Sylvester a cup of coffee so he can wake up and eat!"

Pearl gave Sylvester a gentle scratch behind his ear, and the cat began to purr loudly. "Go ahead and feed him, Nick, and then go wash your hands for supper. I don't suppose either one of you knows where Edward is?"

Shay rolled her eyes. "Chasing girls. But don't worry. You know he won't miss a meal!"

"Well, go wash your hands too, Shay. Supper'll be ready in a few minutes."

By the time Edward got home, Pearl's stomach pains had begun to subside a bit. He walked into the kitchen and kissed her. "Hi, Mama. That sure smells good!"

"Go wash up, son. And what in the world is that on your shirt?"

"Taxi splashed me with some muddy slush when I was crossing the street. I'll change it."

A few minutes later, Doc walked in. "Where's everybody?"

Shay ran into the front room and threw her arms around his waist. "Hi, Daddy! Can you smell that chicken gravy?"

"I sure can. And I sure am hungry. Where's Edward?"

"Changing his shirt. He got splashed by a taxi. Did you see the Christmas tree, Daddy?"

Doc smiled at the tiny tree. "It's beautiful! Did you help your Mama decorate it?"

"Me and Nick did!"

"Nick and I, not me and Nick."

"Yes, sir. Nick and I. But Daddy—"

"Walk and talk, baby. Follow me to the bathroom and tell me everything while I wash my hands for supper."

"Okay. All I was gonna tell you is that while me and Nick—I mean, Nick and I—were helping Mama decorate the tree, Sylvester kept punching the little ornaments off and rollin' 'em on the floor! Oh! And he got all tangled up in the lights too! So Mama had to turn him upside-down to get him untangled. That cat is a mess, Daddy! Edward says he needs to get a job!"

Doc grinned. "You been drinkin' coffee all day or sump'm? Need to wash your hands?"

"No, sir. I washed 'em already. Come on! Let's go in the kitchen. I'm hungry!"

"You comin', Edward?" Doc called.

Edward appeared in the hallway. "Nothin' could keep me from Mama's chicken. And before you ask, I already washed my hands... Twice... 'Cause I know... they're always dirty."

Doc laughed as Shay pulled him by the hand into the kitchen. The racket of chairs scraping and overlapping conversation filled the room as everyone crowded around the small table for their usual noisy supper. But the second Pearl finished serving the chicken, mashed potatoes, gravy, and greens, everyone began to eat and the room fell quiet.

Doc looked around the table and chuckled. "Well, nobody said any kind'a grace, but maybe God'll forgive us since we're obviously a pack of starving hyenas."

Pearl laughed. "There's apple pie for dessert."

"Thanks, Mama," Doc said, smiling at her. "And the Christmas tree looks real pretty. Hey, did my Christmas beer buddy call?"

Pearl nodded as she sat down. "He called. He said he just got back in town and he'll be over later with your Christmas beer."

Edward grinned. "What do you need with beer, Daddy? You got that secret bottle of scotch in the top cupboard. Why don't you just cheer up with that?"

Doc narrowed his eyes at him. "A, it's none of your business. And B, I only drink scotch at the club, not at home. And C, how the hell did you know it was up there? And D, before you ask me *why* it's up there, I keep it for emergencies. Like when I might need a deterrent from knockin' the daylights out of my eldest son for shootin' dice."

Edward groaned. "You just keep settin' those traps, and I just keep walkin' into 'em."

"You'll learn," Doc said, then turned to Nick. "And as for you, when your uncle gets here, you better have a good present for him, 'cause it sure is nice of him to share his Christmas beer with me."

Nick giggled and Pearl shook her head. "Well, don't drink too much. Remember we have to get to church early for Nick's solo."

Doc nodded. "Deal. So when are you planning to visit Magda? In the afternoon?"

"Mm-hmm. Right after church."

"Yay!" Nick yelled.

"Hey! Stop yellin' at the table, boy," Doc said. "Okay. So what else has been goin' on at the homestead while Daddy's been out workin' in the wilderness?"

"I'll tell you, Daddy," Shay said. "I finished my book, Nick played with Sylvester all day, and as for Edward... Nobody knows where *he's* been all day, but I'm sure girls were involved."

Edward grinned and his bushy eyebrows bobbed up and down. "Only one—Sheee-lah!"

Doc groaned. "Your son is a wolf, Mama."

Pearl was staring blankly at her plate and scratching the top of one of her hands.

Doc saw the patch of raw scratch marks and reached for her hand to keep her from making it worse. "You okay?"

"Oh, I'm fine, sugah. I was just tryin' to remember... sump'm I gotta get for tomorrow."

"I hope it's more pie," Edward said. " 'Cause this one won't last the night."

"Can Sylvester have some pie?" Nick asked.

Doc was still looking at Pearl. "Boy, you know cats don't eat pie."

"What that cat needs is a job," Edward said. "And besides, cats eat birds."

"Shut up!" Shay cried. "You know I love birds! Sylvester *better* not eat a bird!"

"Shay..." Pearl said. "Young ladies don't say shut up. It's vulgar."

"Sylvester would *never* eat a bird, ya old telephone-pole neck!" Nick cried.

"Don't call your sister a telephone-pole neck," Doc said. Then he stopped and looked at him. "Okay, wait... Nick, *what* is a telephone-pole neck and *where* do you get this stuff from?"

"It's a long, boney-neck *girl* and Sylvester would *never* eat a bird!" Nick said, glaring at Shay. Then he broke into a grin. "But he ate a cockroach the other day though."

"Oh, yuck!" Shay cried. "Isn't *that* vulgar, Mama?"

Doc laughed. "Okay, boy. You know that's not supper table conversation."

"It's certainly *not* supper table conversation," Pearl said.

"Sorry," Nick muttered, "but he did."

"He did *what*?" Edward asked. "What are you talkin' about *now*, runt?"

Doc held up his fork and pointed it at Nick's arm. "Better think about your answer, boy."

Nick grimaced and squeezed his eyes shut. "Yes, sir. Okay... Sylvester ate... I mean, Sylvester *did* sump'm that wasn't... um, supper table conversation."

Doc laughed and leaned over to kiss Pearl. "Where'd these kids come from?"

* * *

Hours later Pearl was standing alone on a snowy sidewalk with that supper table conversation still echoing in her ears. The laughter, the playful bickering, the way Doc grinned at the children's groaning as he told his corny jokes. It was all pulling at her, calling her home, but, once again, she was losing the battle to that street with no sign.

She had hoped that visiting Magda at the hospital would strengthen her resolve to go home. But after only a few minutes, she had become too sick to stay. *And here I am again.*

She pulled up her collar against the cold air. "Come on, Pearl," she whispered to herself, "just put one foot in front of the other one... and go home."

But a sudden stab of pain nearly doubled her over, changing her hopeful footsteps to a blind, desperate stumble up the steps of the quarter house. She kicked and pounded on the door until it opened. In the yellow light spilling out into the darkness she saw Margaret's lurid smile. Pearl hated her more than ever.

"You waited too long, baby," Margaret was saying. "I been expectin' you."

As Pearl hurried past her, she fumbled in her coat pocket for a twenty and held it out.

Margaret pushed away her shaking hand. "I don't want your money, tonight, baby. I want sump'm else tonight. And if you wanna get right with the Hydra, it's time to pay up."

Pearl stared at her and felt a convulsion rattle through her body. She squeezed her eyes shut tightly. There was a high squealing in her ears, like the deadly screech of some predatory bird. When she tried to swallow, the dry air scraped until it caught in her throat. Unable to swallow or breathe, she felt herself being pushed down onto the sofa. Rough hands yanked her coat open. She knew she had to fight. She had to wrap the coat around her body for protection. She opened her eyes, expecting to see Victor standing over her with his belt. She could see her own reflection in a pair of eyes, but they were not Victor's eyes. It was Margaret who was staring down at her, and the cold fingers unbuttoning her blouse were Margaret's fingers.

"You want that Hydra, baby?"

Pearl managed to push her off, and the screeching sound broke. As she stumbled out the door, Margaret's laughter followed her: "You'll be back, baby. And I'll be waitin'."

Pearl wrapped her coat tighter and hobbled down the street. She barely made it to the corner, then fell down on her hands and knees. Her stomach began to convulse, but there was nothing left in it to expel. *I'm fixin' to die... right here in the street... Oh, God, I'm dying....*

The violent physical beating her insides were taking had left her mind so weary it began to surrender. She closed her eyes and drifted into a deep, welcoming darkness. The flickering image she had always feared was still there, but now it was strangely comforting. She wanted to sleep. *Guess I'm fixin' to die....*

The thought was soothing—a faint angel's song of eternal sleep. No more fighting. No more failing. It seemed such a gentle fall, and now she was lying in the street. The snow was cool on her hot face. From some distant place in her memory, a little boy giggled. *Make a snow angel, Pearl! Sing me a song!*

Then an echo of a little girl singing: *...My little sugah boy... got some little sugah toys....*

The little boy giggled again and Pearl smiled. Just as she reached out for him, she felt a pair of hands grabbing her shoulders and roughly turning her over.

"Lady? ...Hey! You okay, lady?"

Pearl looked up and saw a thin black man standing over her. He had a scruffy gray beard and his tattered clothes reeked of cheap liquor, cigarettes, and body odor. But in his eyes was something that looked like a deep kindness.

"You come from that quahtah house, ain'tcha?" he said, as he helped her to her feet.

Pearl nodded.

"That lowdown bitch is the devil," the man said, casting a bitter look toward the street with no sign. "Come on with me, lady, and I'll get you fixed up. It ain't strong as that shit she pushin', but at least it won't kill ya, and it sho' will keep ya from hurtin' so bad."

Pearl's hand shook as she fumbled in her pocket. "Oh, no! I lost my money," she sobbed.

The man sighed. "Lady, you in bad shape. I'ma help ya get right tonight, and you can—"

Pearl was barely holding on when he suddenly yanked her into an alley. The shrill sound was back, and she began pleading with him, "I need it, but please don't make me do this...."

"Naw, wait a minute, lady! I ain't tryin' to make you do nothin'! I'm tryin' to get you out that street! Ain'tcha hear them sirens? Listen... Them's cops comin'!"

As the man craned his neck to peer around the edge of the building, the sirens began screaming louder and red strobe lights bounced a crazy dance on the tenements across the street.

The man ducked back into the alley. "Lawd! Must be ten cars in front of that damn quahtah house! They finally gon' get her! Lady, you got out'a there just in time!"

Pearl felt her grip weaken, and she began sliding to the ground. "Please help me...."

"Oh, Lawd! Hang on, now, lady. We goin'. But we can't go out there where them cops is, now can we? So we gonna cut down this other alley. Hang on to me now. I got'cha."

As they stumbled through the alley, Pearl gazed at him. "Why you bein' so kind to me?"

"Somebody was kind to me once, that's all." He smiled sadly. "Not lately, but once."

Pearl held on to his arm as tightly as she could. "Thank you... sir."

Dying could wait.

* * *

She was still shaky when she got home, but at least the sickness and convulsions had subsided. She quietly unlocked the front door and peeked in. Doc was sprawled on the sofa with one foot on the floor. He was snoring, and on the coffee table was his bottle of Johnnie Red.

After the fight they'd had over her leaving the house so late on Christmas Eve, Pearl had expected the bottle to be empty, but it was unopened. As she quietly closed the door, she realized why he hadn't opened it. He wanted to be sober in the morning for the children. As she stood there gazing at him, she wanted to tell him how sorry she was, but instead, she tiptoed into the bedroom. She needed a shower, but she needed to lie down for a few minutes first.

When she opened her eyes, she blinked at the alarm clock. It was 5:45, and the house was still quiet. She scrambled up and hurried to the bathroom for a shower before everyone woke up.

She scrubbed herself from head to toe, feeling a much milder high than she had ever experienced. It wasn't the terrifying sexual ferocity of the Hydra; it wasn't even the euphoria of Perry's product that had always chased away her blues. But it was enough to stave off the sickness and bring her some peace. At least for now.

As she stepped out of the shower and began drying off, she smiled. Through the bathroom wall, she could hear Nick and Shay murmuring and Edward's deep voice trying to shush them. As Pearl shook the water out of her ears, she tried to shake Margaret out of her mind. She combed her wet hair away from her face and took a long look at herself in the mirror. She knew that she didn't look her best, but she looked clean. Then she heard Shay giggle from the next room, and the sound of it gave her strength.

"You can do it now, Pearl," she whispered sternly to her reflection. "Whushu got in this house's strong'n any blues. You can quit." She licked her lips. "Ssstop slurrin'. Talk right."

She jerked up her chin and smiled. Then she opened the bathroom door and went to the kitchen. By the time she started making coffee, the children were filing in.

Edward walked over and kissed her forehead. "Merry Christmas, Mama," he whispered.

"Merry Christmas, son. Lord, you look a inch taller'n yesterday!"

He stared at her with troubled eyes. "Did you and Daddy make up?"

"Don't you worry about your Daddy and me, baby. We're just fine. And I'm fixin' to make pancakes in a few minutes."

Shay wrapped her arms around her waist and smiled. "Merry Christmas, Mama!"

"Merry Christmas, baby. Where's Nick? And why's everybody whisperin'?"

Nick walked in and smiled up at her. Sylvester was clinging to his shoulder, as usual. "Shh! We're tryin' not to wake up Daddy so early!"

Pearl laughed. "It's Christmas! He's supposed to wake up early, don'tcha think? We got folks comin' over any minute. And Merry Christmas, Nick. You too, S-sylvester."

Sylvester blinked at Pearl and yawned just as someone knocked loudly on the door.

"See?" Pearl said. "Told'ja folks gonna start gettin' here early. Shay, you go get the door, and Edward, you turn on the radio. I'll get your Daddy's coffee ready."

Within minutes, the apartment was filled with noise and Doc finally opened his eyes. The radio was blaring Dave Brubeck's "Blue Rondo a la Turk." As he sat up, he muttered, "Turn that down a little, Edward... Where's your mother?"

Pearl walked over to the sofa and handed him his coffee. "Right here, baby."

Doc reached up and placed his palm on the side of her face. "You all right?"

"Mm-hmm. I got in about two. Here, sugah. Drink it 'fore it gets cold."

Doc took the coffee and handed her a small white box. "Sorry I didn't wrap it."

"What's this? ...Oh, Lord! *Eau de Joy*? My God, baby! This stuff costs a fortune!"

"It's just a quarter ounce. I wanted you to have sump'm nice this year—for a change."

"Oh, baby," she said softly, "I don't deserve this."

"Shut up and kiss me," he whispered.

Sinking down next to him, she kissed him softly and leaned her head on his shoulder. She peeked over at the Christmas tree and rumbled a low laugh. Sylvester was suddenly wide awake, leaping around under the tree and batting ornaments across the floor.

"Hey," Edward said, "I finally figured out a job for Sylvester. Christmas tree demolition!"

"Shut up!" Nick cried. "He's just playin'! Hey, what did you get, Shay?"

"A new high-fashion model paper doll named Babette! Thanks, Mama!"

Pearl sat up and dabbed some perfume behind her ears. "You're welcome, sugah!"

"Hey!" Edward said. "A transistor radio! Cool!"

Pearl settled into Doc's arms and closed her eyes. She sensed the movement of friends coming in and walking into the kitchen, and she heard the distant warm buzz of their voices. She pressed her face against Doc's chest and heard his heart beating strong and steady in her ear. She could feel the vibrations of him talking to people and laughing, but she didn't need to hear the words anymore. It was all a jumble of sweet music. Then she felt him nudge her.

"Pearl?"

"Mm-hmm?"

"You see Sylvester under the tree tearin' shit up over there?"

Pearl smiled. "I saw him. What'cha want *me* to do about it, trumpet man?"

"Nothin'. But I really ought to slip that cat a mickey. Calm his hairy ass right down."

She chuckled softly, but didn't open her eyes. Nat King Cole was on the radio singing "The Christmas Song" and Pearl reached for Doc's hand. "Baby?"

"Mm-hmm?"

"Squeeze my hand."

Doc squeezed her hand, and she squeezed back. "You remember that?"

"I remember everything, Pearl."

His sigh was deep and melodic, and Pearl wanted to freeze everything about that precise moment: the reassuring grip of his hand; all their memories; the sweet, crazy chaos of their house on Christmas morning; the kids and the cat and all their racket spoiling Nat King Cole's crooning.

"Merry Christmas, Esperanza," Doc said softly.

She smiled up at him. "I'm still your Esperanza?"

"Yes, you are. Did I ever tell you what it means?"

"No, you never did. And I always meant to ask you."

Doc squeezed her hand again and smiled. "Esperanza means… hope."

In the song
there was a secret little inner song
hardly perceptible, but always there
sweet and secret and clinging
almost hiding
in the counter-melody
And this was the Song of the Pearl That
Might Be....

~ John Steinbeck, *The Pearl*

ACKNOWLEDGMENTS

This book, along with all my others, would not have been possible without David, the man whose head rests on the pillow next to mine. For all the love and laughter, the talks, serious and silly, the joy, and even the heated debates, I thank you. On a daily basis, you encourage me to think, extend my intellectual reach, sharpen my skills, and achieve true balance in my life. You are my heartbeat.

To all the pearls in my life — Theresa, Ina, Celestine, Minerva, Sonya, Danielle, Erika, Celeste, Roxie, Liz, Milana, Kia, Lynnette, Rene, Michele, Brittany, Ashley, Heather, Elandis, Nailah, Taryn, Devorah, Cindy, Iman, and the first and truest Pearl I ever knew, my mother. All of you have inspired me and filled the world with pure love.

Special thanks to Oliver Law, Salaria Kea, Harry Haywood, James Yates, Evelyn Hutchins, Alonzo Watson, James Peck, Paul Williams, Langston Hughes, W.E.B. Dubois, Asa Philip Randolph, Ernest Hemingway, Martha Gellhorn, Federico García Lorca, Albert Einstein, Paul Robeson, John Steinbeck, Eleanor Roosevelt, Dalton Trumbo, Richard Wright, Howard Fast, every member of the International Brigades, and every reporter, artist, activist, and citizen who stood up to Hitler, Franco, Mussolini, the KKK, and the House Un-American Activities Committee in the fight against global racism, fascism, and any other methods of dividing the human family.

The fight for unity continues....